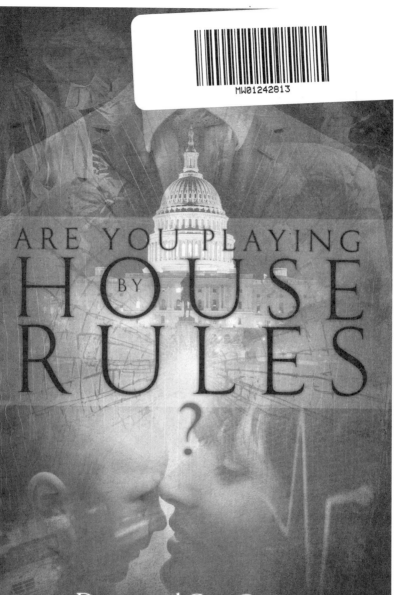

ARE YOU PLAYING

HOUSE

BY

RULES

?

Darren and Cara Grant

21stCENTURY
P R E S S

READING YOU LOUD AND CLEAR.

ARE YOU PLAYING BY HOUSE RULES?

21st Century Press is an evangelical Christian publisher dedicated to serving the local church with purpose books. We believe God's vision for 21st Century Press is to provide church leaders with biblical, user-friendly materials that will help them evangelize, disciple and minister to children, youth and families.

It is our prayer that this book will help you discover biblical truth for your own life and help you meet the needs of others. May God richly bless you.

21st Century Press
2131 W. Republic Rd. PMB 41
Springfield, MO 65807
800-658-0284
www.21stcenturypress.com

ISBN: 978-0-9838359-6-7
Cover: Keith Locke
Book Design: Lee Fredrickson

21stCENTURY
P   R   E   S   S
READING YOU LOUD AND CLEAR.

DEDICATION

It is difficult to put together a comprehensive list of everyone who has taught and encouraged us in the act of writing this book. We have benefited from the wisdom of many authors and speakers too numerous to mention. We would like to thank Lee Fredrickson for working with us to get this book in print. We would like to thank our friends at Legacy Family Church who ministered to our family after our house fire, dusted off the ashes, and lifted us up in prayer during the last eight months. Though we might differ on some things, you are truly a ministering Body of Christ to us. We would like to thank Justin and Jocelyn Humes for their help in the intermediate stages of this book. Special thanks to Mason and Debbie Jacobson, and Jon and Michaele Day for reading the book and making many helpful suggestions and comments before it went to press. Thank you Kitty Schneider for editing the book in a timely manner for us, and being such a blessing to our family. Thank you Ahnna, Keziah, Tabitha, Charis, Aletheia, and Justice for your patience and prayers for Mom and Dad while we worked on this long project. To Sharon, Mick, Clyde, and Wanda thank you for giving us life and giving us a desire to search for the truth at all costs. Our acknowledgement page would not be complete without acknowledging the work of the Lord Jesus Christ in our lives, guiding us in truth, and teaching us each step along the way. Ultimately, this book is dedicated to our Lord Jesus Christ. We pray this book will be used by Christ to start the process of freeing many churches and individuals from bondage, and directing them toward the true worship of our Creator.

TABLE OF CONTENTS

CHAPTER 1

A small jet taxied onto the private runway. The pilot, knowing his passengers would not tolerate even a moderately bumpy ride, had taken extra care in landing. Bernard Thomas, a wealthy Canadian with thinning silver hair, peered down through his window to view the glassy blue waters of Lake Michigan. Carol, his wife of 40 years, sat beside him. On the other side of the cabin sat a private nurse, a woman, in her mid-forties. "The lake looks beautiful and peaceful today," Bernard spoke in an enthusiastic, but gentle tone. "Not right now," Carol snapped. Her dark eyes, accentuated by her thinning hair and frail body, cut him a sharp look. "There's too much pain."

Bernard's flawless 3-carat diamond ring and the costly gems on Carol revealed their obvious wealth. Together they owned a large partial interest in a Canadian diamond mine, and they took pride in displaying their product. A private limo waited at the end of the runway to escort the three Canadians to their suite, at one of the finest hotels Chicago had to offer. Bernard had spared no expense in trying to make everything as comfortable as possible for his ailing wife.

The luxurious penthouse in which they were staying had large spacious windows with a spectacular view of the lake, the city skyline, and many of the other sites that made Chicago so famous. Rare Italian tapestries decorated the walls of the penthouse. Carol had no interest in the tapestries, the lake, the city, or even the plush, spacious rooms of the penthouse. For now, all she wanted was a quiet, dark room, so she could rest, and she let Bernard and the nurse know this in a few abrupt words. Sensing a tongue-lashing was on the way, the nurse led Carol into the spacious master bedroom, complete with a skylight, jacuzzi, and mahogany wet bar, while Bernard called the hospital and told them of their arrival. Once Carol and her nurse were settled in their rooms, Bernard left to make some arrangements at the hospital. He hoped to talk with...what was the man's name? His secretary had e-mailed the information about the hospital administrator to him before they left Canada. Scrolling through his e-mails, he found the contact information he sought. Mr. Verde. Hopefully, with enough cash and a generous charitable contribution to the hospital, they'd be able to obtain a liver transplant in the United States.

Anxiously, Bernard fretted, "Could they find a match?" He hoped, as he had innumerable times before. He even prayed awkwardly to someone called God, just in case He was out there. Although Bernard had faithfully *attended* church for years, he didn't know if he truly believed in God, or if God could care about him. He was just one man among the six billion in the world. But he was covering all of his bases, praying this would somehow be the place where his hopes would become reality. Chicago was their last hope; they must find a liver for his wife. For the last two months they had been flying from one transplant center to another in an effort to find a match.

In a rare attempt at humor, Carol had explained to Bernard "if she had as many needles sticking out of her, as had been stuck into her on this trip, she would look like a big silver porcupine." A new hospital drew blood every few days and she had lost count of how many hospitals across the United States had offered them little or no hope. The stress of the trip was taking its toll on both he and his fragile wife, mentally and physically. Carol often vented her frustrations, and anger on her nurse, her husband, or the pilot. Presently, she was dealing with a pounding head ache, and all she wanted was to be left alone in her own bedroom to rest.

Back at the hotel, Carol lay on yet another strange bed pretending to be asleep, hoping her vigilant nurse would think she was comfortable and leave her alone for a while. The nurse flitted about the room, straightening the already immaculate suite, as if looking for something to do. Her actions only aggravated Carol more. *Why couldn't she see that I just want to be left alone?* Carol thought. After a few moments of watching Carol's even breathing, the nurse assumed she was asleep and retired to her adjoining room, away from her charge.

With considerable effort, and leaning on one arm to raise herself, Carol looked around at the plush accommodations. "Where is Bernard?" She couldn't remember. A sharp pain cut through her back and sides. Grinding her teeth, she silently cursed the airplane pilot, her nurse, and that inept Canadian healthcare system that couldn't provide her with a liver transplant in time.

Carol knew a match for her AB negative blood type would be nearly impossible to find, but the Canadian doctors kept telling them one could become available at any time. Carol didn't have time to wait and be patient. She was learning that cancer could be very unpredictable. So far, the cancer had stayed contained in the liver, but the growing cancer continued to interfere with the proper liver function as it grew. The Canadian doctors had advised Carol to hope for a transplant within three months, or the cancer would have advanced too far, and it would be too late. Carol knew, her long-term prognosis was not particularly good, even with a liver transplant. Statistically, she may not live much longer, and that bothered her. It was this fact that made her ponder life and her purpose on this planet more than she ever had before. She thought she was a good person, but now she wondered. What lay on the other side of death? It was the *unknown* that had begun to haunt her.

As these thoughts drifted around in her head, Carol instinctively reached for the pill bottle and glass of water her nurse had carefully left on the night stand. She swallowed another morphine tablet, not caring whether it was time for another dose or not. Trying to focus her mind on something other than the intense pain she felt in her back, Carol randomly opened the drawers next to her bed. She pulled a book from the drawer and began thumbing through it; two little religious booklets fell out into her lap from inside the cover of the Bible. She had never spent much time reading the Bible, but maybe she'd take it to the hospital and look at it there. She was certainly going to have plenty of time on her hands, waiting. It always took longer than Carol thought necessary to complete the endless mountains of paperwork the hospital required, and drain the blood from her body. She decided she could read while she waited. As she balanced the Bible on her lap, she tucked the papers back inside the cover.

Her glance caught the remote to the wall-sized television in their suite, and she shook her head. Since her illness the TV had become a complete waste of what precious time she had left. It amazed Carol to think how the programming on the TV had once been so relevant to her life and how she lived it, but now death preoccupied her mind. She laid the Bible on top of her silk pajamas in her overnight bag and dragged herself back to bed. Maybe, somehow, just having the Bible with her would bring her into some sort of good favor with God. Possibly she'd read what that ancient book had to say, when she felt up to it. As the morphine began to take effect, she slid beneath the covers. All she really wanted right now was sleep.

A warm summer breeze played with Joe's mousy brown hair, making him look rather boyish. Spring was well underway in Chicago, and a spirit of euphoria filled the air in the courtyard of the Christian school. With Joe's average height and medium build, light complexion, and brown eyes, he was the picture of a typical American male. He was almost thirty, but at a quick glance, he could easily pass for one of his high school students. On this particularly beautiful spring day, he was no less excited about the end of the school year as any of them might have been. Joe leaned against the wall of the building in a small patch of shade and waited. A smile of satisfaction and a look of anticipation spread across his face. Grades were turned in, school was over, and Joe was free to enjoy his summer.

A tall, lanky man with salt and pepper hair stepped out of the old brick school building and walked past Joe, who appeared to be studying the road ahead. "Enjoy your summer, Mr. Smith." Mr. Elder, the headmaster of the school, spoke to Joe as he would one of his own sons. He stopped and looked directly at Joe with a sympathetic smile. "I'll be praying for you and Mrs. Smith. I hope things will work out well."

Joe gave a quick "thanks" as he admired the godly gentleman passing before him. Joe appreciated the "old-school" politeness and sincerity that flowed from Mr. Elder. He was, to Joe, a picture of godly character to be emulated. Watching him cross into the parking lot, Joe wondered if he would, or could, ever be like this man. *Oh God, help me to be more like Mr. Elder, and help me to know the truth.*

Joe scanned each vehicle as it approached the corner, intently looking for his wife, Mary. She was as average in appearance as Joe was, except for her gentle blue eyes, and Joe longed to look into those eyes once again. His mind strayed as the minutes passed so painfully slow. *Would she ever get here? Would she come or wouldn't she?* Mary had left a message with the school secretary earlier that day saying she would be by to see him after school was out. *Was there hope she would move back in soon?* Joe remembered her assuring him she didn't want a divorce—just some time to get comfortable with this new *religion stuff.* Joe's anxious mind wondered if that was too good to be true. Would he see Mary soon?

He had such grand plans for their future together. Everything seemed to hang on whether she came this afternoon. Mary had said she would. Joe wanted to believe her, but why was she so late?

School had ended thirty minutes ago. She had told him earlier that week that she would be coming to talk their problems over after school on Friday. It was Friday after school, and where was she? Joe grew more and more anxious and impatient with each second.

In his hand he held an envelope containing the signed copy of his school contract for next year.[1] *Would Mary be pleased with his continuing this job? No, she probably wouldn't.* To be sure he had taken an enormous pay cut to come to this little Christian school. Working as a web manager for a leading firm in Chicago had paid much more than a Christian school ever would. Besides the pay, there was nothing impressive about being the wife of a Christian school teacher. In her mind, he spent even more time away from home than he did in his previous job, and Mary had pointed out that getting out of debt on his salary would be virtually impossible. However, in Joe's mind, he felt confident he had made the right decision. Optimism and hope had replaced the negative apathy that had once dominated his life. Even Mary noticed this significant change in his life since he had "got religion" as she called it, and this new outlook on life made him feel assured he could win his wife over, if she would only come to talk with him. Had he misunderstood the secretary's message in his eagerness to see Mary . . . ?

There it was, the car he'd been looking for! His wife's baby blue Ford Accent was less than half a mile away. Mary was coming and there was hope for their relationship. *She really did want to move back in with him!* His young jubilant heart skipped a beat. One or two minutes more and he would embrace his beloved. He'd explain everything, reassuring her of his desire to make things work. Despite all the changes in his life, one thing was certain, he still loved her. That would never change. Joe was sure they could have a happy life together because he'd made a new commitment, first to God, and second to her. His new relationship with God would equip him to love her more perfectly. With the help of Christ, he was now able to be the husband to Mary that he had never been before.

Joe nervously glanced at his watch. . . one more minute . . . Oh how he wished he could feel her body against his, her kiss on his lips, her blond shoulder length hair brushing his cheek, and her arms wrapped tightly around his neck. Oh . . . but she was stopped at a traffic light. A few more minutes of agony before he could be with the desire of his heart.

As Mary eased to a stop she checked her freckled face in the rearview mirror for the fourth time. There was Joe! She shut off the radio. *"I can't wait to tell him. He will be so happy."* She was as giddy as a kid at Christmas-time. She felt like it was their first date once again. "Come on light, I can't wait any longer!"

Joe could see the night ahead play out in his mind. Chinese from their favorite restaurant. Carry out, of course. He could smell it; he pictured it on the coffee table before them in the living room. A quiet dinner together with her snuggled up beside him on the couch. Some sincere tears, a patient listening ear, and more explaining. He certainly had a lot of that to do. More kisses, along with forgiveness. And then, when the time was right, they would walk up the stairs together and into their peaceful bedroom and... no more of Mary staying anywhere but their home.

Mary glanced at the light for the cross traffic as it turned to yellow. Not much longer! She revved up the little engine and prepared to take off toward her husband Joe. She released the seat belt buckle—she didn't want anything slowing her down when she got there. The light was about to change. Her car would be the first into the intersection.

Joe's attention was drawn to a large trash truck racing up the road toward Mary's car. The driver didn't seem to have any intention of stopping before he entered the intersection. He would *have* to stop and wait his turn. Didn't the driver realize the light was about to change, and there wasn't time for him to make it through the intersection? And what was Mary doing? She didn't have a green light yet, but she was entering the intersection! Why didn't she slam on her brakes? What was she thinking?

The truck approached at an ever faster rate. "Step on it

sweetheart," Joe screamed, but she couldn't hear him. Time seemed to stand still as he watched. The truck driver didn't even see Mary's car before he slammed into the little blue Accent, pushing it across the road into the oncoming traffic. Mary's head hit the windshield, shattering it into a thousand pieces. Glass covered the hood of the car, and her body slumped lifeless inside. Then another car slammed into the Accent, throwing Mary around in the car yet again.

Joe could see her. She seemed to be bouncing around like a child's toy doll. The car was spinning and the nightmare continued as he watched her car—crumpled and twisted—hit the median, flip up, and roll over onto its side. Joe watched in horror as all the traffic finally came to a stop. Several people were calling for help on cell phones. Joe stood in shock, feeling as if his own body had been thrown from the massive wreckage.

Something inside Joe snapped him into action. What was he doing standing here on the sidewalk, while his wife lay battered and bleeding in that mess? Dropping his contract next to his bag, he sprinted toward his wife, the sidewalk disappearing beneath his feet. He vaulted over the debris to the front of the car. Reaching through the glass with no thought of anything but getting Mary to safety, he dragged her limp body toward him, mindless of the damage he was inflicting on his arms from the gnarled metal of the hood.

Sirens roared in his ears, as he laid Mary gently in the grass of the median. Two paramedics arrived and took her from his arms. He wanted to cry, to sob, to clasp her to his chest, but he couldn't. A large, brawny paramedic approached and forcibly loaded Joe onto a stretcher and into the second ambulance.

"Is she still alive?" Joe pleaded with the paramedic, "I've got to stay with my wife." "They are doing the best they can for her," the big, thick paramedic answered calmly, though he had no real hope for the situation. From what he had seen, it would be a miracle if this woman arrived at the hospital alive.

When the paramedic momentarily turned to reach for a splint, Joe recklessly dashed for the ambulance door. A sudden thud shook him as the paramedic forced him to lie down. "Stay down! or I will have to restrain you," he demanded in a firm voice. "Let me look at your arm." Knowing Joe didn't need the shock of watching his wife die, he added, "They're doing the best they can, and I know you wouldn't want to be in their way."

Joe's blood rushed, pounding in his ears. It had all happened so fast. It felt like a terrible nightmare, but the blood-soaked bandage on his arm, and the roar of the siren, reminded him of how terribly real it was. As Joe lay there watching the blue and red lights through the window, his mind raced. A fleeting thought passed through his head, *the paramedic was only doing his job*. During the remainder of the trip to the hospital however, Joe's one consuming thought took the form of a prayer, *Oh God . . . save Mary's life*.

Chapter 2

Then they cried out to the Lord in their trouble, And He saved them out of their distresses (Psalms 107:13).

My brethren count it all joy when you fall into various trials (James 1:2).

"You're the spouse?" asked the doctor in scrubs with a stethoscope around his neck.

"Yes," Joe numbly mumbled back. His wounds had been treated, and several stitches and butterfly bandages were underneath the gauze on his right arm. The ER staff had given Joe a local to help with the pain, but it wasn't needed. He felt no pain as he sat in a stunned state of shock in the ER. A few hours had passed since the accident.

"Could I get you to step down here to the family room, where we can speak more privately."

Joe nodded, mechanically following the insensitive doctor to the indicated area. Once they had entered the family room, Dr. Bartlett slowly pulled his cap off revealing a bald head. "I'm sorry, but there's nothing I can do for her—your wife?" Joe nodded. "She has sustained severe head injuries. Based on the few tests we have already run, I am almost certain she will not wake up. I can order some more tests if you wish, but in my professional opinion, I believe there is a more than 90% chance that she's already brain-dead."

Joe collapsed in a heap into a chair. "Oh God," he clinched his fists as he fought to control his emotions, "help me."

"Her spine, amazingly, was not broken but there is severe spinal swelling. As hard as it is," the doctor spoke in a matter-of-fact way "I suspect, it's better to let her pass. As much swelling as she has, she would probably be a quadriplegic the rest of her life and be severely mentally handicapped as well. If she does survive this at all, she wouldn't want to spend the rest of her life in a wheelchair with limited mental capacity, would she?"

Without waiting for an answer, the doctor continued, "She's on a respirator; we had to apply the paddles to get her heart going when she arrived here in the ER. Her heart may stop again at any time, and she has severe damage to her kidneys. At this time we aren't even sure they are functioning at all. Once they've lost three organ systems like that—they never make it. We are just prolonging the inevitable at this point, trying to keep her alive. We can pull her off the life support whenever you're ready. If you would like a few minutes alone with her before we start the process, we can arrange that."

"A few minutes alone with her." Joe thought, *"how about a lifetime? I don't care about his professional opinion. He doesn't care about my wife whether she lives or dies: he just cares about her 'quality of life.' He isn't God. He is just a man, and he can be wrong!"*

Joe stood transfixed, blankly gazing at the doctor, for how long he did not know. Turning at the sudden opening of the door, he saw his mother-in-law enter. "How had she found out about the accident?" Joe mused. In his disoriented state of mind, he had completely forgotten the paramedics had called Mary's mother from the ambulance on the ride in. If he had been thinking clearly, he would have wondered why it had taken her so long to get to the hospital.

His mother-in-law, Jane Jones, a stout woman with dyed red hair and swollen green eyes, who prided herself on speaking her mind, being a good person, and not polluting herself with religion, stepped forward. The grief stricken martyr complex marred her countenance as always. A lifetime of assumed wrongs and frustrations were trapped inside her. Like an active volcano, she was ready to explode at a moment's notice. She was angry, bitter, and hurt, and more than anything she needed someone to blame. As usual, Joe would be the target of her wrath.

Jane had spent most of her adult life on anti-depressants, her personal therapist helping her learn to focus her wrath on others. The glare in her green eyes told of the contempt she bore for her son-in-law. There had been a time in the past when she had not loved, but tolerated Joe. That time had long since passed and now she let everyone within ear shot know she hated her worthless, fanatic, religious son-in-law. Obviously she took Mary's side in their argument and separation. And to make matters worse, Mary's father, who had been a stabilizing influence in both Mary and her mother's life, had died three years ago shortly before he and Mary had been married.

The doctor wasted no time in explaining the bleak situation to Mary's mother after Joe reluctantly introduced her to the doctor.

She broke forth in a torrent of rage toward her son-in-law. "You selfish, lazy, no good . . ." foul words spilled from her mouth. "Why Mary wanted to go and see you this afternoon, I'll never know. I tried to stop her. Did everything I could to delay her." Without stopping for more than a breath, she continued her rampage. "After you became a religious fanatic, you had to quit your good paying job and go work for that Christian school at below poverty level—never thinking of my dear Mary. She was right to leave you, and then as if my daughter didn't have enough problems, you had to go and get her pregnant. I wish to God it was anybody else's child but yours. I don't think Mary wanted the child, but she pretended like she did. I wanted her to have the baby taken care of, but ..."

Joe didn't hear the rest. "Pregnant." The words changed everything. Mary, pregnant with his child—their child. When was the baby due? Mary hadn't told him this. She must not be very far along. Maybe his mother-in-law knew, but now definitely wasn't the time to ask. The night, what was it, two months ago leapt back into his mind.

Mary had come over to talk. They were going to work out some of their differences, or at least try. Had he been wrong in changing so radically in such a short time? In his changing so fast, Mary didn't have time to adjust. He was so focused on Jesus, he had forgotten to focus on his wife as well. His mother-in-law had been right about that at least. He had been a no good, selfish husband before he got saved, and a clueless, distracted one since. Apologizing, his eyes filled with tears and he blubbered like a baby.

In Mary's heart, she knew the tears told how very much she meant to him. He'd been so wrong, so many times. Selfish and self-seeking, he never thought about Mary, her life, or what her desires were. Their whole lives had been caught up in working, in having to have more and more stuff, presenting the image of success. It had been a very selfish existence for both of them. And of course, there is no room for kids in that kind of world.

"Mary, I love you and since Christ came into my life, I've realized how much it means to me for you to know what happened to me. I found that little comic book on the back of the toilet in the men's room at the hardware store down the street. I shared it with you, remember? I was there for a while with nothing else to do, so I started to read it and look at the pictures. I thought the little book would be funny, but it wasn't. That little book was written about me. I was on every page, and I didn't like what I was reading. It was true. I was a sinner. I had rebelled against God's plan."

"At the end, it told me there was hope, and I could be delivered from the life I was living, and that God was willing to love me and help me change. I started to cry, sitting there on the toilet with my pants around my ankles, and—" he paused as he reflected on what he had been, "and I realized for the first time in my life that I was a wretched mess headed for hell. I also saw for the first time, through this little comic book, that there was a God with a Son called Jesus, that loved me enough to die for me. I was very confused and didn't understand much, but the book said I could read more about it in the Bible. As I washed my hands and rinsed off my face, I wondered where I would get a Bible. I had to know more! I looked at my reflection in the mirror and said, "God, I need a Bible." I grabbed my cart of items that I had parked outside the men's room and headed for the checkout, and my first miracle occurred standing in the checkout line. Right there next to the register on the counter was a stack of paperback Bibles with a sign that read, "Paid for by the blood of Christ, Free take one!" So I did. "I needed a Bible and Jesus paid for that too! When I checked out the clerk handed me another book and said it was another gift from Jesus, you know that Mark Cahill book I gave you to read, *One Heartbeat Away*?"

Mary nodded. She remembered him reading the book and asking her to do the same. She started to speak but he held up his hand and said, "Hear me out." He remembered how she sat there politely listening, even though she didn't seem to understand the importance of what he said. Joe searched her face for some kind of reaction. Her facial expression seemed to say, "*If this religion thing works for you that's fine, but don't try and push it off on me.*"

Hoping he was misreading her expression, Joe continued, "As I began to read my new Bible, I was searching for God, and I found Him, rather, He found me and saved me from my rebellion against him."

He remembered Mary's observation, "You started reading the Bible, going to church and, and hanging out with those religious people."

"You're right," Joe nodded in assent, "but Christ Jesus changed my whole life. I was a sinner. I was terrible and wrong. I shouldn't have done so many things and gotten involved with all of that. . . stuff at work. When I returned to my job after getting saved, it soon became obvious to me I couldn't continue working for a company involved in online gambling and porn. Before I got saved, I could justify what I was doing at my job, billing, accounts receivable—just normal business transactions I thought to myself. I was writing nice neat programs and protocols for people to easily pay for what I now know was destroying their lives. I just couldn't do it anymore. Mary, Christianity is not about church or religion, but about a person— Jesus Christ," he recalled.

The deluge of words poured forth as he again reassured her of his love for her. "I'm convinced that next to my salvation, you are the greatest gift God has ever given to me. I regret I didn't value and treasure you more. I don't deserve your love and forgiveness, and I can understand if you don't trust me, or if you think this is fake."

She placed a gentle hand on his head and tousled his mousy brown hair. Did she still love him he wondered? Her actions at that moment seemed to indicate she did. "Something certainly has changed in you." She took his hands in hers and kissed them. Her tender lips met his and their tears mingled together as they both realized how much they had missed each other. It was hard living apart. Her shoulders slipped from her loose shirt she wore and he instinctively kissed the bare smooth skin. Her tender eyes said yes, and a slight smile played on her perfect lips. "I have to tell you. I meant to tell you sooner, but I haven't taken my pills in quite a while and. . . "

"That's all right," Joe mumbled between kisses, "God is in control. We'll let him decide when we have children."[1] Mary only smiled and rolled her eyes.

Maybe she was more open to this God thing than he had thought. He could only hope and pray, but what had he just said? Was he allowing God to be in charge of that too? In the excitement of the moment however, the thought had escaped his mind and was replaced by another.

Could it be? Could that one night have made him a father? It had to be. It was the only time it could have happened since Mary had moved out. Mary had been living with her mom for the six or eight weeks prior to the fateful evening that had destined Joe to become a father. God was so good to him.

Without a word he slipped from the room, leaving the doctor to deal with his overwrought, bitter mother-in-law. She was right to be angry. How much did she know? Had Mary told her mother about their many long talks and discussions? What had she revealed about their arguments? Had she shared with her mother that she still loved and was committed to Joe? And what twist had Jane Jones put on what she had heard? It seemed to Joe that Mary's mother always perceived things in such a way as to put him in the worst possible light.

But he couldn't focus on that right now. The baby, his baby and wife, they needed him right now—he must go to Mary.

He regretted she hadn't told him about the baby. Looking back now Joe suspected she had tried two weeks ago. He had noticed she had been very nervous when she had dropped in just to talk. She said she wanted to tell him something but she wasn't sure how. Then she clammed up and stared at the floor. Before she left, she asked if they could go for a walk along the lake shore sometime soon, like they had when they were just newly married. She had said she wanted a nice comfortable place to talk, but then she left in such a hurry that she had forgotten to tell him why.

Silently, he passed through the emergency room partition again. It was late evening now. He felt the slightest hint of a headache coming on. If Joe had been in his right mind, he would have looked around and realized how crowded and overrun the emergency room was becoming. Being so focused on Mary, and now their child, he failed to realize a curtain partition had been pulled to conceal her from the family that had just been placed on the other side of the room. He briefly glanced at the six stair step girls similarly dressed in pink outside Mary's ER partition. Again, if he had been thinking, he would have noticed, they were like little clones of the woman and their injured sister who were sitting on the other side of the curtain waiting to see the doctor.

Joe spoke aloud to Mary, hoping she could hear him. "Mary, oh my Mary," he stroked her bruised and scraped cheek. It was hard to believe this was Mary. It didn't even look like her. Her face was swollen and bruised along the left side, and scratches covered her once smooth skin. A deep split starting at her left eyebrow disappeared into her bloody, matted, hairline "Were you going to tell me about the baby tonight? I can't let you . . . .go." Joe tried in vain to choke back the river of tears willing his voice to work again. It was several minutes of violent sobbing before his will could overcome his emotions and he could continue speaking, "Our child, our only child. Right now I'd give anything to hold that child for just five minutes."

Had he spoken those last words out loud, or were they just in his head? Joe lost all track of time as he sat beside her holding her hand and stroking her right jaw just below the cheek on the only little patch of skin that had been spared damage from the wreck.

He was interrupted by the head nurse of the ER as she walked in. Another staff member waited just outside the door. The nurse, a tall broad woman approached Joe where he sat by the bed. She had been given a difficult job to do, and it was obvious she was determined to get it done quickly.

"Mr. Smith," the commanding businesslike manner in which she spoke showed no signs of sympathy or care for Joe or Mary. She remained cold and detached as she mechanically performed her duties by asking, "Have you finished your goodbyes? Your mother-in-law would like a few minutes alone with her daughter before they remove these," she said pointing to the machines keeping Marry alive.

Joe was startled by the nurse's message. "Take her off life support?" Did they not know she was pregnant? "You can't take her..." His words faltered, unable to complete the sentence. "I want to speak with Dr. Bartlett," He pleaded.

"Dr. Bartlett will be here in a few minutes when he has time. He is busy doing paper work right now. She pulled back the curtain to allow him to pass more easily, "But I need you to leave now. . . "

"I'm her husband." An intense emotion, uncommon to his usual mild manners, came through. "Don't I have a say?" There was an urgent pleading in Joe's voice.

"You are her ex-husband," the nurse coolly reminded. "Since

you are in the middle of divorce proceedings, your mother-in-law now has the only say that matters."

"Are you saying my mother-in-law is the legal guardian of my wife?"

"Yes." The nurse looked evenly into Joe's eyes without blinking.

"We're *not* divorced." Joe sat down in disbelief resting his head in his hands. "She's pregnant. You can't take her off life support even if she is dead. That's my child. Why does this all have to happen so quickly? What's the rush? I'm her husband and I have the right." He bit his lip trying to control his emotions. "I have the right . . to decide in this situation."

The nurse backed up a few steps and collected herself. She was just doing her job: *why was this so difficult for him to understand. Maybe if she said this a little more forcefully, he would do what she wanted. Then again, maybe not.* She decided to try reasoning and common sense first.

In her most professional manner, talking slowly for effect, she began again: "First of all, your mother-in-law told me you were in the middle of a divorce. That makes your mother-in-law the legal next of kin."

Divorce? Joe's mind whirled. Mary hadn't said anything to him about a divorce. In fact, they had talked specifically about it and they both agreed they didn't want a divorce. Joe began to sob in disbelief.

"Secondly, any child not viable outside the mother's body has no legal rights. Thirdly," and here the nurse paused, "I've worked ER for over ten years and most women, say 85% to 90% of women in car accidents of a lesser magnitude than this, lose their fetus, and the few who do survive are so deformed from the mother's injuries and the meds she has to take just to survive that..."

"I don't care!" Joe yelled out between sobs.

The nurse took a different approach trying, rather unconvincingly, to sound more sympathetic. "It's a hard thing to do, but in the long-run, it's what's best for everyone. Your mother-in-law understands this and is willing to make the hard decision. You don't want to see her suffer. You don't want to have a handicapped child with a substandard life dependent on the state. I have seen these cases before, and I can assure you, she is clinically dead. The fetus is most likely dead by now too, or will be within a few more hours, and even if by some miracle these machines could keep her body working until we could take the fetus, the baby would probably die shortly after birth. I've seen it happen before, let me tell you. . . . And the expense . . . ." The nurse shook her head.

Joe was silent. In his current state he just didn't know what to say to this worldly woman.

"You can do this Mr. Smith. We're here to help you. Dr. Bartlett is a trained medical professional. He knows what's best. You have to trust him in this situation. He can advise you as what's best." The nurse wrapped up her argument by saying, "Your wife is an organ donor, and the fetus can be used for research. In this way, their lives will go on helping others."

Like an angry bear, Joe rose to stare the nurse in the eye. "Go get the doctor now!"

The nurse turned to the waiting orderly leaning against the door frame. "Kevin, get hospital security." Kevin snapped into gear and disappeared like a well-trained pet obeying his master's voice.

"Mr. Smith, I've tried to politely ask you to leave. Now, here's your last chance. Your mother-in-law wants you out of here. You can leave peacefully, or you can go kicking and screaming with hospital security. You've got about two minutes to decide." Joe looked up toward heaven and gave a heartfelt cry. This was not an act of religious show, but a helpless plea of a desperate man with no other hope calling to his Risen Savior in a time of need, "Oh Lord Jesus, send angels to help me!" The nurse, obviously uncomfortable at Joe's sudden change of focus became unsure of what do do next. "Don't start pulling that religious stuff on me," the nurse shrieked; an unexplainable sense of panic arising in her empty soul. She took a step back and reminded herself, in an attempt to deal with the fear she was feeling, *security will be here soon!*

From behind the dividing curtain a massive man in a pullover shirt and slacks appeared. Joe was trying to decide if he looked more like an NFL linebacker or a professional wrestler as he pushed back the divider curtain and ducked under the bar. Robert Forbes, a man who looked to be in his mid-forties with greying temples, was no angel, but he had no trouble seeing who was in the right, and who was in the wrong here. He quickly sidestepped the nurse, as a small crowd of bystanders began to gather in the area, wondering what all the commotion and noise was about. "Nurse"..... the intruder looked at the embroidered name on the jacket with narrowing perceptive eyes, "Williams, I think you better do what the man says and get the doctor." Robert's steel blue eyes peered deep into hers, and she knew what he meant. She had lost round one, but she wouldn't lose round two; hospital security was on the way. "All right, I'll get the doctor." The nurse turned and left with a cool air of professionalism.

Joe kneeled in the chair. "Oh God, help me. Mary and I don't deserve your mercy. God, Mary is not saved! I can't let her go to eternity like this! God have mercy on her. Spare her life so she might repent and be saved, and please God, spare my child." Robert placed his burly hand on Joe's shoulder as Joe shook with emotion. In a faint Scottish accent, Robert began to speak, "lovin' Savior, please hear this man's request. Give this woman one more chance to repent and be saved that she might spend eternity with You. Savior. . . . Deliverer, we give back to you the life of this unborn child, this special gift from you. Protect this child with your loving care. Amen." Joe looked up into the eyes of the concerned man with thanks and gratitude for one brief moment. Before he could speak, five hospital security officers in matching uniforms, followed by Dr. Bartlett, filed into the room. Joe stood and turned toward the men.

Joe's mother-in-law stood just outside the door, looking on in angry contempt, tears streamed down her scowling face. *How dare he question the doctor!* She loved her daughter, but the doctor had told her that Mary was already dead. She respected and trusted what the doctors had told her: she had *no* respect for Joe. He wanted to prolong Mary's pain and suffering. As for the baby, she had no desire to keep *his* child if Mary was gone. The bitterness and pride that filled her heart had squeezed out any love for this helpless little one now growing within Mary. In her mind, it wasn't a child—just a fetus, and deep down she felt embarrassed to admit she was old enough to *have* grandchildren. She glared at Joe, the cause of all her problems. If looks could kill he would have been dead.

Joe cleared his throat, trying to look less desperate and more reasonable. He ran his fingers through his disheveled hair in a vain attempt to gain control of his emotions. "Doctor you said we could run some tests? Could we give this a little more time and make sure we're doing the right thing?"

———

Mr. Verde set at his large burled walnut desk in his spacious top floor office. One half of the office was luxuriously furnished; the other half of the office was tastefully done and resembled a studio apartment. Mr. Verde spent much more time in this office than he did at home. His first two wives had resented the fact that his job came first, but he and his third wife had an understanding. She enjoyed all the perks that came from being married to a successful businessman, and she had understood from the start that his job came first. Mrs. Verde was the dutiful wife; she was there when she was needed, but not a bother or an obstacle to his career when he needed to work late. Mr. Verde mused about his relationship with his wife as he picked up the phone. They were both good people, and he took pride in that. They gave to charity, put in their weekly appearance at the church each Sunday morning, were active at the country club, and were concerned about the environment. Mr. Verde subconsciously congratulated himself on how much good he was doing as the phone rang on the other end of the line. He had already ordered the staff in the transplant center to do whatever they needed to do to check for compatibility of Mary Smith as a donor for Carol Thomas, and he had been assured by his staff the liver was compatible. He was about to help save a woman's life, and hopefully have a new wing built onto the hospital in the process. At the prospect of this, his heart filled with pride.

Carol and Bernard Thomas sat side-by-side in the back of the limousine, her head resting on his shoulder, his arms encircling her. He had ordered the nurse to ride in the front seat with the chauffeur, with the privacy glass up, so they might have some quiet time together. A tear slowly traced its way down Carol's cheek as she snuggled in close savoring the aroma of Bernard's cologne. She inhaled deeply and thought to herself *I love this man*. One of the worst parts about dying was thinking about leaving Bernard behind. The trip to Chicago had been like so many others: the registration, the blood work, the waiting. At Bernard's request, she'd agreed to expand the search, but, at this point, she didn't have much hope. She closed her eyes, enjoying the simple pleasure of just being in his arms. For once it was like old times, and Carol let the bitterness, frustration, and anger slip from her and not sabotage their relationship.

As she lay there in her beloved's arms, head nestled on his breast, Carol became aware of a bizarre sensation against the side of her head and a sound faintly reminiscent of an electric razor. She was thankful Bernard had remembered to change the setting on his phone to vibrate mode as she realized how deafening the ring would have been with her ear so close. She became irritated that her perfect moment had been disturbed. She lifted her head and looked up at her husband as he reached into his breast pocket to retrieve the offending cell phone. He squinted slightly to read the caller ID and his heart skipped a beat as he noticed it was a call from the hospital.

"Mr. Thomas, are you on the plane yet, Sir?" Bernard glanced out the tinted window and replied, "No, we are still on our way to the airport. What do you need?" Mr. Verde paused a moment for effect. "I have some news that could be potentially very good for you and your wife. A young woman who has filled out a donor card and has AB negative blood has been in our hospital for the last few hours. The attending doctor tells me the lady is completely brain dead, and her liver appears to be in good shape. Her legal guardian has agreed to take her off life support, and we need you to return to the hospital as soon as possible."

A complex maze of emotions flew through Bernard's head. He was sorry someone had to lose their life in order to save his own wife. Pushing all these thoughts to the back of his mind, he looked at Carol and forced a smile, "good news!" He toggled the intercom button and relayed the information, the limousine accelerated as it moved into the exit lane and they made their way back to the hospital.

A look of great relief and hope was on Bernard's face. They had registered at so many hospitals, and it was hard to believe they might now have a liver, after all this time. Carol thought about what this transplant could mean for her and Bernard. Maybe there was a God who cared about her after all.

———————————

The doctor followed hospital protocol as he explained, "Mr. Smith, I can no longer discuss the situation with you. You are not the patient's legal guardian. Those decisions are her Mother's, and I'm more than willing to follow her wishes."

"We're not divorced!," Joe shouted as he stepped forward to face the men.

"Gentlemen," the doctor called out in a voice that conveyed he and the hospital security had already talked this over. Two men took Joe by the arms and began dragging him down the hall while three stayed beside the doctor. Joe fought, for the first time feeling the pull on the stitches in his right arm, but it was of no use. Robert stepped past the doctor and into the hall as he looked on for one brief moment. With everything in him, he wanted to believe that the young man before him was in the right, but he didn't know the man. How could he be sure? What if he was a criminal? *If you hesitate a moment more Forbes, it will be too late*, he thought.

Lord show me what to do! Stepping in front of the security officers, Robert addressed them, "Gentlemen, can you explain to me your legal right to do this?" They gave him an annoyed look that said, *you obviously have no idea of how things work around here.* "We don't have to explain anything to you," one of them answered. They walked on down the hall ignoring Robert. "Do you have a warrant for this man's arrest or reasonable cause to arrest or detain him?" Hospital security pushed forward ignoring Robert's question, and pushing Robert down the hall ahead of him. *Something has to be done, and fast, Forbes.* Robert shouted to Joe, "Have you ever had divorce papers served on you? Have you ever signed anything?" "No!" Joe pleaded for help with his eyes as he continued his forced trip down the hall. "Stop," commanded Robert "he's not divorced! He is her legal guardian!" The hospital security continued dragging Joe down the hall as if nothing had been said. Robert made a life and death decision at this point. *Why do you always get yourself in these messes?* With a form that would make an NFL player proud, Robert tackled both of the guards, dragging them down, and leaving them a jumbled mess on the floor, somehow freeing Joe in the process. The experience of nearly two decades of playing rugby in his native Scotland allowed Robert to be the first one up on his feet. He hadn't quite lost all of his accent from his past, and he certainly hadn't lost his athletic ability either. Without taking time to adjust his clothing, he pulled Joe from their reach as the security guards regained their feet. It was clear from the look on each man's face, that his maneuver had gotten their attention!

Robert turned to Joe, as he regained his composure, and asked in a calm tone, as if they had merely been sipping tea and eating crumpets, "Would you like to retain me as legal counsel in this matter, Sir? I would suggest that to be the wisest course of action, under the circumstances." Joe accepted with a grateful nod.

"Listen up Doctor! This lad is his wife's legal guardian. They are not divorced. As his legal counsel, I was wondering if you would like us to take action against you, these security officers, and this hospital?" Robert's eyes flashed. "If that woman dies, if she's taken off life support without her husband's consent, if her baby dies, we will take you to court on murder charges, assault and battery, and whatever else I can think up later." Just as the other three security officers were about to get involved, Dr. Bartlett, stepped in and said, "Let's all slow down and rethink this. Security, could you please wait over there for a few minutes. I will call if I need you further." The security guards moved to position themselves between the nurses' station and the exit to wait the doctor's further instructions.

With slow, deliberate, words Joe spoke, thankful for any chance he might have to save Mary, "Sir, I've never signed any papers or had any legal documents served on me. I've never been before a judge either, and this is the first I've ever heard of divorce." Robert, fully aware there were two lives hanging in the balance, asked, "Doctor, you are familiar with the Terri Schiavo case are you not? I am sure someone in your position will remember back in February 2005, the Court declared the parents had no rights in the decision regarding life support as long as the wife and husband were still legally married." Doctor Bartlett heard and understood exactly what Robert was saying. He was also acutely aware of what he was inferring. Making no comment the doctor directed Joe back into the room.

The two looked on as Mary's Mom said a tearful goodbye while a medical team assembled outside the doorway; a young lady from the business office held a stack of legal forms for the legal guardian to sign. Dr. Bartlett put a halt to the proceedings. "We're going to have to wait on taking this woman off life support until we can get some more legal counsel, and determine who the true legal guardian is." At this time Robert entered and queried, "Do you have a state marriage license, lad?" Joe nodded. "What state and county were you married in?" Robert didn't even know the name of the man he'd stepped in to rescue. "Here in Chicago, Illinois County, Illinois." Robert turned to the doctor, "Get your legal staff down here and have them look it up doctor." "It's after 5:00 and the county offices are all closed for the weekend. I doubt . . . ," the doctor trailed off in mid-sentence and began a new thought, "We may have to hold her over the weekend. In her critical condition, I think she'll probably pass over the weekend anyway, and this will be a non-issue."

Mary's mother, who had been unusually silent while listening to the exchange, now felt she had to make her presence known. It wouldn't do to let Joe think he was in charge. "Are you going to let my daughter lay there and suffer all weekend? You don't love her! You'll be hearing from my lawyer, you!" Jane Jones then stabbed her finger into his chest, and stormed out of the room. Robert thought, *good riddance.* The doctor took the opportunity to step outside and make some notes on his chart. He dismissed those waiting outside the room except for the young lady from the business office. He took her aside and spoke to her in hushed, private tones. "Better see what kind of insurance this fanatic has," he whispered, "and get someone to run a background check on him."

Joe collapsed in the chair, stunned and shocked by the turn of events that had taken place. He wanted to rest, he needed to sleep, but he couldn't. He was way too nervous, and he didn't trust anyone, not even Robert Forbes. "Oh God, thank you for saving Mary's life." Joe's breath still came hard and fast. Just then he realized his chest hurt from the pounding of his heart. He looked down and cradled his throbbing arm, and for the first time became aware of the blood seeping through his bandage.

Chapter 3

"While there's life, there's hope." **Cicero**, (106 BC - 43 BC)

Robert Forbes' wife sat in a chair next to her injured daughter in a corner of the ER room trying to relax and look calm, after her husband had tackled the security guards. Her five uninjured daughters crowded around her, presenting a loving, homey atmosphere, while their baby peacefully slept. Each of the girls had their mom's long, flowing brown hair, but all of them except the baby, who now lay asleep in the carrier, had their father's steel blue eyes. The girls' features seemed to be a balanced mix of both mom and dad. With amazing quietness they played and entertained themselves. Several of them looked at books, and the oldest daughter, nearly 14, busied herself combing, braiding, and then combing and braiding again her younger siblings' hair.

Mrs. Forbes tried to move her legs into a more comfortable position, but there was little room left on the floor for her feet with the girls entertaining themselves there. Life was always interesting being married to a zealous Christian man with more than his fair share of vision and purpose, but today had certainly ranked as one of the larger adventures, dare she think challenges, they had faced in their marriage. Robert sat back quietly in his seat in the crowded little room looking almost like a normal American dad. His wife closed her eyes tightly, trying to block the happenings of the afternoon out of her mind. *Why did their family always have to be so different?* She knew anything normal about Robert was only a mirage, but then as she smiled and winked at him she remembered, normal really was quite boring. Boring would never be a word used to describe life at the Forbes house. His wife loved Robert and wouldn't change him for the world. But on days like today, she couldn't help but wonder, *Why couldn't they just blend in and be normal here at the hospital?*

Their baby was asleep in her carrier on the floor beside Mrs. Forbes's chair, and the 23-month-old child lay asleep in Robert's lap. As she leaned close to him to whisper in his ear, she kissed him lightly on the cheek,"How do you get yourself into these messes?" Robert lifted his hand from underneath his daughter's sleeping head and gingerly moved his daughter into a position where she was asleep on his shoulder. Gently stroking his wife's cheek with his free hand, he whispered back. "Divine providence, my dear, God's divine providence."

Robert's four- and five-year-old daughters, the two everyone mistook for twins, were snuggled up on Mom's chest, one straddling each leg. Sarah, almost seven, sat on the examination table taking in all of the sights, smells, and sounds of this strange new place while holding a bandage on her still bleeding leg. Every time she moved, the paper on the table rattled making an annoying sound. A cut about two inches long and one inch deep was on Sarah's knee. The bleeding had just about stanched, but Mrs. Forbes feared there might still be gravel and dirt deep in the wound. Their three older girls, sitting on the floor near the doorway, were looking at some Living Science books Mom had checked out from the library the day before. The books still happened to be in the van when they came to the hospital.

Robert glanced at his watch, almost regretting the decision to bring all the children to the emergency room. He had assumed the hospital trip would only take an hour or two when all of the sisters had pleaded to go with him to see the hospital.

Once before, when he had taken their now ten-year-old to the emergency room, he had refused to let anyone else come. For several months afterward, the four who were old enough to speak had tormented both parents, and the injured daughter, with endless questions as to what had happened at this strange place called the emergency room. When it became obvious that Sarah's accident would require stitches they quickly decided to turn this trip into an educational opportunity. Now he came to realize, had his wife not been with him, he would have been unable to help Joe Smith. So he accepted the decision as from the Lord as he continued to wait for the doctor.

A few minutes later, a white-coated intern walked past the curtain into their side of the room as he carefully stepped around the girls sitting on the floor.

"Well what do we have here—a skinned up knee?" The doctor took a quick look around the small partition attempting to count the children as he passed them. "Still trying for that son? Gotta hand it to you. Most people would have given up by now. How many have you got here? Five?"

"Seven," Mrs. Forbes replied as she had done so many times before.

"All yours?" the doctor questioned.

Robert replied for her, "Yes, they are all ours, and no, we don't run a daycare." He had grown tired of people putting his wife on the spot and asking this question about three children ago. Many people wrongly assume if you have a large family all the children must not be out of the same union or that you're running a daycare. Divorce and remarriage happens, but why do so many assume it to be the norm? He did not mind explaining to the doctor why he had a large family if he truly wanted to know, but now was not the time, or place to explain why they had a large family.

Pointing to Sarah on the examination table, Robert tried to direct the conversation back to his injured daughter. "Doctor, she fell on a sharp rock while playing. That happens when the walk doesn't get swept before you skate," Robert replied with a knowing look to the other children. Robert helped Sarah carefully lift the gauze from the wound, so the doctor could examine the injury.

The doctor took little notice of the wound as he continued to talk. "Ouch, that's deep." the doctor said as he looked at her face and forced a smile. Are you sure someone didn't beat you up," the doctor asked Sarah as he pointed to a large bruise on her cheek where she had hit heads with her sister while jumping on the trampoline a few hours before. His steady stare and his obviously fake smile made Sarah uneasy. He paused for a moment to listen to her comment.

"I was skating really fast, and I fell and hit a sharp rock I didn't see when I swept off the driveway," Sarah said. "Mom washed me off." The doctor suspected that was all the answer he was going to get from this small patient with her parents in the room. The doctor quickly decided the best course of action was to see about getting the rest of the family out of the room so he or the social worker could determine what really happened by questioning the child further.

Approaching the situation from another angle, he continued. "We need to wash that wound out really well, and she'll need a local and a few stitches, then you can go home. Glancing at the curtain behind him, the doctor said, "Why did they put you down here in the trauma center? You friends with that guy?" the doctor pointed at the curtain with his thumb. "Not previously," Robert answered.

Robert knew why—*God had planned it that way.* "I guess all the other rooms were full," his wife added, trying to sound nonchalant.

"Nurse," the doctor called out into the hallway, where a nurse was hurrying past, "we are going to need a local anesthetic and some stitches, so we can get these people out of here. Turning back to the Forbes family, he coolly addressed them, "If you and your family can step out into the waiting room, we'll have her stitched up in no time." He examined the bruise on her cheek with a small pen light again and asked, "When did she have her last tetanus shot?" Casting Robert a subtle look, his wife said nothing as their eyes made contact for a brief moment, and then Robert spoke breaking the awkward silence.

"She's never been immunized."[1] The doctor raised his eyebrows," Don't believe in that sort of thing? Clicking a button on his computer, he looked at a new screen. "You indicated a religious objection on the paperwork. Are you religious?" *So the doctor knew that already*, Robert surmised.

Robert began to weigh his words more carefully. He'd been down this path before. He knew very well that in some people's minds admitting you were religious was an admission of mental instability. "I wouldn't call myself religious, but I am a follower of Jesus Christ."

The doctor methodically asked, "Attend church somewhere?"

"Actually, we are the church," his wife slowly said. "If you'll look at the forms we filled out, you'll see we have an immunization exemption form,"[2] Robert added.

The doctor had known about the exemption form before he came into the room, but he was trained by the DCFS (Department of Child and Family Services) staff to ask these seemingly innocent questions to check for child abuse, and see if he could get any further information from the parents. The doctor's irritation level was rising. He wasn't sure what he should do next. In his recent training class, the attractive social worker had explained most of these Christian fanatics were child abusers, but he had been so distracted by her skin-tight top and miniskirt that he had missed the part about what he was supposed to do.

Trying to remember what he was supposed to do next, he spoke to Sarah, "Where do you go to school?" His mannerism to Sarah was overly sweet to the point of being almost funny, and even Sarah felt uncomfortable around him. The child would have liked to have hugged Mom, and retreat into the safety of her arms, but Mom was busy with her sisters and couldn't be reached. "I don't. Mom home schools me."

Joe Smith listened closely from the other side of the room

behind the curtain. He couldn't help but be curious about the man who had come to his rescue. *Why was the doctor asking so many questions*, Joe wondered. *The doctor sure was curious about the Forbes family.*

The doctor's questioning continued: "Are you on WIC with all these kids? I suspect you could sure use the help." At this point Robert was getting really annoyed. *Did he not provide well enough for his family?*

"Doctor," Robert said as he cleared his throat, "we don't qualify for government aid, nor would we apply for it if we did. We don't believe it is the government's responsibility to take care of us. It is God's responsibility."

Before the doctor had time to ask another question, the emergency room receptionist appeared in the doorway, interrupting the doctor. "Somehow," she spoke slowly as she flipped through some forms in her hand, "we didn't get a Social Security number on your daughter at the registration desk." "She doesn't have one," Robert said as a matter of fact. There was a long uncomfortable silence on the Forbes' side of the curtain.

Joe sat there in stunned disbelief as he continued to listen. *What type of man was this Robert anyway? Didn't he understand that everyone has to have a social security number? How would his daughters have access to society if they didn't have a social security number?*

"Some type of religious objection, I assume?" the doctor replied.

"Well, doctor," Robert flashed an inviting smile; he could think of several remarks he would like to make to this overly inquisitive Doctor. His preference would be to tell the doctor it was none of his business, but he knew that wasn't the wisest course of action. "If you are really that interested in what we do and why we do it, this isn't really the time or place. I already have two sleeping children and the others need to go to bed as well. If it is all the same to you, we would like to go home as soon as you have stitched

Sarah up. My wife and I would be willing to have you over for supper some night next week and discuss it, though. Is Monday good for you?"

The doctor looked a little embarrassed and awkwardly left the room without making any reply. More knowing looks passed between Robert and his wife, who despite her look of composure, gave out an exhausted sigh. "Not this again," she whispered to Robert as a worried expression crossed her face.

Joe felt like he was intruding into the Forbes' private life, but he couldn't help it. Rising from his chair, Joe walked from the room in search of a water fountain so he could take the pain medication in his pocket. His curiosity was piqued as he thought about Robert Forbes. He had to like the guy, and yet, he could not help but think the guy was a little too extreme. The guards had been none too gentle on his injured arm, and his headache had finally arrived with a vengeance. He was bent over drinking when the doctor, completely unaware of his presence, pulled one of the young nurses aside.

"Get Department of Child and Family Services down here right away. I think we've got a couple of child abusers here. They home-school their tribe of kids, and they're obviously religious to the point of extreme. That's 2 out of 3.[3] I think we need to have some psychiatric evaluation done on these people."[4]

"I don't for a minute believe that roller skate story. Did you see the size of that bruise on her cheek, and anyone who doesn't immunize or have Social Security numbers shouldn't be allowed to have children, in my opinion. Doesn't believe in taking government aid? Anyone who won't get involved with the government has gotta be up to something." The nurse nodded her head and turned to leave. "Hey," the doctor added pointedly, "be careful what you say. He's a lawyer. If it hadn't been for him, we'd already have the room next door cleared out and ready for the next patient."

Robert wasn't what most people considered a lawyer. He hadn't taken the bar exam, nor was he licensed to practice law, but he had spent many years studying the Constitution, the documents of the Founding Fathers, as well as international law. In many ways though, Robert was more qualified than a member of the bar to represent Joe as his "legal counsel." Robert was wise in the ways of the world. He knew there was nothing like a lawyer to bring things to a grinding halt, at least for a time, and nothing like the word "lawsuit" to strike fear in the hearts of men.

The doctor returned to the door of the small room with a wound care and suture kit. Hoping for a chance to be alone with Sarah, he said, "Everyone will have to leave the room while I stitch your daughter up. We can't risk someone bumping me while I'm working. It's just too crowded in here."

"Dear, take the girls, and I'll stay with Sarah," Robert replied in way that sounded loving and yet carried the force of a command.

"I said everyone needed to leave," the doctor added assuming Robert must not have understood the command.

"Yes, but I'm staying with Sarah anyway," Robert answered with a look that conveyed to the doctor he knew what the doctor was up to, "I'll sit on the other side of the table while you work on her, so I won't *bump your arm.*"

Returning to the room to be with his wife, Joe knelt on the floor in deep, earnest prayer. If he was honest with himself, he had to admit Robert wasn't *exactly* what he had been praying for.

Robert's little girl, Sarah, was stitched up and ready to go home. It was nearly midnight, and five of Robert's seven daughters had fallen asleep in the waiting room chairs. As Joe finished his prayer, he looked up to see Robert who had stopped in for a final word with Joe.

In a caring, compassionate way, he put his arm on Joe's shoulder. Robert placed a card in Joe's hand with his contact information on one side, and John 5:13 on the other. Joe briefly glanced at Robert's phone number, address, and e-mail along with the Bible verse. His wife looked kindly at Joe from the doorway, where she waited with the girls.

"If there's anything we can do, just call. We'll be praying for all three of you. By the way, what is your name, so we'll know who to pray for?"

Joe wiped his nose, "Joe Smith, and this is Mary," Joe said, gently grasping Mary's hand. "Thanks, lawyer," Joe said wishing he had the strength and the words to express how much he appreciated what Robert had done. He decided a handshake was the best he could do now, as he raised his hand to Robert. He wondered if he could trust Robert. *Was it safe to make a friend of him?*

Along with his firm grip, came the sincere reply, "I'm no lawyer—just a citizen who tries to know our rights under the constitution, and live by the laws as they are written."

Joe paused for a moment, searching in his mind how to respond.

Should he tell them what the doctor had said? "I don't know exactly how to to tell you this. . . I overheard the doctor say they were going to call DCFS on you."

"I know. They've done it before, but they really have no true authority over us, and I feel confident they will leave us alone, eventually."

"Leave you alone?"

"Affirmative, lad, it's a long story best left for another day. Maybe sometime when we have more time, I can attempt to explain it to you. For now you have enough to deal with, without worrying about us, thank you for letting us know though."

"In dealing with your situation, I'd just exhort you to keep praying and reading your Bible. Do you have e-mail?" Robert handed him a crayon and a Big Chief Tablet. Feeling rather childish, Joe scribbled a quick address and gave it back to Robert.

After the Forbes' departure, Dr. Bartlett ordered a transfer to a private room in the ICU. During the transfer, Joe never left Mary's side. After the hospital staff finally left, Joe took a deep breath and enjoyed the silence while he cradled his injured arm on his chest. The last thing he remembered was the bare white wall and the mechanical breathing of Mary's respirator.

When he awoke, he saw a short Hispanic man, with straight

black hair, bending over Mary examining her abdomen. Joe sat up, dazed and unsure of his surroundings, as the events of the past twenty four hours flooded back into his fatigued mind.

The doctor, turning from examining Mary, was the first to speak. "Sorry, I didn't want to wake you. I thought you might need the rest. Looks like you've had a pretty hard day. I'm Doctor Rodriquez, OB," he said extending his hand to Joe with a warm smile. "Congratulations Dad, your wife's blood work shows her progesterone and HCG levels are elevated and at a healthy level for a normal pregnancy. I've been called in for a consult. I'm the obstetrician on duty this weekend. I wanted to check on the extent of her abdominal injuries. Fortunately, all the internal organs seem to be functioning for now: I emphasize *seem*. . . I won't know for sure until we get some testing done."

Joe searched the doctor's eyes for some glimmer of hope. "Doctor, I'm not a medical person. Can you tell me what's really going on—use small words, please? The nurse earlier today gave me a rather depressing outlook on Mary's situation."

The doctor questioned, a hint of a smile playing at the corners of his mouth, "You mean yesterday?"

Joe looked at his watch and nodded, "Yesterday."

Dr. Rodriquez sat down in the chair next to Joe, "I don't want to give you false hope—the situation here is bleak, but I will do whatever I can to preserve this baby's life as long as possible. I believe this baby has a right to life, whatever type of life that may be. Is that your wish?" A convulsion of sobs broke forth from Joe as he tried to answer, but was only able to shake his head amidst the sobs indicating his agreement.

"Good. I'm glad we are speaking the same language," the doctor said, "Your wife has sustained severe injuries. Often times in these situations, the baby will be lost due to the trauma to the mother's body. If it does happen, there is little I can do to save the baby. I want you to be aware this may happen, or may have already happened. If your wife dies, the baby will die, but if she stays in a vegetative state

41

until the baby's lungs are developed enough, there is a chance we might be able to save the baby. It's very controversial, and I want you to know that due to all your wife has been through, and the quality of nutrition received from this point on, the baby will probably have some problems—very likely major problems—like retardation."

Joe dropped his head, vainly searching for a dry spot on his handkerchief. He finally gave up and used his one remaining shirt sleeve, and then raised his head to stare deeply into the doctor's caring eyes. "I don't care doctor. Just save my child, if you can. I'd give *everything I own,* to hold that child for five minutes."

"Five, ten minutes may be all you get, but..." Here the doctor paused for a moment to weigh his words, as he hurried into the bathroom and grabbed a box of tissues for Joe, "but I'll pray God gives you a lifetime with this very special child."

Joe relaxed a bit, realizing the doctor *had* given him a little hope to cling to. He and the doctor were speaking the same language after all. Joe thanked the Doctor for the box of tissues as he dropped another one in the trash. Something within his spirit told him he could trust Dr, Rodriquez. "Doctor . . . do you think my wife is brain dead?"

Dr. Rodriquez looked down at the chart in his hands. What he had to say wasn't easy to communicate. "What did the neurologist say?"

"Neurologist? There hasn't been any neurologist, yet."

"Have they conducted any tests, like an EEG, or a conventional . . ."

Joe interrupted the doctor in mid-sentence. "They haven't tested anything since the ER doctors ran the preliminary stuff."

"Well then, they really don't know if she's brain dead or not," the doctor said flatly. "You could have an apnea test run, but I don't think we have anything to gain by running that test."

"Please explain that Doctor."

"Well, to run the apnea test, they would take your wife off the ventilator, and I don't want to do anything that would compromise the baby's oxygen levels for even one minute. Also, if your wife is brain dead, the powers-that-be will push to take her off life support, and then you will definitely lose the baby. So you see, either way, it's not going to do you any good to request that test. The best thing for you to do right now is to wait-and-see. This coma may simply be caused by bilateral damage to the reticular formation of the . . ." He paused in mid-sentence, as Joe's facial expression changed to a confused stare. He finished simply, "We won't know for a while. If that's the case, whatever happens, don't let them convince you to do a pharmaceutical coma to preserve higher brain function. The drugs they use to do that would definitely hurt your baby."

Joe looked at the floor again as his mind mulled over what the doctor had just said. "There's no fear of that," Joe said in a dejected voice. "Dr. Bartlett doesn't think she has any brain function to preserve. He keeps saying she's dead—her body just hasn't quit, yet."

Dr. Rodriquez flipped through Mary's charts. *Why had the medical staff given up on this patient? Why were they writing her off as if she was already dead? Certainly her situation was bleak, but why weren't they at least trying to save the baby?* Dr. Rodriquez continued, "The first thing I need to do is get a sonogram and see how this amigito is doing."

Rising from the chair, Dr. Rodriquez pulled out his cell phone placed a call to the OB floor. "Martha, is Rachel here this morning?" Joe heard only the doctor's part of the conversation. "Probably at the crisis pregnancy center, huh? Well, I'm going to need our new machine, up here in the ICU. . . Yes, the 4D that came in last week. . ." the doctor said shaking his head up and down in an exaggerated almost comical way, ". . .I know it's inconvenient to move it all the way up here, but please do it for me. . . That would be fine, thank you."

Scrolling through the numbers on his cell phone, the doctor found the number and dialed. "Hello. Good. I'm glad this is the Crisis Pregnancy Center, and I didn't hit the wrong number on my phone again. Is Rachel Washington working today?" Another pause. The doctor seemed to be getting nervous for some reason. "Dr. Rodriquez. . . Thank you"

Joe noticed his discomfort and wondered what was going on. "Rachel," the doctor cleared his throat nervously, and tried to sound confident. ". . . I really need your help this morning in the ICU." The doctor stepped out into the hallway to avoid any undue stress it might cause Joe if he heard what he was going to say next. "I've got a really critical case, and well—I know you and I share the same views on this. . . Thanks, I really appreciate your willingness to help save this baby."

As Joe watched the doctor leave the room, he felt alone, almost abandoned. Instinctively, he bowed his head in prayer, *O God, give me strength and courage for this situation. I don't think I can handle it.*

As Joe lifted his head, he saw Dr. Rodriquez standing in the doorway of the room.

"Miss Washington is going to be down here in an hour or so to take a look at your wife and baby. Would you tell her to call me when she gets here? I've got to go see my other patients."

"I can do that," Joe replied.

Not long after the doctor left, a cart loaded with wires, probes, a computer, and computer screen was pushed into his room by an attendant. A short time later, an attractive dark skinned lady in a pink dress tapped lightly on the door, "Hello, I'm Rachel Washington," her voice was low and pleasant to listen to. "Do you mind if I examine your wife?"

Joe nodded yes, and looked on in anticipation.

With no more explanation, she exposed Mary's stomach and squirted some gel onto her abdomen, smoothing it out with something Joe thought looked very much like a very large computer mouse. Her face was silent and expressionless. He could tell she was concentrating.

Joe studied her face, trying to read her facial expression. The anxiety of the moment was killing him. *Oh God, protect my son,* he silently prayed. Rachel tilted the display screen to a better angle and repositioned the probe, seemingly unaware of Joe.

Was she having trouble locating the baby? Still, no expression on her face. Finally after what seemed like forever, she turned the monitor toward Joe, "There," she said with a sympathetic smile, "There's your child."

Joe studied the screen, to see the rough outline of his precious, little baby. "Is he alive?" Joe asked, fearing the worst.

Rachel pointed to a heart rate scan circling the bottom of the screen. "You've got a good healthy heartbeat at this point—about 160. There may be other problems, but the preliminary scan looks good. I can see that the placenta is still attached, and there is good cord formation."

Joe sat back down in his chair as Rachel moved the probe across Mary's abdomen and captured some images on the display and saved them to show the doctor when he came. Joe felt like laughing, and he felt like crying. His baby was alive and well!

Dr. Rodriquez peered into the room and silently admired Rachel Washington as she worked. Both Rachel and Joe were so intent they neither one noticed him standing just outside the door. Rachel Washington was a perfectly gorgeous lady. Black, kinky hair, held back by a pearly pink head band, lined her perfectly oval face. Her glistening ebony eyes were framed in the thickest black lashes. Her smooth, flawless brown skin needed no make-up, but she did wear some soft pink lipstick which highlighted her full lips. A loose, modest dress, which reminded the doctor of a red bud blossom in the spring was gathered at the waist with a wide belt. He admired her beautiful, well rounded, feminine figure, and slender tiny waist. She was young, maybe 27. She wore no engagement rings or wedding bands, but Dr. Rodriquez wondered if there was a man in her life. She was beautiful, but it was her gentle, quiet spirit and her love for God that was even more attractive to the doctor. Dr. Rodriquez held her in such high esteem that he could almost believe she was an angel instead of a human working there at the hospital. Just being around her intimidated him.

He reminded himself that saving this baby was more important than his feelings and budding interest in Rachel Washington. He tried to put his feelings aside as he pulled the door shut behind him, and he began to wonder what Rachel had found out.

Rachel glanced to her side and saw the doctor enter the room. Turning her attention to Joe, she spoke, "You've got good news. Aren't you going to call your family and tell them?"

A sharp pang stabbed Joe's heart. He didn't really have any family to share his good news with, but he didn't want to tell Rachel about that. "You're right, maybe I should call some of the guys at work. I'm going to run down and get a cold drink."

As Joe left the room, Rachel timidly addressed Dr. Rodriquez, "Doctor, I've only done a preliminary scan, but I want you to take a look at this bruising on the uterus wall. I imagine that's where the steering wheel impact was. . . I'm concerned about head trauma." "Give me just a minute to change screens, and I'll do a closer scan on the head."

Dr. Rodriquez put his hand lightly over Rachel's hand, effectively stopping her from changing screens. His haunting black eyes stared deeply into hers, with a mixed look of tenderness and concern. She bowed her head, and felt her face growing hot. *Could he read the interest she felt for him in her face?* "Let's not go there Rachel. Sometimes it's better not to know the worst," he said. Rachel understood what he meant, and had to agree he was probably right.

"Can you give me some good news Rachel?" Rachel smiled and nodded at the doctor as he reluctantly let her hand go. "Well," she said sweetly, "the cervix is not compromised, the placenta has good attachment and looks fine. We have a good cord, and we have a strong heartbeat on the child. Here are all the vitals."

Dr. Rodriquez put his hands on the back of Rachel's chair and leaned over next to her to look at the data on the computer screen.

Rachel could feel his white lab coat brushing against her back, as he leaned over the back of her chair. *He's so handsome and gentle too*, she thought. *Doesn't he know how intimidating he is with his mysterious dark eyes, olive skin, and jet black hair?* Instinctively, she gracefully slid from the chair, offering it to the doctor.

The doctor took the chair. *She doesn't want to be around me, or near me. She doesn't want me too close,* his fragile ego told him. Turning from his own fears, he looked into Rachel's beautiful face trying to read her thoughts. He couldn't tell what she was thinking so he fell back against the safety net of keeping a "professional distance."

As he spoke to Rachel, he found himself wanting to be lost in the beauty of those dark eyes, but needing to stay focused on the life of this mother and baby. "Don't give me any news on this report that I don't want to hear," he said holding up the printout. Again, Rachel knew what he meant. "We are going to try and save this child at all costs," he said, looking into her eyes this time with less intensity. "If we don't know the child's age, they can't say it's not viable, and if we don't do a head scan, we don't have to report cranial damage." Rachel didn't need to perform the measurements to know how old this baby was. She did this all the time at the CPC several days a week, and she had a pretty good idea just by looking at what she had already seen. "Looks like I'm done for now," Rachel stated, as she grabbed a tissue to wipe the gel from Mary.

Doctor Rodriquez asked, "Before you do that, can we take a look at her kidneys?—off the record."

She placed the probe on Mary once again, and took a look at the kidneys as he requested. "The left one appears to have undergone some serious trauma doctor . . . from what I can tell the right kidney looks just fine, what do you think?"

"I think it looks very good indeed. Thanks Rachel I owe you for this one."

Rachel asked, "Are we done here, Doctor?"

Dr. Rodriquez helped Rachel wipe the gel from Mary, and prepared the machine for its return to OB, as Joe returned to the room. As the doctor held the door open for Rachel to wheel the sonogram from the room, he asked, "Would you send the OB nurse up here, please? I want to get some extra things in her IV. She is eating for two."

Joe had been so excited when he saw his baby, his son.

Dr. Rodriquez went over to sit beside Joe and talk for just a moment. "There's a lot of water in there that cushioned the baby during the accident, almost like it was designed to work that way, and one of Mary's kidneys appears to be undamaged, which reduces our concern of renal failure tremendously." Dr. Rodriquez glanced at his watch. *Wow, where had the day gone?* "Excuse me please, I need to go and do my rounds; I hope this has been a better day for you Mr. Smith," he left Joe alone with Mary.

Later that night, Joe sat numbly looking out the window at the lights along the shore of the lake. The Head doctor on the floor that night took a quick look in on Joe and Mary. Joe, dazed by all that had happened, didn't even notice him. The doctor left Joe, without saying a word and then went to the nurse's station.

"Nurse, let me know if anything changes in room 2A. I need to know when that lady passes. . . or if the family is willing to take her off life support. She's a donor with a rare blood type. If she passes, we may have an opportunity to save or improve several other lives this evening," the doctor said. The nurse nodded knowingly and went back to her duties.

CHAPTER 4

Misty Sellers turned the key in the door of her penthouse apartment and headed for her bedroom. Entering her bedroom early Saturday morning, she noted the time, 2:37 AM. No wonder she was exhausted! She threw her purse in the chair as she began to undress herself, leaving a trail of clothing on the floor behind her as she made her way to the bed. She had been out on the town with her girlfriends, and she was finally calling it a night. As she turned the satin coverlet back, she leaned over to check the caller ID on the blinking answering machine, on the night stand beside the bed.

An irritated frown crossed her face. "The hospital? Don't they realize I've got a 9 to 5 government job?" She dropped a decorative accent pillow on top of the blinking machine as she slipped beneath the inviting sheets. Misty checked the clock again, 2:53. Irritation was rising within her, sleep wouldn't come! . . . *Who called?* . . . The suspense was killing her. *I'll bet it was that tall, obviously-interested intern from the training session at the hospital. He is the only one who managed to get my home number.* She smiled as she thought of the young doctor, "Yes, it must have been him." With that nagging thought put to rest, she flipped her bed pillow to the cool side, rolled over and went to sleep.

Weaving her shiny silver sport coupe through the traffic on the way to work the following Monday morning, Misty pondered her job and position. Just two years ago she completed her Masters degree, with honors. She now trained doctors how to recognize child abuse in the patients they saw at the area hospitals. She also did field work leading a team of veteran police officers in removing children from dangerous situations. When they were with her, she was in charge of her own little police force. To Misty the most rewarding part of her job was rescuing children from dangerous situations of abuse and neglect. Having the authority to rescue defenseless children, made all her hard work to get to this point more than worth it. Having the power and authority to place these abused children in a place of safety where they could be properly fed, schooled, and cared for was a very satisfying part her job.

Misty Sellers had made it her mission in life to protect young ladies from the abuse she had experienced as a child. She was no longer that helpless little girl. Misty wiped away a tear, as she forced herself to focus on something besides what *he* had done to her.

She thought about the two wonderful women who had rescued her from that life. Her high school teacher, Ms. Dixon, and her therapist, Dr. Astra, who had helped her get her life straightened out with the help of meditation and yoga. These two role models had helped prepare her for life at the university.

During her days at the university, she had become heavily involved in the women's Lib movement and Students for a Democratic Society (SDS). Since she graduated, nothing had changed. She was more involved than ever in these worthy causes. In fact, her SDS connections had helped her land this job, and she still maintained those close relationships. The friends she had made while in college had become her family. Misty had a family now, filled with people who cared about her for the first time. Family was something her abusive alcoholic mother, with her endless string of *boyfriends* had never been.

As Misty entered her office, she lifted the screen on her laptop and checked her caseload for this cloudy Monday morning. Grabbing the day planner from inside her leather purse, she began mapping out her day. She remembered that she needed to check the hospital report to find out what had been so important at midnight on Friday. As she located the report and began to scan through it, Misty became filled with righteous indignation, which gradually transitioned into anger as she read further. *This situation must be resolved ASAP. She would handle this one herself!*

From what Misty could glean from this report, seven vulnerable girls were being held hostage by an abusive, hostile, religious-zealot father. As she read further into the report, she discovered the father had attacked hospital security. With no indication as to *why* he had done so. As she studied the additional comments at the bottom of the report she became even more exasperated with the case. *The father and mother had FAILED to protect these children by having them properly immunized! They were being denied an appropriate education in the public school system, and they did not have Social Security numbers. These girls don't even have access to state services and benefits. Anyone who refuses social security numbers must be up to something. . . What's he hiding from us? . . . How can we find them to provide what they need if they aren't in the system? . . . People like this should not be allowed to have children!*

Misty Sellers scrolled through the numbers on her phone. *Well, he wouldn't have them much longer if she could help it!*

After the girls were taken into protective custody and processed through the state system, they would require several foster families. *. . or one with a very large house. I wonder if. . .* She closed her phone and headed to check some information in her files.

Keeping this many children together was usually a practical impossibility. Most foster situations were limited to one or two kids, but Misty knew of a special Christian couple that had been preparing for just such an eventuality, and she suspected they would jump at the chance of saving these children from this abusive father.

Two of her closest friends had decided against marriage and had moved in with each other about six months ago. They each completed the foster parent process as singles, and they had also completed additional training for children classified as 'specialized and treatment situations.' They were prepared, in case their involvement was needed in this unique situation. They were faithful church attenders, so there would be no objection, based on religious grounds, to the placement of these girls with this couple.

Misty had recently been their guest at what they called their "worship experience"—not *her* cup of tea—but it worked for them. The pastor, a short thin woman, used a new, modern translation of the Bible, which was easy to understand and used gender-neutral language. She liked that part anyway.

The pastor was careful not to offend anyone there in the audience with her sermons. She alluded to some spiritual force that she had tapped into. What was it she had said? Faith was a force, words were the container of that force, positive attitudes yield positive results. It sounded like transcendental meditation to Misty. She was into meditation already. No need for her to hear a religious pep talk once a week. After all, Sunday was her day to sleep in.

Crystal and Star were active in their church, and they would be able to take these endangered children with them every week, satisfying the DCFS requirements. Who better to take in the seven abused girls than two of the most loving, patient, and caring women she knew? She could always divide the kids up into several separate homes if this placement didn't work out, but if she played her cards right, she believed she had enough connections to get all seven children placed with Crystal and Star. They were both Ivy-league educated professionals with great salaries and flexible schedules, and they had just purchased a 6000 square-foot, ten-bedroom home, so there should be plenty of room. *It should be a great match for these seven abused girls*, Misty thought as she re-read the home study documentation.

Crystal had recently told Misty that she and Star had intentionally purchased this larger home to allow them the room to care for several abused children at once. She could see no reason at this point why these seven abused girls should be divided up, since there was such an ideal placement available.

Misty could now see the wisdom of Crystal and Star selecting a home so near the grade school. They wanted to live close enough to be able to take the kids to school every day, and be involved in school community events. Each of the nine children placed with them in the past had been transitioned out of their foster care, and these ladies were still keeping in contact with them. These ladies had a great track record as foster parents, and they were currently awaiting some new kids to love and equip to take their place in a progressive global community. Misty knew that they hoped to adopt eventually, and if this situation was as bad as it looked on paper, she would help make that happen too. Both Star and Crystal could show love for these children like they showed for each other.

Punching the speed dial, she waited for Crystal to answer, "Crystal this is Misty, and I have seven girls that need your help..."

Misty flipped her cell phone closed with a smile. As Misty had expected, Star and Crystal were thrilled at the prospect of pouring their life, and love, into seven needy girls. Being able to shape and nurture them, so they would be able to integrate into today's rapidly changing, progressive culture, would be a privilege for them.

A few hours later, a very determined Agent Sellers ordered the driver to pull up to the Forbes gate in the mini-bus she had signed out from DCFS. She glanced in her rear view mirror to see her police escort pulling up on either side of the mini-bus. Before them stood a large iron gate almost entirely obscured with poster boards containing Bible verses and a sign, obviously made by a child, advertising goat's milk and farm fresh eggs. Centered in the middle of the clutter was a neat, orderly, strangely worded legal notice.

As they stood looking at the gate, they were startled by the loud barking of a farm collie. Misty had never seen a collie that big, and her natural reaction was to get back into the bus and wait for animal control. This dog looked like Lassie from the movies, but he sure didn't act like Lassie. From what she could tell from the behavior of that dog, anyone reaching to open the gate would not be able to do so without getting their hand chewed. Misty decided she liked that big iron gate being between her and that guard dog for the time being.

This wasn't going as planned. She told the police to get an animal control officer out here, in case they needed to force their way past the dog.

Robert Forbes looked out to the front gate from his bedroom window and prayed silently to God that they would just go away. Robert Forbes' wife nearly tripped over her own feet as she scurried the children away from the windows looking out onto the driveway. Picking up his two-year-old daughter, Robert hoisted her onto his shoulder, carried her into the living room, set her down on the floor with her favorite stuffed animal, and kissed her on the forehead.

"Stay in the house my bonnie lass," he smiled, kissed her on the forehead, and then winked at the children reassuring them that all was well. Robert beckoned his family to join him in front of the couch as he knelt before it and leaned forward in prayer, asking God for wisdom, guidance, and deliverance in this situation.

As he watched the animal control vehicle pull up, he realized he was going to have to visit with the people at the gate, or they might hurt his faithful dog. As Robert approached the gate, the dog stopped barking and stood quietly by his master, awaiting his command. Robert called out, "Greetings in the name of the Lord Jesus Christ. Do you greet me in the same name?"

Misty's eyes narrowed and her face grew red. She hated *these* religious types—such hypocrites. She wished they could be more like the people at Crystal and Star's church. *Why did they always have to identify themselves with the Lord Jesus Christ?*

Misty replied in her most authoritative voice, "My name is Agent Sellers, and I demand that you restrain your animal and open this gate in the name of the State of Illinois Department of Child and Family Services! This is official state business, and you will comply, or face the consequences. We are here to take your children into protective custody until a full child abuse investigation can be conducted."

Robert looked up from stroking the dog's head and replied, "Ms. Sellers, I suggest you read that notice on the gate in front of you very carefully before you go making any demands. If you would rather go to the court house and read it in better lighting there is a notarized copy on file there as well. I also suggest you go talk to your superiors so they can apprise you of my status. We've dealt with DCFS before, and they will be able to explain to you *why* you have no legal jurisdiction over anyone in my family. To your *escorts*, I suggest they radio in to their headquarters and check with their superiors before doing anything illegal.

"Please," Robert paused for effect, "Read the legal notice on the gate, ladies and gentlemen. I do not wish to continue this discussion any further. God bless *you* and *do have* an enlightening day." With that, Robert confidently turned his back on the visitors and returned to the house followed closely by his big collie.

Misty Sellers was mad. No, she was furious! She slammed her clipboard to the ground in an attempt to vent some of her frustration. *How could this Forbes be so cool, calm, and collected? Had he no respect for the law? Why didn't he FEAR her?* Misty was determined to rescue those girls! They were in danger. They needed her help, she wouldn't let them down. She still had the police.

Turning to the officers she said, "There are seven helpless girls in there being abused. It is our duty to protect them. We need to provide them a safe place away from. . . She thought of her own abuse and helplessness as a child. *Why hadn't someone rescued me from him?* With a pleading look, she gave orders to the police officers, "Go in and rescue those seven girls at once!"

For the first time in her career, her orders were ignored. The ranking officer radioed in to headquarters for instructions. He then walked up to the gate and began reading the posted notice into the microphone on his shoulder.

Misty was growing more impatient and angry by the minute. Why weren't they following her orders? Why did they have to check back with their superiors? She was their superior right now, and she had given them a direct order.

The officer returned to his car after he finished reading the legal notice into his radio. Dispatch had advised him to wait until the legal notice could be deciphered, and informed him they would also be contacting DCFS to find out if there had been any previous dealings with the Forbes family. Faced with this unacceptable delay, and what she considered insubordination, Misty became even more insistent that they go rescue the children.

Fighting hard to maintain her professional image, she went and conferred with the police officers, "I demand to know what the hold up is? Why can't you just do your job?" Shrugging their shoulders without ceremony, they informed her, "We are waiting for an interpretation of the legal notice before we proceed."

Misty climbed into the passenger seat of the transport vehicle, and slammed the door. "This is ridiculous!" She mumbled to herself, "What are those idiots waiting for?" She had never before had police officers refuse to follow her orders. Didn't they realize those girls were in danger? A tear of anger and frustration traced a line down Misty's face. She couldn't let those girls down. They needed her protection.

The driver wisely sat in silence, realizing no response was required from him. Misty folded her legs and rested her forearms on her knees palms up, and closed her eyes, forcing herself to relax.

The driver and Misty both jumped as they were startled by the police officer knocking on the door of the transport vehicle. As the door opened, the officer informed her, "Agent Sellers, Dispatch has ordered us to return to our patrol assignments. We will be leaving the area now." Why had their superiors ordered them to leave the area? She needed them to save the girls. Their job wasn't done. They couldn't leave yet! Misty stared in disbelief as the police cars drove away, and the animal control officer waved to her as he shut the door of his truck and turned to follow.

This had never happened before, and Misty was going to get to the bottom of it. No man was above the law, and she was the law. A sense of guilt filled her being. She had failed to rescue those helpless girls. While the driver turned the small bus around to return her to the office, she dialed her boss on the cell phone. Somebody was going to have to explain this to her, because she definitely did not understand what had just happened.

A little shout for joy erupted from inside the Forbes' house as they had first watched the police and animal control drive away. Now as that big, ugly bus pulled away from the house, the girls could conceal their elation no longer. Dancing and shouts of joy erupted from the children and parents alike. Kneeling beside the couch at the direction of their father, the Forbes family knelt in prayer to give thanks to the Lord Jesus Christ for frustrating the plans of the enemy. After prayer, the girls went back out into the yard to resume their chores and schoolwork.

A deep sigh of relief escaped from Robert's wife's chest as she sat down beside him on the family couch and tenderly laid her head on his shoulder, softly placing her hand in his. Robert had to breath a deep sigh of relief too as he turned to kiss his wife affectionately. He was thankful the DCFS was still obeying the unchangeable written law, and respecting the written notice at the gate.

Robert suspected that some-day soon the powers that controlled their local government would no longer care whether or not they appeared to follow the written law. He knew written law to be the foundation of the freedoms of the individual people. Written law and an informed public had been the only successful way to limit the authority and power of the state and local governments, without bloodshed. Tragically, a proper understanding of written law was being systematically removed from the public conscience by omission at every level of society by the public education system, and by the mass media. True education had been replaced, for the most part, by entertainment.

Robert believed a day was coming when administrative policy, within the various governmental agencies, and judicial decree would replace the written law as the final authority in the minds of the general population.[1] When agency policy and judicial decree become legitimate reasons in the minds of the general public for ignoring the written law, the written law would become meaningless. Robert understood that when the authorities no longer felt the need to be restrained by the written law, and ultimately the state constitution, things would get much worse, especially for true followers of Christ.

CHAPTER 5

Carol Thomas, out of breath and weak from the fatigue of her last trip to the bathroom, lay in her own private room in the transplant section of the large Chicago hospital. It seemed like a lifetime since they had turned the limo around in such high hopes and hurried back to this hospital.

The hospital staff had been in and out of her private room all morning, taking blood and running various tests and scans to make sure the cancer had not spread. Of course Carol and Bernard had dutifully made sure all of Carol's extensive medical history and records were sent to the hospital before they left Canada, but the hospital insisted on repeating a majority of the tests just in case anything had changed. The Canadian medical system had done everything they could for her: test, diagnostics, endless waiting. *Healthcare?* "What a joke" Carol said aloud to nobody in particular. She thought back on the whole ordeal—*it was definitely health rationing at best.*[1] To make the situation even more difficult, Carol had a rare blood type. Finding an AB negative liver for her would be difficult, if not impossible anywhere they were, but the phone call from Mr. Verde had given them some hope.

Hope was in short supply these days. The cold, hard reality was, the Canadian socialist medical insurance had left her with no hope. The chances they would find a liver for her in Canada were slight, and if they did, there were other people on the waiting list ahead of her. Carol was certain she would have been dead before it was her turn if she had waited in Canada.

As her breathing returned to normal she lamented the fact that a trip to the restroom felt like a marathon, and she dreaded the day when her liver was not going to allow her to make the trip without assistance.

Bernard had convinced her to fly across the border into the United States with great hopes and high expectations on his part. Emotionally depressed, and physically exhausted, Carol felt more desperate since they had entered the U.S. leaving their beloved Canada far behind. In Carol's mind, she almost felt disloyal to her homeland by coming to the United States. She had told Bernard, *nothing good could come of it,* and she was more disappointed with each passing day. She drifted off into a drug induced sleep, as she thought of nothing but her own misery.

As Carol lay sleeping beneath the white sheet asleep, Bernard, her devoted husband, gazed lovingly at her puffy face and thought back over all the years. They were both in their 50's now, and there would be no children from this marriage. For some reason, nature had never allowed them to become parents. Bernard never doubted that coming to America, and paying astronomical amounts of cash for an American hospital stay, was the right thing to do.

But, now, as he lay gazing at his wife's fragile form, he hoped he had made the right decision. He would never admit it to Carol, never crush her hopes, but his doubts were mounting. To bring his wife to the United States under protest had not been easy for him, but he still felt it was the only option with any hope of success.

In all her arguing and resistance to the idea, Carol had failed to see his emotional needs. How could he survive without her? His life would be worthless without Carol—she'd been the motivating force behind him—the source of all his business inspiration, and his greatest cheerleader.

They had been a couple ever since high school Algebra class, and Bernard cherished every year more than the last. True, she had been unhealthy for the last few years of their married life, but they shared a happy life together. Even now as he contemplated life without her, he wondered, *would he want to go on living if she did not?*

Bernard would trade all the riches in the world to have his Carol spend the rest of her days with him. Without her there to motivate and cheer him on, life would be meaningless. *What would be the point of ever being successful in business again without her there?* Her health problems had often driven him to work harder, to be more successful, to make more money in order to give her that better, easier life. To compensate for the financial drains of late, Bernard was seriously considering selling off most, if not all of their interests, in the diamond mines. He would willingly liquidate the investments that had gained them most of their wealth in order to have more liquid assets to spend on Carol's survival.

Now in a quiet moment, Bernard ran his fingers through his thinning grey hair and grew introspect. *Why was all this happening to them?* By most anyone's standard, Bernard was a good person, unselfish in many ways. He and Carol had given liberally to many charities over the years. *Why was God allowing this in their life?* But then again, *who was God?* God had always been a vague fuzzy someone, somewhere out there, in Bernard's mind. Up to this point, Bernard merely acknowledged God out of social convention and nothing more. Now there were questions in his heart and mind that he didn't have answers for.

Bernard had never before considered a God who was a personal friend. Before Carol's illness he had never thought about God much at all. He figured he would get to whatever heaven there was by being a good person. In his case, giving generously to charity and attending church regularly were his works to earn his way to heaven. He wondered if there really was such a place as heaven as he watched the slow breathing of his sleeping wife. *Was heaven just some fairy tale for adults made up to ease the grief of losing a loved one?*

If God did exist, He certainly wasn't answering Bernard's prayers. He didn't seem to care about Bernard and Carol Thomas at all, from what Bernard could see. Having a loved one so close to death had caused Bernard to seriously ponder questions about eternity for the first time in his adult life. *Was there a life after this one?* He doubted it. *If there was a heaven though, what would it be like?* He just didn't know. Pushing these thoughts from his mind he wondered, *how much longer until that liver is available?*

———————————

The remainder of the weekend passed with little incident for Joe. After the first few days, his mind became less befuddled, and he was slowly adjusting to the emotional shock he had suffered. There were times of tears, times of dreamy hope as he thought of his son, and times of deep anxiety as he tried to come to accept how he and Mary's lives had changed. In the midst of all this emotional upheaval, he found himself turning more and more to the word of God, and to prayer.

Mary's condition changed very little over the weekend and the subsequent days. She looked terrible. Her face was puffy, and bruised, her hair ratty and tangled. One of the nurses had suggested shaving Mary's hair off so they wouldn't have to take care of it, but Joe wouldn't have her pretty blond locks taken away. It was one of the few things that still looked like the Mary he loved.

The spinal swelling was still present, but the situation had not worsened. Dr. Bartlett, the ICU/trauma doctor, was listed as Mary's primary doctor, but a host of other medical professionals were in and out of the room introducing themselves to Joe. Still somewhat in a daze, he struggled to put names and faces together. It annoyed him the staff came in and out of the room at their pleasure, with no warning, and without so much as a knock on the door.

As Mary's situation failed to change, Joe began to wonder in times of discouragement, if the hospital staff was right. Maybe he should just give up, admit she was brain dead, and let her die. *But what about his son?* His mind was riddled with fear. No, whatever might happen, he would persevere for the life of his child, even if he was severely handicapped.

In addition to the fate of his child, lay the eternal destiny of his wife. *Was it too late? Could Mary still accept Jesus Christ as her substitutional payment for sin and spend eternity with Him, or had she missed her opportunity, and was she forever condemned to hell?* A sickening feeling arose in Joe's stomach as it twisted itself into a knot for the fifth time that day.

Adjusting to the fact his wife had been in a serious car wreck was difficult enough, but contemplating Mary's eternal destiny on top of everything else was much too disturbing for him to deal with right now. With all the emotional turmoil going on in his mind, he was in no state to make eternal life and death decisions, and yet he must! Still the question continually played in his mind, *Why is the doctor in such a hurry for Mary to die?*

As Joe contemplated Mary's death and Dr. Bartlett made predictions of its eventual certainty, he felt utterly helpless. Being a relatively young Christian, he had never before wrestled with the idea of when life began or ended, and now he was forced into a situation where he needed to make these very decisions. These decisions weren't hypothetical mental exercise for him. Such decisions involved not only Mary's physical life, but her eternal destiny. Joe had no frame of reference for making a choice of this magnitude. For now, the two thoughts that plagued his mind were the fragile life of his child, and the eternal destiny of his wife.

Sighing deeply, Joe glanced out the window again, as a nurse entered the room, checked the respirator, and left without a word to Joe. Joe was beginning to understand a little more about the routine and operating procedures of the hospital. Amazingly, no one had brought up, or seemed to care, if Joe and Mary were still married. The legal side of things for the moment had lapsed into nothingness, or at least it seemed that way to Joe.

Another lonely weekend had passed for Joe, and as a new Monday morning was getting underway, a cold breakfast of the hospital's cardboard toast, tasteless eggs, and some greaseless, dry bacon brought Joe back to the world of reality. It had been a difficult night, trying to sleep in the vinyl chair the hospital had to offer him. The business office had been closed for the weekend giving Joe a break from their ceaseless calls and questions, and now as Monday was getting underway, Joe dreaded the inevitable calls and inquiries the financial powers-that-be would again be making into his monetary situation. He had already filled out several documents detailing his limited assets.

Their financial situation was: hopelessly exhausted. He was young. He owed money on his school loans, on his house, on his two used junker cars, and on his credit cards. The large manufacturing company Mary had worked for had downsized almost six month earlier, and Mary's job had been terminated. Fortunately, she had been able to carry her insurance for these six months, but this would soon end as well.

Mary was under consideration for a new job as an administrative assistant, and she had felt certain she would get the job. It offered great benefits, a really nice insurance plan, and all those extras employees like to brag about as they climb the corporate ladder. Mary had been counting on that job. Now, sadly, that job was all a far off dream.

Joe sighed once again, as he mulled over the situation in his mind. She would never get that job she had dreamed about, and what was worse, at the end of the month, this month, June 2007, she would have no insurance.

Joe tried not to think about it. *What could he do?* Maybe Mary wouldn't need insurance by that point, but Joe didn't want to think about that scenario either. That was an even less desirable option. The only somewhat bright point in this whole problem was that their auto insurance would pay the first $5,000 of her medical expenses.

It isn't to be supposed that all the hospital administration and the staff were completely insensitive to Joe's dilemma. Most of them were just working from a very different mindset than Joe had developed since his salvation experience, and the staff had been trained to never question the doctors.

As for Dr. Bartlett, he wasn't a Christian, and he didn't claim to be. When he was young, he had experimented with meditation and Eastern religion, but he had finally settled his faith in mankind. Man was, in and of himself, his own God, and when man died, who knew where he went, and furthermore, why should he care?

Years of evolutionary public education and medical school had left him insensitive to the sanctity of human life. Dr. Bartlett believed man was just a higher evolved animal.[2] When a life was no longer useful to society, there was time to let that life pass. Of course, if harvesting the organs for transplant could improve the quality of life for others then that is what doctors like himself were here for.

Over the last two decades, he had watched many trauma patients die, thus becoming desensitized to, and detached from, death. He believed it was his responsibility not to prolong life when it reached a certain point, when the quality was compromised. In addition, he believed the limited resources of the hospital, and society, should not be wasted on hopeless cases.

Who was to decide when and what that quality of life was, or when too much money had been spent, or resources drained? Well, he was of course. He was the trained medical professional.

Dr. Bartlett held the prevailing view among so many of the medical professionals of his day which allowed them to offer advice on when it was wise to end life. Being an organ donor made it even easier to let a patient, merely a higher evolved animal, pass. Beating heart donor, Dr. Bartlett supposed, offered hope and encouragement to the loved ones of the deceased. Their body, he would assure them, could be used to better the lives of others. Thus, in a tangible way, the deceased was living out their life in the body of another.

It was a repulsive thought to some, but at this point, this woman was basically "spare parts," in his mind. The reality of a human being made in the image of her Creator never entered Dr. Bartlett's mind. To him there was no afterlife, no heaven or hell, only this mortal animal life, such as it was.

Realizing Mr. Smith's unreasonable behavior stemmed from his unscientific religious ideas, Dr. Bartlett had arranged for the Head of the Ethics Committee to try to talk some sense into Joe this fateful Monday morning.

Carrying his Bible and appearing quite religious, a small man in a dignified black suit entered Joe's room introducing himself as the hospital Chaplain, and asked if he could sit down to speak with him.

Joe willingly assented, but with his immature biblical understanding he was ill prepared for the arguments the cunning Ethics Committee advisor was about to offer. After the customary introductions, the Chaplain asked in a serious voice, "Joe can you tell me why you are not willing to let your wife be taken off life support?"

Joe glanced down at the man's Bible, and falsely sensing he had a friend near, let his guard down and gave an honest, sincere, heartfelt reply, "Well, you see sir, my wife isn't saved, and I don't . . .want her to spend eternity in the lake of fire."

Joe didn't even have time to mention the unborn child his wife carried before the grey-haired gentleman launched into his prepared speech in a sing-song voice, which reminded Joe of the old black and white Billy Graham re-runs on TV.

With a soothing smile and a look of concern, he was laying a cleverly devised trap for this one so young and inexperienced in the faith. "Son, can you show me in the Bible where it says your wife is going to hell?" Before Joe could answer, the man continued as if answering his own question. "You see, the Bible is a beautiful book, and God is a loving God, and He could never condemn a nice person like your wife to hell. I'm sure your wife was a good person. Let me ask you young man, do you believe what the Bible says?

"Yes," Joe replied.

It says, "God is love! If God is a compassionate, loving God, he would suffer eternal pain over a single soul being condemned to hell."

A light tap was heard on the door, and Robert Forbes stuck his head in with his customary "Your legal counsel has arrived" greeting.

Joe motioned him into the room with a wave, as the Chaplain continued. "If God suffers pain over souls condemned in a literal burning hell, God himself would be in a sort of hell, or torment, for eternity, and we know this is not true don't we?"

Joe's mind swam. This young believer wasn't sure how to answer and find the fault with this logic, but deep in his spirit he knew what he said was a lie.

Robert Forbes' blood boiled as he took in the situation at a glance. Who was this clown coming in here playing mind games with Joe in his vulnerable state?

Again the chaplain stated, "The Bible is a beautiful book of poetry, but it is not meant to be taken literally on issues like hell. Hell is probably just a state of deep sleep. Most people who are good go to Heaven, if they believe in some type of a god or eternal being. Only a few of the mass murderers of the world enter into that state of deep, forever sleep. All the good, innocent people of the world go to Heaven. A loving God could not condemn an Indian of the rain forest to Hell, just because he had never had a chance to hear about God."

At this point, Robert was compelled to speak. With all of the subtlety of a chain-saw, he spoke, "Since you seem to have about an 8-year-old's understanding of scripture, let me show you a response to an 8-year-old on the subject of Hell. It is from a newspaper article written, back in 1897 that you may have heard of. Pulling out his laptop, Robert pulled up a website.

Putting on his eye glasses, the chaplain skimmed over the article. "These are just the opinions of one man. Hell is a state of mind, not an actual place," the self-confident Chaplain began to reason. Joe looked over at the website. Scanning the single page, he found his faith renewed by the clear presentation of Scripture, and found the courage to address the Ethics Committee Chaplain.

"At this time," said Joe, taking on an air of confidence brought on by the truth of the Scripture, "I am not willing to take my wife off life support. Until you can prove to me that my wife and child are dead, I will not do so!"

A quiet rage was directed at Robert Forbes. The Ethics Committee Chaplain took one more stab at the weakened Joe, "You have to use common sense. God is a God of forgiveness and grace. He wants us to enjoy life and his creation. Your wife will never again be able to do that. If it weren't for modern technology, she never would have lived to this point. God gave us this technology, and he has also given us the knowledge to know when to take people off of it. He would not have given us this technology if he didn't expect us to make these tough choices." [3] And then, adding as an after thought, "How are you going to pay for all of this?" Joe had no answer for the chaplain at this point.

Sensing the despondency this man had brought over Joe, Robert took the man's hand and pulled him to his feet, shaking it vigorously while less than gently escorting him out the door with the other hand, "Sorry you have to leave so quickly. If you would like to continue our discussion on hell later that would be fine. Until then, may I suggest some further reading?" Reaching into his bag, Robert grabbed a paperback book with a dark cover and gave it to the man. "This is a great book, I think you should read. Pay extra attention to Chapter four "The Flames! The Flames!" Finding himself being forced out of the room by the less than gentle giant of a man, the man left with another book in his hand and a confused look on his face.

Joe smiled a thank you at Robert and asked, "What book did you just give him?" Robert reached into his bag once again and lifted out another copy holding it up for Joe to see the cover, "*One Heartbeat Away*, by Mark Cahill," Robert replied with a smile. "I give them out by the case to people I talk to at gas station pumps, and waiting in line to checkout at the store. Would you like one?" Joe looked at the book as if it were a long-lost friend and nodded in the affirmative.

"Actually, take the five I have left in my bag. You can give them to the hospital staff, or to the nice ultrasound lady, Rachel, you were telling me about on my last visit."

Joe smiled and took the books, placing them on the table. The smile was short-lived, however as Joe began to ponder the last comment of the man that had just left. "He may be a jerk, but he's right," Joe said, looking up at Robert in a hopeless manner. "I have no way to pay for all this."

"How do you stand as far as insurance?" Queried his friend. "I have one of those Christian medical sharing groups called Samaritan Ministries[4] for myself, but Mary has another plan through her last employer. She was laid off the first part of the year, but she still carried her employer's insurance—at an insane price per month." Joe leaned his head onto his arm and stared off into space. "The end of this month she'll be totally without insurance," Joe said, shifting around despondently in his seat. "I don't know what I will do. I hadn't thought about it. I guess she will end up going on state aid. I don't like that idea, but sometimes it's what you gotta do." Then, as an afterthought, he added, "Her auto insurance did agree to pay $5,000 of the ER bill."

Robert shook his head, and paced back and forth across the room like a caged lion. Joe could tell something was coming, and he wondered what this eccentric friend would come up with next. "Joe, a lot of problems can develop when you start taking state aid. The number one problem I see for you, Joe, is you become a slave to the system, forced to play by their rules and meet their standards." "Borrower is slave to the lender, ever hear that before?"

"But, I'm not borrowing anything from them." Joe retorted. "What am I supposed to do if I can't pay the bills?" Robert stopped pacing back and forth and looked Joe square in the eye. "Joe, I believe it's the place of family and church to reach out and help Christians. You see, when you take government aid, you're not trusting God to help you. You're putting the state in the place of God. The state is becoming your father."

"Robert I have to be honest with you," Joe scratched his head and sifted through his mind trying to find the right words. How did he tell the man who saved his wife's life he thought he was crazy. "I think you are a little radical."

"I am not radical," Robert replied with a comical smile that made his eyes twinkle. "I am actually a little off the charts on the reactionary side, but we can talk about that later. Don't get me off track. Joe, I'm telling you that you're setting yourself up for trouble when you start receiving government aid. The founding fathers never intended the phrase 'promote the general welfare,' to turn this country into a welfare state. Look at Rome, and many of the other great empires of the world. What was their downfall? God says that if any man will not work neither shall he eat." There you go Forbes. Now you overstepped your bounds. Why did you let that slip out?

Now it was Joe's turn to be irritated. He worked. Who was this man to accuse him of being a freeloader. "I know what you're saying," Joe said with a little bit of agitation slipping into his voice, "but I work. I have a job. I just need a little extra help right now."

"I know, but do you want their help? Their help comes with some serious strings attached![5] What happens when they say she's clinically dead, and you have to pull her off life support? Are you going to be able to refuse their help at that point? I know it's a big step of faith Joe," Robert sat down, straddled the folding chair backwards, and looked into the face of the young man, "but going on government aid isn't the answer to your problems short term, or long term. Trusting in God to provide is always the best plan."

"OK, I'm going to level with you man." A look of embarrassment infused Joe's face. He didn't like telling people about his family situation. "My mother is dead. She was never married to my father, and we basically survived on welfare. If it hadn't been for state programs, I would have grown up a beggar on the streets. I only met my biological father one time when I was a young child. I wouldn't even know how to contact him to ask for help, nor would I want to if I could." A note of bitter hurt entered his voice. "He's never taken much interest in my life, and if you think I'd go begging to him, you don't know me very well."

Robert didn't need to be told he had hit a nerve with Joe. He paused, putting his hand on the young man's shoulder, "I can empathize with you. My father . . ." Robert's slow lilt of an accent fell off. How could he explain his problems to this young man? He'd just look like a rich spoiled aristocrat. "I'm estranged from my father as well." Robert stood up and walked away from Joe. Now it was his turn to hide his deep emotions. Joe's sensitive spirit identified with the hurt this Scotsman felt at the loss of his father's affection.

Screech! The emotional brakes of both men turned on. It would not do, to get all emotional here and now. Pushing the pain-filled past out of their minds, as only males can do, the two started talking again, changing the subject and moving onto something less sensitive to their male minds. Simultaneously a deeper bond of Christian friendship and fellowship was forming between the two men, and Joe was beginning to think, even if Robert was insane, he liked this reactionary Scotsman.

"You don't think they are really that mean do you?" Joe questioned. "Who?" Robert was still in that elite world of his childhood. "The state, government, medicaid. . . whoever. Do you really think they would make me, or could make me pull my wife off life support?"

Robert paused. What should he say? Should he crush the hopes of this fragile youth by telling him the state was all powerful if you sign up for their "help." He weighed his words carefully. "They are a cold impersonal lifeless monster that follows regulations and rules no matter what the consequences," Robert explained.

"The hospital nearly pulled the plug that first night." Robert continued. "Yes, but that's just because they thought we weren't married," Joe reasoned. "Joe this is becoming a very real issue in our society fueled even more by the rising costs of healthcare." Robert was back up on his visionary soap box. All thoughts of his upbringing faded, as he focused on the question at hand. "I know this is hard for a young man like you, but I truly believe you're setting yourself up for more trouble if you take their money."

"Robert, I don't have any savings. My house is worth less than I owe on it. I have no rich relatives. Mary's car was totaled, and mine's a piece of junk. I have little hope my wife will live, and if the child survives, he will be severely handicapped and need medical attention and care all his life." Joe paused, trying to imagine what the future might hold for him and his son. "Possibly down the road, when I'm more financially secure, I can adopt your standards if I feel convicted to, but for the time being I'm stuck with the state plan. Besides, I've paid my taxes all my life. Don't they owe it to me? I don't see how I can do it otherwise."

Robert sighed deeply in spirit and gritted his teeth. It was the same old story he'd heard dozens of times before. No one seemed to have the faith or conviction to do the absolute right, the absolute best thing, right from the start. Christians who haven't known persecution always want to wait and put their faith in God later, at a more convenient time when the first hint of the seemingly impossible presents itself.

Smiling a sad smile, Robert made one more futile attempt at reasoning with Joe. "Joe I would love to try and explain the Cloward Piven's strategy of the Communists to you. And tell you social programs are the tools of the elite, One World Government types, to gain control over the common man and enslave him, but I don't think you would have a clue what I am talking about right now.[6] Maybe later on I can explain that to you. I do need to say, you're leaving out one factor: you are factoring God out of this equation. Let's have a word of prayer, and ask him what he'd have you do." After a word of prayer, Robert started to take his leave.

A heavy weight pulled at Robert's heart. There was so much he wanted to say, so many ways to defend his point, but Joe was not ready for these. He needed milk. Joe needed to develop a proper mindset for freedom. *Joe has no clue what I am talking about.*

Pausing at the door, hesitating, Robert spoke to Joe, "If I brought you some material to read, would you read it?"

"Sure," Joe said with a sigh of relief. "I sure have plenty of time to read." Robert walked back into the room and set his laptop down in front of Joe. "Ever use a Mac?"

"I think I can figure it out. Maybe that computer programming degree will come in handy," Joe said tongue in cheek.

"Good." The old carefree Robert was back.

"My wife is frequently complaining we have too many computers. She says when you have more Mac's than you have children, you have too many." The thought of his family brought joy to the weary visionary's heart. "This one has an airport card. Maybe you can get online from here in the hospital."

Fishing around in the briefcase Robert frequently carried with him, he dug out a tattered copy of *The Law*, by: Frederic Bastiat. Handing it to Joe, he commented, "This is a short book. You can easily read it in a few hours. If I leave it with you, will you promise to read it cover-to-cover?" Joe snatched the book from Robert's hand like a hungry child. "I'll see you in a few days, Lord willing, Lad. Maybe then we can discuss Bastiat."

Another few days found Joe even more adjusted to hospital life. It no longer bothered him when the hospital staff walked into the room he and Mary now shared. To keep from going crazy, Joe did a lot of reading. He could have watched the television all day, but it just seemed like useless background noise, and a complete waste of time. Picking up his Bible, he found himself frequently turning to it for encouragement and comfort, as his mind tried to grasp what had happened to him, and how his life had been permanently changed. He also spent a fair amount of time on the computer Robert had left, researching and reading the links Robert was sending him.

A few days later, Dr. Rodriquez stepped in to check on Joe, Mary, and the baby. "How are my patients?" he asked with concern.

"Ok, I guess," Joe replied. Dr. Rodriquez made a thorough

check of Mary. Everything was as good as it could be. The PEG tube was working fine, a great relief to Dr. Rodriquez. "Where's Rachel, the sonogram lady?" Joe asked candidly. He was curious about the woman who seemed to make this normally confident doctor so nervous. "I don't know. She only works PRN in the OB. I don't see her very often."

Dr. Rodriquez's professional mannerism was outwardly confident, but on the inside, on a much deeper level, he felt like an immature teenager whenever he thought about Rachel. "What's the story on her doctor? She has a little bit of an accent I picked up on." Joe curiously asked.

It was an innocent enough question, no malice intended, coming from a married man. It could have been answered in a few words, but where did he start, and where did he end? He didn't want to give out too much information to this almost complete stranger. As he made notes about his patient, his mind recalled how he first met Rachel.

He was a new intern at the hospital at the time, and he had been invited to a pro-life banquet. She was there sitting at the round table across from him, always an eye catcher. He couldn't help but notice the stunning woman in the red beaded dress with beautiful eyes and perfect proportions. During the meal, he had tried to visit with her, but found himself constantly bending his head to see around the oversized centerpiece, which blocked his view of her charming face and dark expressive eyes. After the meal had ended, she was invited up onto the stage to speak. She introduced herself, gave her testimony explaining how she had been raised in a Christian home, immigrated to the States from St. Vincent as a child of three, and had come to know Jesus as her personal Savior as a teenager.

She told of how she felt God had called her to minister to the women of their area crisis pregnancy center, particularly those women of color. Rachel sat down. Another man stood up and went on to explain how important sonogram equipment and technicians like Rachel were to the crisis pregnancy center. The image of her

74

beautiful face and that red sparkly dress danced before his mind's-eye as he remembered that night. Everything about her seemed perfect to him. Since that night, he had wanted to get to know her better, but for some reason when he saw her, all his confidence melted away. Around any other woman, he could laugh, joke, and be his usual outgoing self, but something about Rachel intimidated him. To make it more difficult, he didn't see her very often.

Joe repeated the question. The doctor hadn't seemed to hear him.

"She's from somewhere in the Caribbean. She works at the Crisis Pregnancy Center most of the time. About every single guy on the planet would like to get to know her better."

Joe sensed from the doctor's tone the subject was closed. "Everything seems about the same here. I'll see you in a day or two."

CHAPTER 6

At first Joe was completely overwhelmed by the cards, flowers, and letters of sympathy, along with the endless deluge of visitors who arrived daily. He had given up trying to keep track of the numerous cards received. Many of them were from students and read something like this, "Mr. Smith: we are so sorry to hear about you and your wife. You're an awesome teacher. I hope you get to come back to school when it starts again. We are praying for the recovery of your wife. In Christian love; Chris." Joe developed systems for dealing with the cards and flowers, like a true Computer teacher would. He started by using trash cans but realized this would look very undignified, when visitors showed up—to see trash cans filled with sympathy cards.

On one of the rare instances when he left Mary, he ventured past the gift shop and noticed some very large wicker baskets on sale there. Those would work just fine he thought to himself. Joe left a few minutes later carrying a large pile of empty wicker baskets. This allowed him to arrange and deal with the incoming sympathy cards in an methodical manner.

He organized them into several categories within the baskets. There was a basket for sincere, heartfelt, and appreciated cards. One basket was filled with cards from students who care. Another basket contained cards that arrived with gifts or flowers. There was even a basket titled people I don't know, but they obviously care for me a great deal. A larger basket was filled with cards that had not yet been opened, with more being added every day. His briefcase was open on a small table next to him. In this he placed any gifts of money, or gift cards that occasionally showed up in the envelopes.

Joe arranged a chair with the baskets surrounding it. When he was alone he would sit in the chair and process the cards. He pictured himself as the CPU in a computer. The big basket was the input that he would process, categorize, and then output into one of the smaller baskets. As he sat there "processing" cards, he thought to himself, "Am I a computer nerd, or what?" Joe laughed out loud, *LOL he thought to himself*—yes I'm definitely a computer nerd!

During the first few days after the accident the visitors were many, but gradually as the days wore on, most of the visitors stopped coming, and the card basket was empty. Joe felt alone, he knew he wasn't really alone however, as he prayed almost constantly to the Lord Jesus Christ, begging Him to let Mary wake up.

Not all of the visitors quit coming: Robert Forbes was a faithful visitor coming several times a week, and Mr. Elder showed up faithfully every Tuesday and Friday. Joe suspected Mr. Elder had put him on his calendar as an appointment each Tuesday and Friday. From what Joe knew about Mr. Elder his headmaster, he was probably right. He did care, and he just wanted to let Joe know it. His other visitor was more sporadic. He didn't seem to be on a set schedule, and when he showed up he was really there to spend time with Joe. Most of the time, he would enter the room with a knock on the door and say, "Your legal counsel has arrived."

Joe did not know what it was about Robert Forbes that made him so different. Yes, he was raised in a different culture and still had that hint of accent betraying that fact. From what Joe could tell, the man was a genuine Christian, not the cookie cutter, fake plastic smile, just go-to-church-on-Sunday type, but someone who truly genuinely trusted and loved Jesus. Joe was discovering more each day how different someone radically in love with Christ could actually be. It seemed as if everything Robert said and did flowed from the pages of Scripture. This man whom God had placed in his life in a moment of desperate need was quickly becoming Joe's closest friend on this earth. He'd only known him a few weeks, but he was much closer to him than men he had known his entire lifetime.

Down deep in Joe's soul he knew he could trust Robert. He didn't understand the man, but he did trust him. Robert had shown a spiritual insight and closeness to God that Joe admired and desired to emulate. However, Joe knew that would take a very long time to accomplish, or rather, for the Lord to accomplish within him.

Right now Joe was sitting in his CPU chair having nothing left to process. He stared at Mary willing her to wake up. He stared at the monitor displaying heart rate, blood pressure, respiration, IV status, etc. As he stared at the monitors, he consciously checked each number hoping for a change, but saw none.

CHAPTER 7

"The moment the idea is admitted into society that property is not as sacred as the laws of God, and that there is not a force of law and public justice to protect it, anarchy and tyranny commence. If "Thou shalt not covet' and "Thou shalt not steal' were not commandments of Heaven, they must be made inviolable precepts in every society before it can be civilized or made free." —John Adams

Psalm 18:16-19 (NKJV)
¹⁶ He sent from above, He took me;
  He drew me out of many waters.
¹⁷ He delivered me from my strong enemy,
  From those who hated me,
  For they were too strong for me.
¹⁸ They confronted me in the day of my calamity,
  But the LORD was my support.
¹⁹ He also brought me out into a broad place;

  He delivered me because He delighted in me.

It had been another monotonous day at the hospital. Nothing had really changed with Mary and the baby's situation, and Joe began to wonder if he should just go home to his average suburban two bedroom home, but then he feared something might happen while he was gone, and what did he have to go home to? His whole life, everyone he loved and cared for, lay here in the hospital. His whole future rested on what happened to Mary and to their child.

Joe had finished reading *The Law* by Bastiat, the day Robert gave it to him. Two days later, Robert left several other books[1] for Joe to read and he spent large portions time reading.

Leaning back into his vinyl chair, he looked around the room wondering what time it was. Outside, the afternoon storm had cleared, and the sun was setting on a beautiful, breezy Chicago day.

As he sat staring through the window at the peaceful lake, his mind contemplated the future. Joe wondered if he would be able to enjoy a day like this with his son. A tear trickled down his cheek. He had almost given up hopes of being able to enjoy a day like this with Mary again, but maybe his son would live. Pushing Mary's situation from his mind, he gazed at the sunset and dreamed of holding his toddling son's hand and walking him along the lake's shore. He envisioned himself stopping to throw a stone in, but maybe that wasn't reality. Maybe he would be wheeling him along in a wheel chair; or maybe he wouldn't even have a son. If his mother-in-law becomes Mary's legal guardian, Mary would be taken off life support as soon as possible. Joe had not heard a word from his mother-in-law, but that didn't surprise him. It would take time for her to get a lawyer and make all the necessary legal arrangements.

Forcing the accident from his mind, Joe's eyes ran down the wall of the room. He caught a look at himself in the mirror. He looked worse than Mary. At least this week he had been able to comb Mary's beautiful blond hair and make it look a little more presentable. Looking at his wrinkled shirt and rubbing his bearded chin, Joe seemed to remember one of the nurses mentioning there was a public shower down the hall he could use. Was the nurse hinting he needed a shower? Joe rummaged around the room for his personal effects and some clean clothes. Unwilling to leave Mary for any time at all, but desperate to get a shower, Joe slipped down the hall to the showers for a quick cleanup.

None of the nurses had seen him leave Mary's room. Hopefully he wouldn't be missed. He didn't trust anyone at the hospital. They all seemed intent on pulling the plug. Fifteen minutes later, he returned to the room feeling a little more human. As he finished drying his hair Joe was once again thankful for Mr. Elder, who, with his quiet servant's heart, had gone by Joe's house after the accident and brought some of his clothing and personal belongings to the hospital.

As Joe tried to eat the meatloaf the cafeteria worker had just brought him, he opened his Bible. Joe mechanically stumbled through Psalm 18. Verses 16-19 stuck in Joe's mind and rang in his heart. Kneeling on the floor against the uncomfortable vinyl chair, Joe began to pray. "God deliver me from the strong enemy, be my Stay. Show me what I am to do," he added as an afterthought. Joe moved the vinyl chair, that converted into a "bed," next to Mary.

Placing his hand over the small left hand, which still displayed her wedding band, he fell into a deep, but troubled, sleep. Water swirled in Joe's dreams. A small child with mousey brown hair and Mary's penetrating blue eyes, his son, sat on a rock in the middle of a gushing torrent. He was screaming for Joe to save him, but Joe, confused and unsure of himself, sat on the bank of the river, unsure what to do.

Joe awoke for a moment. Shaking the disturbing vision from his mind, he looked over at Mary. It had only been a bad dream, but it had seemed so real. Joe looked around the room and out the window. Everything was fine. Mary and the baby were still there beside him. Her once small, but now puffy, hand with the wedding band, was still clasped inside his hand. Shifting around in the chair, he tried to find a more comfortable position. Oh, that is much better, he thought to himself.

Again he lapsed into a deep sleep, but this time, instead of being beside a rushing river, he lay in the hospital room. Nurses and doctors rushed around him in a disordered fashion. In his mind, he heard screams, but this time it was not the screams of his child, but the screams of Mary. Screams of pain, of torture, escaped her lips. "Oh God. . . it's so hot!" Her hand clenched Joe's hand as if she was trying to keep from falling into some deep pit. She pleaded, "Joe don't leave me!" Someone was shaking Joe, yelling, "Mr. Smith! Wake up!"

Instantly, he was awake, glaring lights all around him. Nurses filled the room. No longer did he hold Mary's hand — she was now clutching his hand faintly, weakly, but yes, her hand was clutching his. She's alive his mind thought in an instant, but as he struggled to wake himself he was unable to articulate what had happened. Dazed he asked a nurse, "What's going on here?" A middle-aged nurse in purple scrubs addressed Joe, a little irritated that he could sleep through all the commotion. "Your wife tried to flat line," the alarms went off, and we came. "Flat line?"

"Yes, her heart stopped. Probably won't be long now. Her bodies tryin' to tell us it's time to let her shut down." Ignoring the insinuation the nurse was making, Joe looked at Mary. "Amazingly," the nurse changed her tone after a few moments of silence, "she seems for the time to be stabilizing. She's breathing on the ventilator again. Her heart rate and breathing are returning to normal now. Look her oxygen levels are back up in the 90's," the nurse commented as she watched the computer screens, making sure everything was back to a normal range.

"You were dead to the world." The nurse emphasized the words 'dead to the world' for effect. "I don't know how you didn't hear those alarms going off." As the nurse left the room, Joe slipped into a kneeling position on the floor beside the chair. Joe's mind had a hard time forming sentences but in his heart he pleaded with his Savior for the eternal destiny of his wife.

When the nurse returned five minutes later to check on Mary and adjust the flow rate on the IV, Joe tried to communicate to the nurse what had happened.

"My wife, Mary, clasped my hand." The nurse looked down at Mary's motionless hand now lying beside her seemingly lifeless body on the bed. Not wanting to appear to doubt Joe, but believing most Christians were a little 'off their rocker,' she said, "Sometimes your mind can play tricks on you. Make you think what you want to think really happened." The nurse's doubt didn't faze Joe. Now more than ever, Joe was convinced Mary's eternal destiny lay in the balance. As the nurse left the room, Joe slipped into a kneeling position on the floor beside the chair yet again and with all his heart he pleaded with his Savior for the life of his wife.

CHAPTER 8

My people are destroyed for lack of knowledge. . . (Hosea 4:6).

Mr. Verde, the hospital administrator, looked at the computer screen in the nurses' station of the transplant center and took in the scene before him. No luxury, the hospital could afford, had been spared the diamond mine owners. Mr. Verde knew this wealthy Canadian had come to him as his last hope. AB negative donors were rare. If their hospital could save his wife, they would be heroes, and Bernard Thomas had promised a large donation toward their new building project. If she died, the huge monetary gift Mr. Thomas alluded to would be lost. Mr. Verde's ego and pride were on the line. This man's wife was dying, and without the liver that currently resided in his hospital, she would perish within months.

In truth, Mr. Verde had long ago become numb towards the situations he encountered at the hospital. He had conditioned himself over the years to ignore the feelings of compassion for the one who had died to make the transplant possible. Liver transplants, and decisions about life and death, were purely business at this point in his life. Each life and death encounter was a chance to further his own personal ambitions and career as a hospital administrator. His hospital was known as the leading transplant center in his area, and he had every intention of keeping up that reputation at all costs.

Although he attended church regularly and had memorized several passages in the Bible to quote at appropriate times, the values set forth in the Bible had no application in his everyday life. Verde used his limited knowledge of the Bible and the passages he had memorized to keep up appearances and manipulate others. In truth, he relied on his own intellect and the medical expertise of his doctors to make life and death decisions for those under the hospital's care. Any talk about the Bible and what was right or wrong was disregarded, by what was left of his conscience.

When the Thomas couple had first arrived, Mr. Verde honestly had little hope to offer them, but he had prolonged their stay as long as he could by having his staff authorize more testing than were customary in order to stall their departure. *It was no hardship for the Thomas's; they could afford it.* He had played his cards well, taken a gamble, and he had hit the jackpot.

The day following Verde's stall tactics, a donor had arrived, the victim of a tragic car wreck. Verde's call had turned their limo around and returned them to the hospital. He remembered the scene of their return as if it were yesterday.

He had met them at the door and escorted them to the private suite they had recently vacated. Once they had returned to the hospital room, a nurse made a quick examination of Carol checking her vitals and making a few notes on her laptop. While the nurse continued, he addressed Bernard casually asking if they were comfortable in this room at the hospital. Bernard answered in the affirmative. "I wanted to be the bearer of good news in person," He had proudly proclaimed, "You are in luck. I think we may have located a donor, which is amazing since your wife is AB negative, and less than 1% of the people in the world have that blood type. We've done the preliminary blood work, and everything looks good. The patient is still on life support, but definitely brain-dead. She's an organ donor, young, and I think she would be an excellent match for your wife, and to make things even easier, she's here in our hospital." A notable sigh of relief escaped from Bernard. "I am so glad we made the decision to come here." Turning to Mr. Verde, Mr. Thomas continued his praise of the hospital and it's staff, "I'm really impressed with your hospital, and I would like to be able to add it to our list of charitable contributions at the end of the year after Carol has recovered." Verde had expressed his thanks, adding, "the hospital could really use the extra assets to help others who were less fortunate."

That trip to the hospital two weeks earlier seemed so long ago to the impatient Thomas's. The liver still wasn't available, and things were growing more critical for Mrs. Thomas as her health was continuously getting worse. The Canadian Doctors had suggested chemotherapy and radiation, but as serious as the cancer was, it would only prolong the inevitable. Carol and Bernard had decided as long as the cancer remained localized in the liver they would try for a transplant, since it offered the greatest chance of recovery and a normal life. If chemotherapy became their only option, they had decided to go back to Canada and have this treatment done there, so she could spend her last days in her own country.

Verde drummed his fingers on the desk in impatience as he looked about the hall of the hospital, and his mind explored the options. What he really needed was legal advice, and he knew just the person to help him. The next day over a leisurely game of golf, Verde consulted a friend who was a judge. He spelled out the whole situation, in detail, between holes.

He could speak freely to Ken. Ken, a savvy lawyer, age 55, knew the way things were in the legal system, and had been a personal friend of Verde since high school. For the past three years, Ken had spent three weeks twice a year on the Mediterranean island of Malta, at the University of Malta studying with the International Maritime Organization.[1] He had been specially selected to receive this honorary training by a representative from the World Banking Center.

Ken, having just returned from Malta the week before, had called Mo (a reference to Verde's first name Guillermo which he had called him since high school) to inform him of his return stateside and to invite him to play a round of golf and catch up on old times. Ken was respected by everyone in Chicago, and in the North Central region of the United States, as a top-notched lawyer. Verde watched Ken as he made his tee shot on hole number eight: his white-blond hair fell down in front of his blue eyes, as his muscular 6-foot frame completed the follow through like a pro golfer. Verde smiled as he remembered back to high school and the "ken doll" jokes his friend had endured. The tan he had gained during his recent trip to Malta made him look even more like Barbie's counterpart. Verde needed some legal advice, and there was nobody he trusted more than Ken to give it. A few holes of golf would be, "fun." As they chatted, over the 8th hole, Verde asked him "off the record" what his legal options were for getting life support removed from this brain-dead patient against the will of her husband enabling her organs to be used to save the life of someone in need of a transplant.

"Well Mo," Ken said as he tried to estimate the distance of his next shot, "this patient doesn't have any directives, living will, or durable power of attorney?"[2] Verde nodded no, as he took a sip of his soda. "The indirect route would obviously be much preferred to direct removal by court order, which should only be considered as a last resort. You don't want to have a mob of protestors outside the hospital," Ken further explained, "The mother-in-law gaining custody through the court system would be the best route, since she has already indicated a willingness to take the donor off life support. I'll see what I can do on my end to help speed things along in that direction," he promised. "Mo, your hospital staff working behind the scenes would obviously be the fastest way to achieve your ends. Have you had your doctors and ethics committee representative tell him she's dead?" Mr. Verde nodded yes as he set his soda down in the cup holder in the golf cart and picked another golf club from his bag. "Won't take the advice of the medical professionals huh?"

Ken the lawyer continued. "You may have to get the courts involved with a case like that. I can swing things your way on this end, should the case make it to court. I know most of the judges here in Chicago and can talk to them for you, but the court system is slow, and it sounds like time is of the essence in this case. Keep me posted, Mo. I will check on some other options just in case. Actually the International maritime law I have been studying abroad could possibly be used here as well, but I will need to check a few things first. I could shoot you an e-mail later on when I find out for sure."

———————————

Joe had now been at the hospital for what seemed like an eternity, but really it had only been three weeks. Other than Mary's temporary lapse in breathing which the hospital staff considered a sign she was truly brain dead, little had changed in the situation. Her face was healing up, and it seemed she would have no scars on her face. Her cheeks looked less puffy to Joe, but maybe that was his imagination playing tricks on him. He wanted so bad to have her look like her old self. The beautiful blond-haired, blue-eyed girl, with that spark of determination in her eyes, was who he had fallen in love with three years ago. However, frequent calls from his mother-in-law reminded him Mary's return to the person she was before the accident would likely never happen.

In recent days, his mother-in-law had telephoned twice to yell at him and blame him for the situation. Secretly, she hoped to change his mind and make him see things her way. Inwardly frightened by death, she refused to come to the hospital. Her excuse was, she *could not bear to see her daughter in 'that state'—she preferred to remember her as she was before the accident.* Jane's therapist recommended she practice detached compassion in this situation, and she was following her advice.

To the hospital staff, everything seemed to be at a standstill. Joe retained legal guardianship of his wife: no one could prove they weren't married, and until his loud, overbearing mother-in-law tried to take some type of legal action, they could do no more. Joe refused to take his wife off life support, no matter how much the hospital administration reasoned and argued with him.

The following day after his round of golf with Ken, Mr. Verde, the hospital administrator, purposely stepped onto the floor of the ICU. The hospital staff took note, and tried to look busy. It wasn't every day the hospital administrator and CEO came onto their floor. An air of irritation hung over Mr. Verde and showed in the wrinkles on his high forehead. His hospital expansion plans and his reputation were on the line. It had been three weeks now since the accident, and in his worldly mind, a brain dead woman and her unreasonable husband, were all that was holding up a successful liver transplant, which would better the life of a wealthy, Canadian woman and several others waiting for transplants of various organs. The Canadian woman's husband was growing impatient and didn't mind letting this hospital administrator know it rather loudly. Verde didn't like being yelled at. He feared the whole situation was slipping through his fingers, and was determined to make sure that didn't happen.

Mr. Verde didn't have to wonder what the "right thing" was in this situation. In his mind the greater good would be served by getting that brain dead corpse into surgery as a beating heart donor, allowing them to harvest the organs before they became damaged, and then let the corpse finish dying on its own. [3]

As hospital administrator, he had access to all the patient records and charts. With little ceremony, he peered into a computer screen on the ICU floor and looked over Mary's charts making sure everything was in order. Yes, the consent form for organ donation was signed and ready. A color copy of the woman's driver's license was scanned into the computer. Mr. Verde's greying black eyebrows arched upwards as he smiled to himself. He knew this was the best type of organ donor. A beating heart donor, not yet completely dead, made for a much higher rate of success. Calling Dr. Bartlett over to him, in private tones, he discussed the situation with the doctor. "So you can assure me this woman is clinically brain-dead?" "Yes, there is no way she has any brain function at this point." "Tests?" Mr. Verde inquired. "None. Don't need them," the doctor replied confidently. Mr. Verde made no comment. He trusted Dr. Bartlett knew what he was talking about. Dr. Bartlett continued, "Test might only complicate the situation, give the husband a false sense of hope. I can't believe she's still alive. She flat lined a couple of days ago, but at this point she's still a beating heart donor.

I think her husband would be willing to take her off—if it weren't for the fact that she's pregnant." "Pregnant?" Mr. Verde seemed even more irritated: *yet another complication!* "How far along is she? Is it viable?" He asked as an afterthought.

"I doubt it. I don't know. Let's look at the sonogram. Her husband didn't know about it until the day of the accident, and he doesn't seem to think the baby's viable." The doctor flipped a few more screens and found the ultrasound report. "That's strange, there is no fetal age given anywhere on the sheet. In fact the report is rather incomplete to be honest with you. Look down here in the corner. The technician left a note; baby seems healthy and normal— no fetal trauma or malformation found." Verde paused for a moment wondering if he had made a mistake. "What's your gut feeling Doc?" How far along is this pregnancy," Mr. Verde questioned. He knew the law. If the baby was past 24 weeks, he could run into legal problems. "I guess we could take a blood level test to determine that, but she doesn't appear to be showing much. I would say first term definitely."

Mr. Verde weighed the situation in his mind for a brief moment. If he was honest with himself, he had to admit the life of the child was of little consequence to him. In fact, it wasn't even a child to him. It was just a parasite. Society had trained him to look upon it as a disposable inconvenience.

In the liver transplant section of the hospital lay a woman dying, a woman of a sound mind—dying. With this brain dead woman's liver, she could once again have a healthy life.

"This sonogram was taken shortly after the accident. This fetus may not even be alive now. "I wonder what we could do to prove to Mr. Smith it was dead?" Dr. Bartlett perceived his boss was asking for his help as a medical professional. He knew from his facial expression the man implied more.

"I think the pharmacy might be able to help us," Dr. Bartlett said with a knowing smile. "I propose we give Mary Smith a little methotrexate in the IV to help with spinal swelling." "Will that affect the liver function Doctor," Mr. Verde asked. "I'll watch it closely." Dr. Bartlett assured his boss. "Then in a week or so, we can do another sonogram, and, I think Mr. Smith will be willing to work with us at that point. Is that what you want me to do?" Mr. Verde never said yes, but he never said no. A pleased smile spread across his face, and the doctor knew he had his answer.

Joe was a little surprised to see the doctor again so soon. The doctor had been in earlier that morning when on rounds, and he and the doctor were never on the best of terms. But now, the doctor seemed unusually friendly and comfortable with the situation. "Mr. Smith, I may not agree with the decisions you've made, but I would like to discuss what I perceive the future to hold. The fetus, has a very small chance of survival. I anticipate seeing it self-abort in the next 1 to 2 weeks. In fact, I would be willing to bet if we did another sonogram, we'd see it was already dead."

Despair filled Joe's countenance as his eyes filled with tears again. "*Oh God, no, not this,*" Joe's soul poured forth as Joe fought to hold the tears back. He didn't want to appear weak and vulnerable to this insensitive doctor. Joe wondered if he should suggest they do another sonogram right now, today, but he was afraid of what the results might be. "I'm going to say when, not if the fetus is dead," here the doctor paused for effect, "would you allow us to take your wife off life support?" Joe staggered and sat down, unable to make this decision.

"I would have to pray about it. If the baby," Joe stuttered nervously, "I—I mean my child was no longer. . ." he had trouble saying what was on his mind as his voice trailed off. Joe sat there in silence, he didn't want to consider the life of his child might already be snuffed out. He saw the Doctor staring at him, he willed himself to finish his thought, ". . . alive, that certainly would change everything." "Mr. Smith let me assure you, your wife's death would not be a complete loss. She is a young woman, and as an organ donor she would help many other people." Joe let out an exasperated breath of air, as anger flooded his being and his face turned red. *Why did everyone keep mentioning his wife was an organ donor?* Every day he heard this same synopsis from at least one of the hospital staff. He felt like they were always pushing him to make a choice he wasn't ready or prepared to make. *Did they want her dead for some reason?* Joe quickly pushed that evil thought out of his mind. *This was a hospital. They were here to help people not wish them to die. What was wrong with him? Why did he suspect everyone?* He was under way too much pressure, and it was starting to show.

"Now I'm not going to overload you emotionally right now," the doctor continued, realizing from the expression on Joe's face he was on shaky ground. "You just think about these things. In the meantime, I'm going to prescribe a drug to help with the edema. In response to Joe's confused look, the Doctor explained, "edema means swelling. It's an off the label use for this drug, but I have had success with it in the past, and it may help. If we can get the swelling down, maybe we can see what's really going on with her spine. Joe glanced over at Mary's puffy face. "Is this O.K. with you?" "Sure," Joe somewhat eagerly, replied as he hoped this would somehow make a difference. "I'll be back to talk with you in a day or two." Joe numbly shook his head acknowledging the doctor's words. Why was it that Dr. Bartlett always left Joe with a sense of hopelessness? His sensitive spirit always felt oppressed by the doctor's visits. On his way out, the doctor flagged down a nurse, and gave her his explicit instructions. Twenty minutes later with syringe and vial in hand a nurse entered the room. Joe smiled and spoke to the nurse. *No need to make any more enemies than you need to,* he thought.

Glancing out the window at the storm clouds moving in from the lake and the early darkness moving into Chicago, Joe didn't realize the storm brewing in his own room. The nurse, like a professional, carefully measured out the lethal medication with extreme precision. Poking the syringe into the IV bag port, she shot the injection into Mary's IV. That was it. It was done. Only a matter of time now until Dr. Bartlett's prediction of the baby aborting would come to pass. The nurse checked the flow of the lethal solution as it dripped into the tube that was attached to the unconscious woman's arm. It would indeed help with the swelling, but at a murderous cost. Joe turned his attention again to the clouds rolling in off the lake, as the nurse began giving the IV pump one final check. The doctor had said this medicine would help with Mary swelling. Innocently, in his mind, Joe hoped it would.

The Holy Spirit was at work orchestrating the events that would soon come to pass. He prompted Dr. Rodriquez to check on Joe earlier than he had planned. The doctor repeatedly tried to refocus on his paperwork to no avail: Mary Smith and her baby kept jumping into his mind. In the end he dropped his writing pen, stretched in his chair, and headed toward the Smith room to pay them an unannounced call.

In his jovial way, without bothering to knock, Dr. Rodriquez stepped through the door into Mary's room. "How's she doing today, Joe?" The nurse gave a slight jump as if she had been a kid caught with her hand in the proverbial cookie jar. Joe stepped forward to offer the doctor his outstretched hand he thought, *at last someone who will at least give me a little hope.*

"About the same, doctor. There seems to be no change. Dr. Bartlett was here about 30 minutes ago. He didn't seem to have any good...." Shoving Joe aside, the rest of Joe's words were lost on the doctor as he looked at the empty vial of rheumatrex on the tray next to the nurse. In an instant his mind perceived what was going on. The nurse had just finished increasing the flow rate on the pump to speed the fatal injection on its course.

Pushing the nurse aside with his elbow and reaching for the tubing clamp he quickly slid it down the tubing to within a centimeter of the connecter. Rolling the clamp foreword he pinched the IV tubing off, stopping the flow of the lethal liquid before it had a chance to reach Mary's arm. In one fluid motion with his free hand Dr. Rodriquez yanked the tubing from the bag on the stand causing the contents to slowly drain onto the floor. The fatal fluid continued to stream onto the floor as he stepped out of the way to avoid the mess.

With a flame in his eye, Dr. Rodriquez glared at the nurse. "Do you know what you're doing?" She tried to replicate the look that had worked so well in school when she had been caught cheating on a test, and looked innocently at him with no answer. "Who ordered this?" "Dr. Bartlett, I am just following orders" was her only reply said over her shoulder as she opened the door leaving the room not wanting to incur the doctor's wrath. Not missing a beat, the doctor quickly dialed the pharmacy on the room phone beside Mary's bed. After identifying himself he said, "I need a bag of IV parent natal solution added, nothing else. Get it up stat, that's English for pronto, now! room 612 as fast as you can!" The doctor paused ready to slam the phone down on the night stand next to the bed, then, as an afterthought, he said "Thank you," and placed it a little more gently back in its place, than he would have just moments before. Still holding the tubing in his hand, the doctor called over the intercom for a staff member to bring a mop bucket to room 612 ASAP.

Once again Joe sat back in stunned silence. He realized that now, right this minute, was not a good time for questions. Like a bystander watching a play, he felt detached and unconnected. A sense of utter helplessness, in the face of the bureaucratic monster of healthcare, filled his soul. After a few moments he decided to risk a question, "What's going on here Doc?" "Joe, they're trying to get your baby to self-abort." Holding up the empty vial he questioned Joe, "the doctor discussed this drug with you, and you gave your consent?" Dr. Rodriquez's critical eyes questioned Joe as he dropped the empty vial in his pocket. Joe walked around the room, disoriented, scratching his head with his arm, trying to remember exactly what had happened. He felt stupid and hopelessly dependent. It had all gone by so fast. Recounting the scenario for Dr. Rodriquez, "The doctor said he was giving her some medicine for swelling." "And you gave your consent?" Dr. Rodriquez prompted a little impatiently, "I guess I did. The doctor said it might help." Joe replied with a nervous glance at Mary, "I didn't think about questioning the doctor about any effects on the baby."

Dr. Rodriquez was mad. No, angry would be a better word, but it wouldn't be professional to vent his anger in front of Joe, or even worse at Joe. If there was one thing medical school had taught him, it was to never let his guard down—always maintain a certain aloofness from the situation, be professional. Speaking with what seemed like little emotion, he spoke to Joe, "I'm not your wife's primary physician, but if we are going to save this child, you're going to have to refuse all drugs given to your wife. Can you do that for me?" Then with a hint of irritation in his voice, he held up the IV tubing for emphasis, "You can't let them sneak anything in here. Also," Dr. Rodriquez shook his head, "I'm not supposed to be recommending physicians to patients, but if I were you, I would refuse the care of Dr. Bartlett and start looking for another doctor." Joe scratched his head in disbelief. "Who do I ask for? Can you be our doctor?"

"I don't know. I doubt it. But you can try and request me. I'm an OB doctor, I don't know if they will let you do that. Here's my card," Dr. Rodriquez scribbled his cell phone number on the back and handed the card to Joe. Joe stroked Mary's face and placed his hand on her stretching abdomen. "Oh God," he silently prayed. "Thank you for protecting our child." After the pharmacy had brought up the new IV bag, Dr. Rodriquez returned to the OB floor to try and get caught up.

Dr. Rodriquez was late finishing his rounds that night. He had lost time getting the IV situation under control with Mary Smith. Joe was now really upset. Guilt flooded his mind, and he felt like he could trust no one on the 6th floor ICU.

Back on the OB floor, Dr. Rodriquez was busy finally filling out paperwork which had been interrupted earlier to save the life of little Baby Smith.

Rachel swept into the nurses' station. She looked so stunning arrayed in her dark purple scrubs. The dark purple complimented her glistening dark skin. A wave of shyness swept over her as she noticed the doctor bent over his papers. "Are you working this evening?" Rachel asked with a hint of timidness in her warm voice. The doctor looked up and quickly took in the beautiful form before him. His deep piercing eyes haunted her soul. How she longed to be in his favor, to have a closer friendship with this interesting doctor, and yet, it seemed so allusive to her.

To Dr. Rodriquez, she looked so fresh and clean, and she smelled of roses. Just then he didn't feel so fresh and clean. A fourteen-hour shift and delivering a breach baby, on top of averting the crisis with the Smiths, had left him less than fresh and clean.

A sense of nervous inferiority passed over the doctor. Breaking gaze with Rachel, he turned his eyes from her to look back at his paper work. "No," he answered flatly, "just finishing up some paper work before I leave." Oh how Rachel wished he would take more interest in her, but then again what could she expect? He probably had a girlfriend. Both stood there in silence for one awkward moment. The doctor's mind raced. What should he say; a nice relaxing dinner with Rachel would be so nice, refreshing, but then he remembered their last meeting. When he had put his hand on the back of her chair, she had fled from him. She had no interest in a looser like him. She probably had some tall, dark, and handsome boyfriend. A girl like her could have her pick of any man she wanted.

Then, like a lightning bolt, it hit him. He needed to thank her or do something for her for coming in and doing the sonogram for the Smiths. "I," the doctor began slowly, "wanted to thank you for coming in the other day and. . ." before he could ask her out for dinner, Rachel began to answer. "It was fine. I was glad to be able to help. Don't mention it. Say, how's she doing?" Dr. Rodriquez's mind shifted gears as he recalled the situation which had so angered him that afternoon. "The wife's still in a coma. It doesn't look good. Her internal organs seem fine, but her kidneys are not where I would like. . . " Dr. Rodriquez stopped mid-sentence realizing he was probably saying too much and violating patient confidentiality. Going back to Rachel's original question, he continued, "Her primary care physician seems to have little respect for the Hippocratic Oath, and tried to give the mom some methotrexate today. He reached into his pocket and pulled out the empty vial handing it to her. I caught it just in time." "You're kidding me!" Rachel said in disbelief. "No, I wish I was." "Mr. Smith didn't realize what was going on?" Rachel further inquired. "No. No if he had a clue he'd be dangerous. Like a simpleton, he trusted the doctor completely. The doctor told him it would take the swelling down. Like he was worried about swelling in a patient he believed to be brain dead." Dr. Rodriquez was careful not to mention who the doctor was, although he intended to make a full report of the incident to his superiors. He reached out, taking the bottle out of Rachel's hand, and placed it in his desk drawer for safe keeping.

Rachel giggled with a mocking, amused smile at the doctor's cockiness. *She's mocking me*, he thought in his mind. *I deserve that.* "Well you can't expect everyone to be a genius like you doctor." Rachel's reply was meant as a compliment, but the doctor took it offensively. In his frustration he had spoken out of turn in his criticism of Joe Smith. *She thinks I'm a haughty, cold, jerk.* Oh how he wished he hadn't come across so poorly. He wanted so bad to ask her out to dinner, to show her another side of him, but his fragile ego couldn't handle another rejection from her.

Rachel moved and stood with her back to the doctor, while she looked through some files on the counter top. *Here's your chance. Ask her out you fool.* "Well, all the same, I wanted to thank you. I owe you something. I'll," the doctor shifted nervously in his mind for the words to say. The right words just wouldn't come. "I should buy you dinner." Rachel stood still as her heart jumped into her throat for a moment. *Was he, could he, be asking her out to dinner?* For one brief moment Rachel lived on the hope that it was so. *But, no, it wasn't a dinner date. 'It wasn't could I buy you dinner?' Or, 'Would you go to dinner with me.' It was I owe you something, and I wouldn't want to be beholding to a lowly sonogram tech.* Rachel rested her forehead on her open palm for one brief moment and took a deep breath before answering. It was good the doctor couldn't see the hurt expression on her face. A look of disappointment filled her eyes. *He doesn't want my company she thought. He'd as soon hand me a $50 bill and tell me to go get my own supper.* "That's generous of you, doctor," she began slowly, weighing her words, "but you don't owe me anything. I've got to get back to work." And with that, Rachel's beautiful form passed through the half door of the nurses' station and glided gently down the hall. *She can't stand you, you jerk.* Yet another rejection from the woman he so admired. His paperwork was done. Closing his laptop, he, unceremoniously, left the OB ward.

Once out of the doctor's sight, Rachel slipped into the bathroom and dabbed her eyes. Trying to focus her emotions on something besides her own bleeding heart, Rachel thought about Joe Smith. Her sensitive spirit empathized with the helplessness of this fellow Christian. Putting her own personal disappointment in Dr. Rodriquez aside, she longed to do something to help Joe, or at least comfort his hurting heart and mind. A couple of hours later, when things slowed down in the OB ward, Rachel went down to the ICU to see Joe. It was late. Almost everyone who wasn't working was asleep, but Joe wasn't asleep. He was too worried to sleep.

From the cracked door, Rachel could see Joe inside, sitting in his chair crying. It was hard to see a grown man weep. Rachel's tender compassionate heart wanted to weep with him.

She had brought her Doppler along hoping to reveal some good news to Joe, but she didn't want to fail to find the baby's heart beat with Joe in the room. Before entering the room, Rachel placed the Doppler in her deep pockets. Lightly she tapped on the door giving Joe a minute to dry his eyes before she entered. "You want to go get a drink or something? I'll watch her while you are away." Joe calmed himself, tucking in his wrinkled shirt. "Dr. Rodriquez told you what happened?" Rachel nodded. "You need a break. Get out of here," she said with a sympathetic, put playful smile. Joe obeyed. Picking up some change from the table, he headed for the candy machine. To take in a bite or two of something that actually tasted good would be a welcome change to his bland diet of hospital fare.

As soon as the door was closed, Rachel pulled the Doppler from her pocket. She did this all the time at the crisis pregnancy center, but just now she felt a little nervous. What if she couldn't find the heartbeat? What if the baby really was dead? She didn't want to be the one to break this to Joe. "Help me God. Help me give this man some hope and encouragement." Pulling the blanket off Mary's stomach, she went to work. Joe returned to the room only a few minutes later munching on a candy bar. Rachel smiled a merry, carefree smile at him. Her black eyes danced with pleasure as the Doppler played back the sound of the baby's heartbeat. "There it is. Hear that." Joe nodded and a noticeable amount of tension left his body. "My son?" Joe questioned, "is that his heartbeat?" "That's your baby. Steady as a rock." Rachel remarked confidently. With a playful smile she teased, "I think the baby is doing better than you are."

CHAPTER 9

A merry heart does good, like medicine, But a broken spirit dries the bones (Proverbs 17:22).

Joe squinted at the sun streaming through the hospital windows. He stretched lazily and yawned. The utter despair of the night before had disappeared with Rachel's visit. After she left, he was able to sleep the rest of the night. With the new day, the situation looked a little brighter. Joe picked up the piece of dried-out toast from the serving tray. The cafeteria worker had left it there, not wanting to disturb Joe's sleep. Joe munched away at the toast, and hummed to himself in happiness. A good night's sleep, and the simple knowledge that his baby was still alive, left him with a more optimistic mindset than he had experienced in quite a while. Joe turned his eyes upward and gave God thanks for Dr. Rodriquez saving his child the day before. Reproaching himself inwardly, he vowed to be more vigilant in monitoring what each medical professional did while in Mary's room.

A light tap on the door interrupted his prayer. Upon entering the room, Dr. Rodriquez was surprised to see a peaceful, well rested Joe. "Well you seem happier," the doctor commented. "Yes. After Rachel's visit, we are doing much better." "Rachel's visit?" The doctor questioned out loud while inwardly he once again felt the rejection and pain of their last encounter. "Yeah, didn't you send her? She found the baby's heartbeat. The baby seems to be doing fine," and then as an after-thought he added, "according to her." "Good. I'm glad to hear that. A strong heartbeat is a good thing," the doctor said in a professional manner. He scanned the room looking for some way to change the subject and said, "How do you think Mary is doing?" Joe sighed deeply, his facial expression visibly changing. "Well, her doctor gives me no hope. They see no changes in her conditions. She still is not breathing on her own, her heart is holding steady, and you know the results of the renal test better than I do. Sometimes it's hard for me to believe that is really her. She doesn't move. It's like she's asleep, but no matter how much I talk to her, I can't wake her up."

Joe paused for a moment, not willing to ask what was on his mind, yet feeling he must. "Doctor, do you think my wife is brain dead? Dr. Bartlett keeps telling me she is."

Dr. Rodriquez didn't know what to say. No amount of medical school could ever prepare someone to answer a question like that. "I don't know. I don't have a good answer for you Joe. I guess only God knows the answer to that one." Trying to change the subject again, Dr. Rodriquez went on, "what tests have they performed?"

"None that I know of, other than that renal test they ran a few days ago," Joe began to choke up a little. "The day before yesterday, Dr. Bartlett said he wouldn't be surprised to see her go into renal failure at any time."

Dr. Rodriquez checked Mary's records on his laptop. "Her renal enzyme levels are about the same. Not good, but okay. I don't think we need to get worried about that right now." Dr. Rodriquez kept a close eye on her renal enzyme levels and anything else involving her kidneys. "What other tests have they run?" the doctor asked again thinking, *Joe must have forgotten something.* "How about the swelling on her spine? Have they checked that lately?"

"No, not since that first night in the ER." Then as an after-thought Joe added, "maybe it's better they didn't. I don't know if I could handle any more bad news right now."

Dr. Rodriquez was understanding the situation a little better, after each visit with Joe. Inwardly, he questioned Dr. Bartlett and the hospital administration's motives. *Why weren't they being more attentive to her and giving her the care she needs, and why had Bartlett tried to abort the baby yesterday? There were a lot of other options besides rheumatrex for swelling, if that was really the doctor's concern.* It was true, the spinal condition should have been monitored more closely. It was as if her doctor and the hospital staff had completely given up on the patient, and were just waiting for her to die. Dr. Rodriquez left Mary Smith's room pondering what he should do about this obvious problem.

As regular as clock work, Mr. Elder appeared for one of his twice a week visits with Joe. Today's visit with Mr. Elder was a particularly pleasant relief. It gave him a reason to hang up on his annoying mother-in-law who was once again threatening to get a lawyer, and who had called to give Joe yet another round of tongue lashing and a 'piece of her mind.' *Joe wondered how many pieces of her mind she could give him 'till he had the whole thing,* as he smiled to himself. *He was sure she couldn't have much mind left at this point.* The light hearted side of Joe, which seldom appeared these days, imagined his mother-in-law without a brain as he shook hands with his visitor and tried to focus on what he was saying. Mr. Elder continued, "so if you think you are up to it, I will bring them by next week then?" Joe had missed the first half of this sentence as he mused about Jane Jones having an empty head. Joe questioned with a blank look on his face, "Bring what exactly?" "The red books and the reading plan of course," was Mr. Elder's reply. "O yes, that . . . would be fine," Joe replied.

A smile stole over Joe's face as he set back in the chair and relaxed. He had come to look forward to Mr. Elder's visits. Since Joe had two regular visitors, an extra folding chair had been placed in his room. Mr. Elder now sat on the folding chair conversing with Joe in his easy manner. Joe was sorry to see their visit come to an end. Both men bowed their head in prayer as Mr. Elder prayed for Mrs. Smith, and the baby which he affectionately called 'Baby

Smith', and Joe.

As Mr. Elder stood up to go, Joe held out his hand but, Mr. Elder held out his arms saying, "my dear Mr. Smith you look as if you could use a hug right now." Joe felt a bit awkward at this. Having never hugged his dad growing up, this man hug thing was a bit strange to him. Joe was expecting the typical three pats on the back awkward thing he had seen at church. Much to his surprise, Mr. Elder simply gave him one firm squeeze in a loving fatherly sort of way. Joe's arms hung awkwardly at his sides during this strange new experience. Mr. Elder smiled at him and promised to see him again next time. Turning in a slow manner, he left the room.

After a days contemplation and some prayer about what he would say, Dr. Rodriquez decided to go and speak with someone about the use of methotrexate, and the substandard level of care the hospital staff was providing Mary Smith. His supervisor was powerless, especially in a case involving the ICU ward. Finally, after some contemplation, he decided to go all the way to the top. He had been told that Mr. Verde, the hospital administrator, was a Christian. Surely he would sympathize with his concerns.[1]

Early in the morning, before his shift began, Dr. Rodriquez dropped in on Mr. Verde in his office. A slim, young secretary in a pencil-straight, black skirt and high heels escorted him into the office. Pulling up a comfortable seat for Dr. Rodriquez to sit in, she left the office, closing the door behind her. Sitting in the plush surroundings, he put the situation as bluntly as he could to Mr. Verde. He explained how he felt Mrs. Smith was being denied her rights to proper care; routine tests were not being run; and her Primary Care physician was violating the hippocratic oath, by endangering the life of Joe Smith's unborn child.

As he placed the empty Methotrexate bottle on the desk, he explained how he felt the doctor had misled Joe Smith, by not informing him of the potential harm this drug posed to the baby. Dr. Rodriquez went on to explain how Dr. Bartlett's behavior was bordering on malpractice, cautioning that such substandard care could pose risks to the hospital, if allowed to continue.

A cold glare flashed across the desk in Dr. Rodriquez's direction. Dr. Rodriquez had wrongly assumed Mr. Verde was ignorant of the situation, but he could see by the hard set to Verde's jaw, and the irritation on his face, he was more than aware of the situation. Rodriquez was more than a little surprised at the response from Mr. Verde. He knew Verde to be a regular attender of the denominational church that owned and operated the hospital, and he had assumed, they both would share the same opinions, convictions, and worldview on this subject. It was now painfully obvious to Dr. Rodriquez, Mr. Verde had *no* such convictions. Verde made it quite clear to his *employee* that he deeply resented his interference, and went on to explain in detail that his interference would no longer be tolerated.

Dr. Rodriquez sensed the conversation was at an end. He had anticipated Mr. Verde praising him for his attentiveness to the needs of individual patients; but, instead of receiving the praise and admiration he felt he deserved for saving the baby's life, Mr. Verde reprimanded him for interfering with another doctors patient. Verde reminded him he was JUST an OB doctor. Dr. Rodriquez kept a cool head and placid expression on his face, but inwardly he seethed with anger. He didn't know why, but it was all too clear to him Verde had wanted the Smith baby dead. Rodriquez was clearly being punished for his interference in the matter. He cried out in prayer to the only Power in the hospital, greater than Mr. Verde. God was still in control. The Holy Spirit had prompted him so clearly the day he had saved the Smith baby. He knew the powers-that-be here on earth would not stop him from saving this child's life, if it could be saved. Dr. Rodriquez didn't need to be told the subject was closed and the conversation was over. Rising from his seat without another word, he headed for the door. Without saying good bye, he left the office.

With only ten minutes remaining before he needed to begin his shift, Dr. Rodriquez realized the situation was urgent. With no second thought, he began running through the halls of the hospital, dodging staff and visitors. Not even stopping to apologize to a nurse he nearly ran over in the hall of the ICU unit, he rushed into Joe's room. Dr. Rodriquez understood Mr. Verde's unspoken body language, and he also felt confident after the conversation he had just finished that he would be removed as the Smith's OB doctor. He must speak with Joe, before it was too late!

Relieved to find Joe in the room, Dr. Rodriquez paused to catch his breath while he leaned against the door. Joe smiled and seemed relieved to see the doctor. "What brings you down here so early Doctor?" Joe casually began.

"Listen Joe," the doctor gasped between breaths, "I don't have time for small talk. I fear I am going to be removed as your OB doctor if I haven't been already. Pay attention. You have got to be ever vigilant about this IV bag and Peg tube. You can't let them put anything strange in there. Also, you have got to make sure they keep her hydrated and fed regularly. Can you do that?" Dr. Rodriquez questioned.

"What's going on," was Joe's only response.

"I don't know, but, like I said, I don't think I'll be your doctor much longer. If things really get bad, you need to threaten to leave the hospital, file charges, and/or call in the newspaper or television." A nurse, on a routine check, opened the door. "I've got to be on the OB floor in one minute," Dr. Rodriquez said, and left the room without another word. Panic should have gripped Joe, but he had a hard time believing any hostility on the part of Dr. Bartlett. Sure he and the doctor didn't see eye-to-eye on a lot of things, but he wouldn't try and purposely hurt his baby, especially since he believed the baby was already dead. Amidst all the stress and guilt, any ideas of leaving this hospital quickly slipped from Joe's mind at present.

Dr. Rodriquez entered the OB floor and reluctantly went to his box. Pulling out the pile of reports, he noticed on top of the stack an odd-looking, yellow sheet. Unfolding it he glanced over it, realizing what it was in an instant, but who would take his place? He was being officially removed as Mary Smith's OB doctor. He was no longer allowed to see, visit with, or have any contact with that patient. A violation of this would be grounds for being fired, and *if he lost his internship*, Dr. Rodriquez didn't even want to think about that. . . . A formal reprimand for removing the IV bag was stapled to the back of the yellow sheet. Unbeknown to Dr. Rodriquez, he had violated some unspoken rule by interfering with Dr. Bartlett's (or was it Mr. Verde's?) intentions for his patient and Dr. Rodriquez had no other line of recourse.

The Head OB Doctor, a single, heavy-set woman in her mid-fifties, removed her glasses and looked up at Dr. Rodriquez from her paperwork. She had always been fair with him, and he thought he could trust her. Rodriquez questioned, "You knew about this?" "Just found out and placed the notice in your box not more than five minutes ago," she replied. "I've been instructed to cut your hours in half effective immediately. If you don't comply with the order to stay away from the Smith's, I have been ordered to suspend you until you can be fired. You could lose your career over this one." "And will you?" Rodriquez questioned. "Got to do what Mr. Verde says. I can't risk my job. Remember, we're *only* OB doctors." she coolly replied.

"Who's replacing me to care for the Smith baby?" Dr. Rodriquez asked. "Nobody. I don't know that they really need a OB doctor on that case. The patient's Primary doctor thinks the baby's already dead," the Head OB Doctor commented as she left the room, and walked into the hall. She clearly did not want to get involved.

Is no one willing to take a stand for what is right? Oh God show me what to do!

The door to the nurses' station swung open again. As if an answer to his prayer, Rachel's beautiful form slid through the door. She was wearing a pleasant smile on her dark, glistening face. She looked so beautiful he thought. *Rachel, here was the answer to his prayer!* Rachel returned his gaze with a warm, sympathetic smile. She could tell he was upset about something, but *what was it?* "Everything OK with the Smith baby," she casually asked. The office was vacant, and they were left alone for once. "Rachel," the doctor began, "I need your help!" Sensing the seriousness of the situation, she walked to his side and sat down in a chair near him. Rodriquez sat down too. "I've been removed from the Smith case." "Removed?" Rachel questioned. Dr. Rodriquez handed her the yellow sheet. Rachel gave a swift look over the page. "They can't do this," she continued. "They can, and they already have," he explained.

Rodriquez continued, "I know I. . . " Dr. Rodriquez looked deeply into those beautiful black eyes. He could have spent a lifetime looking into them, but he didn't have time for that now. His courage was failing fast as he looked at her flawless smooth skin. "I know I . . ." his mind searched for just the right words. He wanted to say, *I was a real jerk the other night,* but instead he found himself saying. "wasn't very diplomatic the other night. I. . ." Awkward silence followed.

Rachel felt compelled to say something. "I know you're really busy and I was taking up your time," Rachel continued, and *I'm not important to you* she thought to herself. Dr. Rodriquez cut to the chase. He assumed by the look on her face, she had no feelings for him. "I need your help. I need someone to look in on the Smiths. I need someone to make sure everything is alright with the baby and Mom, and more than anything," Dr. Rodriquez put his hand on top of Rachel's small dark hand, "Mr. Smith needs someone to give him hope. If he gives up...If they convince him this baby is dead, it's all over. Can you do that for me?"

Rachel's eyes closed, she bit her lip, and a tear fell down her cheek. Dr. Rodriquez reached for a tissue and handed it to Rachel. He wanted so bad to take her in his arms, to hold her close and tell her how much he cared for her, but he couldn't. She wasn't his, and besides, she didn't seem to care for him. He had struck a deep nerve with Rachel, a conviction, the sanctity of life, which they both held dear. Rachel struggled to regain her composure. *How could they have so many things in common and still be world's apart?* He was quickly winning her admiration, even if he failed to realize it. She had better be on the alert and guard her heart, or he would break it. "I've been put on nights for the next month, and you work days." Rachel explained. "Will you check up on them for me? Leave me a note in my box, no. . . better yet, here's my cell phone number. Call me if anything changes."

He quickly jotted down his number on a sheet of paper and pressed it into her hand.

"Dr. Rodriquez. You're needed in Delivery Room A," a voice announced over the intercom.

"Call me, please! They are going to stop all care and try to get this baby to abort," was the last thing he said as he hurried from the room.

It was true, Mr. Verde had hidden motives for wanting Mary to be taken off life support. His Worldview and professional training had convinced him Mary Smith was brain dead. One of his best doctors had told him so.

But Verde was not the only one with an agenda in this situation; there were other unseen Forces at work in this situation. As with most of the wrongs in the world, one man or a group of men could not have orchestrated and executed the evil plan that was underway. The demonic Prince of this Principality was hard at work doing the work of our ultimate adversary, the Devil. Yes, man would make his evil plans; and yes, men would carry out their evil plans; but, there was a stronger, Supernatural Force behind all these trials.

CHAPTER 10

... In the world you will have tribulation; but be of good cheer, I have overcome the world" (John 16:33).

While Joe puzzled over what had caused Dr. Rodriquez's abrupt visit and what the ramifications of it would be for himself, Mary, and their baby, Mary's mother, Jane Jones, reclined by her pool behind her comfortable suburban home having yet another rum and coke with one of her few friends on this lazy summer day. Truth be told, Mary's mother really didn't have many close friends. She was much too selfish, and her mood swings way too unpredictable for most people to endure being around her for very long at all. She did however, have a few friends from her Bridge club who tolerated her so they would be invited to play bridge in her beautiful, Victorian-style home on the north end of Lake Shore Drive.

Iris Wethers, a tall, slender woman in her early fifties with medium brown hair and a long narrow nose, was one of these fair-weather friends. A recent addition to the bridge club, Iris, for some strange reason, seemed to enjoy the company of Jane Jones on this fair afternoon. If the bare truth were known, Iris primarily appreciated Jane's beautiful home; lavish taste in food, which she often shared; the fact that her bar was never dry; and the ability to brag to her friends that she had spent the afternoon on Lake Shore Drive. In return for these amenities, Iris must put up with, endure, even seem to sympathize with her host's latest laundry list of complaints. Of late the only topic of conversation Jane seemed capable of speaking on was the loss of her daughter.

She spoke and acted as if death had already happened. *Hadn't the doctors told her that her only child was dead?* In her mind, there was only a temporary delay in the funeral, caused by her heartless son-in-law's unwillingness to cooperate. She had come to blame Joe for all of her current problems, both real, and imagined. She wanted to have the funeral, get this whole terrible loss behind her, and move on with her life.

As the sun reached its full afternoon intensity, the two ladies applied another coat of sun tan lotion and leaned back in the recliners beside the pool. Iris Wethers helped herself to yet another generous serving of shrimp scampi as a lull came over the conversation. For a moment, Jane Jones was quiet, her green eyes impatiently shifting back and forth in her head as she was unable to think of a new way to slander her son-in-law. She searched for some new topic to gripe and complain about. Having exhausted the topic of Joe completely, she finally decided to vent her feelings by insulting the people at Joe's Christian school. She quickly tired of the usual stereotypical comments about how all Christians are hypocrites, self-righteous bigots, holier-than-thou, and so forth. In an attempt to keep Iris engaged in the conversation, she went on to explain, "They wouldn't even hire hard working experienced people like you and I, because in their eyes we aren't *good* enough to work there. Those self-righteous..." and here, she made a repulsive, almost demonic face, and spit out the word, "Christians!" Totally unaware of the actual demonic influences guiding their slightly inebriated minds, the two women laughed.

"I wouldn't want their money anyway," Jane Jones criticized, as a Power, not of this world, was carefully guiding the conversation of these two bitter women.

"I would," Iris announced. "I really need a job."

In jest, Jane Jones retrieved the phone book from the drawer of the wet bar beside the pool. Quickly finding the number for the school, she dramatically pressed each button with a wave of her arm and presented the ringing phone to Iris. A volunteer mom answered the phone, "Grace Christian Academy, how may I help you?" "Do you have any opportunities for employment," Iris asked as she nearly belched into the phone. "Yes, as a matter of fact we do. Our secretary has just had a baby, and we will be needing a replacement for her immediately." Iris smiled and replied, "I've been a secretary for almost 30 years. Could you mail me an application, please?" The unsuspecting volunteer took the appropriate information to mail the application out to Iris, not realizing what eventual problems this simple act would create. The Demonic Prince, knowingly, guided his charge, Iris, along the path he had chosen for her.

Iris Wethers was serious about her inquiry into employment at the school. She wanted a secretarial job, and she didn't care who hired her. Newly divorced, she needed a way to support herself for the next few years until she was old enough to qualify for Social Security. Two days later, Iris appeared at the school with her completed application and references. She looked like an excellent applicant on paper. She wore an attractive two piece suit, and on the surface she appeared to be exactly what the school was looking for.

Iris sat in the reception area of the office as Mr. Elder scanned over her application and resume. *Her qualifications and references were excellent, and she can begin work right away!* Mr. Elder was so excited about finding such an experienced person; he failed to notice the statement of faith was unsigned. Leaving the door to his office open so the volunteer mom in the hall could hear them, he asked Iris to come in to his office and he conducted an informal interview for the secretary position. He nonchalantly added as the interview was closing, "The pay isn't much, but it is a great opportunity to serve the kingdom of God with your talents." Not wanting to loose this applicant, he scheduled her for the second interview in the hiring process, for the week after the next Board meeting.

A few days later, at the board meeting, Mr. Elder brought up the subject of the school's need for a replacement secretary for the main office and passed out copies of the only application they had received. He explained that several of the student's moms had been volunteering as secretaries until the space was filled, and they needed an employee right away so they could complete the training necessary before school started. As the board members read through the forms, one of them happened to notice the statement of faith wasn't signed. Mr. Elder was aggravated with himself and impatiently drummed his fingers on the board table as he stared at the unsigned statement of faith. His oversight would delay the hiring process, and they didn't need any delays.

The next day, Mr. Elder called Iris on the phone, explaining the simple oversight, and asked her to come in and sign the statement of faith so they could continue the interview process. Thinking it must have been a simple oversight, he politely explained all applicants must sign the statement of faith before they could continue the interview process.

Iris's initial response to Mr. Elder and his request for signature on the statement of faith, was a slight chuckle under her breath. "Mr. Elder I didn't sign that piece of paper because I didn't understand half of what it said, and I make it a practice to never sign anything I don't fully understand. I'm a da__ good secretary," Iris continued, "and I am more than qualified to do what your school needs done. Your school is incorporated as a business, right? Well," Iris paused and her voice was altered as she seemed to be reading something verbatim, "Title VII of the Civil Rights Act of 1964 prohibits employers with at least 15 employees, as well as employment agencies and unions, from discriminating in employment based on race, color, religion, sex, and national origin. It also prohibits retaliation against persons who complain of discrimination or participate in an EEO investigation. In other words, you can't not hire me because I refused to sign that piece of paper."

Mr. Elder was flabbergasted! He strained his ears as he seemed to be hearing another voice in the background talking with Iris.

With a slight delay, Iris resumed the conversation, and the other voice grew silent, "That pledge not to drink any alcohol is sheer foolishness," she continued on her tirade, "I understand I will not be allowed to drink alcohol during business hours, and obviously, will not be allowed to show up to work drunk. But, do you honestly think that an employer can dictate their employee's behavior during the time that they are not at work?" Mr. Elder was about to answer in the affirmative, but Iris kept right on talking, not giving him a chance to answer.

"*When* I take this job, I will happily and cheerfully do whatever you ask me to do while I'm at the school on company time. What I do on my own time, however, is quite frankly none of your business. You obviously realized right away, I'm more than qualified to do this job, or you would not have scheduled a second interview with me. I need a job Mister. You have an opening. I am more than qualified to fill it; and you admitted to me during the initial interview that you had no other applicants for the position. If you refuse to give me another interview just because I won't sign a piece of paper agreeing to let you dictate my behavior when I am not on the clock, I suppose that would be discrimination wouldn't it, Sir? And," Iris continued, "It's against the law for a business to discriminate in its hiring practices isn't it, Mr. Elder?"

"Ms. Wethers," Mr. Elder began in his calm, mild-mannered way, "I can assure you, if you are unwilling to agree with the statement of faith by signing it as well as the no drinking pledge, you will not be considered for this position. This is a Christian school, and we only hire Christian people who are willing to hold to a high moral standard. We can't expect the students to abide by these rules if the staff doesn't. And for your information, Christian schools are exempt from the legal requirement pertaining to religious discrimination in hiring.[1]"

"I need a job Mr. Elder and you can't do this to me. It's illegal! You may think you can get away with this, but I assure you, you are sadly mistaken, Sir. I have a good friend with a good lawyer who I'm sure will be more than willing to help me change your mind on this matter. Good day!"

And with that, Iris slammed down the phone ending the diatribe. Picking it back up again and smiling she handed the phone to Jane Jones who promptly dialed her lawyer, while the unseen Powers guiding Iris laughed a sinister laugh, inaudible to human ears.

CHAPTER 11

Of equal importance to the health of a community, is a good civil Constitution or frame of government. This is the foundation on which political life and happiness are raised and secured.— Sermon by Chandler Robbins, pastor of the First Church in Plymouth

It had been five days since Mr. Elder's disturbing conversation with Iris Wethers. Since he had heard nothing from either Iris or her supposed lawyer, he dismissed the case from his mind and assumed there would be no further retaliation. It was Tuesday morning at 10AM sharp, and Mr. Elder was again at the hospital to visit Joe, but this time, he carried a fair sized book bag on his arm. Mr. Elder tapped lightly on the door, "May I come in?" Joe turned from his trancelike staring at the monitors on the wall, "Sure—always nice to have a visitor."

"I've brought the red books and your reading plan," Mr. Elder smiled as he placed the satchel on the table. "This is your reading plan. It takes you through your required readings, and it is broken down into the different principles of America's Christian history." Mr. Elder transitioned into headmaster mode and began going through the reading plan in an official, dry manner. It starts with number one, God's principle of individuality, and then progresses on from there, number two: the Christian principle of self-government, number three: America's Heritage of Christian Character, number four: conscience is the most sacred of all property, number five: the Christian form of our government, number six: how the seed of local self-government is planted, and number seven: the Christian principle of American political union."

Joe stifled a yawn and pretended to be interested in what Mr. Elder said, but his mind couldn't help but wander. When Mr. Elder stopped talking about the *red books*, he and Joe went through the traditional chit chat about how Mary was doing. Taking a slow but steady stand, the discerning Mr. Elder stood up. Doing something rather untraditional, he placed his hands squarely on Joe's shoulders and began to pray without ceremony or introduction. "Dearest Savior, strengthen Joe. Give him wisdom. Heal his dear wife Mary that she might be saved from eternal damnation. Prosper Joe's time reading in the red books. Reveal new truths to him through this tool. We beg your blessing on the school, the students, and the faculty in this time of trial. Our Father in heaven, Hallowed be Your name. Your kingdom come. Your will be done on earth as it it in heaven. Give us this day our daily bread. And forgive us our debts, As we forgive our debtors. And do not lead us into temptation, But deliver us from the evil one. For Yours is the kingdom and the power and the glory forever. Your will and desire be done in all of this." The beeping alarm of Mr. Elders watch sounded as he said the final "Amen." Mr. Elder sighed and extended his hand to Joe, giving him a firm hand shake as his other hand reached for the door. "Sorry, I've got a meeting in an hour. I'll stop in again soon."

A reading plan! Oh joy! Joe's satirical side exclaimed in disbelief. But then upon further reflection, Joe decided reading a dry book had to be better than staring at the heart monitors hoping and praying for a slight fluctuation, or listening to the monotonous sound of the respirator all day.

Joe wiped his hand slowly across the cover, studying the golden letters written on the red background, *The Christian History of the Constitution of the United States of America*. Under the beautiful gold embossed eagle, he read *Christian self-government*. Not exactly

116

a light read, Joe thought to himself as he felt the massive book in his hands noting the author, "Verna M. Hall." He'd heard the names of Ms. Hall and Ms. Slater spoken reverently at the school, and as he glanced at the spine of the smaller of the two books, he noticed the metallic luster from the second name shining forth: Rosalie J. Slater, *Teaching and Learning America's Christian history-the principal approach.* It was the *American Revolution Bicentennial edition!* He had just been born when this was printed. Sliding a scratched up Mac out of the way, Joe placed his feet upon the makeshift table, grabbed the required reading list Mr. Elder had brought, and settled back into the familiar hospital chair which had become his second home.

Pausing for a moment, Joe prayed for his sleeping wife and then, almost as an afterthought, asked God to bless his reading of this big red book. As chills began running up and down his spine, Joe realized whatever information the books held, God would do just that. Before the accident, Joe had to admit, he had been dreading the required reading of these massive red books, but now something deep down in his soul was actually looking forward to the experience to learn more about America. He would learn not only about America, but what Christian self-government was really about. Was he experiencing the leading of God? Yes, that's exactly what it was. God was preparing his steps, and he would walk in the path that God had prepared for him.

Somewhere deep in the recesses of his soul he sensed Christian self-government wasn't what he saw and experienced around him today in America. He had grown up thinking, or being taught rather, America was a free, Christian nation. *Was it really truly as free and Godly as our founding fathers had intended, or had things changed over the last 200 years?* With those deep thoughts forming in his mind and heart, Joe carefully turned six pages and began reading the preface Ms. Hall had written on September 17, 1960.

Joe traveled back several hundred years in the next few hours from the Magna Carta to the Mayflower compact, the pilgrims and William Bradford. Page after page of truth, line after line of legacy, and paragraphs of promise poured forth from the pages. As he set the book down and rubbed his tired eyes with a yawn he stretched, "Why? Why wasn't I taught this in school?" Joe questioned aloud.

Looking up at Mary for what seemed like the millionth time —*Did her face just twitch?.. Did her eyes just move?.. Maybe it was just the ventilator.* With his eyes strained from reading, he reasoned, they must be playing tricks on him. A small sense of guilt spread over Joe. He had been so absorbed with his reading for the last few hours that he'd hardly paid any attention to Mary. Standing, Joe walked over to his wife and kissed her lightly on the cheek. Then sliding to his knees, he called out to his Father God once again for her recovery.

A light tap on the door stirred Joe from his time of prayer. "May I come in?" Robert's request was quickly granted with a smile and a nod. As both men settled into their familiar seats, Robert set down a grocery sack. Catching a glimpse of the big red book Joe had been reading, Robert began. "They say you can't judge a book by its cover, but this one looks mighty impressive. How is it lad?"

"To tell you the truth Robert," Joe began, "It's blessing my socks off. It's. . . it's challenging me to my core, and," here he paused "driving me crazy all at the same time. Learning American history from original documents! What a novel idea! All throughout my education, all I got were sentence fragments and summaries . . . and, come to think of it, I am beginning to understand that the viewpoint of the summarizer was often antithetical to what the actual document says." For the first time, some of the old pre-accident Joe was back. His mind was less worried about Mary, and he seemed more at ease.

"It isn't exactly a cover-to-cover read. This reading plan Mr. Elder has me following has got me jumping around this book like I'm on a pogo stick. Compared to today's modern English, it seems as if some of the writers have taken a creative spelling class." Here Joe paused again, and smiled in a joking manner, "Or maybe they've taken some lessons on diction and grammar from you."

Robert grinned from ear to ear and said with an overly

exaggerated accent. "Aye, Your jus' jealous because ye canna' speak the queen's English."

Joe handed the book to Robert for him to examine and pass his judgment on. The expression on his face softened, as Robert cradled the book in his giant hands and pulled it near to his heart. The bottom lip of this seemingly tough man seemed to quiver and his eyes grew moist, "We've met before." A puzzled look came across Joe's face. Robert continued, "This book and I, we go way back, as the expression goes. It was this beloved book that started me on the journey of falling in love with my Savior Jesus Christ, and growing to love this country as if it were my very own."

Joe's questioning expression urged Robert to continue. Robert could tell Joe wanted some type of a follow-up on that comment. "Well here's my life story in a nutshell, Lad. You can probably tell by my accent that I'm not native born here in Chicago." Joe nodded. Robert continued as he tried to gauge just how much to say and what not to say. "You see, I'm the second son of a Scottish Lord. My older brother will inherit the land, and the title. I was sent to the US to study law, but God obviously had other plans for my life."

"It's a little bizarre I must say. I have always found the United States Constitution fascinating; it being the basis of the oldest continuous functioning government in existence today. Let me see—it would have been 1985, yes that's about right, I had only recently arrived in the United States and I was walking around taking in the sights and sounds. I happened across a rather large old bookstore, with a very unusual sign. Since I was in no hurry, I decided to go in and take a look. I love the look and the smell of old books, the way they feel, and the places they can take you. It reminded me of the family library at home. I had just recently converted some of my English pounds into U.S. Federal Reserve notes and decided on a whim, right there on the spot, a book would be my first purchase with them.

"As I walked the aisles in search of the perfect book, the red cover caught my eye. The book, as it turned out, was an earlier printing of the one I now hold. The sales clerk who rang up my order, gladly took my new Monopoly money[1] in exchange for the book, did a most peculiar thing: he reached under the counter and placed a brand new, still in the plastic, Giant Print New King James Bible in my bag. He said there was 'no charge for the second book, since it would be impossible for me to understand the book I was buying without the one he was placing in the bag beside it.' I am a prolific reader if I do say so myself, and since this is the nutshell version, I'll just tell you, I read both books and somewhere along the way I found myself on my face crying a river of tears and calling out to the Beloved One whom I now call my Lord and Savior Jesus Christ." Now both men were crying unashamed, happy tears of joy, as for a brief moment they forgot their unemotional male side. This friendship that had started in a hospital emergency room would continue for eternity.

When he could speak again, Robert continued, "I was raised as a spoiled rich brat by a father who lives enslaved to debt and has never worked an honest day in his life. I will not try to explain how his title, position, and lands allowed him to continue this for so long, even to this day. Just suffice it to say this—the borrower is slave to the lender, and my father is one of the many votes the bankers control in the House of Lords in my country. My father was furious when he found out I was now the son of the King of Kings. He offered to buy me my own estate—which I suspect he always wanted to do anyway, but with borrowed money and a built-in debt to the bankers, included in the bargain. I believe that's why I had been sent to the United States, to study at the prestigious law school I was enrolled in."

Joe looked confused. It was hard for him to grasp what Robert was saying. Why would a nobleman need to borrow from the bankers? Weren't they supposed to be independently rich?

Robert began again, trying to explain. "So I could return and join my father in the House of Lords to be one more vote in the banker's pocket. It's our hybrid system of monarchy and Parliament that most people see, but the real power that controls the country of my birth as well as most of the others is the banks." Robert could tell he was quickly loosing Joe. *Too much information for the lad,* he reminded himself mentally. He had introduced some new ideas Joe was having a hard time believing. "Sorry Joe, back to the nutshell—I did study law, constitutional law, graduated with honors. God put me into a peculiar little church where I met the most wonderful woman on the planet. No offense to your own lass there," he said with a nod and a wink at Mary, "I got to know her family and allowed them to get to know me. I asked her father's permission to pursue his daughter with the intent of marrying her. Several months and several interrogations later," Robert doubled up his fist slamming it into his other open hand for comic effect "he granted my request and I proceeded with fear and trepidation to try to convince my future bride to be that the match would be a good one. We went to a rather large Christian conference together with her whole family. I later convinced her to marry me. Her father actually did the ceremony, and we now have seven beautiful daughters." Ending the story, Robert said, "I love this country, or maybe I love what the founding fathers intended it to be."

Looking for a new subject, Robert glanced over at Mary, "you know if Mary's accident had occurred in Scotland, or England, or Canada she probably would not still be alive. Each of those countries has socialized health rationing, and Mary would've been pulled off life support long-ago."

Mary lay in a semi-conscious state vaguely aware of Joe talking to someone. She desperately wanted to wake up. This had to be a nightmare. *Where was she; how did she get here?* She tried to open her eyes and sit up. Her body would not respond. She could hear though; she could hear this man with an accent talking about her.

An accident? Life support? Why can't I move? Mary tried to swallow but quickly found she could not. Something, some tasteless hard piece of plastic was holding her mouth open. She tried again to talk, to moan, to make some type of noise, but to no avail. Giving up, she tried to focus on what Joe was saying, but then she felt so tired, so very worn down, and she couldn't stay awake any longer... Listening to Robert's accent, she was quickly lulled back into a state of unconscious sleep.

Jumping up from his folding chair, Robert said, "Oh, I almost forgot! My wife asked me to bring you these." From the grocery sack he had brought with him, Robert produced two large blocks of cheese, some homemade bread, and a big glass pickle jar filled with milk which had been on ice in a small collapsible cooler. With a broad smile Robert said, "I made the cheese myself. My daughter made the bread, and the milk is yesterday's vintage. Do you like fresh, raw milk[2]?"

He also pulled from his sack some plastic cups, plates, forks, and a large bread knife. Robert smiled as he set the items down, "Please excuse the fine china, but I don't like doing dishes in the hospital." Robert bowed his head and said a short sincere prayer of thanks. "Well let's eat," he followed up without ceremony. Joe marveled at this nobleman who could be so informal.

"This stuff is amazing." Then as an afterthought Joe added, "It's funny to think about a nobleman raising cows. This is the best milk, and this cheese has such an amazing flavor. What kind is it?"

Robert smiled. The joke was definitely on Joe. A humorous look crossed his face. "You've been eating way too much hospital food Lad. My lovely wife thought you could use some real food in your diet. We don't have any cows though."

Joe stared at the plastic cup that he had recently refilled which was halfway to his mouth. Joe wondered to himself, *what have I been drinking? He said this was milk, and milk comes from cows doesn't it?*

"No cows?" Joe inquired.

"At my place we have no cows," Robert responded obviously enjoying Joe's confusion. Robert inquired with a sly smile, "Joe, are you familiar with Proverbs 27: 27?"

Joe grabbed the Macintosh from the floor and launched the online Bible program. After a few keystrokes, Joe looked up with a smile, "'You shall have enough goats milk for your food, for the food of your household, and nourishment of your maidservants.' . . . Goats milk?" Joe inquired.

"At my house," Robert said proudly, "we call it Proverb's 27:27 milk."

Joe reached down and looked into the glass with a smile. After finishing the milk off in one long drink, he spoke, "Thanks. . . for not telling me it was goat's milk before I drank it. I probably would have refused to try it, and I would've missed out on a very good thing."

The teacher in Robert couldn't help but say, "There are a lot of things in life we miss out on, just because we won't take the time to try them."

Robert reached for another wedge of cheese, and handed the large red book back to Joe. "You said this book has been blessing your socks off and challenging you to your core? What have you been reading and studying?" Joe made a feeble attempt over the next hour to explain what he had been reading, realizing the man he was talking to had been pouring over these books since the time Joe had been in grade school. Out of habit Joe was typing notes as he talked and listened.

As he discussed with Robert, he better understood the first principle; *everything in God's universe is revelational of God's infinity, God's diversity, God's individuality.* God creates distinct individualities. God maintains the identity and individuality of everything which he created. They discussed God's view of man, wicked, evil and sinful. They discussed the pagan view of man: man is basically good-given the right environment. They talked about the second principle which basically says, a man cannot control or govern anything outside himself without controlling himself by reason, and obedience to God first.

Joe was just starting the third principle when Robert, glancing at his watch, realized he had been gone from home way too long. Promising to listen to what Joe had discovered later, Robert left the remaining food and milk and excused himself until another day. All throughout this discussion, Joe's fingers transferred the spoken words into notes on his laptop. Joe didn't completely understand it all, but he had gotten most of it down so he could study in detail later. He definitely had some food for thought now, and this day at the hospital had definitely been a little less monotonous.

CHAPTER 12

Joe passed a long, quiet weekend at the hospital followed by a slow Monday. The long weekend would have drug by slowly, but the reading material, left by both Mr. Elder and Robert, coupled with his Bible reading, had nourished his thirsty soul. It kept his mind sharp and occupied during these long, dark days. Late on Monday, Rachel made a visit to the room. She didn't stay long, but Joe was glad to see her again. With Doppler in hand, they listened to the baby's heartbeat.

"Have you noticed anything different Joe?" she casually asked.

"No," was Joe's only reply.

"Joe," Rachel began hesitantly, "Have they talked with you about taking the baby at some point?"

Joe walked over to the window and looked out across Lake Michigan, "No. Nobody has said anything about that, but in one way I'm kinda glad."

"Why?" Rachel asked giving him a puzzled look.

Joe turned and faced Rachel. "Well, I. . ." Joe stammered, "I'm just not ready to make that decision. I'm afraid a C-section might kill Mary; or even if she made it through the C-section, the doctors would see no reason to keep her on life support after the baby was born. Besides the doctors don't think the baby will be born. They keep telling me it's going to die and abort. . . and with all the head trauma to the baby from the accident. . ."

Joe sat down on the folding chair, dropped his head, and clasped his hands behind his neck. Rachel wished she had said nothing. *Why did she have to bring up this subject which was obviously so painful to him. She had come down here to be an encouragement, not bring discouragement.*

"I can't make any promises Joe. But," she said with a smile, "that baby's got a really good heartbeat for being near death." Then, on a lighter note, trying to change the subject. she asked, "When is the baby due? Dr. Rodriquez didn't want me to calculate gestational age when we did the sonogram."

Due. No one had said anything about when the baby was due. "I don't know. No one has asked that." Joe's spirits lifted a little as he thought about something more positive.

"Do you have any idea when the baby was conceived?" Rachel queried, as she pulled an odd-looking plastic wheel from the backside of the Doppler case.

"March 20th," Joe answered as his interest was being peaked by the interesting device she held.

"Around March 20th?" she asked.

"No, not around, *on* March 20th." He said in an all too affirmative way. Rachel moved the appropriate dials, and Joe for one brief moment thought he was going to die of excitement, if he didn't find out soon.

"Let's see, that puts us at about 15 weeks, and the baby being due Dec. 25, a Christmas baby." The beeper on Rachel's waist buzzed. Rachel looked at it. "I've got to run. We'll talk later." Picking up the Doppler and pregnancy wheel in one quick motion, she raced from the room.

Christmas, if they could just make it until Christmas, Joe reasoned. *I'll have the best Christmas gift in my life.* Joe opened his briefcase which Mr. Elder had been good enough to bring up to the hospital for him. He pulled out a small desk calendar and opened it up, thinking he would hang it on the wall or in some other conspicuous place and start marking off the days, until the baby was born.

Now, what was the date? Wow, where had June gone? Joe flipped the calendar over to July and put a slash through Sunday the first and Monday the 2nd. *It was nearly the 4th of July. Maybe he could see some fireworks from the hospital window. Time was sure traveling fast. July. . .*

Joe stopped in his tracks suddenly remembering what July was. Mary no longer had insurance. He was now responsible for her bills. A sickening feeling rose in his stomach. *How would he ever pay for all of this? Of course, he could always go on Illinois Medicaid.* Picking up the pamphlet "Not Yours to Give" on the top of a stack of books, Joe thumbed through it mechanically. His eye quickly ran over the books in the stack: *The Law, The Tragedy of American Compassion,* and *Using Your Money Wisely* by Larry Burkett.

Those books were all fine and good, Joe even agreed with their premise, but none of them had lived through what he had lived through. Medical expenses were not what they were in Davy Crockett's day, and Robert Forbes, that spoiled rich child, had never had a tragedy, let alone a tragedy of this magnitude in his life. Yes, he would have to go on Medicaid to pay for all this. After it was all over, he could adopt Robert's high standards, but for now it was what he was stuck with. Maybe tomorrow he would start dealing with that problem.

Carol Thomas's nurse/personal attendant was off duty for the day. Every Tuesday was her day off, and Carol felt particularly alone on this rainy Tuesday morning as she looked out the window. The pain in her abdomen was growing ever sharper. Her husband Bernard had left, forced to return to Canada for business reasons.

A large vase of red and white roses was on the nightstand next to Carol's bed. Beside them sat a large white bear with a Canadian maple leaf sweater on him. Bernard had, lovingly, sent them to his wife with a note explaining how much he missed not having her with him on Canada Day.

The flowers were no good. They only made Carol miss Canada, Bernard, and her life there even more. In a fit of anger, she swept everything on the desk, except the flowers and the bear, onto the floor. A sharp pain like a knife cut through her abdomen. The simple action of pushing a few papers and magazines into the floor had been too much. Reaching for the call button, she pumped it like a fire button on a video game. Her nurse soon came, annoyed that she had been called again for the third time this morning.

"Pain medicine," she gasped between breaths, "I need my pain medicine!" a crazed, desperate look shone in her eyes.

"I'm sorry." The nurse replied flatly, "It'll be an hour before you can have another dose of medicine. In the meantime, use your morphine pump."

The nurse started to leave the room. "Don't leave me. Pick this junk up off the floor." She waved toward the things she had raked into the floor. The nurse did what she was commanded, and stood to leave the room. As the door closed behind her, a large crash and the shattering of glass was heard on the other side of the door.

Sinking into a fit of despondency, Carol began to muse and think back over her life. Had it all been worth it? Why was she even on this planet? What was her purpose? She had no offspring. For whatever reason, she and Bernard had never been able to conceive. She had spent her life doing good works and charities. By most people's standards, she was a good person. Why was her life filled with so much physical pain and sickness? Why, now, was she being cheated out of the last twenty years of her life? What was the meaning of it all? Good? What was good anyway? She believed good people went to Heaven. What was Heaven? What would it be like there? A childhood image of an angel sitting on a cloud strumming a harp flashed in her mind. *NO thanks. . .,* she thought sarcastically.

Is there something after this, or do we just die and cease to exist? It all seemed so much more acute now that she was facing death. Is there a Hell? Was she headed for Hell? That single thought terrified her more than anything. "Oh God! If you are God, show yourself to me!" Fumbling in the drawer of the desk, she found the Gideon Bible she had placed there and opened it up. "In the beginning was the Word and the Word was with God and the Word was God." (John

1:1) Her mind mulled over those words. What did this mean? Who was this Word? Was He a person, or a thing? It all seemed so ambiguous. She slammed the book shut, and tossed it aimlessly back into the drawer. "Why is the Bible so hard to understand?" she asked herself aloud. How could she understand such nonsense? Surely there had to be an easier way to seek God: some psychic or mystic who could reveal him to her. Aimlessly she turned on the television, hoping to drown out the reality of the real world, and distract herself from the pain she felt not only in her body but in her heart.

A janitor entered the room with her cleaning cart and began to clean up the glass, water and flowers. Carol had fallen asleep, but for how long? At the nurses desk, the nurse pulled Carol's chart and called her husband. He had left his number in case they had a problem. Retelling the morning to Carol's husband, she explained how they needed someone there to sit with Carol on the nurse's day off, or they would have to restrain her or worse yet, sedate her.

Bernard hung the phone up and retreated into the bathroom in his office to dry his eyes. *Why had he left her there all alone? She wasn't doing well. The hospital wasn't doing their job. They obviously were neglecting her, or she wouldn't be so difficult. What was wrong with the hospital? Either they had the liver or they didn't. What was the hold up?* Choosing a clean wash cloth from the cabinet, he washed his face and returned to his desk. After locating Mr. Verde's personal cell phone number, a number few had access to, he called him.

Mr. Verde's Arctic Silver Porsche was just pulling out of the driveway on this warm summer day, when his phone rang. Pulling the car back into the driveway, he took Bernard Thomas's call. "Could you update me on the state of that liver Mr. Verde. It's been nearly a month now, and we are still waiting. I don't know any hospital that would hold a patient off this long."

Mr. Verde cursed himself for not checking his caller ID before he answered the phone. This was the last thing he wanted to deal with on the way to work today. He was already running late. "The liver should soon become available," Mr. Verde tried to reply patiently, "Listen, could I give you a call when I get to my office?"

"No!" Bernard snapped impatiently. "You listen to me. You told me you had the liver of this 26-year-old woman for my wife. Now either you do have a liver, or you don't! If you don't have the liver in a few days, I'm taking Carol to Houston. Baylor and Texas Medical Center will be more than happy to accept our money."

"It's not like you think Mr. Thomas." Not wanting to violate patient confidentiality, Mr. Verde stumbled with his words trying to find the right thing to say, "The patient is . . . well, we know she's brain dead, but the husband . . . isn't willing to take the patient off life support yet. We are trying to . . . negotiate. . . this." Both men paused, and there was an uncomfortable silence on both ends of the line. Mr. Verde didn't know what else to say, and Bernard, for one brief moment contemplated the pain this 26-year-old woman's husband must be feeling, while being pressured to take his wife off life support.

After a moment Bernard Thomas spoke. " I'll be in Chicago at the end of the week, and I expect to be able to talk with you face-to-face about this issue."

Mr. Verde heard nothing on the other end of the line, but he was glad he didn't have to deal with the situation any more. Throwing the car into reverse, he backed out and drove to work, as his mind contemplated what to do next.

Once he was in his office, he opened his email and looked for Ken's address.

Ken,

I spoke with you the other day about at situation here at the hospital. The situation is no better, and the foreign clients grow even more impatient as the days go by. What is my legal recourse? I want to get this situation resolved and deliver the product to the buyer. What legal rights do I have? Mo

Clicking the send button on the email program, Mr. Verde sat back in his office chair, and contemplated what to do next. He would go visit this, Mr. Smith. In his arrogance, he thought a visit from the hospital administrator would carry enough clout to somehow change Joe Smith's mind, and allow them to proceed with the transplant. Maybe a chat with a personal touch to it would be just the thing to remedy this situation.

Mr. Elder sat in the folding chair behind the partially open door to Mary Smith's room. Bringing Joe up-to-date on the events at the Christian school, they leisurely talked on this fateful Tuesday. There really wasn't much new to say, so both men sat quietly for a moment, as Mr. Verde approached Joe's room with a determined stride. He was prepared to offer Joe a reduction in his hospital bills if he would agree to remove his wife from life support and . . . *let nature run its course.*

Not far behind Verde was Jane Jones' lawyer, Mr. Brown, who was coming to serve papers on Joe Smith for a custody hearing. Mr. Brown's goal that day was to serve the papers he held in his hand quickly—and get out fast.

The door was open, and there was no need to knock. Mr. Verde took one glance into the room, and was quickly repulsed by the less-than-pleasant scene before him. Turning his eyes away from Mary, he stood in the open doorway and addressed Joe. "I'm Mr. Verde, the hospital CEO. Could you step out into the hall so I could have a word with you please?" Joe was about to comply with the request when an odd looking, short man in a suit pushed past Mr. Verde. A uniformed Chicago police officer stood looking on from the hall. Mr. Brown, Jane Jones lawyer, papers in hand, entered the room.

Joe exhaled an exhausted breath from his body and stood from his chair as the lawyer walked in. The two neatly-pressed suits and professional images stood out, in stark contrast to his own wrinkled pants and two-day-old T-shirt. Mr. Brown walked right up to Joe with no hesitation. "Mr. Smith I assume," he said in a stiff, impersonal tone. Joe nodded in reply as Mr. Brown continued. "I represent your mother-in-law, Mrs. Jones. I have here a subpoena requiring you to appear in court, to assess your ability of guardianship of Mary Jones-Smith."

Joe's mind reeled! Since when had Mary ever been called Mary Jones-Smith? Since the day of their wedding, she had always gone by her married name, Mary Smith. Joe looked at the summons he had just been handed and thumbed through the papers uncertain of how he should reply.

Seizing the opportunity, Mr. Verde began to speak, blocking the door, as the lawyer sought to exit the uncomfortable scene before him. "Sir, could you please remain one moment more. We may need your legal counsel." The lawyer waited for a moment with his back turned to the hospital bed. Mr. Elder, partially hidden behind the door and unseen by Brown and Verde, sat back in his chair and listened to the conversation unfold.

Mr. Verde began, "Mr. Smith, I think upon assessing the situation, this legal dilemma could all be avoided if you would just *consider* pulling your wife off life support." Mr. Verde placed a strong emphasis on consider. "We don't have to do it right away. Let's just set a goal. Say one week. If we don't see any improvement by then, we will remove life support. I think that would be a good compromise."

Turning to Jane Jones's lawyer, Mr. Verde continued, "Would your client be willing to work with that?"

"Indeed she would," the lawyer added. "Your mother-in-law has added a clause stating that if you will agree to take your wife off life support so her suffering would be ended, or if her daughter dies on her own, the case will be dropped."

So his mother-in-law wasn't bluffing Joe thought. If Mary was still alive in a week, if the baby was still alive in a week, and if this whole mess was still continuing, Joe would be required to stand before a judge to defend his right to be a husband and father to the two humans he loved most on the planet, his only remaining family, his wife and child.

"But the baby..." Joe stammered.

"Mrs. Jones has spent a lot of time consulting with me, concerning the need to allow nature to take its course. Mrs. Jones is not insensitive to her daughter's situation. She realizes her daughter is already brain dead. It is not that your mother-in-law didn't love her daughter, but, she is being responsible. Removing the machines will allow her body to finish dying with dignity. She is willing to put her own emotions aside, and do what is moral and ethical in this situation. Your mother-in-law is looking at what is the best for everyone involved. I think you need to do the same thing Mr. Smith. I'm afraid you're just not willing to let her go. In addition, we've been told by the hospital staff that it is very unlikely this fetus will survive. Have others spoken with you about organ donation? I am pleased to know your wife is an organ donor. As an organ donor a part of your wife will continue to live on and help someone else live a full productive life," Mr. Brown explained.

"Mr. Smith," Mr. Verde added, "I know you don't have the resources for a long-term legal battle. Your hospital bills are getting rather large, and I don't know how you plan on paying for them since her insurance expired July 1st. Let me be blunt Mr. Smith, I have no desire to bring this hospital into any long term financial entanglement necessitated by your refusal to be reasonable, nor do I want to subject the hospital to a lot of undue publicity in this situation. I would much prefer for you to agree with your mother-in-law, and make the right choice in this matter, but if I'm forced to do so by your lack of cooperation and refusal to be reasonable, I will use the hospital's resources to help you come to the right decision in this matter. Ultimately, we don't need your permission to do the right thing, Mr. Smith. The doctors and I can make the right medical decision for you, if you continue to refuse to do so."

It was a veiled threat, but Mr. Elder, unseen behind the door, more than understood what Mr. Verde was saying. Angered by what he heard, Mr Elder felt a little powerless. *Did the hospital really have the right to pull a patient off life support? This was America;*

this couldn't be happening here. Mr. Elder could very quickly see the energy and vitality of this young Christian being drained from him by the combined words of these two men, and he feared the resolve of this young believer was being quickly destroyed.

When the hospital administrator had finished speaking, Mr. Elder poked his head around the door and spoke to the unsuspecting Verde, who suddenly wished he had been a little more cautious about what he had said. "Sir, if you attempt to do what you have just threatened, I will personally see to it that you have groups of Christians protesting outside this hospital. As Christians, it's our duty to defend the weak, the helpless, and the unborn."

"That is up to the courts to decide," the lawyer said in a matter-of-fact tone, adding in his professional opinion. "I have no doubt in my mind, reviewing the allegations of Mr. Smith's physical and emotional abuse of his wife and what a bad husband and provider he has been, that the courts will award the protective custody of this woman to her mother Mrs. Jones. I would not have taken this case otherwise."

Mr. Verde nodded his agreement with the lawyer, and then, looking for a way to quickly end this controversial conversation, turned and walked silently from the room before either Joe or Mr. Elder could make any comment in their defense. He had overstepped his bounds, and making a personal visit to Mr. Smith had been a mistake. Mr. Smith was not as easily dissuaded as Mr. Verde had hoped, and he may have only succeeded in stirring up a hornet's nest. The lawyer, seeing that the door was no longer blocked, made a quick departure as well, along with his police escort.

Placing his firm, fatherly hand on Joe's shoulder, Mr. Elder bowed his head and prayed out loud with Joe. After a few more words and a Bible verse of encouragement, Mr. Elder left, promising that he would continue to pray for Joe.

Mr. Elder's words about "groups of Christians protesting outside the hospital" were not without effect on Mr. Verde. The last thing he wanted was a bunch of Christians from that man's church and school protesting outside of HIS hospital. The cultural war may be over. Christians may have little influence left in society, but the last thing he wanted was a bunch of do-gooders and fanatics milling around in front of the hospital with Protest signs. Verde was a firm believer in the old saying, the best defense is a good offense. Working his way back to his office, he began to form a plan in his mind of what his good offense would be.

Once back at his office, Mr. Verde flipped through his business cards, until he came across the number of an old acquaintance. The card read, Building Inspector—Bill Marshall. Verde called the State office. He hadn't spoken with the building inspector for at least two years, but after arranging to play a round of golf with the man on Saturday at The Beverly, he told him what he really called about. "This Christian school principal, I fear, could become a big problem for me and my hospital. I suspect that if you were to look into his school and church, you would find they aren't on the up and up with the building code."

"I get your drift Verde. I'll have some of my men down there looking into it. I can pull a few strings in the other departments as well. I imagine we can find something better for them to do than to send some church goodie-goodies to the hospital to cause you trouble."

"Thanks Bill, I knew I could count on you. I'll look forward to seeing you on the green Saturday and, I'm paying."

Dr. Rodriquez pulled a stack of papers from his box in the OB office. It had been the first break he had had all day. He quickly glanced over the papers tossing half of them in the trash. He wondered how Joe Smith, his wife, and their baby were doing. It had now been a week since the whole incident. *Had he made a mistake not staking his career on this case? He could have refused to follow Mr. Verde's orders.* As if in answer to his questions, a hand-written note quickly caught his eye.

Dr. Rodriquez,

Mr. Smith and his family are doing well. I talked with Joe today about conception dates, and based on what he has to say, I would say the baby is due around Christmas. Based on what I remember of the ultrasound, I would have thought the baby was much older than that, but he is confident about the conception date, and assured me he was sure. Otherwise, they are fine. Rachel

---

Dr. Rodriquez smiled and put the note in his pocket. It was strange what love could do to a man.

Chapter 13

The rain pounded against the window of Joe's room, but he didn't seem to notice the weather. His head pounded from lack of sleep, stress, and the depression of being cooped up inside the hospital room. This was not the worst day Joe had ever had, but it was close. He swallowed 4 aspirins and prayed they would take away the headache, but he knew they wouldn't help the dull ache he felt deep down inside.

Joe's two unwelcomed visitors today had given him an emotional beating, followed by doctor Bartlett who had made another depressing appearance, filled with the same bad news he always brought. Joe was glad this day was coming to an end. Joe thought back on the day: *Mr. Elder's visit was all too short, and had been interrupted by Mr. Verde, that jerk in the custom tailored suit that wanted his wife to die quickly, and the parasitic lawyer representing his mindless mother-in-law. Each successive visitor this miserable day brought more bad news and depression than the one before.* Sitting under the glare of the reading lamp beside the bed as the hand of the clock sped its way past eleven, he examined the paperwork he had been given. It seemed to be written in a foreign language. '*What did it all mean?*' He wondered as he scratched his head.

Joe stared at the legal documents which had been served on him summoning him to appear in court one month hence to decided who should have legal custody of Mary, if she lived that long.

Joe's eyes scanned the third page and noticed a paragraph highlighted in yellow highlighter. He stumbled over the legal jargon trying to comprehend what it meant. After reading it over several times, he realized this must be the clause His mother-in-law had added giving Joe the option of taking Mary off life-support of his own free will. The highlighted clause also stated that the whole case would be dropped if her daughter died on her own. *What was he going to do? He had no money to hire a lawyer to help him fight this case.* His mother-in-law had deep pockets and an expensive attorney. He tossed the papers to the floor and tried to pray, but the words wouldn't come.

He passed out from exhaustion some-time after midnight, but he wasn't sure he had slept much. He tossed and turned all night from the disturbing dreams, and sweat saturated his sheets. Doubt ever assailed Joe as he slept and as he awoke to face yet another day. It was morning, but it certainly wasn't a good morning. As he mechanically went about his daily tasks, the littlest thing said or implied by the hospital staff was enough to make him doubt himself, his motives, and ultimately his core convictions. God had not left Joe alone in these dark days; a steady stream of friends and prayers were ever around him.

Robert's wife took every opportunity she had to send him a home cooked meal, which Joe was always grateful for. The food was not what he was accustomed to eating. Often he wasn't even sure what some of the foods were, but Joe felt he might have starved to death if he had been forced to survive exclusively on the food the hospital offered.

He missed the smile of the nice sonogram technician, Rachel. She hadn't been in today, and Dr. Rodriquez had been taken away. The loneliness began to eat away at Joe's joy. He knew Rachel was probably working at the crisis pregnancy center today, and Dr. Rodriquez had been removed as their OB doctor, but that didn't make it any easier to deal with.

Joe reminded himself, *they had a life outside of this hospital even if he no longer did. At least not for now.* Joe, true to his word kept a vigilant watch over Mary and was becoming keen enough to know what should, and shouldn't, be put into the IV bag.

The manipulative ethics committee's chaplain paid Joe yet another unwanted visit and begged him to be "reasonable." Joe could still hear his irritating voice echoing in his mind, "The baby is probably already dead. . . Set yourself a time limit. . . If Mary has not changed in one week, could we get you to agree to take her off life support?" He had tried to convince Joe that he would be better off without Mary. "You are a young man and you could remarry, have a healthy wife, and healthy children." Part of Joe had wanted to punch that guy right in the nose when he said that. He still had a wife, and a child. He didn't want a different or better wife. Even in his tailored suit and smooth sounding words, Joe had decided he was a snake that had slithered in, bit Joe in the heart, and slithered away.

His hospital dinner came; the deliverer had been as unwelcome as the delivery. He raked the food back and forth on the metal plate with his fork, making a sound much like fingernails on a chalkboard, as he stared at Mary. Joe could not bring himself to lift one bite of it to his lips. He had lost his will, and he was quickly losing his strength.

His eyes misted as he dropped the fork and started searching for his handkerchief to wipe his nose. *Had the last few weeks been all for nothing? Was the baby dead, and Mary a vegetative corpse?* Mary lay motionless in the bed. Dead to Joe, and yet the living shell of her body still remained as a token reminder of what once had been, and of a life Joe wanted to re-embrace with all of his being."

This whole day stunk, and Joe decided he probably did too. He ran his fingers through his unwashed hair and across his stubbly chin. He didn't remember the last time he had dared leave Mary to catch a quick shower. The past several days were like a never-ending bad dream, a blur in his memory. Only the occasional visits from Mr. Elder, Rachel, and Robert gave him any hope at all. Personal hygiene was definitely not high on his priority list now, but

Joe decided anything that might make this putrid day stink a little bit less was worth a try. Grabbing a change of clothes and his duffel bag, Joe slipped into the shower for a quick cleanup, afraid to leave Mary out of his sight for any length of time. He didn't think the nurses had seen him leave Mary's room. Hopefully he wouldn't be missed.

He returned to the room and finished drying his hair deciding he would shave later. Opening his Bible, he mechanically stumbled through a Psalm attempting to read a few verses. Joe moved the vinyl chair that made into a "bed" next to Mary. Placing his big hand over her small one, he collapsed into a fitful, restless sleep.

CHAPTER 14

When my spirit was overwhelmed within me, Then You knew my path (Psalms 142:3).

The red books and the literature Robert had left for Joe to read had been a life saver for Joe in his time of despair and grief. Joe rubbed his blurry eyes and yawned, as he looked up at the clock on the wall. It was nearly 11:30PM. *Where had the time gone?* Life at the hospital was not easy for Joe, but the reading program Mr. Elder had left with him at least gave him something worthwhile to occupy his time, instead of just staring at the clock worrying about Mary and their unborn son.

Joe walked around the room, and then thought about turning in for the night. Getting good, quality rest was still a challenge for Joe though. Nurses and hospital staff were in and out of Mary's room every few hours making it difficult to sleep for any period of time. Joe could have ignored the nurses, rolled over and gone back to sleep, but he was a very light sleeper, and every time the door opened letting in the ever present artificial fluorescent daylight from the hall, he was wide awake. In addition, after the metho-trexate ordeal, he felt it necessary, to get up and inspect what each nurse or staff member was doing, lest they slip something in the IV bag and take his son's fragile life. Consequently, Joe would sleep some, but he was not getting any real deep, rest. The vinyl covered chair which folded out into a bed, was less than comfortable, and the fitted sheet the nurses had given him to put over the vinyl chair for sleeping seldom stayed on the bed. Most nights, Joe woke up with his sweating cheek stuck to the vinyl. The hospital did quiet down some between 1AM and 5AM. At this time the staff seldom entered. It would have been an ideal time for Joe to get some sleep, but Joe had found this a good time to get up, leave the room, and get a shower and attend to his personal hygiene without fear of anyone disturbing Mary or the baby in her womb. Putting down the Red books, and picking up *Debt Virus* by Jaques Jaikarin,[1] Joe hoped he had found a book that would put him to sleep.

An hour-and-a-half later, Joe sleepily lay *Debt Virus* on the floor and dozed off to sleep, but restful sleep was not to come to him. Sad dreams usually accompanied Joe's sleep. Grief, guilt, remorse. . . all these flooded Joe's mind. *If only I had said this, maybe Mary would have been more open to the gospel. If I hadn't been involved in this sin before I was saved, maybe Mary would have been more open to the gospel.* In addition, he couldn't put out of his mind the terrible dream of Mary's screams of torment. Giving up on sleep, Joe mechanically got up and found his towel and shaving gear. *He would feel a lot better after a good shower* he reasoned.

Joe gently pushed the hospital door open, trying not to make a sound. Nervous, and afraid to leave Mary alone, he jutted his head forward and looked out into the always bright lights of the hospital hallway. The hall seemed vacant. Gingerly, Joe proceeded into the hall, when he saw a male nurse and his friend step into the hall down the corridor. He took the handle of the door and went back into the room to watch them through the crack he had left open in the doorway. The men went on about their business, and Joe resumed his path to the shower.

Joe didn't much care for these two men. They seemed to have an unnatural male friendship. Joe suspected the worst, but trying to give them the benefit of the doubt, he pushed them from his mind, and walked on down to the shower.

142

The door to the shower room squeaked on its hinges destroying Joe's secrecy and the silence of the night. Anyone on the floor could hear the shower turn on from the hallway and would know Joe was occupied for the next few minutes. He would love to stay in the shower 20 or 30 minutes, but only allowed himself 10 minutes.

With the shower running, Joe could hear nothing of what was about to take place. The two nurses heard the shower door squeak. They had been waiting for this. "Come on, quick, now is our chance." Like the Grim Reaper, the two male nurses silently entered Mary's room. The shorter of the two pulled a rubber glove off the wall mount holder and put it on out of habit. The instructions came in a whisper to his partner, "Pull the ventilator. Hook it on her arm so it looks like she did it. It's always best when it looks like the patient wants to go on her own. You go on and turn off the hall lights. I'll stay and make sure things go as planned."

Mary gasped and sputtered as the tubing was removed from her throat. "*Oh God. Don't let me die this way* she thought, but only a very weak moan escaped her throat. The tubing hurt her throat as it was rapidly removed. Her right hand began to grasp weakly for Joe. *Joe where are you when I need you? God, I hear Joe talk to you so often PLEASE send him to me now. I need him so badly.*

The shower was warm, relaxing, and pleasant. Joe just wanted to stand here and wash away all of the bad news over the past few days. He allowed the warm water to soothe and relax him. It felt so good to just stand here and shut out the world for a while. Suddenly a chill ran down Joe's back. A panic came over Joe; something wasn't right with Mary. The Holy Spirit brought back to Joe's remembrance the dreams of her torments and screams in a split second flash of his mind's eye. He knew down deep in his soul that she needed him, even if he could hear nothing. In an instant, he pulled his clothes over his dripping wet body, not bothering to dry off. Grabbing his towel and bag, he threw the door open. Why were the lights off? Had the power gone out? Would Mary's ventilator go on backup power? Adrenalin pumped through his veins, as he sprinted down the hall toward their room, his wet feet slipping on the tile. In a few seconds, Joe was at the door.

Quickly he threw it open, but the room was pitch black as well, even the curtains were pulled blocking out the moonlight. A slow, labored gasping noise was all he could hear. Mary was gasping for air, and every breath sounded like it would be her last. He rushed to Mary's side. *Where were the alarms. . . and the nurses?* Mary coughed and made some more loud wheezes, and then all was silent. *Was this it?. . . Was she already gone?. . . What had gone wrong?* In the dark, he struggled to see Mary. *The curtain! Open the curtain and let in the moon light.* Joe groped for the curtain cords but when he did, he ran into another person, someone was in his path.

The waiting nurse pushed Joe down slamming his arm into an unseen object in the dark. Joe staggered to his feet, disoriented and in a panic. The nurse ran for the faint light of the open door, knocking Joe to the ground once again and falling to the ground in the process. The unseen person grabbed Joe's injured arm and twisted it hard. Twisting his arm around behind him, the male nurse pushed Joe into the bed rail then onto the floor, causing a stab of pain to shoot through Joe's already injured arm. Joe clutched his arm in pain still unable to see who his attacker was. The door to the room opened, but with no light in the hall, Joe could see almost nothing. His nose was spraying blood on the floor and his forehead throbbed from being rammed into the rail of the bed. Torn with pain, Joe felt his way across the floor and pulled the cord to call for the nurse at the desk. Light, he had to have light. He strained to hear Mary's breathing. *I'm too late,* his guilty mind reasoned.

If Joe hadn't been in such a state of shock, in the silence, he could have heard the sound. It was a weak rasp of a sound, but it was the sound of Mary, breathing. The feeble breath she exhaled sounded like it would be her last, but she was breathing. Crawling across the floor, he found his way to the door and pulled himself up to the light switch. Bumping it with his shoulder he turned it on. *Where were the nurses? One of them should be here by now!* Walking back across the floor to Mary, Joe tried in vain to put the ventilator in with his clumsy left arm as his nose dripped blood on the sheets. The door flew open. A female nurse entered. Without waiting for a greeting or question, Joe yelled, "Someone was in here and they pulled Mary's ventilator... I think they broke my arm... I can't get the hose back in!"

The nurse flipped the code blue alarm as she surveyed the scene, realizing that what Joe said was true. The nurse hesitated, and stood there with the ventilator hose in her hand debating what to do next. Joe wanted to curse himself for taking a shower, the 'if only" doubts were beginning to flood his mind. The nurse could see the distress on Joe's face, "Look... Mr. Smith! Come here!" Joe didn't want to look, to see that beloved face expired, dead, departed into a lost eternity, and to think he would never hold his son. *She had gone so fast, so quickly. Was this the end?*

The voice of the nurse caught Joe's attention, "Hand me that stethoscope on the wall" she commanded. Joe did as he was told knowing all to well what had happened, and dreading what the prognosis would be. Putting the stethoscope to Mary's chest the nurse confirmed what she had suspected, "She's breathing on her own." *Breathing on her own? How... could this be?* Joe had been so sure she was dead. He had heard the cough, the sputter, her last breath. "We've got to get the doctor down here. Why are these alarms turned off? Did you unhook these?" Before he could answer, the nurse was calling for the doctor.

Joe fell back thinking he'd land in the vinyl chair. In a combination of shock and exhaustion, he hit the floor. He hadn't realized the chair had been pushed aside in the scuffle and was no longer in its usual place. Joe sat there bleeding on the floor in a state of shock, unable to focus on what was happening.

As his injured arm was being examined by a nurse, Joe cried out. The stab of pain brought him back to his senses. Hospital staff flooded into the room surrounding Mary like a swarm of angry bees. Joe clutched his arm and gave thanks to God that his beloved was still alive. The doctor called out, "Where is all this blood coming from? The patient doesn't appear to be bleeding anywhere."

The nurse explained, "Joe, the husband is bleeding and his arm appears to be badly injured."

After Mary had been stabilized, a doctor Joe had never seen before turned his attention to Joe. The bleeding from his nose had slowed substantially, and he was still clutching his arm. His hair was still wet from the shower and his slightly damp clothing was covered in his own blood.

The compassionate new doctor inquired of Joe, "Mr. Smith can you tell me what happened?" Joe spent the next few minutes relaying the details of the event to the doctor, as well as he could remember. The doctor applied direct pressure to his nose and got the bleeding stopped. He then turned his attention to Joe's arm. "Mr. Smith" he began "I'm going to order a scan of your arm. It appears to have sustained serious trauma in two separate areas. It will most probably need to be in a sling for a while. I will send someone here to help you get changed. Your wife," the doctor paused, "appears to be breathing well on her own currently. We may need to put her back on the ventilator later but, I would like to gradually wean her from it over the next few days if she's up to it. This unfortunate set of circumstances may turn out to be a blessing in disguise. This seems to indicate your wife is not a complete vegetable. She is obviously getting better and improving. If she can breathe on her own, and if we can keep her from losing anymore organ systems, I think she may continue to improve." Looking at Joe and sensing the mental anguish he felt at the thought of leaving his vulnerable wife, he continued, "I'll call hospital security and have a guard at the door of her room until you return from your scan."

Oh, God what is happening here? he thought. Numbness clouded his mind as he tried to sort out the events that had just happened. After his arm had been scanned and his clothing had been changed, Joe returned the room. Gently clasping her hand, he gazed lovingly into Mary's face. A prayer of thanks to God for His mercy welled up from Joe's heart, and he prayed aloud to the Savior who had spared his wife's life one more time.

Mary listened intently to Joe's prayer. She didn't mind his praying so much anymore. Somehow in the foggy recesses of her mind, she knew God was hearing him, and answering his prayers. She was getting better, slowly. Her mouth hurt less, and that hard uncomfortable piece of plastic was gone. Her tongue could feel her teeth once again. Mary wanted so badly to speak to Joe, to let him know she still loved him, but she still couldn't speak no matter how hard she tried to break loose of the dreamlike fog enveloping her mind. For now though, she was content to hear Joe's voice, just to know he was near and cared about her. Her heart rate steadied, and her respiration became more even.

She desperately wanted to communicate with Joe somehow. She tried to squeeze the hand he held, but he seemed unaware of her efforts. Unable to do anything else, she tried to smile at him. Joe looked at his wife's face. The slightest hint of a smile played on the corner of her mouth. It was as if the dimple in her cheek on one side was showing. As Joe smiled back at her he cried out "I love you Mary!" She was smiling at him again! It was enough to fill his heart with an inexpressible joy. He didn't care if it was only his imagination, or the swelling in her face, for one brief moment his wife had smiled at him.

The attack on Joe Smith had everyone confused. Of course Joe implicated the two male nurses, but they both had valid alibis for where they were at the time of the attack. Mr. Verde personally saw to it that the two male nurses were re-assigned to another floor. Of course, they insisted on being on the same floor when they were moved, and the "on call" doctor, who had been floated from another floor to work in the ICU, was sent back to his regular duties. Mr. Verde assigned some hand-picked security officers to investigate the incident. The outcome of the investigation had of course been pre-determined by Verde. They found nothing.

CHAPTER 15

Saint's fellowship, if it be managed well, keeps them awake, and that in spite of hell.—John Bunyan, The Pilgrim's Progress.

The day after the attack dawned, and found Joe sore and very uncomfortable. As Joe lay in the hospital chair, his faith in a loving God was seriously being tested. *Why had God allowed this? What good could come of this? Was God hearing his prayers?* Doubts and fears flooded his mind. In the midst of this trial, he failed to see the good side—Mary was off the respirator! In the aftermath of all that had happened, Joe's physically exhausted body was leaving his mind and body open to emotional and spiritual attack. Joe had no more to give. He had reached the end of his physical ability to persevere. Sleep, a confused state of bad dreams and fears, came for short periods of time, but not a restful, long sleep like Joe needed. Frequent visits by hospital security and the usual visits by the nursing staff only exacerbated the problem.

Although Mary's situation was more stable, the long-term outlook for her still did not look good. She still appeared to be a lifeless body, void of personality. Mr. Elder, faithful friend that he was, phoned or came by almost daily now, and, of course, Robert Forbes, the radical or what was it he called himself, reactionary, stopped in if not daily, at least five times a week. Without the prayer support and help of these men, it is doubtful Joe would have continued to do what he was convicted to do. Joe, though he had a strong faith in God and a desire to do right, did not possess the leadership skills or vision of these other men. God had begun developing the skills of leadership, vision, and faith in God in Joe, but they were still in their infancy.

Joe's arm, fractured by the attack, was put in a sling. The bone was not broken seriously, only a hairline fracture, but Joe could see nothing in this to be thankful for. As Joe looked at the injured arm, he studied the site of the recently removed stitches and his thoughts went back to the day of that terrible accident. His world and even his thoughts had changed so much since that dark day of the accident. As Joe sat quietly in his chair, the still, small voice of the Holy Spirit caused Joe to remember the prayer he had uttered just moments before the accident on that fateful day, "Oh God, help me to have the faith and character of this Godly man, and help me to know the truth." Joe had to admit dealing with this accident had been the hardest thing he had ever done, and yet in the midst of the trials and testing of the last few weeks, he had been drawn even closer to God. God had become his intimate friend and sustainer. Every time Joe read the Bible, it seemed to come alive with some new word or hope or encouragement for him. God's Spirit called Romans 8:26-28 to Joe's mind,

Likewise the Spirit also helps in our weaknesses. For we do not know what we should pray for as we ought, but the Spirit Himself makes intercession for us with groanings which cannot be uttered. Now He who searches the hearts knows what the mind of the Spirit *is,* because He makes intercession for the saints according to *the will of* God. And we know that all things work together for good to those who love God, to those who are the called according to *His* purpose.

Joe pondered the truth of those verses in his life. Had God's spirit helped him in all manner of weaknesses making intercession and groanings for him? *What could that possibly mean?* As Joe meditated on these verses, he realized God had even worked out this terrible accident for good in Joe's life. Joe didn't know exactly how this would all end, but he was beginning to trust God to work it out for good. He thought about the words of the doctor the night of the attack, calling it a "blessing in disguise." Joe thought about Joseph in the Bible, how he had gone through slavery and imprisonment for years only to be brought out and made ruler over all Egypt, putting him in a position to save the very brothers who had sold him into slavery. *But how was he, Joe Smith, to survive? He was exhausted physically, and at this moment, he was ready to give up the good fight.*

Joe looked again at his injured arm and then back up at the ceiling again. *There was only one of him, and he couldn't do it all. If the attackers came back again while he was out using the toilet, he didn't even have a good arm to defend his wife and son.* Joe was certain he knew who his attacker had been, but without having seen the attacker in Mary's room, he knew his story seemed weak to the hospital security officers. If it hadn't been for the wounds inflicted on Joe, he would probably have been blamed for the whole incident. Joe knew he should fight his natural inclination to hate the men who had tried to take his wife's life. He knew that, instead, he should pray for them and for an opportunity to share Christ, but deep down in his heart, he didn't want to do those things.

Besides, Joe suspected, *the hospital staff didn't really like him.* The rumor being spread around the hospital was Joe was so sleep deprived, mentally unstable, and desperate, that he might have tried, or done, anything. Many of the staff on the ICU floor, suspected Joe, the crazed husband, had disconnected Mary's alarms. *Maybe the doctors were right, maybe his mother-in-law had a point, and maybe he should just give it all up. So many people were against him. Maybe he was the one who was in the wrong and not everyone else. Oh God, if I am to continue this fight, you are going to have to send some help.* Big tears slid down Joe's face as he wondered if or how God would *answer his prayer.*

A familiar light tap was heard on the door before Robert Forbes stuck his head into the room. Robert started to make his normal, comical comment to the effect of, 'your legal counsel has arrived, but one glance at Joe's forlorn face told him this wasn't the time for that comment. Dark circles lined Joe's eyes, and it was obvious he needed rest. As Joe started to tell his story, Robert wanted to ask, "Why didn't you give me a call?" But he quickly decided Joe didn't need any more pressure or criticism. Pulling up the ever present cold, steel folding chair, Robert sat down. Joe began to fumble through his story, telling all that had happened. Without ceremony, Robert interrupted him, "Lad, run to the bathroom, and when you get back, you can tell me."

Five minutes later, Joe was back and just sat down in the vinyl chair when Mr. Elder knocked and entered the room. Joe's cell phone rang before Mr. Elder could even shake his hand and give his formal hello. As Joe answered the phone, a professional, booming voice addressed him, "Mr. Smith," the caller on the other end of the line addressed Joe. "I'm .... Jane Jones' lawyer. You have been summoned to appear in court in a few days, and we were wondering if you would want to try and settle out of court. I have here in my hand a living will signed by your wife, and it very explicitly says, she has no desire to be put on, or left on, life support." Tears filled Joe's eyes again, and no matter how unmanly it looked, he couldn't help but cry. *How could he contest a document like that. Mary had never mentioned anything to him about a Living Will. It had to be a forged document, but how could he contest it.* The speaker on his phone was turned up loud, and Robert and Mr. Elder could not help but hear every word. "I... I don't believe you," was all Joe could say.

"My client and I would be willing to let you review this document if you will agree to take your wife off life support once you see this document and verify your wife's signature." Joe was stunned. "I'll have to think about that sir," was all Joe could say as he hung the phone up without even saying goodbye. Stunned, Joe walked around the room. *What should he say; what should he do? He never knew of the existence of such a document, but would the courts believe him if he called it a fraud.* As he stumbled about the room, he tripped over the foot of Mary's hospital bed. Robert Forbes was on his feet in moment, quick to help Joe back up. "Now Joe, you just lay down here," Robert said, as he led Joe to the reclining vinyl chair. Mr. Elder placed his hand on Joe's shoulder and began to pray. It was the only thing to do in that tenebrous moment. Robert prayed next, and then Mr. Elder, having just received a call from the school detailing yet another surprise inspection, left saying he had other pressing business at the school he must attend to, but promising to return the very next day, if not sooner.

Even though Robert had other pressing matters, they would all have to wait. Joe Smith needed him right now. He would call his wife and make the necessary arrangements as soon as he could. Then in a soothing, fatherly accent that only Robert could master, he reassured Joe: "Rest, shut your wee eyes, and listen to me read a passage from the Good Book to ye and your lass here. Won't do the wee bairn any harm either to hear a little of the King's English from the Good Book. Aye, I understand. Nothing goes in that IV bag without your knowledge. No drugs. I got it. You eat a bit of my wife's fine cooking, listen to God's word, and shut your eyes and rest."

Paralyzed in mind, unable to reason what to do next, Joe obeyed Robert, one of the few people he felt he could trust. "Robert, with the help of the most high God, will stand watch. I may be a bit older, but ye saw me bring the security guards down that day in the hall. Ye know there's still fight left in my bones. I'll be waking you if I need your help. Here eat this, then get some sleep man. You need your rest. We can decide what to do when you wake up."

Robert's exaggerated accent added a light tone to the moment, and Joe, even though he wasn't able to laugh in the face of adversity, relaxed just a little as Robert began reading in the Book of Galatians. Joe awkwardly ate his meal of meat loaf, green beans and scalloped potatoes with his one good arm. Left-over meat loaf had never tasted so good to Joe. About the last thing Joe remembered was Galatians 6:2, "Bear one another's burdens and so fulfill the law of Christ." *Thank you Lord God for Robert who is bearing my burden.*" Without another thought, Joe drifted off into a deep sleep as Robert's voice droned on.

Joe slowly drifted into consciousness, gradually becoming aware of his surroundings. He became aware of the sling on his arm, the fuzz coating on his teeth, and the stiffness in his back caused by lying on one side too long. As Joe regained full consciousness, the sun seemed to be streaming through the windows of the hospital room with a new brightness. The curtains were open, and the room seemed bright and clean. In place of the metal folding chair, another vinyl recliner was set up for Robert. Joe looked around in amazement. While Joe had slept, Robert had asked the hospital staff to come in and clean the room. He realized a clean room would do a lot to lift Joe's morale. "Did you have a good sleep lad?"

Joe answered in the affirmative with a nod and asked, "Where did you come up with another chair?"

Robert smiled, "Ask and you shall receive."

"What time is it? Boy I'm hungry. Is there any more of that left-over meat loaf?" Asked Joe.

Glancing at his watch Robert replied, "Nearly 11AM, and I don't suppose you would want any of that three-day-old meat loaf now." In shock Joe exclaimed, "Three days! Have I been asleep that. . ," anxiety gripped Joe's heart as he suddenly remembered what happened the last time he was awake. "You let me sleep through the court hearing!" "Relax man," Robert seemed all too cool and collected for Joe. "They called yesterday, Tuesday, while you were asleep, and said they were going to reschedule the hearing." Joe breathed a great sigh of relief. Robert continued his update as if there had been no interruption.

"I came Monday afternoon, and this is Wednesday. All day yesterday, ye did not stir, and I let ye sleep. Run to the bathroom, and then I'll catch you up on what has happened. Your lass has continued her rest though, I fancy she's been winking at me some, and once she gave my hand a slight squeeze. Your friend, employer, Mr. Elder stopped by." Joe looked on amazed. "Go to the wash room man and scrape the moss off of your teeth," Robert held out a new tooth brush and a fresh towel. "Get yourself a drink, and I'll tell you when you get back." Joe quickly complied.

Upon Joe's return, Robert continued his account of the day Joe had missed. "Mr. Elder came by to see you. He said the school lawyer has offered to defend you in the case your mother-in-law is bringing against you—free of charge. Mr. Elder had stopped by Monday to tell you that, but he didn't get the chance to on account of some surprise inspection at the school. He, the lawyer, wants to see you when you wake. I told him I'd pass along the message. Also Mr. Elder, he's a fine chap; he and I see eye-to-eye on many things I can tell; has lined up four or five of the older ladies from the church to come in once a day and sit with Mary for an hour so you can get a shower at a decent time instead of at 2AM. I suspect that will help ye rest some. You'll be wondering about your lady. Well, Monday night when you were sleeping so sound I could not wake you, her breathing wasn't what I thought it ought to be." A worried look crossed Joe's face. *What had he missed while he was asleep?* "I called the nurse, and they put her back on the ventilator for most the night. They say it's not uncommon to need to wean them some. But, I dare say they wouldn't have thought of it if I hadn't said something. Yesterday, she went all day without the ventilator, and then last night, about midnight, they put her back on for six hours, but as you can see she is off of it this morning. Her body is still weak, and she just needs a little help I imagine."

"Did the doctor have anything to say?" Joe asked. Robert shook his head no. Joe paused looking for just the right words to say to Robert. He wanted to say thanks, but somehow "thanks" just didn't cut it.

Robert felt the awkwardness of the moment as well and spoke

up trying to alleviate the situation. "Now, don't be standing there lad. Ye got some business to tend to, and I need to be going." Picking up a stack of five books off the table and another small stash of tracts Robert had been handing out to the hospital staff, he dropped them carelessly into a bag along with his large print Bible. "I owe you a thank you Lad. Thanks to you, I had a good excuse to take two days off from work and get some rest." Robert opened the door to leave, "and I got to finish nearly five books I have been meaning to read, but just didn't have the time to get to 'till now. I'll see you in a few days," and with that Robert Forbes left.

Joe found his cell phone, and called Mr. Elder to get the lawyer's phone number. Fumbling with his phone, he nervously called Corbin Cutler's office. The secretary answered. She had been expecting Joe's call. She took his number, and informed Joe that Mr. Cutler had left early for an appointment and she would call Joe tomorrow and arrange a meeting at the hospital, since he and the secretary both understood it was difficult for Joe to get away. Joe thanked the secretary, feeling a little apprehensive about the whole meeting, but he really didn't have any other choice at this point. Joe really didn't know Mr. Cutler, the school's lawyer. He had been introduced to him in passing, and he remembered him as a large intimidating figure of a man with a stern, cold, impersonal manner.

Corbin Cutler was an intimidating figure. Six foot five inches tall and broad shouldered, he looked more like an ex-NFL player than a lawyer. His deep set blue eyes only accentuated the firm set to his jaw, which gave him that determined look everyone expects a lawyer to have. His nose was large and broad—not at all handsome or refined, and his hair, what was left of it, was coal black and swept back from his forehead. His thinning hairline and ever increasing forehead only made him appear more experienced or shrewd. Everything about the man portrayed strength, but those who knew him well, knew the events of the past year had come close to shattering this seemingly strong man.

Chapter 16

Any Transformation in government must begin with the church.

Corbin Cutler buzzed through traffic on his way home from work. He had already called David, his future son-in-law and told him where the key was to let himself in, because he was running late. As Corbin sat in the car, he congratulated himself on the almost perfect son-in-law he was about to get in just a few short months. The great personal losses he had suffered in the last year seemed a little less painful knowing his family was going to expand instead of get smaller for a change. Corbin always knew Katie, his only daughter, would marry well. Her beautiful face and light-hearted disposition were a winning combination. And David Brogden, the almost perfect homeschool boy, had wasted no time in realizing the treasure Corbin's daughter was. The match seemed perfect. David was a prize any father-in-law could brag about. Six foot tall, with dark complexion and warm brown eyes. From a physical standpoint, Katie had done well. But, Katie had done well in other ways too. David had everything a Christian father would want for his daughter. David came from a stable Christian family. He had graduated first in his class at college just 6 weeks ago, and he had a strong faith in Christ that impressed not only Corbin, but many other Christians in the area. Corbin had taken an immediate liking to this young man. On the surface he seemed very sincere in his faith, and he was definitely on fire for the Lord. This kid witnessed to people about Jesus more than anyone he knew.

Corbin reasoned he would make a better missionary than accountant, but at least the boy had a way to support his daughter. When David asked Corbin for permission to pursue Katie, his daughter, he had checked this young man out thoroughly. All those who knew him loved, trusted, and respected him. There were no red flags to warn Corbin of what was about to take place.[1] Corbin's active mind shifted back and forth as he changed lanes wondering what David could want with this meeting. Yesterday afternoon, when David had called and asked for this meeting, Corbin had suspected it would have something to do with his daughter. Maybe David wanted some fatherly advice on picking out an engagement ring, where to go on their honeymoon, or maybe he just wanted to ask him how many grandchildren he wanted? While this meeting did have everything to do with his daughter's relationship with David, it was not to be what Corbin was expecting.

Corbin's stomach grumbled, and looked forward to the meal Katie would be bringing home later this evening. *I wonder what she'll bring home? Mexican?. . . Chinese? Chinese from a restaurant sure sounds good. At any rate, it would be a nice relaxing time at home with the family, almost like old times.*

David sat nervously, no anxiously, in the front room of Corbin Cutler's house. Glancing up at the family picture taken two years ago, he admired his future wife Katie Cutler. She looked so much like her mother with that long, flowing auburn hair gleaming in the sun, but her tall frame with broad shoulders and slender waist and hips very obviously favored her father's side of the family. David's eyes looked at Katie's father, Corbin, and for a brief moment, the uneasiness returned to his stomach. Three weeks earlier, he had come to Corbin asking for his daughter's hand in marriage. That had seemed easy compared with what he had to share now, but yet he felt the Holy Spirit was demanding him to share his convictions with Katie's father now, not later. David bowed his head and prayed his father-in-law would be open to his convictions, or at least tolerate them.

For Katie, despite all the tragedy of the last year, life was perfect. She was in love, marrying the perfect young man; and tonight would be another enjoyable evening with Ashley, her dearest friend and the one she had asked to be her maid-of-honor. Along with her father and the Love of her life, David. Katie knew nothing about this secret meeting. As Katie picked up the phone to call in an order of pizza from her and David's favorite Italian restaurant, she had no idea David was already at her house waiting to talk with her father.

David jumped, knocking a large notebook to the floor, as he heard the garage door open signaling the arrival of his future father-in-law. Picking up the notebook, David stuck a few loose pages back into the binder. The notebook was the compilation of several years' work. It contained evidence and documentation for not only one of his deepest held convictions, but what he felt the Holy Spirit would have him share with Katie's father.

After Corbin had loosened his tie, fetched himself a glass of ice water, and sat down on the couch, David suggested they begin in prayer. Both men bowed their heads. Corbin's prayer was short, direct and to the point. David's prayer was more of a request of a child to his beloved Father asking for the blessing over the meeting and time together.

"Mr. Cutler," David began nervously. He cleared his throat and started over, trying to be respectful and more confident. "I would like to share this with you, and I hope and pray that you will understand it. I believe that as a lawyer you have the ability to grasp legal concepts that others may not possess. Please forgive me if I explain too much, but I'm used to explaining this sort of thing to people who have no idea whatsoever about any of these principles. I often find myself having to explain simple concepts to enable the listener to understand the big picture."

David took a deep breath and started. His mind raced on ahead of him. He could see Katie's pretty face, and somehow he feared his future with her depended on this one meeting with her father. "One of the rules governing God's creation is the *rule of creation*. The one who creates a thing controls that thing, or rules over that thing and possesses that thing. God created everything, therefore he has the right to control, rule, and possess—everything."

Corbin nodded, not sure where this kid was going with this line of reasoning, but willing to follow along.

David continued, "If I invest my labor to produce a widget, I, by my labor, have created the widget. Therefore, I possess and control what happens to the widget. It is my property."

"OK, get to the point," Corbin urged. David timidly ran his fingers through his hair trying to alleviate some of the tension rising in his being.

"Corporations are created by the state; therefore, the respective states control, rule over, and possess the corporations these states have created. In short sir, the creator and controller of all corporations is the state that created them. The creator and controller of the church of the Lord Jesus Christ is, the Lord Jesus Christ. If the church incorporates, it ceases being the church and removes God as its ultimate authority since the state is the ultimate authority of every corporation. [2] Incorporation destroys the church, and creates a legal entity whose creator and authority is the state, instead of God. Scripture makes the point clearly when Christ said, it is impossible to serve two masters.

Corbin sat in complete silence, hoping his ears were deceiving him. Could this boy, this idealistic kid Katie loved, be so deceived? David stood and paced the room. He didn't like the silence and he was beginning to feel even more awkward.

"Let me try another way," David continued trying to rescue the situation, "God created people, and because He created them, He is the absolute authority over them. The state creates corporations. Because the state created them, it is the absolute authority over them. The only difference is God and people are real, and corporations and the state are imaginary fictitious entities that represent people, or groups of people. But, the analogy is the same; the creator controls that which is created. The creator also controls what is under the jurisdiction of the created. In the biblical sense, this means everything I own belongs to God. In a corporate sense, this means everything the Corporation owns ultimately belongs to, or is controlled by, the state."[3]

Mr. Cutler, President James Madison vetoed a bill to incorporate the church during his presidency. David handed Corbin a loose copy of a paper from the back of his notebook.

JAMES MADISON'S VETO MESSAGES

VETO MESSAGE From President James Madison, Thursday, February 21, 1811:

To the House of Representatives of the United States:

Having examined and considered the bill entitled "An Act incorporating the Protestant Episcopal Church in the town of Alexandria, in the District of Columbia," I now return the bill to the House of Representatives, in which it originated, with the following objections:

Because the bill exceeds the rightful authority to which governments are limited by the essential distinction between civil and religious functions, and violates in particular the article of the Constitution of the United States which declares that "Congress shall make no law respecting a religious establishment." . . . [4]

David studied Corbin's face trying to determine if this was making sense as he scanned the document. Corbin's facial expression betrayed nothing; it was blank, expressionless, and disinterested as he read the document. David continued speaking as he sat on the edge of the couch in anticipation of Corbin's response, "So you see when a group of Christians incorporate, they cease being the church under Jesus Christ as their head, and they become a nonprofit corporation with the state as their head and final authority, thus replacing

Jesus as such. Do you understand? Jesus Christ gets replaced by the government bureaucracy. While the individual members may still claim Christ as their Lord, the group as a whole has acknowledged the state of Illinois as their ultimate authority."

David handed Corbin another sheet of paper and read it aloud to him. It said "The second provision within the first amendment about free speech also applies to a church. Free speech (which does not constitute treason) is guaranteed to those within the church. *The church* can take a stand on abortion, homosexuality, marriage, and support or oppose bills presented within civil government. A free unincorporated church can endorse a candidate if they choose to do so. Not-for-profit corporations are forbidden to do so! Speech of this nature is labeled propaganda if you are a Not-for-profit corporation and will result in forfeiture of the tax exempt status."

David handed Corbin yet another loose paper from his notebook. It was a quote from the late Rev. D. James Kennedy stated before his death about his 501(c)3 incorporated ministry:

"The federal government has proved a tremendous impediment to the ongoing work of Christians. In all the laws that they have passed against Christian schools, *gagging the church,* taxation, and all kinds of things that they have done, they have made it harder for the church to exercise its prerogatives and to preach the gospel.

"Take the last presidential election. There were numbers of things that I knew that I was never able to say from the pulpit because if you advance the cause of one candidate or impede the cause of the other you can lose your tax exemption. That would have been disastrous not only for the church, but for our school and our seminary, everything. *So you are gagged.* You cannot do that. *The IRS, a branch of our government, has succeeded in gagging Christians."*

Corbin had heard enough. As he rose to his full height and threw the papers onto his desk he began with an accusatory finger pointing at David, "Listen David, I don't know where you have been getting this nonsense from. Who told you that incorporating is giving up Jesus Christ somehow? Incorporation of the church is done for the protection of its members! Incorporation creates a barrier, a legal barrier, between the members of the church and any potential lawsuits that may be brought against the church. Without incorporation, a lawsuit brought against the church could go after the assets of the individual church members. By incorporating you are limiting the assets that the lawsuit can go after, to only those owned by the church. Furthermore, being incorporated guarantees gifts to the church will be able to be counted as tax-deductible gifts in regards to the IRS. Being incorporated also allows the church to sue, and be sued in a court of law."

In Corbin's mind, his arguments were solid and indisputable. Corbin had expected his reply would cause David to tuck tail and run, so to speak. David, however, was not that easily intimidated. His intellect had not been sitting idle as Corbin made his reply. He had been taking notes, and pulling papers from his notebook as the arguments were brought up. David organized the papers and was ready to answer each of Corbin's points. Much to Corbin's surprise David's response, though simply put, was anything but retreat. Humbly, David questioned, "May I make some observations, Sir?" "Certainly," Corbin said as he sat back down, hoping to salvage this discussion and talk some sense into David.

David began methodically, "I will deal with your arguments in reverse order. Sir, you implied that the church must be incorporated in order to sue and be sued. I see nowhere in Scripture where God commands us as a Body of Believers to bring a legal suit against anyone. I do see, in 1 Corinthians chapter 6, an admonition not to go before the judges of this world, but to establish judges within the church. I realize this is talking about two Believers going before an unrighteous judge, and that Scripture calls this an utter failure! Paul makes it clear it would be better to accept the wrong, instead of going to court. I obviously don't see the ability to be sued an advantage gained by incorporating, but doesn't it follow that if incorporation is necessary to sue and be sued, that the unincorporated church cannot be sued due to lack of jurisdiction?" He handed Corbin a stack of legal decisions and rulings.

"Next argument," David continued. He grabbed his notebook and opened to a photocopy of the IRS code. "According to IRS Code § 508(c)(1)(A) churches, their integrated auxiliaries, and conventions or associations of churches are exempt from having to apply for 501(c)(3) status. At the federal level incorporation is not necessary, and my research shows it is not necessary at the state level either. I will show you the research if you wish. He handed Corbin another stack of papers.

David shut the notebook. "Next, if the church is indeed functioning as a church, individual believers should look to the Body of Christ, and to Christ Himself, for protection and not need some legal construct to hide behind. If the church pulls together to take care of her own, and they take all their cares and problems to the Lord Jesus Christ, there is no need for any other asset protection. It all belongs to Christ anyway, and He is perfectly capable of taking care of it, wouldn't you agree, sir? I don't need a legal barrier to protect me from the world, the Lord Jesus Christ promised me that he would protect me and there is no better protection than that. Chapter 1 vs. 18-24 of the Book of Romans, talks about men who suppress the truth in unrighteousness. As a general rule that's what we have in the system today, sir. They have exchanged the truth of God for a lie and they worship and serve the creature rather than the Creator. This idea that we have to 'fight it out in court' is a pagan concept, Sir, not a Christian one."

Corbin started to interrupt, but David wouldn't let him. "Let me finish please." David continued, "All 501(c)3 churches are listed as corporations in the Secretary of State's office of their respective states, Am I not correct?"

"Yes, that's correct," Corbin acknowledged.

"What happens if the government takes over all corporations in the case of Sweden, Holland, and Denmark?"

"No, that won't happen here," Corbin snapped.

David asked, "Why not?"

"Because lawyers and people like me won't let it happen here in the United States," Corbin thundered.

David shook his head in disbelief. "Well for the sake of argument, what if it did happen? Won't the state then have control of our incorporated non-profit corporations to do with as they please? Look, Mr. Cutler, please." David said in a pleading way, "Please, study my notebook. I have made a copy just for you. I have answers and documentation here for every issue you raise, plus a dozen more which you are probably ready to give me now. Sir, I have prayerfully considered this issue and know beyond a shadow of a doubt that incorporating a group of saints amounts to rendering unto Caesar that which is God's. It is wrong, and it needs to stop!"

Corbin rose again. It was all he could do to not lose his temper and completely blow up at this insolent, foolish youth. He didn't need to study some goofy notebook put together by a kid half his age. He knew the law. He was a lawyer! Church incorporation was something he had been studying for years. "No young man." Corbin's eye's narrowed and his brow wrinkled as he interrupted David, "It is you that needs to stop. I won't listen to this anymore. It is quite clear to me you have no idea what you're talking about. I have personally helped incorporate several churches and ministries, and will continue to do so. That poses the least risk to the Church Bodies and members of the church. It is accepted by both the church, and the legal powers-that-be. All this talk about Christ protecting our assets is great until you get into the real sin-filled world. When you get a little older, and you're less idealistic, I fear you'll come around and see my side of the issue, and then it may be too late. The damage will already be done."

Corbin walked out of the living room and into the kitchen. He needed a moment to think. *If this boy had so little respect for him and for the law, how would he treat Katie? What would be next? Would he refuse to get a state marriage license? What sort of protection would*

Katie have without a state marriage license? Would his grandchildren be raised with no respect for the law? He wanted Katie to have a normal, all-American life. He wanted Katie to be accepted by other Christians and not be branded as a weirdo. David was not at all what he had envisioned for Katie. How had he been so deceived? Deep down in his heart, if he was honest with himself, he resented the fact that this 22-year-old pip-squeak of a kid thought he could match wits with, even persuade Corbin Cutler, a lawyer with twenty five years of law study and experience, to accept the idea that church incorporation was wrong. Corbin spun around suddenly in the kitchen turning from the cabinet he was leaning on. *No! No! No! He couldn't let this happen! He would protect Katie from this fanatic at all costs.*

Corbin didn't like what he was about to do, but it was the only right thing to do. He couldn't prevent this starry-eyed youth from continuing in his legal stupidity, but he could keep his daughter's life from being ruined by it. As for David, he sat calmly on the couch praying for wisdom. He didn't need to be told Corbin was less than happy with the situation. Corbin entered the room and stared down at that miserable pup of a man on his couch, "Mr. Brogden, David, I'm sorry I have been so deceived by you. I cannot with a clear conscience grant my permission any longer for you to pursue my daughter. It is my desire that you leave my house this instant, take that notebook with you. Never try to contact myself or my daughter again. I'll see you to the door now, goodbye."

"But," David began.

"No, I will hear no more of your ideas." And with that a very worked up Corbin Cutler escorted a very disappointed David Brogden to the door.

David struggled with his emotions. For one brief moment he was willing to give up all these views for Katie, but he couldn't deny what he believed—even for Katie, the woman he loved more than anyone else on the planet.

As he was being forcefully escorted out the front door, David begged in a desperate attempt to reason with the man he wanted for a father-in-law. Attempting to appease the angry father, his voice was thin and shaky as he held out the notebook, "Please Sir, let me explain. Look at my research and study it for yourself. Don't you see? I came to you with this information. I could've waited until after I was married to bring this up! I could have deceived you, but I didn't!" David was pleading, and crying, and looking Corbin directly in the eye. David continued, "I love my Lord Jesus Christ, and I love your daughter. I will not deny Him for her, or for anyone else. Just know this, I have spoken truth to you today. I'm leaving you to the conviction of the Holy Spirit. God bless you, Sir. I pray you will change your mind soon."

"Goodbye." And with that, Corbin shut the door, closing that little nutcase out of his life forever.

David's tears flowed heavily as he dropped himself into the seat of his small car. He tossed his notebook into the seat beside him and rested his head on the steering wheel. "Lord," he began "I was obedient to share all that you gave me to share with Mr. Cutler. Things are not looking well at this point, but I choose..." Here David struggled. "Lord, help me to trust in you in this situation. I don't know how you're going to work it out. You have shown me that Katie is to be my wife. So I trust You that this will all work out according to Your plan. I don't understand how, but I claim the promise You made to me in regards to doing this." David broke into uncontrollable sobs and reached his hands to the heavens, "Lord, why is this so hard?" The Spirit of God filled David's soul with a peace that passes understanding.

Corbin continued to watch from the window and shook his head slowly as David drove away. *That kid is nuts*, he told himself. Then the question formed in his mind, *How was he going to tell Katie what just happened? What would Katie think of him?* Suddenly he wasn't looking forward to dinner at all.

Corbin slowly walked upstairs and entered his room. A large portrait of his wife hung on the wall. Corbin placed his hand on the portrait, somehow wishing he could touch his wife or just be near her. Corbin heard Katie and Ashley arrive downstairs. Walking into the bathroom, he blew his nose and washed his face. As he came downstairs, he could hear Katie and Ashley talking.

Corbin stood outside Katie's room and watched the two girls through the doorway. Katie stood in front of the mirror, her wedding veil trailing down over her auburn tresses an open book of wedding flower bouquet designs on the bed beside the girls. "Daddy wants us to have a big wedding, but I think a small, intimate wedding in the early evening is more romantic." Corbin had no time for such silly talk, but he hated what he had to do. "Katie, I need to speak with you. Ashley could we have a few minutes alone?" Ashley left and went into the living room wondering what on earth was wrong.

"What's up Dad?" How did he tell his daughter there would be no wedding? "Katie, David and I have been talking, and there's not going to be any wedding."

Katie looked at her dad in a state of shock. "No wedding? . . . What on earth are you saying?" Picking up her cell phone, Katie headed for the door and walked out of the room. Corbin followed, "Katie, don't call him. He's not worthy of you." Katie wasn't listening. Corbin walked out into the hallway and tried to take the phone way from Katie. A look of defiance he had never seen before flashed in Katie's eyes as she looked at her father.

"I have the right to call him at least one last time. You won't deny me of that."

Corbin backed away, "Please don't call him."

As Katie dialed the phone Corbin raised his hands and turned his head in defeat. It wouldn't hurt Katie to call him one last time. Katie's eyes met her father's as she slowly let her breath out between clinched teeth. Moving quickly past her father, she darted toward her room, slammed the door and locked it. Katie would hear David's side of the story first, and of course, she'd side with him.

Corbin looked down into the living room. Ashley sat meekly on the couch trying to pretend she hadn't heard their conversation.

What did Ashley think of him? Oh well, it didn't matter. Corbin thought about blaming Ashley. He had let Katie go to that home church with Ashley's family, and Ashley's brother had introduced Katie to his best friend. Oh well, blaming Ashley wouldn't do any good now. The harm was already done. All he could do now was protect his only daughter from a life as an outcast. Corbin walked down the stairs into the kitchen and saw the carryout pizza sitting on the table. Suddenly he didn't feel hungry, and whatever Katie brought home for supper didn't seem to matter.

Walking back upstairs, he paused outside Katie's room. Katie was sure making a lot of commotion in there. What was she doing? Corbin put his ear to the door: "David I will always love you. You are the only man God has for me. I will wait for you forever." *Oh boy, this wasn't going to be easy*, Corbin thought.

Corbin walked back down the stairs and out the front door. Maybe a walk around the block would do him some good. It couldn't hurt. Fifteen minutes later when Corbin turned the corner to approach his house, he saw Ashley's car driving off. Good. Now he'd have a chance to talk freely to Katie. Hurrying up to the drive way, he saw Katie in her car backing out. Stepping behind the car, he forced Katie to stop. Katie rolled the window down, and Corbin walked around the car to speak with his daughter. That new determined look he had not seen before in his daughter shone in her tearstained face. Maybe she was more like him than he had thought. Katie didn't waste any time letting her dad know what was on her mind. Her feelings were transparent. "Dad, I thought you were doing pretty good with Mom and Justin's death, but I see now you aren't."

"Katie, this has nothing to do with your mom and your brother."

"Yes, it does. You can't bear to let me go."

He never should of let her talk to David first. "David put these ideas in your head."

"No, no he didn't. I knew my marriage was going to be hard on you, but I didn't think you would resort to this. An argument over whether or not a church should have some silly license is nothing to end a marriage over. You can't do this. You gave us your blessing, and I love him. It's not fair."

Katie was being completely irrational. "I'm doing this to protect you. There will be someone else," Corbin tried to reason with his heartbroken daughter.

Katie put the car in gear, "I don't WANT someone else. David is God's best for me, and I'm God's best for him." The car started to roll backwards.

The authoritative father in Corbin snapped into gear: "Stop that car, now, young lady! Get out and come in the house."

Katie stopped the car momentarily, "I don't have to stay here tonight. I won't marry David without your blessing, but until you change your mind, I can't stay here. I'll be at Ashley's house." Katie's car pulled out into the street and sped away as Corbin felt utterly alone.

CHAPTER 17

An unjust man is an abomination to the just: and he that is upright in the way is abomination to the wicked (Proverbs 29:27).

M r. Elder entered the office at Grace Christian Academy (GCA) in the same fashion he had done for the last 35 years. In the summer, Mr. Elder kept a quiet routine at GCA unless he was interviewing a potential employee. As he walked casually through the office, he checked his daytime planner to make sure he didn't have an interview scheduled that day. He had no appointments and realized it would be a nice quiet day for himself. He smiled and nodded a good morning to Mrs. Ross the GCA mother who had volunteered to work in the office until they could find a replacement. Inquiring of Mrs. Ross if there was anything new he needed to know, she shook her head to indicate "no," and continued her knitting. The joyful headmaster sat down at his tidy desk to resume his normal tasks where he had left off the previous day.

After 35 years of being a headmaster, little ruffled his feathers, or bothered him. Grace Christian Academy was little more than a hole-in-the-wall when he had taken it over 35 years ago, but the Lord had blessed the work, and the school now boasted over 400 students K-12. Mr. Elder took a sip of his iced tea before placing it on the coaster, and sorted through the papers on his desk expecting to enjoy a nice quiet productive day in the office. Little did he know the day was about to get very complicated.

Mr. Elder heard the phone ring, but thought nothing of it until a confused Mrs. Ross appeared at his office door explaining the state inspector was on the phone wanting to know if the school was properly educating its teachers, students, and staff in the area of blood-borne pathogens and uh . . . . Once on the phone, the inspector asked Mr. Elder if their "safe sex education, and alternative sex partner program (spanning all grades) was in compliance with state policy?" There was prolonged silence on Mr. Elder's end of the phone. He didn't know how to tell the inspector that most of the parents at their school sent their kids to a private school because they didn't want their children receiving any sex education from the school at all.

Organizing the thoughts in his head, he began to explain how their school approached sex education from a biblical standpoint, leaving that topic up to the parents. He would have continued, but the impatient state inspector cut him off short, saying she would be by to talk with him later that day and verify their paperwork was in order.

Mr. Elder had barely finished this rather awkward conversation when the phone rang again. Mrs. Ross called over the intercom this time, "Mr. Elder, there is a gentleman from the Department of Transportation on the phone for you." Mr. Elder wondered, *What could he want with us?* He soon knew the answer to that question. The voice on the other end read a quite lengthy list of every single person qualified to drive a school bus for GCA, explaining they had been "randomly selected" for a drug test this afternoon.

Mr. Elder needed to make the appropriate calls and give everyone a heads-up. He had nothing to fear. None of his drivers would have problems with a drug test, but it was an inconvenience and extra expense. The school had agreed to pay everyone extra mileage and two hour's pay for their trouble. Still, Mr. Elder's calm strength showed through. *How had all of the GCA drivers, including the volunteer dads and pastors, been selected on the same day? It seemed too odd to be coincidental.* An ill wind was blowing today, and Mr. Elder didn't like the smell of it.

"Mr. Elder? . . ." the intercom called again. *What now?* Thought Mr. Elder, ". . . Another state inspector is on their way over to inspect the cafeteria," Mrs. Ross, announced. "Thank you," was his wondering reply. That was odd. Usually they called and made an appointment before coming over. To the best of his knowledge the cafeteria complied with all state regulations. But why not come when school was in session and the cafeteria was in use, like they usually did? Mr. Elder wasn't worried, but it was just really strange that all these state officials were coming over at the same time.

Mrs. Ross tapped lightly on his door and stuck her head in, "Mr. Elder, the State Fire Marshall is here to see you. He's here to do a surprise inspection of the building." Mr. Elder stopped and scratched his head in disbelief and shrugged. "I'll be right out to show him around." As Mr. Elder finished up with the Fire Marshall, another "state authority" was waiting at the school office from the state Building Inspector's office. Taking another hour and a half of Mr. Elder's time, he made a thorough search of the building and then wrote a citation: the men's faculty bathroom had a round toilet instead of an oblong. They had 30 days to fix the problem or they would be fined for non-compliance. Hot on the Building Inspector's heels, the state Boiler Inspector showed up. After his hour long inspection, he handed Mr. Elder some documents stating the school needed a new boiler or major repair work by winter, or they would not be able to hold school. He also said something about an asbestos abatement plan, but by that time Mr. Elder was too distracted by what he saw to understand any more. The school office was full of people, standing room only, waiting for him.

Mr. Elder began to pray for wisdom as he took the abatement plan paperwork from the stunned inspector. The Boiler Inspector looked at the office full of state employees looking back at him as they returned to the office. The Boiler Inspector saw Mrs. Ross, the kind lady that had greeted him earlier with her knitting on her lap.

Instead of knitting now, she was almost in tears. The knitting had been put away and her desktop was covered with business cards bearing official state and county seals and a note beside each one. He had wondered why he had been pulled down here to inspect a school boiler in the middle of the summer on short notice with instructions to be extra diligent to "make sure the kids were safe." Now he wondered even more.

Mr. Elder turned to the waiting crowd scanning the faces and the name tags and announced that he would be with them as soon as he could. He turned to Mrs. Ross, who was relieved that he had returned, and asked her to call all of the other school office staff and have them come to the school as quickly as possible. "Tell them we have somewhat of an emergency here, and I need them as quickly as they can come." A worried tear traced its way down her face, as she picked up the telephone.

Mr. Elder retreated to his office and closed the door. Sliding to his knees over a well-worn spot in the carpet, he placed his elbows on the chair and began to cry out to God for wisdom and direction. He then began to thank God for his mercy and praise Him just for being God. He asked God to show him what was happening, and help him understand what to do. As he wiped away the tears, he turned and sat in the chair. The Holy Spirit reminded him of some of the scriptures he had memorized long ago. He pondered the response of Job when his world had also fallen apart around him over the course of a single afternoon. Shall we indeed accept good from God, and shall we not accept adversity? Mr. Elder thought about Job 13:15 *Though He slay me, yet will I trust Him.* Those he loved were still safe, but Mr. Elder sensed GCA's world was falling in around him.

As he sat there pondering what to do next, a Health Inspector for the cafeteria knocked on the door to his office, "May I come in sir?" Mr. Elder recognized this woman. She usually came in the Fall, when school was in session, to inspect the school's kitchen. With a nod from Mr. Elder, she entered and said, "I know you're busy, and

I'll keep this short. Someone at the top has pulled out all the stops, and I'll be praying for you. I knew something was wrong when I was pulled from my regular schedule to do an emergency inspection on a school cafeteria at a school that wasn't even in session. I did some checking, asking what the rush was, since the students obviously weren't in danger during the summer break. My boss said he wasn't at liberty to discuss the matter, and mentioned something about a transfer; or worse if I didn't just shut up and do my job. The bottom line is someone, very high up in government, has painted a bulls-eye on your little church, and school. I don't know what the purpose is. If it is to destroy you, if the state wants you closed down, things could get very ugly and you will eventually be forced to close." The woman eased up a little. She had dumped a lot of bad news on him at once. "It is possible however, the purpose is to harass you and keep you from doing something they don't want you to do; to put you in your place, so to speak, and make sure you know who is in charge; but either way it is going to get a whole lot worse before it gets better. By the way I am sorry to tell you, I need to inspect your cafeteria. The good news is, this shouldn't take too long."

When Mr. Elder returned from the cafeteria, the reception area was still filled with badges and clipboards of state department of this or that wanting to inspect anything and everything that could possibly be inspected in the school. Since the office was so crowded, many had left saying they would be back tomorrow. Mr. Elder actually lost count of the hands he had shaken as his normal day turned nightmare continued to bring more surprises.

Toward the end of the day a Department of Child and Family Services worker with a chip on her shoulder, and not much else, appeared at the school office escorted by a police officer in uniform. She introduced herself as Agent Misty Sellers with the DCFS and shoved her business card in his face. The way Agent Sellers dressed reminded him of a prostitute he had encountered while witnessing on the streets with his church a few years back. He stared at the picture of his wife on his desk and recited Job 31:1 silently to himself

... I have made a covenant with my eyes; why then should I look upon a young woman? The DCFS worker began her attack by asking what procedures the school had in place if they suspected child abuse. Mr. Elder was wise enough not to trust this woman, but he also felt the need to comply with her demands, if he could. After what could only be described as a lengthy and awkward interrogation by the DCFS worker, Mr. Elder could tell by her tone of voice she didn't like the answers she was getting from him, and the fact he would not look at her, but simply stared at the picture of his wife instead, obviously annoyed her.

Mr. Elder, with his gaze firmly locked on his wife's picture, assured her he was just following Board policy, and couldn't do anything else without Board approval. As she was preparing to leave a uniformed police officer who was with her served an official written request to Grace Christian Academy Inc. demanding the names and personal information of all the students Mr. Joe Smith came in contact with during the school year. The DCFS worker explained, since Joe is currently under investigation for abuse, the state felt it important to make sure he had not abused any of the students under his charge during his time of service at GCA. In addition, she dutifully informed Mr. Elder that in the report to her superiors she would recommend Joe Smith not be allowed to return to work at GCA until a full investigation had been conducted.

Mr. Elder tried again to dutifully explain to the uncompromising DCFS worker, that he didn't have the authority to release GCA student records without Board approval, and he didn't know which records were being requested anyway. Misty Sellers placed her hands on the desk and leaned forward in an attempt to get him to look up at her as she explained, "Mr. Elder, Grace Christian Academy Incorporated is under the jurisdiction of the State of Illinois. You have no choice except to comply with my request." Misty Sellers turned to look over her bare shoulder as she left saying, she "would get those records one way or the other," and, "the school must comply with the request, or. . ." as she so poignantly put it, "there may not be a school left." With that last threat, she and her police escort left. He checked his watch—just after five. No more state bureaucrats would be bothering him today.

Mr. Elder stepped out into the office to tell the other staff members they could go home. But before he could speak, Mrs. Ross handed him a large envelope. "This came while you were talking to the Boiler Inspector. They wanted to deliver it to you, but they got tired of waiting, and had me sign for it." Mr. Elder told Mrs. Ross and the other office staff members that had come in to help with the deluge of inspectors they could go home and thanked them for their help. As an afterthought, he asked a few of them if they could come back tomorrow to deal with the rest of the state officials who had promised to return.

Walking slowly into his office, he carefully opened the sealed envelope and pulled the contents out. Iris Wethers had followed through on her threat; the school was being sued for religious discrimination in hiring. He would deal with this later; he needed to call Corbin anyway, this was just one more thing to add to the list.

Mr. Elder slowly picked up the phone. Calling his wife, he told her he would be a little late getting home and would explain when he got there. He returned to the well-worn spot on the carpet behind his desk and dropped to his knees again. He felt like Jesus, in the garden of Gethsemane. He cried out to God, if it be your will let this cup pass from me! Mr. Elder spent the next several minutes in quiet communion with his Lord and Savior. He knew God was sovereign, and he knew God was in control. This day had shown him just how quickly their little school could be destroyed by the powers of the State of Illinois. Unless God directly intervened, he could see no way in the world Grace Christian Academy would be opening its doors at the end of the summer.

When he stood up, he began the routine of shutting off the lights and locking the building. This had been the ONLY thing that had been routine today, he thought. As he walked to his car, he pondered what one of the inspectors had said. "Mr. Elder, Grace

Christian Academy Incorporated is under the complete and sole jurisdiction of the State of Illinois. As a corporation you are at the whim and mercy of the powers-that-be within the state." Mr. Elder had always assumed that being incorporated was no big deal. Until today he assumed the state would always treat their little school equitably and fairly. He had assumed, nothing like this could ever happen. He had been dreadfully wrong.

Mr. Elder slowly walked toward the lone car in the parking lot as he pressed the button on the keyless entry. A sense of dread spread over him. The more he mulled over the events of the day, the more he felt certain he knew why the school was being investigated. Jane Jones and her lawyer would stop at nothing to smear Joe Smith's name, and the Christian school he worked at seemed an easy target. It angered him that the state system could be so manipulated by petty men for their purposes. But then deep in his heart, he wondered if there was a deeper spiritual battle at stake as well. Pausing for one more moment outside the glass doors of the brick school, Mr. Elder called the school's lawyer. Reaching Corbin's answering machine, he left a message for him to call on urgent matters as soon as possible. There was nothing left to do now but wait.

Never in his wildest dreams had he supposed he would own a car like this, a pristine Cadillac Fleetwood with all the bells and whistles, immaculate blue leather interior, and lots of polished chrome. At first he had been self-conscious about driving around the limousine. Now he almost didn't notice the people who stared as he drove by. The car had been an unexpected blessing from an unexpected place. The funeral director in town had heard that Mr. Elder was looking for another car after his last one died. Mr. Elder had been looking for something with a little bit more room, since he often transported large numbers of children, grandchildren, and students. This car certainly did fit the bill. All six of the Perry children had graduated from Grace Christian Academy and Mr. Perry, the owner of the funeral home, had made Mr. Elder an offer he couldn't refuse. The cost was less than one-third of the car's listed price, so he didn't refuse it. The limousine looked brand-new even though it was 15 years old. It only had 38,000 miles on it when he had bought it; now it had that many more.

Mr. Elder came back from his little trip down memory lane as he fired up the limousine and heard the low rumble. As a young man Mr. Elder used to dream of owning a Corvette, but this was definitely better. Although it had the same engine as the Corvette, it had six doors and was much more practical when he had to strap the grandchildren into their car seats. Years ago he had been unable to buy that Corvette. Now he had been given something so much better. True, it was just a car, but he thanked God for blessing him with so much more than he deserved.

His mind was whirling as he thought about his grandchildren on that drive home. He thought about Joe and Mary Smith, and their unborn baby. He talked to his Lord and Savior Jesus Christ about it all as if He were sitting in the passenger seat. They talked about the Smiths, about the insane day he had had at school. They talked about what to do, and how to handle all the situations that presented themselves today. He thanked God for his beloved wife. He knew she would be praying for him as she kept his supper warm and waited. Mr. Elder often kept late hours when school was in session, but it wasn't often he was this late during the summer hours.

What would happen in the Fall? Mr. Elder pondered his options. Up to this point, Mr. Elder had been considering what would happen if, or more likely when, Mary Smith died. He had supposed Joe Smith would return to work there at the school. He'd been a great computer teacher. He knew his stuff, and he had a natural gift for teaching and working with students. But now he was wondering if any of the teachers would have a job to return to at the end of the summer.

Would Grace Christian Academy Incorporated cease to exist? During the end of his conversation with the Creator of the universe, Mr. Elder had become confused. The Spirit of God speaking to his spirit had seemed to indicate that Grace Christian Academy

Incorporated would indeed cease to exist. And yet, he seemed to be assured that the school would go on. *How could Grace Christian Academy cease to exist, and go on at the same time?* What would become of the building, and the church? As he pulled into his driveway and eased his very long car into the garage, that question was still ringing in his mind. *Maybe, just like the corvette he had always wanted, God had something better in mind for Grace Christian Academy.*

CHAPTER 18

Robert Forbes paused in the hall of the hospital to greet a heavy-set cafeteria worker in her fifties that few people would have noticed. As she left, Robert handed her a beautifully illustrated gospel tract with flowers and a magnificent waterfall on the front.

The door to Mary Smith's room was cracked, " . . .One thing they discussed is why this might be happening. The subject came up of you and your continued teaching." Mr. Elder sighed deeply, "Then the Board discussed whether or not there was even going to *be* a school for you to continue teaching at in the Fall." Robert stuck his head into the hospital room. He wanted to hear what Mr. Elder said, and he didn't want to be eavesdropping. "These hospital rooms are not very private are they," Robert spoke as he pulled up the folding chair. Joe sat in his vinyl chair nervously rubbing his injured arm.

Mr. Elder and Joe made no response. Joe was too interested in what Mr. Elder had to say to care what Robert said or did right now. Changing his tone of voice from worry to congratulations, Mr. Elder continued. "I am happy to report that after some prayer, the Board of Directors was unanimous. They want you back to teach the computer classes. If we have a school that is! When this whole issue with Mary comes to a conclusion, you may have a job waiting for you. Let me put that another way, If I have a job you will too. We are placing our trust in the Lord to deliver the school from this attack by the enemy." Mr. Elder smiled and his unwavering faith in God as the ultimate Provider showed in his face, "God will provide for our needs or change the situation for us. Of this I am confident."

The alarm on Mr. Elder's wristwatch started to beep. Shutting it off, he rose to his feet. "Sorry to leave so soon Joe. I have another state inspector from the Department of something or other showing up in less than an hour, and I need to go prepare. This would be funny if it weren't happening to me!"

Addressing Robert Forbes, he continued "Mr. Forbes, if you'll excuse me I must be leaving. However, I would sincerely like to sit down with you sometime and discuss the *red books*. Joe tells me you are quite well read in this regard." Mr. Elder extended his hand to shake Joe's before leaving.

"I'm sorry I've caused the school so much trouble," Joe apologetically blurted out.

Mr. Elder smiled a sympathetic smile. "It's not all you. You didn't have anything to do with the lawsuit," Mr. Elder paused trying to remember how the legal forms had been worded, "the religious discrimination in hiring case we're now facing."

"What are you talking about?" was Joe's confused response.

"I guess you didn't hear. I refused to hire a lady who applied for the office secretary job because she refused to sign the Statement of Faith, and she has gotten a lawyer, and is suing the school." Joe and Robert were silent, neither one sure what to say next. As an afterthought Mr. Elder added, "We are just waiting to see what God is going to do in this situation because it's hopeless from a strictly human standpoint." Having said this, Mr. Elder hastily retreated down the hallway saying he needed to leave if he was going to be on time for the state inspector.

Both men were silent for a moment. Robert seemed to be deep in thought as if wanting to say more, but feeling he shouldn't.

"Robert," Joe turned his attention to his friend trying to draw him out of his melancholy state, "It's so good to see you. I see you've already taken your seat. If you don't mind, I'll stand. I have exceeded the endurance level of my posterior."

"Then I will stand also." remarked Robert, "It sounds like they want you back next year. So tell me, if you can, I'm terribly curious, what is going on with the school, and what was Mr. Elder saying about a state inspector?" Robert added as an afterthought, "How about the latest on your mother-in-law too, while you are at it."

The uneasiness which had come over Joe at the news Mr. Elder brought was heightened by Robert's request of news about his mother-in-law. Robert faced a very worried, annoyed, and defeated Joe. "Things are about the same with my mother-in-law. Her lawyer claims they have a signed Living Will—you know all that. We are just waiting for them to reassign a court date. She calls every day or so. The school's lawyer is supposed to be by tomorrow to talk with me. I guess he'll know what to do."

Robert looked perplexed, "And what does all that have to do with the state inspectors at the Christian school?"

In a few sentences, Joe conveyed to Robert the news of the trials the Christian school was facing. He went on to share how the school was being harassed by the state in every possible way, and Joe believed it was all on his account. "My mother-in-law's lawyer must have called every state office in the phone book. All of the bus drivers have been *randomly* selected for drug testing on the same day," Joe said while making finger quote marks around the word randomly. "They wrote the school a warning citation about the shape of the toilets! They say the boiler needs a major overhaul before winter, or the school cannot remain open. The Fire Marshall is demanding the installation of an expensive alarm system and horn strobes (whatever those are) in all of the science areas, hallways, and stairs. He also mentioned something about the state requiring an intruder site plan, there was much, much more but you get the general idea. And I have no idea what this new religious discrimination case is about! The DCFS has requested the records of any student I may have had contact with during the year so that they can evaluate the potential danger to the students. Anyway, last night, the Board members called an emergency meeting to deal with the fallout from this full court press from the state. One of the board members said 'this is not some Communist country. Why is the state attacking a Christian school?'"

"Because they can!" Robert flatly added.

Joe kept right on talking. "The school doesn't have the money to make all the needed changes before the school year starts, and they say we can't hold school there until we do. We could try and change locations, but no one knows of a site that would or could meet all the regulations they are throwing at us. In addition to the school, the church was also checked by every compliance officer and Marshall immediately after they left the school. They revoked the kitchen certification on the fellowship hall, and said we needed to put new toilets in the church and hall restrooms as well. No more fellowship dinners there until further notice.'"

Robert was silent as he weighed in his spirit what to say. He wondered if he had already said too much. Joe continued his complaining. "Something is seriously wrong when the state can do that to the church! The Board wants to make the school and church as safe as possible, but some of this stuff is really ridiculous, and they certainly can't afford it."

Drumming his fingers on the side of the chair as he looked nonchalantly out the hospital window, Robert asked, "So what is the Board going to do?"

"It seems they aren't sure what to do. They are all in shock. Joe ended his explanation by saying, "And I feel responsible for it. I guess we don't have any more separation of church and state."

"It isn't a church and state issue if the church and school are both incorporated. It is simply a matter of the state controlling and regulating what it has created." Robert coolly commented. Joe wondered what Robert meant. *Was he implying the state should be allowed to control the church in this way?*

Joe listened intently for the next hour asking questions about church incorporation, trying to understand and take it all in.

Robert told Joe when church incorporation started, and why it was such a big deal. Robert explained, "Constitutionally a church is nontaxable and outside the jurisdiction of the federal and state governments. When a church incorporates, the church loses its status as a church and becomes a non-profit corporation which is created by, and subject to, the rules of the state. By incorporating, the church exchanges its nontaxable status for tax exempt status. These may sound the same but they aren't. Nontaxable means the church cannot be taxed. Tax exempt status can be modified, altered, or revoked at any time for any reason. Tax exempt status is a benefit given to a corporation for meeting specific criteria. If you cease meeting the criteria, or the criteria are changed, your tax exempt status can be revoked."

Joe expressed confusion and frustration, "This is purposeful systematic fraud isn't it?" Not waiting for an answer Joe continued, "We are told by the lawyers we have to incorporate our churches, and you are telling me, in so doing, they cease to be the church at all?"

Robert answered, "Right, they become non-profit corporations like the boy scouts or the local men's fraternity." Robert kept right on explaining, "Decades of public school education have trained people to be little robots instead of thinking for themselves. The united States has lost its history, and therefore has lost its purpose. Those living in the fifty states, on the whole, have lost the mindset for freedom. The founding fathers died for these ideas. Yet, today most Americans are willingly giving their freedoms away in exchange for the illusion of security. You see Joe, if you don't know where you've come from, it is impossible to know where you're headed or where you should be headed. In the generation of the founders, as you've been reading in your red books I suppose, many men were self-educated critical thinkers. It was normal and expected to question and understand WHY things were the way they were."

Robert asked Joe, "In your experience at school what is the

more likely scenario? Option #1 — for a student to ask another clueless student how to do something on a computer and follow their wrong advice, or ... Option #2, to read the step-by-step instructions embedded in the program telling them exactly how to do the desired task?"

Joe slowly nodded and held up one finger. He was beginning to understand. He responded, "Software manuals that come with new computer programs — I have always read those. The computer programmer in me knows, if you make one small error, things don't work in the world of electronics and computers."

Robert nodded in agreement as he added, "Students in today's culture are taught to 'Go with the flow,' 'Don't make waves,' 'Don't rock the boat.' As a culture, we are more likely to ask someone else how to do something, than to read the instruction manuals for ourselves."

Robert continued, "Allow me to give you an example, It is amazing to me how someone will spend $30,000 to $50,000 on a vehicle and then not read the owner's manual explaining how it works and how to operate the special features. By now you already know, I'm peculiar by today's standards. I check people's glove boxes sometimes, if they don't mind, to satisfy my curiosity. I find most of the owner's manuals are still sealed in plastic or have never left that really nice case they came in from the factory. Sometimes it just keeps them from using some feature they paid several thousand extra dollars for, but sometimes it can be more serious. For instance, just last week one of the older ladies in our church had her first car wreck ever. She is a very safe driver, but she didn't read the owner's manual, and it could have cost her her life, instead of just her car."

"You see, she bought a newer car to replace the one she had been driving for the last two decades. She had never even heard of antilock brakes before the accident. When she tried to stop quickly to avoid an accident the antilock brakes engaged, and she immediately jerked her feet from the brake pedal, and had a wreck. I asked her why she didn't stop. She told me "when the loud noise started and the brake pedal began jerking up and down under my foot, I pulled my foot off to keep from tearing up my new car."

"Her owner's manual clearly states there will be a vibration in the foot pedal and some very loud noises when the brakes are applied quickly. This is normal, and do not be alarmed. It went on to encourage the new car owner to practice applying the brakes quickly in a parking lot or driveway, to become familiar with the process. The sad thing is, I had just seen her new car in the lot at church and encouraged her to read the owner's manual. I tried explaining there had been several changes in cars in the last twenty years, and her new car had some safety features she needed to know about. She told me she might do that when she got around to it, but I could tell she was offended at my suggestion. "

"You know Joe, people can be told the right thing to do, and they won't do it if it involves changing the way they have always done things, or changing what they believe. She believed the new car was just like her old one. In her mind, she didn't need to read the Manual. She didn't see a need, or a benefit, so she didn't put forth the effort to change."

"She told me after the accident that she had resented my telling her to read the owner's manual. It was as if I was calling her an old lady and telling her she didn't know how to drive. I failed to communicate clearly WHY she needed to read the manual, and I offended her. In hindsight, I should have communicated more clearly to her about the antilock brakes in particular. My suggestion to read the whole thing was offensive to her. I hope I have learned from that mistake. I know she did."

"I have never read my car's manual. I bought used, and my car didn't have one when I bought it," Joe admitted.

Robert inquired, "Have you ever read the instructions to a board game like Monopoly?" Joe nodded in assent.

"You will appreciate this story then" said Robert. "I asked several of the high schoolers from our church fellowship during a lock-in to play Monopoly several months ago, they reluctantly agreed with a 'let's do it for the old guy' look. This was an eye-opening experience for me. Before we began, I asked each one of them if they knew how to play Monopoly. They all replied in the affirmative, saying they had played many times before, although it wasn't much fun, and it took too long to play. I then asked if any of them had ever read the instructions on the inside of the box, or perhaps in the instruction booklet.

None of them had ever read the instructions. They had all been told how to play by someone else. This became a very educational game of monopoly for me as to how things work when house rules are used.

We each selected our markers and placed them on the GO space to begin. One of the students, Kim, was the banker. She began by giving us $2000—the wrong amount of money. I asked her why she gave us this much money to start with, and she replied that was the amount of money they always started with. *She hasn't read the instructions* I reminded myself. Kim then proceeded to place $500 in the middle of the Monopoly board. "What's that for?" I asked. Kim gave me a very strange look and explained to me it was for the person who landed on free parking. She then asked me if I'd ever played Monopoly. I smiled, assuring her I had played many times with my daughters as part of their schooling. I added, "It is an excellent way to teach economics in a properly functioning free-market economy."

"Kim gave me a puzzled, irritated look, and we began the game. Kim's brother Ezra landed on income tax on his first roll and proceeded to pay his $200 to the middle. 'For the one who lands on free parking?' I asked. 'Of course Mr. Forbes' was his flabbergasted reply. When they landed on a property they did not want to buy, they merely passed the dice to the next person. 'I would like to buy that property if you do not,' I said. Kim and Ezra both informed me 'you have to land on the property to buy it, Mr. Forbes.'"

"I must explain to you that what followed was the longest, most boring, and most painful Monopoly game of my life. When they ran out of buildings to improve properties, they started using pennies and nickels and dimes for houses and hotels. Toward the end of the game Eric was almost out of money and he landed on free parking. It was like winning the lottery! The game never ended. The students just got bored of playing and decided to quit. No wonder they don't like playing Monopoly. I wouldn't like it either, if I was forced to play like that every time."

Joe looked at Robert like he often did with a strange confused expression on his face, "I'm sure there's a point here, but it's escaping me at the moment."

"Don't you see Joe? The game of Monopoly is designed after the game of life; not the board game but the one we're living. None of those kids had ever read the rules. They were playing by what are commonly called *house rules*."

"What are *house rules*?"[1] Joe asked.

"Well, you see Joe, *house rules* are the rules that you're being taught to play by from someone else, without reading the rules for yourself. Often house rules are modified from the actual rules by someone who has decided to use a different set of rules in their house. The trouble with house rules is, they may be different in every house and are subject to change at any time by the one making up the rules. Usually they preface the rule change by saying 'Oh, I forgot to tell you,' and then they make up a rule that is to their benefit."

"I love to play board games. You can learn many life lessons by playing them, but only if you play according to the rules. I sometimes use board games to teach my children to follow rules that never change. Like the standards in God's word never change."

"As my children became old enough to play board games, whenever there was a question about the rules to the game I would give them the rule book for the game and have them look it up for themselves. Sometimes, I would purposefully violate the rules to see if my children knew whether or not I was playing according to the rules. Oftentimes my children would say I was cheating. I would then hand them the rule book and say prove it! When they had done so, I was always careful to explain how I was using the game and the rules to teach them about life. I wanted them to understand I was cheating to teach them a life lesson about knowing and following the rules, not to win the game. Winning is meaningless if one must cheat to win. Most of my children have memorized 2 Timothy 2:5 'And also if anyone competes in athletics, he is not crowned unless he competes according to the rules.' At this point my children have the rules memorized for many games as well as what page each rule is on. When everybody plays by the rules, everybody can have fun."

"My children have had the unfortunate displeasure of being called "cheater" on more than one occasion in the past, while playing with friends. They would often play games at church fellowships, or with groups of friends and be accused of cheating. You see my children have been taught to play by the written rules, and the other children are playing by house rules. I would like to say that when my children quoted the rule and page number to them the problem was settled; however, this is often not the case. The other children said things like, 'My dad told me how to play, and I know my dad wouldn't lie to me;' or 'Well we don't play like that at my house;' or worst of all 'That's just your interpretation.' It has gotten to the point where some of my older children will not play games with other children without first reading the rules aloud to the other children. You see the problem with house rules is they're not written down. They are subject to change often without notice, and often to the benefit of those making them up as they go."

"Recently my wife invited Kim and Ezra over to dinner to give their parent's an opportunity for a parent's date night. Our kids had been planning for days to have a rousing game of Monopoly after supper."

"In the Lord's divine providence things will all work out. Ezra and Kim were invited by my children to join the family game of Monopoly. My oldest daughter, in honor of our guests, pulled out the rule book with a flourish and proceeded to do an interactive dramatic reading of the Monopoly rule book with two of her younger sisters. She then turned to Ezra and Kim and said, 'In this house, we play by the written rules which are as unchanging as God's law! If you have a question about the rules, here's the book.' She then presented the book to them as if it was some fine treasure being bequeathed to them by royalty."

"Ezra and Kim turned to each other having finally heard the correct rules to Monopoly for the first time in their entire life and decided to give it a try playing by these *new* rules. About an hour later, Justin was battling it out with my second oldest daughter for the Monopoly championship for the night, and bragging rights for the next week."

"Kim and the others had been put out of the game much earlier, but were watching on to the bitter end to see who the victor would be. When the game was over, Ezra had his first Monopoly championship, and a crash course in free market economics from my children in the process."

"Kim and Ezra both agreed after the game was over, that Monopoly was much more fun when played according to the rules the creator of the game intended. The game was much faster, and made much more sense too. Kim said that was the first game of Monopoly she had ever finished. Always before she had always gotten bored and just quit part way through. They both agreed playing with my kids had been very eye-opening as well. It was a side of my daughters they had never seen before."

Joe had sat down during this long talk. Instinctively, he rose and went and checked on Mary and gave her hand a firm squeeze. Robert stood and stretched. "Bear with me a little longer. Joe it works in life as well. A church friend of mine is a truck driver. He follows the rules to a fault, and he knows the rules. His load was being inspected by a new officer who was bound and determined to find something wrong with his load—I suppose to impress his supervisor. The officer finally found a rule about the first chain must be within the first ten feet of the load, and my friend's first chain was twelve feet from the front of the load. The officer wrote my friend a ticket for an improperly-secured load. Later my friend looked up the rule in question, and it was in a section about short loads. The rule didn't apply to the load he was hauling. He was hauling reinforcing bar for cement work that was almost as long as his trailer. He decided to pay the ticket instead of fighting it, since he would lose at least a day of pay to take time off fighting the ticket."

"I, myself, was pulled over by an officer for a supposed violation of a traffic law two years back. I informed the officer the rule he said I violated didn't apply to me since I was not operating a commercial vehicle. He wrote me a ticket and proceeded to leave. I demanded his contact information, and I informed him I would be in touch."

"I found the statute I had supposedly violated, and the law he said I had violated applied only to school buses! I found the officer and showed him the statute the next day. Amazingly, he apologized for the mistake, and said he had never even read the actual statute. I found out from him, the troopers are given a small paragraph on each statute to read which is merely a summary. He explained they don't have time to read all of the new laws that come out, so that is how they stay updated. Most of them just enforce a few of the laws, since there are so many. I am very fortunate he was so understanding. He could have been a hard man, and I would have had to decide whether or not to contest the ticket in court."

"Joe, I can give you hundreds of examples of people and events where the powers that be were playing by *house rules* instead of by the written law. Most of the time the powers that be have never even read the actual law. They're going off of some blurb or paragraph given to them by their superior, or they are making it up as they go. Many times the actual written law is so vague or convoluted that deciphering exactly what it says takes a degree in Law and a legal dictionary."

"I play the game of life like I play board games, according to the written rules not according to the house rules. That often leads me to be misunderstood. I have been called things to my face by people

I have known for years that I dare not repeat. You see Joe, they have been playing the game of life by house rules and to them I seem to be *cheating*, when in reality, I'm actually playing by the law as written—and they just don't understand. As a result, I tend to keep my life rather private, and don't let many people know what I do. I keep my private things private, to avoid offending those who are playing by house rules, and for those who refuse to see the truth."

"The hardest people to deal with are the supposed experts in their field. They have been trained by other experts, and have been studying for years a specific area or aspect of law, business, banking, or whatever. But they were trained by those who were using house rules. They've never been forced to go back to the original documents and read the rules. In all honesty, those doing the training do not want them to know or understand the truth because perpetuating the lie is to their advantage. They 'exchanged the truth of God for the lie, and worshiped and served the creature rather than the Creator, who is blessed forever.'(Romans 1) They have created a hegemony and will use what is in their power to maintain that power. It's a . . . "Joe sat there trying to take it all in and Robert stopped in mid-sentence.

"I'm sorry Joe, once I get started on something I am so passionate about it I don't know when to shut up sometimes. I would love to talk with you some more about this later when Mary gets better, and you're ready. Just know this, one's worldview and what they accept as truth determines how they think and how they act, and what rules they play by. The rules you play by will determine how you play and what the goal of the game is, whether it's a board game or real life. "

Robert pulled up a chair and sat back down, "Back to the problem of the school. There is an easy way to get the state off your back." Joe asked in slight amazement, "Oh really, what is that?" "Well actually, what to do is easy. Getting those responsible to agree to do it is going to be almost impossible," Robert said as he ran his fingers through his brown hair streaked with silver."

"The church and school need to get rid of their Incorporated status. Changing the name is usually the easiest way to accomplish this. Most bodies of Christians hate change, and getting them to change something like the name of the church fellowship is almost impossible."

"You see Joe, most groups of Christians who band together, and call themselves a church, very quickly fall into a rut of tradition. Most assemblies of Believers are so locked into their traditions that they would sooner die than change."

"I know what you mean about churches being resistant to change," Joe interjected, "I've heard of some churches nearly splitting over changing the carpet in the Fellowship Hall, or how many cups to have at Communion." "Changing the name, that would be almost inconceivable," Joe agreed.

Robert continued, "As I said, the process is actually not that complicated. In essence, here is what happens. A new name is decided upon. A group of believers organizes as a church under that name. The leaders of the Corporation then give all of the corporation's assets to the newly formed church as a gift. The assets are transferred. Then people decide to quit going to the corporation and start going to the new church. After everything has been transferred, then the Corporation is dissolved or goes bankrupt or whatever, depending on the type of corporation it is."

"The individuals in leadership position in the Corporation resign. You notify the state in whatever means are prescribed in the Corporation's bylaws, and the Corporation just ceases to exist. No income. No assets. No members. No bank account. The actual nuts and bolts of how to accomplish this is a bit more complicated, but in essence that's what must happen. The newly formed church will then establish an educational ministry as part of what it does. You can organize this ministry as a school if you wish, and even become accredited as such. The school will obviously need a new name as well and can function as a ministry of the church."

"The teachers would either quit or be let out of their contracts and could covenant with the elders of the church to perform as ministers with the job of pastor/teacher, within the school ministry. Since the church and the school are NOT employers, then they will have no employees. Neither of them will register, or apply for a federal employer ID number. The way things are run will have to be completely different. It must be run as a church ministry not as a corporate business."

"There will be some things that you can't do anymore. Churches can't borrow money from a bank. They can't take government grants, and they cannot take part in government programs, faith-based initiatives, and that sort of thing. They cannot bring a lawsuit against anybody, but they also cannot be sued by anyone."

"There's more, but that's enough for now. Most corporations, masquerading as churches, don't want to change. They're quite content on being slaves of Caesar, so to speak. They enjoy the perks and privileges of being Caesar's slave and would not want to give them up. The leaders of the Jews back in the time of Christ were in this same boat. They appeared to be in control but were really in slavery to Caesar."

"Most individuals within the church body are slaves to the world's system, so having the actual church be a slave of the system is not a big deal to them at all. Actually it is a comfort to most people to have their *church* officially recognized by the state, it guarantees their gifts will be tax exempt without a fight with the IRS, should they be audited."

"I suppose I'm getting the cart before the horse. If there is no willingness to change the way things are, change will never happen. As I said before, you have to possess a mindset for freedom, or at least desire that knowledge. If not, you are like the lady I told you about earlier who wrecked her car. If you don't see a need to change as a group, the change will not likely happen.Unfortunately, we've lost the mindset for freedom and the desire to search out the truth in most groups of believers. But then again, if individual Christians don't know change is possible and necessary (and learn how to change) they will never seek to do so will they? Just know, it is possible, for a group of Christian Believers to meet in fellowship together without seeking permission from the government. We already have the right to do so spelled out in the constitution's first amendment. Christians can gather as a church without applying to the secular government for permission to do what God has commanded us to do."

There was a lull in the conversation. Joe viewed what Robert had said as too hard to believe, but what he had said made some sense.

Both men were in deep thought, and then Robert inquired, "Joe, what are the chances that I can have an audience with Mr. Elder?"

Joe scratched his cheek with his good hand. "A hundred percent I'd say, provided you can relate what you have to say in some way to the red books."

"Excuse me," Robert replied in a rather confused tone.

Joe smiled and replied with a chuckle, "Robert, were you listening to what Mr. Elder said? He said he would sincerely like to get together with you and discuss the red books sometime. Do you suppose if you discuss the red books and their contents with Mr. Elder, this topic might possibly come up?"

A smile crept across Robert's lips as he replied, "Aye lad, I suppose that would definitely come up in the course of such a conversation."

Joe gave Robert the contact information for Mr. Elder at the school, and as he did so said, "I think you'll find Mr. Elder a very open and honest man who may be more agreeable to doing what you suggest than you might first suspect. Mr. Elder not only teaches the principles in the red books, but he also believes and lives by them. What you are telling me is in line with what I've been reading and studying in my reading assignments. It just doesn't seem to be in line with everything else I have been taught to believe my whole life. It is all so overwhelming: too much to process at once. Kind of like trying to drink out of a fire hose."

The next day, Robert Forbes walked slowly toward the school while straightening his tie with one hand, and pulling a large box on wheels filled with books with the other. He smoothed his lapel and checked his pockets. He shook his head as he pulled out the wedding program and notes from his niece's wedding. She was the oldest of the cousins in his wife's side of the family.

His niece had insisted Uncle Robert be the one to do her wedding. He flipped through the pages taken from his pocket as he walked. There was a copy of their vows, a copy of their wedding covenant, and the notes from the message he had shared with all that attended, that explained the concept of a covenant marriage before God without state sanction, or permission.

He thought back to the discussion he had with the young man's father and mother assuring them that getting married without a marriage license and a state-ordained licensed minister was indeed legal and proper, and that they would be "legally married" after the covenant had been signed by the witnesses.[2]

After much prayer, discussion, and questioning, the parents not only accepted a covenant marriage, but agreed it was far superior to a state-supervised legal union. The state of Illinois could never grant a divorce for this marriage, since they had not sanctioned and given license to the union in the first place, and were not a party to it. Robert hoped the meeting he was now headed towards would have a similar outcome.

Robert folded the notes and placed them back in his pocket. He would have to remember to take them out and put them in a safe place when he got home. He glanced at his watch. He was going to be about 10 minutes early to the meeting with Mr. Elder. He thanked God, knowing he had made this happen. It was indeed a rare miracle for a man with seven children to be early anywhere.

As he walked to the meeting, he prayed once again all would go well. He had even fasted and prayed instead of eating dinner last night. "This meeting could be a huge step in the right direction

Lord. Please let it go according to your will."

Robert entered the reception area and encountered a lady with a very large sincere smile asking how she may help him. Robert informed her of the meeting he had scheduled with Mr. Elder. The smiling receptionist directed him to a chair and informed Robert that Mr. Elder was with someone currently and should be done shortly. About two minutes before the appointed hour, Mr. Elder emerged with the visitor from his office shaking the visitor's hand and thanking him for coming and setting things up on such short notice.

Mr. Elder welcomed Robert with outstretched hand and an honest smile. "Mr. Forbes, thank you for coming. Please do come in," Mr. Elder said in welcome. Robert was escorted into a very nicely decorated office with a homey feel. It suited the owner well. He saw a very large conference table off to one side with a pile of books next to a digital recorder connected to two microphones on stands and a small video recorder set up in the corner.

"I hope you don't mind Mr. Forbes if I video this conversation? I've been praying about this for a long time, and the Lord has clearly shown me that this should be videotaped for future use. It isn't often I have the opportunity to visit with someone of your background and intimate knowledge of the principles laid forth in these books." He placed his hand softly on the pile of books to which he was referring. A feeling of peace flowed through Robert. In his spirit he knew as well that this conversation must be videotaped. As soon as he saw the camera, he shot up a silent prayer of thanks to God. Mr. Elder placed a basket filled with dry erase markers on a shelf next to a dry erase board mounted to the wall. "Just in case," he said with a smile.

"Would you like to begin in prayer?"

"Sir, there is no other way to begin," was Robert's earnest reply.

During the next two hours, the Holy Spirit led these two men of God in discovering the truth of what needed to happen at the school, both in its philosophy of education, and regarding the restructuring of the school and church to become unincorporated.

They forgot all about the small video recorder in the corner of the room, but the discussion it was recording would later have the power to change the hearts and minds of those truly seeking after the will of God, to those who've been "called according to his purpose."

CHAPTER 19

Corbin Cutler pressed the button on his phone, ending the conversation with Mr. Elder. He threw the phone on the couch. Had Mr. Elder lost his mind? He felt like he'd just spent the last few minutes on the phone with a crazy person, but he'd known Mr. Elder most of his adult life, and he knew he was anything but a crazy man. He began to pace the floor. What he had been hearing just didn't make any sense. A lifetime of legal training and experience was screaming out to him how wrong it all was.

The school was obviously being harassed by the State, and Corbin's legal mind knew precisely what needed to be done. *You take them to court, you sue them, and you get a judgment on your behalf. That's the way things work in the world.* He had tried to explain this to Mr. Elder, but Mr. Elder's calm reply was like fingernails on a chalkboard to Corbin. "I don't want to give the devil home-court advantage. He is the god of this world, and we can't win the legal battle in court. Even if we win, we lose," Mr. Elder had said.

This new way of thinking by Mr. Elder angered Corbin. Corbin knew his way around a courtroom. He could control things there most of the time. He knew the rules in a courtroom; this was a legal battle, wasn't it? Who was this Robert Forbes character Mr. Elder kept referring to anyway? Mr. Elder had said he had a degree in constitutional law. What was that? Constitutional law no longer applied in the courts; it was all about legal precedent now. Past rulings dictate and shaped law and set legal precedents for future rulings. They needed to take this case to court and set a legal precedent. That's how the legal system works. All this nonsense about the original intent of the Constitution and following the laws as written. Were they living in some kind of a dream world?

Exasperated, Corbin sat down on the couch. *And now he wants me and everyone on the School Board to watch some video disk, claiming some video put together by a man named Robert Forbes will explain everything. I don't need an explanation! I'm a lawyer! I know the law, I have power in a courtroom to use the law for right, and what they are doing to the school isn't right! But who were "they" anyway?* Corbin mused to himself. *It was obvious someone high up in the state bureaucracy had painted a bull's-eye on this little, seemingly-helpless school. But who had done it? And why? It just didn't make any sense. Sure there were some issues with the Joe Smith case, but that didn't warrant a reaction of this magnitude. He was missing something. Think Corbin. The "Discrimination in hiring" case Iris Wethers was bringing against the school didn't bode well either, but why was every government office in the State of Illinois attacking the school? Think!* Corbin willed his mind to focus on the facts. *Why would the state bureaucratic monster want to sink its teeth into this little Christian school? The school and the church were both flying well under the radar. They were not taking the American Defenders Foundation tactic of breaking the law on purpose to try to pick a fight in court.*[1] Corbin had worked with the ADF people before. They knew their stuff, and they did good work.

Sitting on the couch wasn't solving his problems. Corbin snatched the phone from where he had thrown it. *I'll call him. He'll know what to say.* Corbin called a lawyer friend who worked for the American Defenders Foundation and gave him a brief rundown of what was happening. "Have the church leadership contact us. I believe I can speak for ADF when I say, we will be right down there," Corbin's friend reassured him from the other end of the line. Corbin replied, "They don't want your type of help. They want to unincorporate the church and school and hope all their troubles will go away."

The voice from the other end of the line replied, "It is our legal opinion that they will still be viewed as an incorporated entity by the state, so they will be gaining nothing, and losing their legal status."

"That's EXACTLY what I tried to tell Mr. Elder our school headmaster," Corbin said with exasperation. "He just wouldn't listen to reason," Corbin hissed through clenched teeth.

"But we can't help them if they don't want our help," a calmer voice on the other end replied. "Just let them know we're willing and able to fight this one out in court."

"Thanks, I'll be in touch," Corbin said feeling completely helpless. He killed the power on the phone and threw it back on the couch again, venting some of the pent up anger in his soul.

Corbin fished his keys out of his pocket as he headed toward the garage, "I'm not waiting for that disk to come in the mail. I'm getting a copy now!" Corbin announced out loud to no one in particular but the walls of the house. Two black tire marks pointed their way to the school as a very determined Corbin Cutler left the driveway. Corbin forced himself to stay calm as he drove. Putting on the bluetooth headset he placed a call to the school. Good, they hadn't yet taken the mail out for today. In business tones, he informed the receptionist he would be picking up his copy in person, if she would please set it aside for him.

Mr. Elder was waiting for Corbin when he arrived. "I had a feeling you'd be here today," Mr. Elder said as he handed the disc to Corbin with a smile. Corbin wasn't smiling. He was agitated and it showed on his infuriated, determined face.

"I don't really want to watch this video. I would much rather talk some sense into you before this gets out of hand," Corbin said in a low disturbed tone.

Mr. Elder placed a loving hand on Corbin's shoulder, "My dear brother would you come back to my office so we can discuss this?"

"That is exactly what I had in mind, Sir" was Corbin's calculated reply. Corbin was in lawyer mode: cold, analytical and factual. He had no patience for Mr. Elder's sentimental, fatherly ways, and yet, in the past, he had held a deep respect for this godly man. When they entered the office, Corbin began, "I've contacted the American Defenders Foundation, and they would be happy to help us out. They confirmed what I suspect. Even if you do unincorporate the church and the school, the state will still consider them corporations."

Mr. Elder seemed unmoved by these comments. His reply was calm and steady: "They can consider us anything they like, but that doesn't make us incorporated just because they consider us so, does it?"[2]

Corbin changed his approach, "Look Mr. Elder, I have been a lawyer for 25 years. I know how things work, and they don't work like you think they do. It's just not that easy. The laws must be interpreted by the courts, not by you." Corbin threw the disk onto Mr. Elder's desk.

Mr. Elder shook his head slowly. He reached down, picked up the disk, and handed it back to Corbin. "Dear brother, I'm about to do something very difficult, and I hope and pray someday you'll understand why. Mr. Elder took Corbin by the arm and escorted him out of his office. Mr. Elder looked Corbin directly in the eye and said, "Mr. Cutler, Corbin, I will not talk with you further on this issue until you've watched this disk. The Holy Spirit made it very clear to me during this recorded conversation the direction He would have his church to travel. The only thing left to be seen is whether you will follow." And with a heavy heart, Mr. Elder turned and went back into his office.

Corbin and Mrs. Ross, the receptionist, both looked at each other stunned. This was a side of Mr. Elder they had never seen before. Corbin was confused. Mr. Elder had never refused his legal advice before. He was hurt by what Mr. Elder had just done, but what part of him had been hurt?

Corbin considered these thoughts as he walked back to the car.

Was it his pride that had been hurt? What does the Bible say about pride? Maybe he'd look that up when he got home. No, he wasn't going home! He was going to find this Robert Forbes fellow and straighten this all out man-to-man. Who did this man think he was anyway? — giving legal advice to HIS school. That was Corbin Cutler's job. He had been doing it for years, and he wasn't looking to be replaced. His kids had graduated from GCA. *He loved the little school and the people, and he was going to protect it the best he could even if it meant confronting a completely unknown legal lunatic.*

As Corbin left the parking lot, he hit the speed dial for his office. Speaking with his secretary, she looked up Robert Forbes' address, and Corbin punched it into the GPS on the dash of his car. "Alright Mr. Robert Forbes, here comes Corbin Cutler!" Pressing down on the accelerator, Corbin's self-confident, prideful self-sped his way towards the confrontation.

Meanwhile, Mr. Elder called Robert Forbes and asked him to be in prayer about Corbin Cutler. He had dealt with his school board enough to know that without Corbin's approval on a legal matter it was probably dead in the water. The two men prayed together on the phone, said the obligatory goodbyes, and hung up. Robert went into his prayer closet, a small room behind his work shed which had been set aside for just this purpose, and, getting down on his knees, cried out to God. Robert's time of prayer was cut short by his barking dog. This was his dog's *"stranger at the gate"* bark. Robert wondered who it could be at this hour of day?

Corbin pulled up to a gate, covered with Bible verses and a rather strangely-worded legal notice that puzzled Corbin. Not understanding something in the legal realm annoyed him. He was trying to decipher the legal notice when he was distracted from reading further by a rather large, barking farm collie on the other side of the gate. *Great,* he thought to himself, *the constitutional lawyer has a legal notice, a stout perimeter fence, an iron gate, and a very large dog who does not appear at all happy to see me.*

Corbin looked around evaluating the situation. In addition to the verses, Notice, and dog, he saw two teenage girls hanging up laundry on a clothesline and a very tall, stout-looking man walking up the driveway. This man, who looked nothing like his preconceived mental image of this constitutional lawyer, was coming to meet him. Corbin thought about double-checking the GPS to make sure he was at the right address. He was at some goat farm it seemed, and it didn't look at all like the residence of a lawyer, but he didn't have time to check the address. The farmer was almost to the gate.

The man with a big smile, blue jeans, T-shirt, and big rubber boots, approached the gate with his hand outstretched. "Greetings in the name of the Lord Jesus Christ. Do ye greet me in the same name?" The dog stopped barking and sat down by his master.

"Well, uh, yes, I suppose I do. Greetings in the name of the Lord Jesus," Corbin replied. This greeting cooled his temper, temporarily, as he tried to focus on the reason for his visit. *Could this goat farmer who didn't look like he had a high school education be the supposed learned man Mr. Elder spoke of? He certainly wasn't the stereotypical lawyer.*

"My name is Corbin Cutler," he said, as the two big men shook hands over the gate, "I'm looking for a man named Robert Forbes," Corbin said as he sized-up the man.

Robert replied with a smile, "Well then I suppose you aren't here after some milk, are you?"

An irritated, puzzled look crossed Corbin's face as he shook his head "no" and said, "I was wondering if I might be able to visit with you for a few minutes?"

Robert stroked the big dog's head and responded, "I know your name from Mr. Elder, but if you don't mind me asking Brother Cutler, what would you like to visit about?"

Corbin wished he were standing in a courtroom right now as he scrutinized the humble homestead before him. He knew the rules in the courtroom. He had the power; he had control. He could make a witness squirm on the stand. But here standing on the outside of this gate talking to the big man in the rubber boots, he felt like a fish out of water. He had no way to answer Mr. Forbes' question. For one of the few times in Corbin Cutler's life, he was completely at a loss for words. "I would like to talk to you about the school, Grace Christian Academy, and the conversation you had with Mr. Elder."

"Oh, so you've had time to watch the disk?"

"No sir I haven't, and I don't intend to. I have been practicing law for twenty five years, and not meaning to sound prideful, but I don't think there's a whole lot you can teach me," was Corbin's sharp reply. Robert paused for a moment and turned his head to look out across the pasture trying to think how to reply. With an all too incredulous smile, he turned back to Corbin, "Well, until you do, I don't suppose there's anything to discuss. Mr. Elder and I have been praying for you, and I will continue to do so Brother Cutler. I am praying that God will open your eyes to the truth. We have both agreed not to talk to you about this matter until you have watched the video of our conversation. Then you will know what we are proposing, and why. Until you watch that video, I suspect you would be speaking from a position of ignorance. I want friendship and fellowship from you, not misunderstanding and hard feelings. Swallow your pride and humble yourself before God and watch the video Brother Cutler. Have a nice day." And with that, Robert walked back to his house leaving Corbin facing a closed gate and a very large, fluffy barking dog.

Corbin got back into his car and slammed his car door shut. He didn't want to watch that disk! You can't cross-examine a disk. You can't interrogate a disk. You can't argue with a disk, and you can't humiliate a disk. You can only watch it, and agree or disagree with it. Corbin had already decided what he thought, and he knew he didn't want to watch that disk. He was not changing his convictions. It would be a complete waste of time!

His tires sprayed gravel on the dog as he drove away from the Forbes' farm. Corbin's pride was seriously wounded, and he quickly decided he probably wouldn't be talking to Mr. Elder for a very long time. *What did it matter what Mr. Elder thought anyway? The school's board would certainly side with him.*

The next day, Robert walked into Joe's room with a very somber look on his face.

"What is the matter?" inquired Joe.

"Well, if it won't discourage you too much, I wanted to tell you about the discussion between Mr. Elder and myself."

Joe nodded his head in agreement.

"The discussion went amazingly well and lasted almost two hours. I think we have a workable plan for getting this school out of harm's way, and in a position that will allow the ministry to the families of the school to continue. There'll be some tough decisions along the way. I just pray the men in charge decide to obey God, rather than follow the worldly wisdom of men."

Robert broke off his conversation abruptly. Now for what was really burdening the visionary's heart. "This discussion with Mr. Elder made me realize there was a discussion I needed to have with you that couldn't wait any longer. There are many evils in our society today, but there are two which God has burdened my heart with. One, as you know, is the corporate enslavement of the church of Jesus Christ. The other is the willing (yet fraudulent) enslavement of our children."

Joe looked at Robert with disbelief. *What had the fruitcake come up with now?* Joe was only just beginning to understand a little about church incorporation.

Over the next hour, Robert read and explained to Joe the dangers of getting a birth certificate, and Social Security number for his child. He could tell he was giving Joe way too much information at one time, and that Joe was becoming overwhelmed. He needed to show Joe the big picture, and the dangers. He could fill-in the details later. Quietly, in his heart, Robert prayed that God would somehow reveal the big picture to Joe. Robert trusted that his friendship with Joe had become strong enough to endure this. As he finished the discussion and left Joe with some reading materials, he wasn't so sure he had made the right choice. Robert again prayed for wisdom, understanding, and spiritual discernment for Joe. He then excused himself, and bid Joe farewell until another day.

Joe felt like he was drowning. He did not need one more thing to deal with. He was being sued by his mother-in-law over custody of his dying wife. He was in a financial hole the size of the Grand Canyon. The school was under attack... and now Robert was dumping this on him? Joe was mentally, emotionally, physically, and spiritually overwhelmed. He was certain he could not handle one more thing. Yes, Robert had been the most incredible friend anyone could hope for. However, Joe found himself getting angry at Robert for dumping all of this on him now. Dismissing the whole incident from his mind, Joe forgot about the whole situation.

A few days later, Joe sat nervously waiting for Corbin Cutler to arrive. In the few times that Joe had met with Corbin Cutler previously, he had seemed very cold and impersonal. Joe was sure he and Corbin would never be close friends. Still, Joe believed that without his legal skills Mary was probably going to die along with their unborn child. So he waited, and he prayed until Cutler arrived.

Mr. Cutler carried a nice briefcase and was dressed in a suit almost identical to the one his mother-in-law's lawyer wore when he delivered the papers that had made this meeting a necessity. Mr. Cutler pulled out a yellow legal pad and asked a series of questions that he'd written down. He needed to get a thorough understanding of all the pertinent information involved in this case. They didn't have much time to prepare before the hearing, and Corbin was making the most of it. Joe found Mr. Cutler to be very focused and efficient at gathering and organizing the information Joe was giving him. He was filling up his second legal pad with notes by the time the discussion ended.

Mr. Cutler assured Joe that his mother-in-law would not be gaining custody of Mary if he had anything to say about it. He could not make any guarantees of course, because so much of the outcome of the hearing depended on who the judge was. He further explained that even though the law and legal precedents may be on your side, sometimes the judge would rule against you anyway. Corbin knew most of the judges in this part of the country, and most of the judges knew him. Corbin went on to explain that Mr. Brown was a very expensive, and very ruthless lawyer. This would not be the last hearing on the matter. No matter which side won the first round, it was certain to be appealed all the way up to the Supreme Court. Corbin assured Joe that by the time the legal proceedings had been exhausted, Mary's medical condition would have run its course, whatever course that may be.

Corbin started to explain legal strategies to Joe, but quickly realized the man was too overwhelmed with what was going on in the rest of his life to even care what he was saying. Corbin decided to leave Joe in peace and ask just one final question before he left. "Are there any other questions you have for me Mr. Smith, before I leave?"

Joe surprised Mr. Cutler with a response, "Yes, as a matter of fact, I do have a question. Would getting a State Birth Certificate and Social Security number on my child enslave them to the world's system?"

Corbin reacted as if he had been hit in the head with a baseball bat. "Who in the world told you that?"

"A friend of mine: Robert Forbes. Most of what he says makes perfect sense, but I'm having trouble sorting through all of the legal mumbo-jumbo. I thought since I had an experienced lawyer here I would ask you what you thought."

So here was the link between Robert Forbes and GCA. Corbin weighed his words very carefully, then responded, "It seems everywhere I turn lately Mr. Forbes is causing contention and problems. I do not know Mr. Forbes personally, but I can assure you in my expert legal opinion, the man's views are completely out of touch with reality. He may be your friend, but he is completely and totally out of touch with the way the legal system works today. He seems to be trying to operate with the outmoded legal views of the late

1700s. To answer your question sir, having a State Birth Certificate and Social Security number are absolutely necessary for your child to live a normal life in this society."

"Do you have any other questions, Mr. Smith?"

Joe shook his head, and then stood to shake Mr. Cutler's hand. "Thank you Mr. Cutler, for your help. Mary and I really appreciate it."

Corbin Cutler picked up his briefcase and headed for his car with yet another reason for his growing dislike of Robert Forbes. Turning the car out of the hospital parking lot, he headed home to prepare for the board meeting later that evening.

A week had passed since the CD of the discussion between Mr. Elder and Robert had been recorded and his last visit with Corbin Cutler. Mr. Elder couldn't remember ever calling an emergency board meeting in the past. Now he was attending the second one in only a few weeks. Mr. Elder had made sure each of the men on the school board had received a copy of the CD of the discussion between Robert Forbes and himself. Each man at tonight's meeting had watched the CD at his special request, except for Corbin. During the quiet talk preceding the meeting, it became clear that the board was polarized into two camps. In one camp, led by Corbin Cutler, were: Mark Martin, a bank president; Brian Davis, a corporate CEO; Gary Hutchins, a CPA; and Dennis Gray, the pastor of the church.

In the other camp were: Dr. Jim Wilson, a medical doctor whose grandparents had been missionaries to China during the Communist takeover; Cecil Klein, an assembly-line worker who was a deacon in the church; Barry Robertson, a mechanical engineer; and Ivan Waters, a Russian immigrant and history professor at a local Christian college.

Corbin had always been included in the meetings as an advisor to the board. He was not an official member, but had become an important part of the board over the years.

All of those on the board who'd spent their entire lives working within corporate America had understandably sided with Corbin. Corbin's frustration was with those on the board who had traveled outside of the United States, or were descendants of people from other countries. They had readily identified with what Mr. Elder and Mr. Forbes had pointed out in their talk. At the same time, those who had no frame of reference outside of corporate America were quick to dismiss the exact same information as foolish and out of touch with the way modern America works. All of these men had watched the exact same discussion, yet had come to two completely different conclusions.

Mr. Elder, his faith unwavering, opened the meeting in prayer and waited in anticipation to see what work God would do in the meeting.

At the beginning of the meeting, Dr. Jim Wilson shared several things his missionary grandparents had told him over the years. He still had close ties with many in China, and explained that the true Christians worship in groups that are not part of the official state-recognized church. Many Chinese Christians that Jim knew personally had faced loss of property and imprisonment for refusing to register the church with the government. Ivan Waters was quick to recognize, and point out, the similarities between the former Soviet Union, and what the United States was quickly becoming. He, and his family had been a part of an unregistered group of Christians in Russia when he was a child. He pointed out that the official recognized churches, at the time of the Soviet Communist takeover, were immediately targeted.

Because they were already registered, they were given the choice to function only within approved Communist Party guidelines, or they would cease to exist and their leaders would be imprisoned or executed. Many of the registered churches were shut down or combined with other registered churches, and their buildings and property confiscated and used by the state for the state's purposes.

The unregistered bodies of Christian believers fared much better at this time, and were free to continue following Christ without putting themselves and their loved ones in jeopardy for the most part. Yes, what they were doing was considered illegal by the government and some were caught and imprisoned, but the majority went on to become the leadership of a growing, thriving underground church. He also pointed out the first century Christians refused to register the church under Emperor Nero. They chose to die, rather than voluntarily place the church under the authority of the pagan emperor.

With great emotion, Ivan went on to note that during times of prosperity the churches tend to wither on the vine. They become apathetic. Whereas, the persecuted church thrives and grows despite the wishes of the government to prevent such growth. Dependence on God, and true faith in Christ become more necessary, and more real, under such circumstances.

Cecil Klein was definitely the least-educated man on the board, as far as formal education was concerned. He'd never even graduated from high school. Since his conversion at the age of 33, he was the most radically-changed man many of them had ever met. His sweet, simple, childlike faith often bewildered the other men on the board. His straight-forward, practical understanding of God's word had more than once humbled the more educated men. Cecil, in his plain, simple, straight-forward way said, "If you can watch that video presentation between Mr. Elder, and Mr. Forbes; and not come to the conclusion that church incorporation is about as smart as sticking your finger in a light socket while standing in a puddle of water, then you either have no spiritual discernment whatsoever, or you watched a different video than I did!"

Barry Robertson only smiled and shook his head in agreement at Cecil's comment. Robertson, considered by most to be the most logical, insightful person on the board had surprised everyone in the group who had sided with Corbin, by not joining them.

Barry opened his notebook, and proceeded to summarize the entire discussion between Mr. Elder and Mr. Forbes point-by-point, that he had watched on the CD. He followed his summary by saying, "Gentlemen, I've spent the last few days praying and fasting, and checking out each and every one of these points against Scripture, against the law, and for historical accuracy. I'm forced to come to the same conclusion Cecil has come to, although," he smiled a little, "I'm certain I would not have worded it as eloquently as he did."

If Corbin had not been there to immediately argue against everything Barry had said, rallying the troops on his side of the argument, a unanimous consent in favor of Mr. Elder's proposal would probably have resulted. Barry's summary and summary statements were so powerful. So were his words and his deep conviction!

While Mark, Brian, Gary, and Pastor Dennis were all fine Christian men, they were more comfortable following Corbin because he was a lawyer, than they were studying these things for themselves. All four men who sided with Corbin agreed this could never happen in the United States. Things would never get that bad here. As each of them had watched the CD, they caught themselves nodding in agreement with what they heard. Each of them however, had rejected the message in the end because it didn't line up with what they had already decided to believe. They were unwilling to even consider the information that was being presented because it was so uncomfortable and foreign to them. They were experiencing cognitive dissonance, and instead of questioning what they already believed, they decided that following Corbin would be the best and safest route to take. Pastor Gray's statement summed up the sentiment of this group, "If you can convince Corbin to change his mind on this issue, I will gladly and willingly change mine."

CHAPTER 20

It was late. Mr. Verde sat at his desk wrapping a few things up. It had been a frustrating day. Bernard Thomas tried to make contact via Mr. Verde's cell phone all day long. He had even called the hospital and tried to reach him through his secretary. His new, attractive young secretary had already left for the day. Glancing at his email, he saw Ken had just emailed him. Opening the email, Mr. Verde began to read:

Mo

Sorry this reply is so long in coming. I took a few days off and went to northern Michigan, and did some sailing. When I got back, I started looking into your question regarding the authority you possess to remove someone from life support. Traditionally, if the patient has no family, a hospital administrator and a doctor together have the authority to remove someone from life support, remove a feeding tube, etc. . . . In this case, the next of kin's refusal of the doctors' advice presents a problem. The best option would be to use the hospital's resources to back the mother-in-law in her custody battle. If they were taking state financial aid or Social Security, I could pull some strings and have this issue wrapped up by next weekend, but alas that is not the case. If you took this case to court our mutual friends would do all they could to insure a favorable outcome, and set yet another good and needed legal precedent in our nation; but in your present circumstances the time that it would take may be too long to be of benefit to the hospital. I understand your concern over the people creating a scene outside the hospital, but I suspect from what you told me that the group in question has been given more than enough distraction to prevent them from being a problem in this regard. I have been researching your question in admiralty/maritime law, and if this woman has a state birth certificate, the state has ultimate authority in this case. If you wish to take this case to court please contact me and I would be glad to advise you. If you have any more questions or problems, let me know.

Ken

The reply was short and to the point.

Ken

I cannot wait on the custody battle. Transplant needed ASAP! The patient owes a huge debt to the hospital. I will see what I can do to *encourage* next of kin to apply for state aid. We need to meet to discuss what strings will need to be pulled as soon as they are on state aid, at your earliest possible convenience.

Mo

Joe sat staring at the monitor screen which displayed Mary's vital signs. He was starting to see fluctuations in her heart rate, and when her heart rate sped up, he would talk to her in the vain hope that she could hear him. It wasn't much of a change, but it was something. He looked up as Robert walked in carrying his small collapsible cooler and a sack. He had brought more goat's milk, cheese, and fresh bread.

"Have you had time to think about what I said regarding the Birth Certificate and Social Security?" Robert studied Joe's face, and did not like what he saw. An annoyed look infused Joe's face. "Yes, I have thought about it, and I even consulted a professional lawyer. He assured me that you were wrong and that my child needed a Birth Certificate and a Social Security number to function in today's society."

"To function as what? As a slave?" Robert emphatically asked. Joe rubbed his hands across his face and sighed deeply, "Listen Robert, I don't mean to be rude, I mean you've been a great friend and all. . . but I can't do it. I don't want to know any more. You may be right. I mean, some of what you say makes sense, but I. . .I . . . have enough to deal with without dealing with your reactionary ideas. I am in a legal battle for the life of my wife and child. I am hopelessly in debt to this hospital for medical care. The school is being shut down, and I don't even have a job anymore, so pardon me if I'm just too sick and tired of this new stuff you're cramming down my throat to swallow it any more. You may have had a perfect life and easy path, but I haven't. The path I'm on right now feels like a minefield, and I don't know where to step next. So cut me some slack if I don't get too terribly overjoyed about this whole new set of land-mines you're placing in my path. You may be right about the whole Birth Certificate thing. I just don't care anymore! Is there something wrong with not wanting to know any more information right now? I refuse to ignore the legal advice of a professional lawyer who is helping me keep my wife from dying. He said you are wrong! That you're trying to live in the 1700's instead of the 21st century! I don't want to buy what you are selling. The cost is too high: I am not willing to pay it."

Robert's initial reaction to Joe was complete disbelief, but as Joe's response began to register, his heart sank within him. He walked over to the window and stared down at the lake. He wanted to scream. He wanted to pound his fists on the wall and make the world listen or at least the Christians hear him. He wanted to shake Joe hard and make him think, but it was clear Joe didn't want to be roused from his current circumstances. Under his breath, Robert mumbled the word "coward." Robert checked his emotions and decided it was time to leave. "I. . . I am sorry Joe, I'm sorry for you, for Mary, and for your child. I'm sorry for myself. It appears I wasted several days of my life here trying to give you a gift that you now refuse to take. I have been giving up time with my wife and children, to come and be your friend. I am not abandoning you Joe, but you are rejecting me. You have my phone number and e-mail. If you change your mind or if you really need me, you know how to reach me. I'm going to leave now, before I say something I'll regret." With that final statement, Robert picked up his cooler and his sack and walked out of the hospital room and slowly down the hall.

An empty feeling inside of Joe's soul rose up. He hadn't meant to hurt Robert. He just couldn't handle any more of his crazy ways. *Maybe in a few days he would give him a call and patch things up. If Robert was willing to drop the whole Birth Certificate/ Social Security number thing, they could still be friends.*

Mr. Elder sat at his desk. It was the last week of July now, and he was faced with some difficult decisions. The board was still hung over the issue of church unincorporation, four against four — with his vote breaking the tie! But he hated to make such a major decision without a majority approval of the board. And without Corbin's approval, the four remaining board members would not change their minds. Yet Corbin's mind would not be changed on this issue. He was firm, rock solid on the issue.

Thinking back over the past thirty-five years, he had a hard time doing what he knew had to be done. The state was requiring a new boiler for the school at a cost of approximately $65,000. The old boiler was about 45 years old, and yes, it would need to be replaced someday, but for now it still ran, and they could make do with it. They certainly didn't have the money to replace the heating system.

The school had never had air conditioning. It wasn't needed much in Chicago since they didn't hold school in the summer. Now the state was requiring they install air conditioning at a cost of $250,000. There were lists of other necessities. The most humorous of which was the requirement they change the standard toilet in the men's bathroom to an elongated and install another urinal. The school could probably afford to do that repair, but $315,000 for the heating and cooling systems was nowhere in the budget. Top that with the legal battle they were facing with the Iris Wethers' case. It was a recipe for disaster. On top of all that, Corbin wanted to take on whoever-it-was in a case of Grace Christian Academy Inc. Verses the State of Illinois. Corbin was hoping the American Defenders Foundation would pay for that case. It was certain the school didn't have the money for it, but would it matter once the school was closed?

Mr. Elder bowed his head in prayer. At the School Board's last meeting a week ago they discussed the very real possibility that the school might have to close. Now, last night, over the phone Mr. Elder and the board members had decided it was best for Mr. Elder to call each of the families in the school and inform them there would be no school in the fall. As a result they would have to make other arrangements for their student's education.

Mr. Elder pulled up the school roster for 2007 on his computer. Abram was the first name on the list, a new family to the school. The Abram family was in the process of adopting a teenage girl, a distant cousin who needed a home. Mrs. Abram home-schooled her other three *or was it four? four biological children,* but DCFS wouldn't let her homeschool the foster child until she was legally theirs. Their school had been a halfway point for them until the adoption went through. Their only other option would be the public school, and of course they didn't want to take that option. Mr. Elder hated to let the Abram family down, but what could he do? Quickly, he looked up their address on Google maps. The next closest Christian school was twenty miles from the Abram's home. He would call the principal there first thing tomorrow and see if they could fit this special situation student in for fall.

Brooks, their seven oldest children had all attended GCA, and their eighth son was a senior this year. They were like family to him. They couldn't be his first call.

Mr. Elder rubbed his eyes. It was nearly three o'clock. Maybe if he started at the bottom of the list he'd do better. Whetler, Mr. Elder dropped his head. How could he call them? They were the most desperate case of all. Just 18 months ago, Mr. Whetler's wife had died birthing his eleventh child. Prior to her death, his wife had home educated their nine school age children. Mr. Whetler's mother, a widow who walked with a walker, now lived in their home caring for the 18-month-old and 3-year-old. But she was not well enough nor did she have the energy to care for the home plus teach the older nine children. The father worked as an auto mechanic, but couldn't afford GCA. Last year, he had paid $2,000 to the school for the education of his children. Other church and school members had paid the rest for the education of the older children. Public school would be their only option or maybe some type of video school, but then Mr. Elder knew the home they lived in was only about 2000 square feet. It would be hard to do a video school for all those different grade levels in such a small area. Mr. Elder sifted through his mind trying to think of a single woman who might donate her time to help educate the children in Mr. Whetler's home. He couldn't think of anyone. Maybe one of the other Christian schools in the area would take the Whetler family on, but he doubted it. They certainly didn't have the money to pay tuition.

Maybe if he tried the middle of the list. Moore, no that was no good. Their situation was nearly as desperate as the Whetlers. The mother had terminal cancer, and their two daughters were being sponsored in the extra mercy group as well. Mr. Elder changed screens again. Nineteen students, the nine Whetler children, the Moore's two daughters, and seven other students were part of the extra mercy group. The parents paid what they could afford and private individuals made up the rest of the tuition. Oh God, what can we do for these families?

Mr. Elder smiled a funny smile as he thought of his favorite group of the students, and how disappointed they would be not to be able to return to GCA in the fall. He didn't believe it was right to show favoritism, but he couldn't help but be partial to this group of thirty one students. Each and every one of them had the privilege of calling him Grandpa.

Falling to his knees there in his office, Mr. Elder bowed his head and sought the presence of the Lord, pouring his heart out. Why God? What good could come of this? Quietly, in his heart, the Spirit seemed to be speaking to him. You haven't asked the parents and student body to pray for this situation. Mr. Elder cringed. Yes, a number of the families knew about the challenges the school was facing, but Mr. Elder had not gone public with prayer requests, for fear of the many questions that would arise. Rising to his feet, Mr. Elder again pulled up the roster for the school and dialed the Abram family. The phone rang on the other end, and a voice picked up the phone.

"Mr. Abram," Mr. Elder questioned. "Yes," a man's voice replied. "Mr. Abram, this is Mr. Elder from Grace Christian Academy. I've called to ask a favor of you. Our school is in serious trouble, and we may not be able to hold school this fall. We are facing the very real possibility of being forced to close our doors. Could you and your family pray for us, that God's will be done in this situation?" "Yes, we'd be glad to," was the reply on the other end of the phone. "Thanks, we appreciate it," Mr. Elder replied as he hung up the phone. A peace that passes all understanding filled Mr. Elder. He wasn't sure what was going to happen, but he felt certain God was already working in this area. Romans 8:28 flooded his mind. If the school closed, God must have some other, bigger plan.

He proceeded down the list with a renewed hope all the way to Mr. Whetler. Within hours thousands of people were praying for the little Christian school, as prayer chain after prayer chain added them to their list. The unified prayers of thousands of praying saints of God were at work. As these saints lifted up the school to their heavenly father they were unleashing the most powerful force in the entire universe and beyond.

As these prayers reached the throne room of God a wave of fear and terror swept over the principalities and powers, and the rulers of the darkness of this age, who were at work to destroy the little school and church. The spiritual hosts of wickedness were being faced with a multitude of warriors in the heavenly places equipped for battle. Unknown to the praying saints, this battle was being extended to the hospital where Mary Smith lay.

At the home of Corbin Cutler, the outpouring of prayer for Grace Christian Academy was about to bring about a divine chain of events that would finally equip an unsuspecting warrior with the truth that had been hidden from him for so long. [1]

Chapter 21

For my part, whatever anguish of spirit it may cost, I am willing to know the whole truth; to know the worst and provide for it. —Patrick Henry

It is better to fail in a cause that will ultimately succeed than to succeed in a cause that will ultimately fail. —Peter Marshall

Blind patriotism is idolatry. —Albert James Dager

But what things were gain to me, these I have counted loss for Christ. Yet indeed I also count all things loss for the excellence of the knowledge of Christ Jesus my Lord, for whom I have suffered the loss of all things, and count them as rubbish, that I may gain Christ and be found in Him, not having my own righteousness, which is from the law, but that which is through faith in Christ, the righteousness which is from God by faith... (Philippians 3:7-9).

The drizzling rain outside made Corbin's heart heavy for the welcome sight of home. In the past, when his wife was alive and children at home, the sight of the house, lit up and waiting for his arrival had always cheered his heart. However, now as he pulled into the suburban driveway and opened the garage door a deep sense of loss filled his soul. The garage was dim, and as he opened the door to the house, it was dark and quiet inside. There were no warm lights to welcome him, no smells of supper simmering on the stove. No tender hugs or kisses to greet him. *If only Katie was there to welcome him home,* he thought to himself. A pang of grief stung his heart as he thought of Katie's reaction to his forbidding her marry or even see David. *She will come around some day,* he reasoned within himself, *when she finds the right guy. Some day she would thank him for not letting her marry that lunatic.* Corbin's gaze locked onto the family picture on the table in the hall. It always reminded him of a happier time when the four of them, his wife, son, daughter, and himself lived together.

Corbin smiled to himself as he remembered what his life once was. Happy memories were all he had left of the dead loved ones in this life. He tried to recall the Bible verse about heaven, and no more tears, but he couldn't remember it. The rainy day fit his mood today, cold and dreary. He dropped the bills, junk mail and a couple of packages on the table as he placed his coat on the set of hooks Justin had made for the family several years ago. He left his coat hanging next to the three empty hooks in the hall and headed for the kitchen.

Life has really changed, he thought as he opened the freezer door and rummaged through the stack of frozen dinners attempting to find something that looked interesting. He missed his wife, and he missed her cooking, especially now as he dropped a rock-hard frozen dinner on the granite countertop. Peeling it out of the box, he compared the contents to the picture that had enticed him to make this selection, "False Advertising" he said as he placed it into the microwave with a vain hope it would look more appetizing when it came out.

Corbin sat alone at the table drinking his water and waiting. A sad mood pervaded his existence. Though not one given to emotion, even Corbin had to admit—he was lonely. Sadly, he also felt too numb to pray. Although he knew he should, he just didn't.

Retrieving the mail, he rummaged through it trying to fight off the forlorn feelings with busyness. His eyes darted across a package written to him in a masculine hand. He glanced at the name of the sender, and a flash of anger swept across his face again: Robert Forbes! *How did that clown get my home address?* Corbin tossed the package across the table. *No use dealing with that now. There will be nothing but bad news in there.* The microwave sounded and Corbin pulled his "savory beef" from the black box, comparing it to the picture once again. *Not much improvement, definitely false advertising.* He left the dinner on the counter next to the box. Inside him churned a hunger that couldn't be filled by a frozen dinner.

He was in one of *those moods* as his wife had called them. His wife always knew how to cheer Corbin up and bring him out of these moods. But since her death, he found himself spending more and more time taking life way too serious. He glanced up again at the family picture. His wife smiled down at him. Her pretty face, green eyes and auburn hair, even now, sent a ray of sunlight into his soul.

Taking the familiar picture into his hands, Corbin sat down and looked at the faces of his beloved family, leaving a fingerprint on the glass as he touched each one with his finger. Katie was the only one he had left, and even now she was somewhat estranged from him, *because he had ordered David out of his house and forbidden her to see him again.* Katie had grown up and become a beautiful young woman since this photo was taken, but to Corbin she would always be daddy's little girl with the toothless smile and freckle-covered nose. Time had only improved her looks in his eyes. It wasn't surprising to him that she looked more like her mother every day.

He studied his son's face in the picture he held as he wiped the fingerprints from the glass with his napkin. The remembrance of Justin brought joy, and yet pain. The tall, handsome, dark-haired boy with a serious look in his eyes had always tried to make his father proud. It pained Corbin to think of Justin's death and the last angry, bitter words he had spoken to his son.

Justin always had a tender heart for anyone who was hurting, and he always had a desire to see people saved from their sins.

Corbin walked to the study. He would read some of Justin's old e-mails and the few handwritten letters he had received from him. It would be *almost* like having his son there with him again, for a little while at least. Sitting down at the computer, Corbin pulled up the special file where he kept all of Justin's correspondence, and began reading the letters one by one. Some were humorous, some serious, some spiritual; but they all brought a smile to the proud father's face. They seemed to bring Justin back, for a few minutes. Corbin wished he had given the letters, and his son, this much time and attention when he was alive.

As he read over a letter telling about Justin's Bible study group in Afghanistan, Corbin leaned back in his chair and was finally able to pray, "Lord help me to be more like my son Justin was —always seeking the truth." Even after his death, Justin was still helping draw him closer to God through his letters. He missed *his boy*. Corbin reached across his desk and held the picture once again. If only he could talk to Justin one more time. *In eternity he would,* he reminded himself. *In eternity he would.*

Enough of this sentimentality, he thought to himself. Corbin forced himself to close the file and focus on the here and now. He had work he needed to do. Pulling the drawer open, he rummaged around for a pen, to no avail. It had been a year or more since he had spent much time at this desk. It reminded him too much of the happy days before he had lost half of his family.

Feeling around underneath the heavy two-year-old Chicago phone book, he felt the edge of a bulk mailing box. *What is this thing doing under here?* Moving the phone book, Corbin pulled out the mysterious package and began studying the handwriting on the envelope taped to the outside of the box. It was written in the same flowing script he had just been reading. To Dad From Justin. A lone tear of joy mingled with grief slipped down his rough cheek. Emotions hard to explain welled up in his heart. A letter, an undiscovered letter from his dear son! With excitement he carefully, almost reverently, peeled the envelope flap back and pulled out the letter from within.

A long epistle lay before him, and Corbin smiled through the tears. The prospect of one final communication from his beloved son, and one of this length, was a treasure indeed. What could Justin have to say to his dad, and why had he not given it to him directly? Did he know he was going to die? Corbin looked at the date on the letter. Just about three weeks before he was killed in Afghanistan! He would open the box later. For now he would read, and continue to remember the only son God had given him. *Work would just have to wait.*

His hunger was now being satisfied. He walked slowly to the couch, he was going to savor this one last communication, and for a short time, fill the aching hole that was left in his heart.

Dear Dad,

I am praying that at the right time, when you can accept what I have to say, you will find this letter hidden in your old desk. I know you seldom use this desk in the study since Mom has gone on. Yet, I am praying God will allow you to find this letter at just the right time. Dad, since I've been in Afghanistan, my views have changed so much. I used to think our Government, the United States of America was just, and right, and good. I viewed us as the new Israel, and I thought, although there were a few problems in our government, all in all we did the right thing. I believed our foreign policy was good. I believed God would bless our actions in the Middle East. In addition, I viewed it as my job to follow the orders of my superiors without question.

I don't think we are the new Israel anymore. I've come to know and understand that we can't claim the promises God made to the nation of Israel. I am so tired of Christians quoting second Chronicles 7:14 and claiming it for the United States.

(If My people who are called by My name will humble themselves, and pray and seek My face, and turn from their wicked ways, then I will hear from heaven, and will forgive their sin and heal their land.)

I now understand that claiming that promise, for the USA, borders on heresy. That verse is part of a conditional promise which is made to Solomon at the dedication of the Temple. That promise is continued in verse 20 which says if we forsake God's statutes and commandments, he will drive us from the land and cast us out of His sight and bring calamity on us. Dad how can a Christian with a functioning brain cell want to claim that promise? This promise was made to a NATION of people, the nation of Israel, the JEWS. It was not made to the remnant of faithful followers within Israel. At that time the entire nation was considered God's people.

As a nation we have turned away from, and forsaken, God. According to their logic, those people claiming that promise would have God cast us out and bring calamity upon us. I don't want that! I throw myself on the blood of Jesus Christ and *His grace alone*! We don't have a national promise. We never have. We have personal individual promises. Jeremiah 3:14-15 says God will take us one from a city two from a family and give shepherds according to his heart who will feed us with knowledge and understanding. It's like Peter said in his second letter chapter 3, These untaught, unstable people are twisting the Scriptures to their own destruction, and being led away with the error of the wicked.

Dad, tonight when we sat at the dinner table, I said, 'If we would pull out of the Middle East tomorrow, I believe all our Arab problems would end.' You were very offended when I even hinted at the fact that our government might have made a wrong choice, and that that choice should be corrected. It's almost like you've set the US government up as an idol, and you can't believe they have let you down. You almost seem to enjoy the excitement and drama of this war, while all I can see are the souls dying and going to a lost eternity in the lake of fire. Sometimes Dad, you are so deceived by what is going on. You seem to hope, or think, if you can just fight the right battles, or elect the right officials we can change the country for the better. The wrongs we've done in the past will be forgotten, and everything will be all right.

Dad, even if there was a major revival in our land, which I am praying for; and even if Americans repented and turned their hearts and minds to God, I still don't think that would stop the coming disaster God has in store for our country. At one time, I believed following the agendas of my government was right. I was being patriotic. How could the US government be wrong? We had a godly beginning to our country, right?

Our pilgrim forefathers tried to do what was right, and they left us a superior form of government. Dad, any government, no matter how good, can be corrupted. Our republic has been perverted from what it was at its founding. In fact, I would go so far as to say our government is no better than the people it rules. The rulers are a reflection of the people. And our average American, and average Christian in the pew, are a far cry from what used to be the norm in this country.

Our churches, for the most part, are full of people with saved Christian hearts and pagan minds. They may be saved from their sin, but they continue to think like the world has trained them to think. Christians who think like the world have "stinking thinking." I believe the culture war is lost. It was lost a long time ago. We need to take the battle for truth and right thinking into the church, not into the world. The church needs to be *trained* to think like Christ. They need to be *transformed by the renewing of their mind*, that they may prove what is that good and acceptable and perfect will of God. (Romans 12:2)

The church is supposed to be salt and light to the world. I'm seeing mostly pepper, and darkness. No, it isn't funny, it is very, very sad. The average person in the pew is a materialistic socialistic, moral relativist that thinks like a pagan, or a humanist, and acts like anything but a godly person. These carnal Christians use the Bible as their guide only for what they consider *spiritual matters*, but in the areas of education, politics, economics, society, family, and everything else they leave their Bible on the shelf and act like the world! They have divided their life into categories. Few of these categories are considered spiritual and the majority are considered secular. Perhaps they attempt to live by the Bible in the spiritual areas, but they live by their own judgment within the rest of the categories. The average American is like the people of Israel during the days of the judges. "In those days there was no king in Israel and every man did what was right in his own eyes."

These carnal Christians are blinded to the problems created by dividing their life into many different categories viewed as sacred and secular. These people often contradict themselves in their thinking and actions. They justify this life of inconsistency since it occurs in a *secular category* of their life, or between a secular and sacred part of their life. These people have developed intellectual schizophrenia!

Dad I know these statements seem really strong, but please hear me out. I joined the Air Force to serve my country. They taught me to fly an airplane, to shoot things, to perform air strikes, and to keep the world "free." Dad, most of the people I shoot at are lost, and if I kill them, it's like I'm pushing them into the Lake of Fire. In the past I thought people who wouldn't fight were cowards. Sometimes they are, but I have now come to believe that there is a right and a wrong time to fight. Most of these people in Afghanistan are just trying to survive. They aren't cowards. They are just average people who have been invaded by a foreign military force (us) [1], and they resent us being in our country.[2]

Dad these people didn't do anything against the USA, and they aren't the real threat to our country.[3] They couldn't attack us on our own soil if they wanted to, but I am here killing them on their own soil. I've come to realize this is wrong!

In their minds we are no different than the Soviet invaders that tried to take them over before we were here. First the USSR tried to enslave these people, and we "helped" them get rid of the Russians. Now we are the ones trying to enslave. Yes the USA is backing thugs who are trying to enslave these people. We are not solving anything by being here. We are making it much worse. Instead of fighting with bottles, sticks, and clubs we arm BOTH sides to fight against each other so they can kill each other faster, and much more efficiently, with high tech weaponry.

The hate doesn't go away. It is multiplied and some of it is directed, and rightly so, toward the US military. They attack us, and we escalate the conflict by launching an air strike causing both sides to just seek more revenge. In many ways we are prolonging this mess. We are enabling them to continue fighting by being here, and supplying them with weapons. If left to them, I suspect they might decide it is all pointless to continue to fight. They might try and get along and quit killing each other. Even if they didn't quit fighting, at least we wouldn't be responsible for causing some of their deaths, as we are now.

I know the recruiters for the terrorists would have a much harder time getting volunteers to fight for their cause if we weren't in the Middle East. Getting support from the average man to go attack an unknown enemy far away, that poses no immediate threat to them, is almost impossible. However, getting support from the average man to defend his homeland against the foreign invaders is much easier. It is even easier to enlist his help if he believes them to be a threat to his home and immediate family. Most, who would not fight otherwise, are getting involved in the fighting here *because we have occupied their country* and they feel they need to protect their family and home against US!

All of this talk about spreading a democracy is insane. Dad, these people cannot have a government like ours. They don't possess the personal self-government, Christian understanding of history, and knowledge of the one true God to make that a reality. Democracy is a LIE. We don't have a democracy, at least not on paper. We have a representative REPUBLIC handed down to us by men with far more understanding of God and His word than we currently have in our churches today, let alone our country at large. Sadly, I fear since most people in our own country do not possess under-standing of these things either, we are well on our way to losing the very things about our country that once made it great. "Liberty can-not be established without morality, nor morality without faith."[4]

We should spread freedom by example, not by gunpoint. These people need an example, not a bigger gun with more bullets. I took an oath to support and defend the Constitution of the United States against all enemies, foreign or domestic. I often wonder if I am violating that oath every day by just being in Afghanistan. Since we've been here, several of us have come to the realization that fol-lowing many of the orders we receive daily is in direct violation of the very constitution we have sworn to protect. Please don't think wrongly of me, but several of my fellow officers and airman have refused to follow orders several times recently. Needless to say, that went over like a pregnant pole vaulter. I am not sure what will come of it all, but I took an oath to uphold the constitution, and I am bound by that oath to refuse to follow these unconstitutional or-ders. My commander suspects we will be reassigned, but where to is anybody's guess. They have forbidden any of us to go to the press with our refusal to follow orders. You aren't the press. You are my father, so I think I am safe in telling you this.

I have been reading some old congressional records of speech-es made by Congressman Ron Paul of Texas that my commander shared with me. He tells me Mr. Paul is writing a book that should come out sometime next year.[5] I have enclosed copies of his speech-es for you to take a look at. Please read the highlighted part very carefully Dad. I have a favor to ask of you. Could you find the time to read these articles for me, please? Maybe we can talk about them when I get home next time. When the book comes out next year, maybe we could buy a couple of copies and read and discuss what is in them like we used to do back in high school.

A tear traced its way down Corbin's rugged face, as he looked up from the letter. He would read that book, even though they would never be able to discuss it. He owed Justin that much. The official government letter had told him his son had died a hero. It explained to the family how his son had died on a classified Top Secret special mission. *You don't send someone who is refusing to follow orders on a classified top secret special mission, unless you know there's a pretty good chance they are going to get killed.* The thought cut through him like a knife, as a sickening feeling came over him. Had his son and the others been purposefully sent on a suicide mission, like King David had sent Uriah the Hittite on, to be permanently silenced? He took an oath to support and defend the Constitution of the United States against all enemies foreign and domestic. Had he encountered a very dangerous domestic enemy who had ordered his execution?

The tears flowed down Corbin's lined cheeks freely now, as the letter he held caused him to begin to question the status quo of his life. *What was God trying to tell him?* Corbin didn't believe in luck. Over the years he had come to understand, and know, God was in charge of everything. Mr. Elder called it Divine Providence when he taught it to his children at the school. Justin and Katie had been taught the principle of divine providence when they had attended Grace Christian Academy, and Corbin had just picked it up from his children as they had lived it out in front of him.

Corbin had to admit to himself as he sat there crying on the couch, *I am an argumentative, hard-headed fool, who has been stubborn to a fault.* Those qualities had helped him become a good lawyer, but they made him rather closed-minded when it came to new ideas. He may be stubborn, but he wasn't stupid. God was beating him over the head with this one, and he was finally getting the message. There was just too much evidence lining up for even hardheaded Corbin to ignore it now. The first blow to the head was from Katie's "fanatical" boyfriend, and that notebook he had put together to show him the truth. The second blow was dealing with the insanity at the school and Robert Forbes' seemingly insane idea of actually following the constitution and law *as written*. The final blow was finding a letter from his beloved son more than a year after his death, beginning with the words . . . *I am praying that at the right time, when you can accept what I have to say, you will find this letter hidden in your old desk.* All three instances of Divine Providence pointed him in the same direction, the direction he had been fighting against with all of his stubborn foolish pride. The Holy Spirit was stirring Corbin somewhere deep in his soul, giving him a burning desire to search out and find the truth. Corbin wiped his tears away so he could once again see well enough to read, and forced himself to read more of Justin's letter.

Dad we need to pull out of this mess and all go home. We need to send MISSIONARIES NOT MERCENARIES if we want to change the people in the one hundred and thirty nations plus that we have troops stationed in on a permanent basis. Most of them need to raise their own armies, and let ours go home. God does not intend the USA to be an international police force answerable to the UN. He wants us to send missionaries to every people group in the world, and we are way behind in fulfilling that mission. I know of several here who have refused to wear the uniform of UN peace-keepers. I was one of them! I am an officer of the United States military not a puppet in a pretty blue beret.

I am convinced that instead of making us safer at home in the united States, this and the many other undeclared wars we are fighting, are bringing us into danger on a much higher level than we have previously experienced. Most of the people I meet are just trying to survive, and they resent the oppressive foreigners (us) being in their country. Dad, the extreme radicals here have been trying for years to draw supporters with only nominal success, but we are helping them swell their ranks beyond their wildest dreams, just by being in their homeland. Men will do extreme things they would not normally do to protect their homes and loved ones. If we weren't here in Afghanistan, the average man wouldn't feel threatened by us and would not perceive us as an enemy. Sadly we are here, and they do see us as <u>the enemy</u>. We are the biggest help to the radical recruiter there is. I am now convinced WE are wrong to be here, and we should leave. I am tired of seeing people go home in a body bag fighting for NOTHING. I have asked my superiors "Why are we here? What are we fighting to accomplish? What is the mission objective?" There is NO objective, NO point, NO overall goal! They say we are just here following orders. *They* aren't even sure who the enemy is, or how to fight this unseen enemy. I know who he is, Satan, and I know how to fight him.

(I am back. I stopped and took a prayer break)

I don't know what lies ahead. I want to tell you Dad: I am getting out of the US Air Force the first chance I get. I know this will greatly displease you, but it's what I believe the Lord Jesus Christ would have me do. I cannot violate my oath to the constitution, and they keep asking me to do so. When I first came to Afghanistan, as you know, those UN peace keepers angered me greatly. I still believe they are wrong, but, beyond the issue of the UN, there are some deeper issues at hand. I went into this battle believing it was a just and right battle. I believed US occupation of the Middle East would make it not only a safer place, but also a place more open to the gospel of Jesus Christ. Since then, I have come to believe this war was a planned conflict by the powers-that-be to gain more control over the American people and the people of the world.

They, (the UN, international bankers, one world types, Communists—it's hard to pin point just one group) are undermining our sovereignty and keeping us too busy with the latest crisis to look at what is really going on in the world; while at the same time enslaving us with a bigger debt than we can ever pay off. [6]

Bringing war and destruction to the Middle East is not going to turn the hearts of these people to the Lord Jesus Christ. Dad there is a right and a wrong time for war. (See the article in the box attached on just war.)[7] This battle does not fall under these qualifications. A couple of months ago, some friends sent me this e-mail and information detailing how the Pentagon and World Trade Center bombings were a set up. (copy in the box) I know you will probably just dismiss this as conspiracy theory junk, but Dad I think if you would look at it, you would see there is really something scientific to it. If nothing else, G. W. Bush sure used the event to push forward the Patriot Act and the wholesale loss of America's freedoms. [8]

Many of those laws are not currently being enforced, and some think the American people will never let this happen. Remember back in the 1950's. No one believed abortion would ever be legal, but it is today, and a lot of people are making money off this murderous market. It's a slow process Dad, but it keeps getting worse and worse by degrees. Remember the story about boiling a frog?

Dad, I've thought and studied long on many of these "conspiracy theory" items, and I've found out most them can be proved well enough to hold up in a courtroom. There is enough substantial evidence behind them to convince me, and enough, I believe, to convince you too, if you will take an honest look at them. These items in the box aren't just theory for me anymore; there is too much hard evidence for these things to ignore them. I call myself a "conspiracy factist" since it isn't theory to me—it's fact. *They* have an agenda, and they are bringing it to fruition. It angers me to see what is going on in our world. I must admit for a time I avoided these issues, because I didn't want to come face-to-face with reality, or deal with the idea of an evil agenda.[9] It was easier to live in my own world of denial (that river in Egypt...Ha ha). I didn't want to have to change my life or my way of thinking to accommodate new ideas.

As I learned and studied more, my worldview began to change. After a time, God convicted me that I shouldn't be afraid of the truth. I need to face up to it. I started reading the New American magazine[10], and it opened my eyes to some things I'd never seen or heard before. I started reading original documents, and I dug out my big red books from high school. (you know the ones: Christian Heritage of The Constitution, etc.) Solomon was right when he said

234

in Ecclesiastes 1:18 "For in much wisdom is much grief, and he who increases knowledge increases sorrow." I was really depressed the more I read and studied about it, but then I started looking to the Lord, our Creator, and praying about these issues and God showed me the bigger picture.

Dad we may not be far from a great persecution of Christians and a world ruled by the UN, or worse. But every day, over 150,000 people enter eternity, many of them unprepared and destined for the Lake of Fire. I want to do something about all those unprepared people who are going into a lost eternity.

Yes, someone needs to be fighting in America for true separation of church and state. Yes, someone in America needs to be fighting for our freedoms which are being lost. But I'm convinced that God has other things *for me* to do. Dad I'm not a brilliant lawyer like you. I AM a soldier: I am a soldier in the LORD's army. I don't fight political battles well, nor do I have an eloquent, witty tongue to tell Americans how to avoid getting themselves entangled as slaves to the government, or how to protect themselves from the government. Warning them against enslaving their children by getting state Birth Certificates and Social Security numbers for them, or warning them against church incorporation—I don't have that gift. Those things are for another believer to do, but Dad I do have a heart for the lost. If I can, or maybe I should say when I get discharged from the military, LORD willing, I am going to go back to Afghanistan as a translator and spread the gospel. I have blood on my hands. Innocent, lost people have died at my hands. Oh Dad, I can almost hear their cries of torment in hell. Guilt for my part in all of this, and for their lost souls eternally in the Lake of Fire, burdens my soul and interrupts my thoughts daily. I want to do something to make a difference. I want to lead the Muslims, Communists, and atheists to a saving knowledge of the Lord Jesus Christ when I come back here to Afghanistan, as a missionary.

Dad, I run across a lot of people who know bits and pieces of what's really going on in this world, and yet, they don't want to do anything about the truth. Often they will say something like "That may be true, but my focus is on winning souls to Christ." That's great if that were truly their focus, but I can't think of the last time I saw one of these people handing out a tract, or talking about the Lord Jesus. Most of them are too busy with their own lives to care about winning souls, or what's really going on in the world.

Dad, it's people like this that you could reach—the average Christian sitting in the pew. They will believe you because you're a lawyer, and a Christian. Dad, someone needs to be out there telling them how to protect themselves, and their churches from encroaching government powers. I am praying God will reveal to you the truth, and make you His instrument. Dad would you be willing to pray that God will show you and help you understand the truth? Could you ask him to show you the truth no matter what the cost? You would probably be disbarred for taking a stand like the one I am proposing, but it is the right thing to do.

I have come to understand we all have a job to do in the Lord's army. You have been specially trained and are uniquely qualified to do things other people cannot do. You have been deceived like we all have. The Father of Lies is a master deceiver, but through Christ we can know the truth, and the truth will set us free. I thank God for what Mr. Elder taught me about government. I am just so very sorry I had to travel halfway around the world to kill my fellow man, and see all this misery to finally understand what he was talking about. Dad, there's a huge difference between the way things are, and the way things should be. As a follower of Christ, I have determined to give whatever time on this earth I have left to fight for the way things ought to be.

I am sorry most of this letter has been very depressing. I'm sorry to have to communicate to you this way, but when I try to talk to you in person, you won't listen to me. Your brain clicks into "lawyer mode," and you are no longer listening to me, you are too busy planning your rebuttal, and counter arguments to hear what I am saying. I pray this message is well-received, when God, in His perfect providential timing, leads you to this package. I have been praying for months that God will bless you with an understanding of the truth.

On a lighter note, I have been visiting with Katie's new friend David Brogden quite a bit, and I am impressed. He seems to be an on-fire squared-away Christian young man. He already knows way more than I do about constitutional issues and the proper role of government. He said his parents made a proper Christian worldview part of his home-school curriculum. He is going to a home church right now, and he absolutely loves it, and Katie does too. He was talking about church incorporation and how dangerous that is. When I get to the bottom of the mountain of books I'm currently reading, I think I'll check into that too. He scanned from his notebook a series of PDF files and e-mailed them to me. I have burned them to a disk for you. It's in the box as well.

Well, unless the *all-wise federal government* changes its mind, I should be done with my deployment in Afghanistan at the end of next month. I look forward to seeing you then.

Love, Your Son,
 Justin

Corbin laid the letter aside. His own dear son, a conspiracy factist. He wasn't sure what to make of all of this new information, but in his heart he knew that in the box Justin had left him there was a huge start at finding out the truth. He walked in to the kitchen table and laid his son's package next to the smaller one he had received from Robert Forbes. He opened the smaller package and looked at its contents. As he had suspected, it contained a recording of the discussion between Robert Forbes and Mr. Elder along with a handwritten note from Forbes saying he had been praying the Lord would place His hand upon him and cause him to see the truth. At the bottom of the page he saw a telephone number with a neatly written note beside it. "Call anytime day or night. Your Brother in Christ, Robert."

He picked up the packages containing David's notebook on CD, the articles, and the book from Justin, along with the contents of Robert's package and went to the library to grab his daughter's copies of "the red books" and his laptop with his electronic study Bible. *This is going to be a long week, possibly a long month,* Corbin thought to himself as he dropped his load on his old desk. But first, he'd start this study time out right by dropping to his knees. His Father was long overdue for an apology, thanksgiving, and some serious repentance. He would need the Holy Spirit to guide him in the way of all truth if he ever hoped to understand all of this.

During his time of prayer, the Holy Spirit placed it on his heart to make some phone calls before he dove into the mountain of information his son had left him. First he would call Katie and David to ask them to pray for him as he began to study the things David had mentioned in his notebook. After that, he would call Robert Forbes and Mr. Elder and asked them to continue praying as he searched for the truth. Once he had loved ones praying for him, he would proceed to chew through this elephant sized pile of information one bite at a time, and that promised to be much more satisfying than the cold microwave dinner of "savory beef" that still sat on the counter in the kitchen. The Holy Spirit recalled John 4:34 to Corbin's memory, "My food is to do the will of Him who sent Me, and to finish His work." Corbin set to work on this feast, with a hunger in his soul he hadn't known for a long time. He would do God's will, God's way, not Corbin's way this time.

CHAPTER 22

"One man with courage is a majority." —*Thomas Jefferson*

"Is it not the great end of religion, and, in particular, the glory of Christianity, to extinguish the malignant passions; to curb the violence, to control the appetites, and to smooth the asperities of man; to make us compassionate and kind, and forgiving one to another; to make us good husbands, good fathers, good friends; and to render us active and useful in the discharge of the relative social and civil duties?" —*William Wilberforce*

Corbin sat leaning back in his chair and stretched as he surveyed his large desk, looking at the organized piles he had arranged by category. The deeper he dug, the more his hunger grew. The Holy Spirit was revealing to him truths that he had been turning a blind eye to for years. He landed his elbows firmly on the edge of the desk and ran his fingers through his hair, resting his head in the palms of his hands. Had it been hours or days since he had slept? He wasn't sure, and he didn't care. It was clear to him by now that God was giving him supernatural strength, and blessing him with understanding he hadn't had before. As he sat there, he remembered the story of Elijah being sustained for 40 days on the food provided by the angel as he fled from Jezebel. This hadn't been 40 days; in reality it had been only four. Corbin was unaware of the passing of time as he studied. He hadn't moved from his desk during this time except to go to the bathroom, or grab another book from the shelf.

He knew he should be hungry, but he wasn't. He knew he should be tired, but he was wide awake. How many times had chills run down his spine as the Holy Spirit revealed another truth to him, or showed him the connection he hadn't previously seen between two seemingly unrelated things?

He had started by watching the DVD of the conversation between Elder and Forbes. He had been avoiding watching the DVD for the past few weeks, but now his hungry mind devoured the information it contained. He had paused it many times to take notes, or to grab the big red books and look things up for himself. From there he switched discs and began methodically chewing his way through David Brogden's notebook. This young man repeatedly amazed Corbin with his thoroughness and documentation. Corbin couldn't count the number of times he had shook his head in disbelief saying out loud to himself, "No, that can't be right!" However, each time he had followed the careful documentation of David Brogden, he discovered the young man to be correct, not only from a biblical perspective but from a legal one as well. *It was a shame this kid didn't want to go into law, Corbin thought to himself. He certainly had the mind for it.* Corbin then ravenously chewed through the books and articles his son had left him. As he pulled out the last of the items Justin had enclosed in the package, he noticed something he hadn't seen before. Stuck in the bottom was a USB thumb drive.

The thumb drive contained several documents filled with hypertext links to research his son had been conducting. It outlined his plans for the mission work he was going to do in Afghanistan. This was something he would have to look into later. Then he noticed the folder of a different color set apart by itself. It was labeled "My vision for Dad." As he opened the file he noticed that it contained three documents. As he opened and scanned the first document he realized it was an electronic copy of the letter his son had given him. The second document was a lengthy Bible study with multiple scripture references titled "Things I wish my Dad would read." The third document was titled "My dream." As he clicked to open the file he read the following. . .

I had a dream last night. I won't say it was divinely inspired, but it may have been. I have been praying and fasting a lot lately that my Dad would see the truth about what is going on in this world. About how Satan has infiltrated almost every major church denomination as we were warned about by Paul the apostle, "and after my departure savage wolves will come in among you not sparing the flock" Acts 20:29. "Woe to them! For they have gone in the way of Cain, have run greedily in the error of Balaam for profit, and perished in the rebellion of Korah.

These are spots in your love feasts, while they feast with you without fear, serving only themselves. They are clouds without water, carried about by the winds; late autumn trees without fruit, twice dead, pulled up by the roots; raging waves of the sea, foaming up their own shame; wandering stars for whom is reserved the blackness of darkness forever." Jude 11-13

This evening, I have been studying those verses and meditating on them. I'd fallen asleep and this is the best I can remember of my dream.

I was at church back home and everybody had on these strange glasses but they didn't know it. We were singing hymns and having church. I reached up and felt my face: I had on glasses too, but they were locked onto my head. I prayed that God would help me take the glasses off. I just felt in my spirit they were evil. Then it got weird and everything changed and I was in a room with David Brogden and he handed me his notebook. As I opened up the front cover, it said "Brother Justin, receive your sight." David turned the page and the book became a key, which he took and unlocked my glasses. David told me to take the glasses off and see the truth. I reached up and took off the glasses and placed them in my shirt pocket. I could see clearly. When I looked down, I was holding a Bible, and I was back in church. I looked toward my Dad who was standing beside me wearing those glasses. I looked around the church, and I saw a very large man wearing a T-shirt and jeans and big rubber boots. He pulled the glasses off of Mr. Elder. Then the man was gone: he just disappeared.

Mr. Elder ran around pleading with everyone to take off the glasses, but they just sang the hymn louder and ignored him, like they couldn't hear him. Then a man dressed in a fancy church robe, like I've seen on the movies, came down the center aisle and everybody smiled and welcomed him there. I couldn't see his face because of the crowd. I looked down and the glasses I had taken off were in my pocket. I held them up to look through them without putting them on, and I could see the man clearly. He was a clean-cut fellow with a broad smile and a friendly face. I threw down the glasses and stomped on them shattering both lenses. When I looked up again the man had the head of a Dragon. I tried to tell the people, but they just sang louder.

Turning to my Dad, I grabbed his arm, pulling him towards me. The glasses slid down his nose just a bit, but he immediately shoved them back on and straightened them properly. I tried to remove his glasses but he just pushed me away and handed me my Air Force uniform. Then I was back in Afghanistan putting things in a box addressed to my Dad. After this was done, I handed the box to a big man in a white robe, and he walked with me into the next room. The next thing I knew I was back at my parent's home sitting at the desk putting the box in the drawer under the phone book according to the instructions of the large man in the white robe.

As I stood up, I was back in the church standing beside my Dad in the pew where we sat growing up. I saw Mr. Elder and the man in the rubber boots each holding a CD that turned into a key. They reached up together, each having a key, and unlocked my Dad's glasses. Then I looked down into my hands and I was holding the box I had placed in Mom's desk. I opened the box and it contained a letter which I gave to my Dad. The letter said "My dear father, In the name of Jesus Christ, please remove the glasses so you can see the truth." He turned to me, stopped singing, and smiled. He then reached up and removed his glasses and something like scales fell from his eyes. There were tears in his eyes, and he reached out to me, but he couldn't touch me.

I pointed to the Dragon in the clerical robes as the Dragon called out a new song. The congregation began to sing the new song. It was a strange song that I couldn't understand, and they were being led by the Dragon. Then Mr. Elder took the key with which he had unlocked my Dad's glasses, and he called the other elders and deacons of the church and school to him. As the deacons and elders looked on, the key became a CD once again. He held it up to the elders and deacons for all to see, and they removed their glasses. The elders and deacons turned to my Dad and pointed to the Dragon in the clerical robes. My Dad walked out to the sign in front of the church and ripped the name of the church from the top of the sign. The name of the church disappeared as soon as he removed it from the sign. Then my Dad and the man in the rubber boots grabbed the beast in the front leading the songs who looked like a dragon, and stripped him of his robe. My Dad grabbed the Dragon, carrying him down the middle aisle of the church and threw him out, never to return.

The next part of the dream was really weird. I'm not sure how to describe it, but I will do my best. My Dad was as big as a giant. He walked around 'till he came to a church. He would then reason with the members and hold up the disk that had become a key which Mr. Elder had given him. He asked if he could remove the name of the church from the sign on the front of the building. If the members removed their glasses and allowed him to remove the name on the building, he would reach through the roof of the church building without damaging the church roof at all, removing the dragons masquerading as men from the churches. He stripped them of their robes and placed them in a bag he carried. Sometimes he would pull out a wolf dressed in the skin of a sheep along with the Dragon. He would remove the sheep skin and stuff the wolf into the bag with the dragons.

Walking throughout the country he went to the churches one after another showing them the disk that had become a key. Some of the churches refused to let him remove the name from their building and refused to remove their glasses. He would reach into their building and remove the Dragon and the wolf showing them to the people, but they would invite the dragon and the wolf to stay and tell my Dad to go away and leave them alone.

He carried the contents of his bag to the state capitol building and dumped them on the lawn. On the lawn, the dragons turned into men carrying briefcases and they walked up the front steps of the capitol building and went inside. The wolves ran to the churches that had refused to have their name removed and the people there clothed them in sheep skin and welcomed them in.

This is what I can remember of my dream. I don't know what it means: I just know it was so real I needed to write it down:

But this is what was spoken by the prophet Joel:
'And it shall come to pass in the last days, says God,
That I will pour out of My Spirit on all flesh;
Your sons and your daughters shall prophesy,
Your young men shall see visions,
Your old men shall dream dreams.
And on My menservants and on My maidservants
I will pour out My Spirit in those days (Acts 2:16-18).

As Corbin finished reading the file he sat there in stunned silence. He didn't understand what it all meant either, but he understood most of it. God had made this whole thing clear to his son more than a year ago, before his death. Corbin's pagan worldview glasses had been removed. David Brogden, his son Justin, Mr. Elder, and Robert Forbes had all been key players in removing the scales from his eyes and helping him see the truth.

"For by grace you have been saved through faith, and that not of yourselves; *it is* the gift of God, not of works, lest anyone should boast. For we are His workmanship, created in Christ Jesus for good works, which God prepared beforehand that we should walk in them" (Ephesians 2:8-10).

"He who has an ear, let him hear what the Spirit says to the churches. To him who overcomes I will give some of the hidden manna to eat. And I will give him a white stone, and on the stone a new name written which no one knows except him who receives it" (Revelation 2:17).

Talking out loud to himself, Corbin said, "Incorporation of the church name allows these dragons to enter and take control of what was once the church. The church is incorporated under a certain name and registered with the state or federal government. The incorporated churches become not-for-profit commercial entities under the complete control of the state. They promise perks and privileges which they can remove for any reason, at any time." Corbin still had not put together exactly how, but in the last few days he had definitely nailed down the what, and why. Justin's dream had been right. The incorporated names must be removed to free the church of state control. This was only a first step, however. If the churches were free, but, the individuals within them were still enslaved to the corporate system, little would change.

David Brogden's notebook had pointed him in the right direction. He needed to research more about Birth Certificates and Social Security numbers. They seemed to be the key to the enslavement of the American people. He needed to do more research to find out how this fraud could be overcome for the people who already had Birth Certificates and Social Security numbers. But how to protect the children that would be born from this day forth was easy. David's research was clear and complete. Christians should never sign their children into slavery by agreeing to a state-issued Birth Certificate contract, and they should never enter into a contract for a Social Security number. Those were the two documents, contracts actually, that were used to lay the foundation to defraud and enslave the people.

Corbin Cutler bowed his head and asked God where to begin. Joe Smith came to his mind. As the Holy Spirit replayed Joe's question in Corbin's mind, "Would getting a state Birth Certificate, and Social Security number on my child enslave them to the world's system?" He had lied to Joe. He had not known it at the time, but Joe was now believing a lie because of Corbin. He was going to enslave his child into the world's system if things weren't changed. He felt overwhelmed. He had done so much damage. How would he ever repair all of the damage he had caused? Well, he had to begin somewhere, and Joe Smith was a good place to start.

He called Joe Smith to apologize for lying to him. Joe was confused and shocked at this news. Corbin explained that Robert Forbes had been absolutely correct concerning the church incorporation issue and he suspected he was right regarding the Birth Certificate information although he had not had time to study that issue out totally. God had recently revealed to him the truth, and while he was still learning, he knew enough now to know that Robert Forbes was speaking the truth. Following the phone call to Joe Smith, Corbin felt led to place another phone call to Pastor Gray.

"Pastor Gray this is Corbin Cutler. At the board meeting you said if you can convince Corbin to change his mind on this issue, I will gladly and willingly change mine. Well, I have changed my mind sir. No that's not right, the Lord Jesus Christ has shown me the truth, and the truth has set me free. Pastor Gray, I was wrong and Robert Forbes and Mr. Elder are absolutely correct in what the school needs to do. I now support their efforts 100%, and I will do everything in my power to get the church and the school to unincorporate as quickly as possible."

Pastor Gray couldn't help but say, "Are you sure?"

"Yes," was Corbin's confident reply, "If you want, I'll get together with you, and I'll show you what I've learned. Pastor, could you please call the other men on the board and inform them of this change?"

A very confused Pastor Dennis Gray agreed to make those phone calls.

Corbin picked up the note from Robert Forbes that read "*Call anytime day or night*, your brother in Christ, Robert." He dialed the number and smiled, wondering what crow really tasted like.

CHAPTER 23

"Most people, sometime in their lives, stumble across the truth. Most jump up, brush themselves off and hurry on about their business as if nothing had happened." —Winston Churchill

"Whether we like it or not the morals to which we subscribe as a people are vital for our survival as a free nation. Concerned citizens are beginning to wonder if we may not be in grave danger of rejecting those things which are the source of our nation's strength." — J. Edgar Hoover

"If to be feelingly alive to the sufferings of my fellow-creatures is to be a fanatic, I am one of the most incurable fanatics ever permitted to be at large." — William Wilberforce

"So enormous, so dreadful, so irremediable did the Trade's wickedness appear that my own mind was completely made up for Abolition. Let the consequences be what they would, I from this time determined that I would never rest until I had effected its abolition." — William Wilberforce

Joe Smith closed the Bible he had been reading, zipped up the cover, and tenderly set the precious volume aside on the table. Reading aloud to Mary and his son had become a normal part of his day now. He rose and went over to Mary, squeezing her hand and reassuring her of his love.

Mary could feel the squeeze of her hand and hear Joe's soft comforting voice speaking to her. She willed her body to move. It just wouldn't respond. Still the fact that she could hear was something. She wondered how long she had been asleep this time. She clung to whatever Joe might have to say. She couldn't move, but she could still listen.

There were days Joe awakened full of hope and courage. Other days he awoke with a sense of despair and discouragement that were almost unbearable. Guilt was the friend of despair and discouragement. The "if only's" flooded his mind. If only he had told Mary to wait until he came to pick her up on that fateful day. If only he had. . . the list was endless and if he wasn't careful this line of thought led him to questioning why God had even allowed this trial in his life. In contrast, the days he remembered to focus on Christ were the ones full of hope and courage. Focusing on Mary and her seemingly hopeless situation caused despair and discouragement, but Joe had not yet made that connection. He did notice however, when he focused on things other than Mary being in a coma, things seemed to go better for him mentally.

Rachel had come last week with the Doppler, and the baby's heartbeat was quick and steady. He wondered why the doctors hadn't suggested they do another sonogram? He'd love to see what the baby looked like now, but since Dr. Rodriquez had been removed as his doctor, no one besides Rachel seemed to take much interest in his son. His son was still alive. He at least had that to still be thankful for. Joe had lost track of time since the accident, each passing day blended with the next in a blur. Joe's hope grew that his son, maybe mentally retarded, maybe handicapped, would survive. But, with thoughts of his precious son, came the realization that each day was a day closer to that dreaded decision of whether or not to try to have the baby taken by C-section. Only last week, Dr. Bartlett had spoken with Joe on the issue assuring him if the baby did survive to a viable age, they would have to take the baby premature by C-section. Mary's brain dead body would never go into labor on its own. It wouldn't be safe for the baby if it did. "What would be the effects of a C-section on Mary," Joe questioned the doctor. The doctor looked at Joe like he was stupid. "We may be able to save your handicapped child," the doctor had impersonally answered Joe as he left the room. Joe's head throbbed with pain and his mind spun. *O God, I have no good choices. If I will save my son's life, I must give up Mary, and if I give up Mary. . . O God show me what you would have me do.* For now Joe's best option seemed to be to wait it out. . . give it some more time. He prayed daily for his wife's recovery, but for now, waiting to see what the Lord would allow was all he could do, and when he thought of Mary's eternal destiny, he begged God to spare her life at least long enough for her to be saved.

Sometimes Joe would think back to the long busy days at Grace Christian Academy and remember how he used to long for, even pray for, some time to himself, just to rest and read. How ironic now he dreaded that very thing. It seemed all he had was time to himself to rest and to read. With all his spare time, he had finished three years' worth of reading assignments for the school in the last month and a half. He had learned more in the last month about the providential history of the United States and the principal approach of education than he knew what to do with. Things were definitely not like they used to be in this country, and Joe was firmly convinced they used to be much better in all of the ways that mattered. There was so much more he wanted to know, but when he got on the Internet he found so much revisionist history and outright lies he became discouraged.

Computer files could be changed or deleted without a trace of the change. Books, on the other hand, once printed, were static and unchanging. He had taken to reading a large number of the books Robert had faithfully brought to him. They made sense and were well written, but sometimes they seemed out of touch with reality. Following a long logical argument laid out in print was getting easier for Joe the more he read. At first he discovered that the Internet had changed the way he processed information. He was easily distracted and found himself wanting a video or a summary instead of having to wade through the whole document himself. He did read a summary or two from the Internet, but when he took the time to read the original and compared it to the summary he had read, he found the summary often said exactly the opposite of what the original document actually said. Joe was getting frustrated at the systematic web of lies he found.

He had asked Mr. Elder to bring his college history book to the hospital when he picked up some more clothing at Joe's house. He was so disgusted at what he read he almost threw it away, but then, on second thought. . . he began to read and compare the college book to the original documents and pictures. He started at the beginning of the history book and highlighted every lie or omission, so he could show these lies to skeptics later when they doubted his word. He made a file on his laptop with copies of the original documents and set up a cross-referenced database by page numbers to his college textbook.

Joe studied a copy of a picture of Pocahontas with an unattractive scowl in his college history book. The caption read, "Pocahontas (circa 1596 - 1616) daughter of an Indian chief aided the first English colonists and later married one of them. She is shown here in the clothes she wore in England where she went with her husband John Rolfe." This picture was being sold at the National Parks Gift Shop near Jamestown. Joe had discovered an actual full-color oil painting with a bright pleasant-looking Pocahontas (a nickname given by her father, her real name was Matoaks) was on display at the Smithsonian. This painting was made from an engraving of the original drawings. The revisionists had turned a beautiful full-color picture of an attractive Christian lady with an amazing history and Christian testimony into a dull, black and white, sterile, scowling, insignificant nothing! The true history had been replaced by meaningless information, devoid of any mention of God or purpose. He slammed the book shut and added another entry into his database.

He had been taught carefully-crafted lies in his public school education, and he was quickly realizing he had become a "public fool." His education consisted mostly of lies, deception, and re-worded summaries of historical documents contradicting the original, more often than not. Any mention of God or Divine Providence was often replaced by three little dots. (. . .) History in the "public fool system" had been so boring: meaningless dates, facts, and places memorized and regurgitated on multiple-choice or fill-in-the-blank tests. It would seem, other than to develop an absolute loathing of the study of history, these tests had no purpose. It wasn't even called history anymore. It was called social studies now. It was more like Socialist studies, Joe was coming to understand. Joe was starting to see he had not received an education, he had received an indoctrination.[1] He'd been trained to be a citizen in the global community, not a citizen of Illinois State. Providential history like he had been studying from original documents was exciting, encouraging, and enlightening. Studying the history of the United States from original documents was like a giant lighted sign with a blinking arrow pointing straight to Jesus Christ. It was no wonder the current powers-that-be did not want students studying history from original documents. They might actually learn the truth, and the truth would set them free.[2]

Now that he had a better attitude, the books Robert Forbes had recommended began to take an effect on Joe's thinking; and in his spare time, which he had plenty of, he had been on his laptop listing some notes and questions to discuss with Robert.

Joe had to admit, Robert had become his closest and most trusted friend. He had rescued his wife from certain death, and he had been his most faithful friend during these long weeks in the hospital. Joe still wrestled with Robert's unusual, even reactionary ideas. When Joe called him a radical, Robert would always explain, "On the geopolitical spectrum I am not a radical, I am a reactionary. I may be off the chart on the Reactionary side; but Radical is at the extreme other end of the spectrum. Radicals attack and try to destroy the status quo by any means available so it can be replaced with a Socialist or Communist dictatorship. Reactionaries, like me, however, are trying to stabilize society by working to restore our American Christian republic to its historic biblical foundations." Joe was learning more and more about the historic biblical foundations of our constitution and country, but he just wasn't sure that it was wise *or even possible* to go back to the way it used to be. So much had changed. *Could it ever be that way again?*

Robert's ideas were just a little too far out there; they were just too extreme! Even if the lawyer, Mr. Cutler, had assured Joe that Robert was right on the legal stuff, some of the things he knew about Robert made Joe rather uncomfortable. He didn't even like to talk about them much, but he felt compelled to know more, to search the matter out and really know the truth, and not to stop at anything short of the whole truth. Joe thought back to the day Robert and he had had that terrible disagreement. The words Robert had shared that night still hurt, "I am not abandoning you Joe, but you are rejecting me." Robert claimed Joe had refused the gift he was offering. After the unsuspected call from Mr. Cutler, Joe had called Robert and apologized for his outburst, and his rejection of Robert's gift. He asked Robert to visit him when he had the time. Inwardly, he hoped Robert would stop by soon. He had some serious questions for him. God had given Joe a hunger for truth, and he wanted the truth to set him free. In many ways he was isolated here in the hospital away from reality. He was free to search for the truth.

By his nature, Joe was a mild mannered man, and he had no desire to stick out like a sore thumb as Robert Forbes seemed to do. Left to himself, he was happy to go with the flow and be considered "normal" by those around him. He suspected the only *normal* at the Forbes residence was the dial setting on the dryer. On second thought, they might not have a dryer at all, they were so outside-the-box, they might just use a clothesline. Which would mean, as Joe first surmised, there might be nothing normal at their house at all.

While Joe mused over the state of things at the Forbes house, without ceremony, Robert Forbes entered the hospital room. Several tracts were stuffed in his shirt pocket, and his hair looked quite windblown.

Robert sat down with a casual "Hello" to Joe and handed him a bag containing a plastic food storage container and a plastic spoon. Without mentioning anything about their previous argument, he began the conversation in a normal enough way, by asking, "How you doin' Lad?"

Joe made no response except to nod his head up and down in a way that said, "Okay," as he stuffed a large mouth full of stroganoff and noodles into his mouth. Even cold, it was five times better than anything the hospital had to offer. Joe finished his meal in silence trying to word a question in his mind, while Robert tried to make casual conversation about all sorts of meaningless things. Robert could tell something was really bothering Joe as he sat there in silence. He could only assume it had something to do with their previous discussion on Birth Certificates and Social Security numbers. He decided to cut the small talk, sit quietly, and silently pray Joe would identify the problem. Maybe then he could be of some service to Joe and talk with him about it.

Finally, after he was done eating, Joe summoned the courage to speak. Without introduction he asked, "Why don't your children have Social Security numbers?"

Robert threw his head back and laughed a loud boisterous laugh. "So, is that what is bothering you today, Lad?" The ice was broken, and both men felt more at ease. "I wondered why you were so quiet. Well, let's see, where do we even begin with that one? From the look on your face, I suspect that is not the only thing bothering you today, but we will start with that and see how it goes. I'm glad you finally asked.

I guess since I don't have anywhere else to be for the next few hours, we can get into that discussion. But first let's have a word of prayer.

Joe quickly bowed his head and Robert started praying aloud, "Dearest Savior, help me to explain this to Joe. Help me not to leave anything out that is necessary for him to understand, and help me not to overwhelm him with too much information. Amen." Robert reminded himself what had happened when Joe had felt overwhelmed by his last attempt and didn't want a repeat performance.

"First of all I suppose I should determine how far back to go. I could go all the way back to Satan in the Garden of Eden, but I suppose that would take too long for today. I guess I should go back to the time of the establishment of social insurance. The Canadians accepted the idea with just this title, but the idea was renamed Social Security here in the United States, so it could be more efficiently sold to the Americans. Hand me that laptop lad," Robert said as he grabbed the little Macintosh and launched the web browser. He typed in the web address...

http://www.gemworld.com/EdMandellHouse.htm and showed the following to Joe.

Edward Mandell House had this to say in a private meeting with President Woodrow Wilson [1913-1921]:

"[Very] soon, every American will be required to register their biological property in a National system designed to keep track of the people and that will operate under the ancient system of pledging. By such methodology, we can compel people to submit to our agenda, which will affect our security as a chargeback for our fiat paper currency. Every American will be forced to register or suffer not being able to work and earn a living. They will be our chattel, and we will hold the security interest over them forever, by operation of the law merchant under the scheme of secured transactions. Americans, by unknowingly or unwittingly delivering the bills of lading to us will be rendered bankrupt and insolvent, forever to remain economic slaves through taxation, secured by their pledges. They will be stripped of their rights and given a commercial value designed to make us a profit and they will be none the wiser, for not one man in a million could ever figure our plans and, if by accident one or two would figure it out, we have in our arsenal plausible deniability. After all, this is the only logical way to fund government, by floating liens and debt to the registrants in the form of benefits and privileges. This will inevitably reap to us huge profits beyond our wildest expectations and leave every American a contributor to this fraud which we will call 'Social Insurance.' Without realizing it, every American will insure us for any loss we may incur and in this manner; every American will unknowingly be our servant, however begrudgingly. The people will become helpless and without any hope for their redemption and we will employ the high office of the President of our dummy corporation to foment this plot against America."

"Remember, one time you asked me about what house rules were when we were discussing Monopoly several weeks back? Here is another way to understand *house rules*. Mr. House helped establish the fraud-based system that unwittingly enslaves so many today. Most people in the United States have been registering their biological property for years by getting state Birth Certificates." Joe looked confused, but he continued to listen to Robert. "The Birth Certificate establishes a primary contract of ownership with the state. In previous generations birth records and marriage records were kept in the family Bible, as our family has done. Applying for a Social Security number gives you a number and puts you in their system so they can control your life. With those two fraudulent contracts you effectively have contracted to be a slave in debt forever. Most, who have studied this out, suspect they use people as collateral for the debt to create paper money backed by nothing else. Once this system had been in place for a number of years, the powers-that-be pulled us off a gold/silver standard and replaced it with a fiat money system.[4] Remember, the Bible says the borrower is slave to the lender. In this condition you no longer function under the protections guaranteed in the Constitution. You function under maritime/admiralty law and/or the Uniform Commercial Code. The beauty of the system they have devised is that each generation enslaves the next generation without even knowing it, while they are still children. The parents sign away legal custody of their children with the Birth Certificate. Application for a Social Security number becomes an application for your tax ID number, and employee ID number. From that time foreword you work for *them*."

Joe interrupted Robert's train of thought with a question, "Why didn't the first generation fight the change?" "Initially some did, but at this point this is the system most people are born into, and they don't know any different." Robert explained, "It's kind of like my ministry group in college when I was a sophomore. We made a major change in the Ministry's outreach from the way it had been done the previous twenty years. By the time I was a senior it became obvious that the change was a bad one, and I and several other seniors rallied to undo the change before we left, but we realized reverting back to the original way of sharing the gospel would be unlikely to happen. You see, the juniors and sophomores fought against us. When I asked one of the more vocal juniors in the group why they were so violently opposed to changing, their reply was, 'We can't change. This is the way we've always done it!' To me it was a bad change that had been made two years earlier; to him it was all he had ever known. I took him to the campus minister, who had been there since the ministry started, and I asked the campus minister to explain the history of campus outreach efforts there. The junior was shocked to learn the change to the only campus outreach methodology he had ever known had been made a week before that student had arrived at the campus. This junior, upon learning the history of the Ministry and how effective the previous method of outreach had been, was more than willing to change back to what had worked so much better the twenty years before he had arrived. He even helped us educate the others and get them to see what had taken place. So, you see Joe, people are very resistant to change from what they have always known. From my perspective it was a recent change that was done on a trial basis and didn't work. From their perspective, it was the way they had always done it, and they didn't want to change to something else.

Do you see how people raised to do something one way, and not allowed to see their history, will resist change? Once the generation that saw the change take place is gone, no one remembers the way it used to be. From that point on, and for every generation thereafter, the way it is, is the way it's always been. . . unless they are students of history.

Joe, you've been reading enough original documentation about the founding of this country to know the way things used to be is not the way things are today. This great country was founded on biblical principles and individual liberties. Many things have changed since then. Do we as Christians embrace these changes toward a pagan relativistic, Communistic slavery? Or do we fight the changes and work to restore this nation to its godly historical biblical foundation? The first thing we must do is break the cycle. That is why my kids do not have Birth Certificates, or Social Security numbers. I made an informed choice not to enslave my children. This is a choice, my friend, you will have to make for your own child very soon, Lord willing. It's not an easy choice, but it is the right choice for all Christians who know the truth.

Back to the quote by Edward Mandell House. You see, it is my understanding that House was a Jesuit priest and a self-proclaimed Communist who followed the ideals of Karl Marx. House wrote a book *Philip Dru : Administrator* in which he outlines his agenda for the United States, and his desire for Socialism and a system of governing society in which there is no private property. People with their 'biological property registered' become property. Registering a person establishes a presumption of ownership. House refers to people as stupid, lazy slaves (chattel), and as sheep going to the slaughter.

Joe, I could go on about him to tell about his Communist ties and how he was the mastermind behind the Federal Reserve Act; an act creating a privately-owned national banking cartel called the Federal Reserve. I could tell you how he was instrumental in the formation of the Council on Foreign Relations (CFR), the Trilateral Commission, the Bilderberg group, the depression of 1933, and how he was one of the many influential persons responsible for getting the US involved in World War I. He also worked to establish a progressive income tax, and initiate the war draft. House is just one man among many that I could tell you about Joe, but I think one is enough for now. I cannot pour out all of my reasoning in one afternoon. It would overwhelm and confuse you. I am not sure that this small bit of an answer hasn't overwhelmed you already. From the look on your face, I suspect this is going to take you some time to process." Joe nodded.

"I'm sure you would agree it is impossible to summarize twenty years of research and reasoning in a single afternoon. Please consider. Even if it were possible, you would not have the background or understanding to appreciate all of my arguments. Please understand that in saying these things, I'm not being arrogant, or proud, and I am not calling you stupid. I am just being realistic. If most of the people I know had brought up the question you just asked me, I would've smiled and given them no answer at all. When you asked me that question, however, I answered you as I would have answered one of my children. No, that's not entirely true. My children have grown up with the background knowledge and understanding of the way things truly are. I have been training and teaching my own children these things since they were old enough to speak. These things are a part of our normal everyday conversations. I answered you with the spirit and heart I would have used with my own children, were they in your situation.

Joe, I view you in much the same way as Paul viewed Timothy.

Yet, I realize you have a pagan past. You do not have the benefit of having a grandmother like Lois, and a mother like Eunice, as Timothy did. I didn't either, but you do possess a faith in the Lord Jesus, and I have seen evidence of the working of the Holy Spirit within your life. You have the same Heavenly Father as Timothy. You have the potential to serve the Lord Jesus that I've seen in few others. You can make your pagan past work to your advantage, if you are willing. You see Joe, you did not get indoctrinated into false religious views like many Christians. You have not had your thinking corrupted by any particular denomination's pet doctrines and twisting words in scripture to alter their meaning. Ultimately Joe, what you have to be committed to is a search for the truth. Most people don't want to hear the truth. It contradicts their preconceived idea of reality, and they don't want to go through the pain and discomfort of changing their worldview. They have become too comfortable with the way things are in their own private little world. I hope you're coming to realize that much of your secular education through the public school system was a lie intended to deceive you and keep you enslaved."

Joe nodded slowly. This, at least, he had come to accept as reality.

Robert continued, "God's word says the truth shall set you free. I believe in the sovereignty of God, and I know that it was no accident that my Sarah fell on her roller skates that day your beloved Mary was in her accident. Romans 8:28 makes us a promise that God will work all things together for good to those of us who have been called according to his purpose. I have been called according to his purpose and I believe you have as well.

Every Christian is asked to play a part in God's overall plan. Some people willingly play the part God has given them, and God does mighty things through those people. Some people resist the leading of the Holy Spirit and never fulfill God's best for their life. They are left with God helping them make the best of a bad situation, a situation that they have profoundly messed up by their rebellion from following His plan.

260

I have been working for many years preparing myself, and praying that God would show me His perfect timing; that He would show me when He has aligned the people necessary to accomplish His will; those who are willing to follow Him, no matter what the cost. Joe, I've come to know and understand, you are one of those people. Or, more correctly, you will be one of those people if you're willing to continue to recklessly follow your Savior wherever He will lead you. There is a battle going on in your life. You are experiencing what psychologists call cognitive dissonance. The new information you are receiving is not lining up with what you believe to be true based on what you have been taught in the past. Ask your Heavenly Father to show you the truth. Don't rely on just your own judgment. Some of these things are spiritually discerned.

These things we also speak, not in words which man's wisdom teaches, but which the Holy Spirit teaches, comparing spiritual things with spiritual. But the natural man does not receive the things of the Spirit of God, for they are foolishness to him; nor can he know *them,* because they are spiritually discerned. But he who is spiritual judges all things, yet he himself is *rightly* judged by no one. For "who has known the mind of the Lord that he may instruct Him?" But we have the mind of Christ (1 Cor. 2:13-16).

When someone is experiencing cognitive dissonance one of two things usually happens. Either that person must form a plan to incorporate the new understanding into their life and change what they believe, or they must reject it and ignore the truth God has revealed to them. Accepting the evidence and truths I have shown you will involve rejecting many of the things that you have held to be true your entire life. I encourage you to be as the Bereans in the Book of Acts were. Search the scriptures and documents daily to see whether or not the things I tell you are so.

There are some tough, life changing decisions that must be made when one becomes a child of God. Most people refuse to make the changes necessary to recklessly follow Jesus Christ as Master and

Lord. They want to go to heaven, but they follow the things of this world and not the leading of Christ. It is like it is in the parable of the sower, 'the ones sown on stony ground who, when they hear the word, immediately receive it with gladness; and they have no root in themselves, and so endure only for a time. Afterward, when tribulation or persecution arises for the word's sake, immediately they stumble. . .the ones sown among thorns; *they are* the ones who hear the word, and the cares of this world, the deceitfulness of riches, and the desires for other things entering in choke the word, and it becomes unfruitful.'[3] You had made many of these life changing decisions before we ever met. You were recklessly and unashamedly following the truth that you understood from the first acceptance of Christ into your life. You had already quit your prestigious pagan job, with its large salary and followed God's leading to take a job below poverty level. You had already put the Lord Jesus Christ above every earthly relationship in your life. You had already made the decision you were not going to fight God for the right to rule your life completely."

Robert locked his gaze on Joe and said, "Pray God will show you the truth no matter what."

"I already have," Joe said, "the day of the accident. That was the last thing I asked of My Lord before Mary's wreck."

Robert wanted to jump up and down and tell Joe *God was answering his prayer*, but it was too early to tell if Joe would really accept the truth. "Get online and do some research on it. Type in 'Birth Certificate and slavery' and see what you get."[5] Robert and Joe said their customary goodbye's, and Robert left the room praying God would open the heart and mind of Joe to further receive the truth.

A few days passed. Mary's situation really hadn't changed. Dr. Bartlett again warned Joe that the protein levels in Mary's urine were not ideal. Dr. Rodriquez had been concerned about this too, before he had been forbidden to care for Mary. Dr. Bartlett called the situation microalbuminuria. Since Joe had threatened to change hospitals, Dr. Bartlett had quit suggesting they take Mary off life support, but his nonverbal communication still screamed it. The kidney function was deteriorating. In a day or two, they would do a protein-to-creatinine test to determine more.

"I'd recommend we do a GFR test, but then you wouldn't let us give your wife any drugs for the test would you?" Dr. Bartlett asked Joe.

Joe shook his head "no," assuring the doctor that he would not allow drugs for such a test.

As Dr. Bartlett was leaving the room, Robert came in. This was the first time Robert had seen Dr. Bartlett in quite a while. "Aye, it's good to see you doctor. I was hoping I would see you sometime."

Dr. Bartlett would have stepped past Robert if he could have and walked out the door without even acknowledging his presence, but Robert filled the doorway. "I have just the book here for you today." Robert stuffed the book in the large pockets of the doctors' scrubs as the doctor passed through the doorway without a word of acknowledgement.

"Friendly guy there," Robert said in jest to Joe. Joe gave Robert a half smile but couldn't say anything. "He didn't have any good news for you did he?" Robert guessed.

"No," Joe continued, "he thinks Mary's kidneys are failing, and there is nothing I can do about it." Robert and Joe stopped and had a word of prayer.

"Tell me what else is going on Joe?" Asked Robert.

"I did some of that research you told me about."

"And what do you think," Robert interrupted before Joe could finish his sentence.

"I don't know what to think." Joe responded. "I'm at a real loss. It seems so crazy to think that a bunch of control freaks have trapped, and enslaved, a large portion of the free world. I mean, if this was true, wouldn't there be a large scale rebellion or something? Why doesn't the president, or the congress do something about it?"

"Some of them know, but don't want it to change, or don't have the courage to change it. Others are just useful idiots." Joe chuckled at Robert's comment. "It's been this way for so long no one is willing to challenge it. Besides, I fear it may be too late. We owe so much on the national debt. We are in so deep, you know, and all those people mortgaged as collateral on the loan. What would they offer in exchange for that? No, it's just easier for them to maintain the status quo and not make waves."

"Well, if it is true, it's the greatest deception of all time." Joe said.

"I don't know about that. Being enslaved to satan is a bigger deception." Robert responded.

"Yea, maybe you got me there," Joe agreed.

There was a lapse in the conversation and then Joe started talking again. "You really believe this stuff don't you? You probably see yourself as the new William Wilberforce."

Robert smiled to himself. "Well, yes, I would like to see people freed from the slavery by consent they are putting themselves under, but first and foremost, it's important that each person be saved from their enslavement of sin and have a saving relationship with the Lord Jesus Christ. That's what counts for eternity."

"I appreciate that about you Robert, but if the salvation of the lost is more important to you than this human slavery, why do you bother with the other?"

A sad expression passed over Robert's face. *How could he explain it all in a few words?* He had been a part of the elite world once, as a child. He had seen the other side of the coin. "We had a freedom here in the united States which few have enjoyed. With that freedom, there comes great responsibility. We have neglected that freedom here in the United States, and it is being taken away from us. The U.S. has sent out more missionaries than any country I know of. Freedom of this type allows unhindered commitment to the cause of Christ and spreading of His gospel. I hate to see that lost."

"You talk like we have already lost it!"

"Largely we have." Robert paused again, wanting to say more, but unsure of how much to say. "I've told you about my father. He's not really one of the power players, but the bankers and other one world types that control him are godless, humanistic, satanic types. If they have their way, the cause of Christ will disappear from the earth."

"Yeah, but God won't let that happen."

"What? The persecution of a rebellious, largely Godless America?" Robert questioned.

"No, I don't mean persecution. But, God won't leave Himself without a witness in this world."

"That may be true." Robert continued, "But the persecution of Christians is at an all-time-high worldwide, and it's coming to America too. It will separate the wheat from the chaff, but I hate to see this great nation lose its freedom of religion. Any sensible person should be the same way. God has worked mightily through this nation in the past to spread the gospel and send out missionaries. Not that He can't use some other source if He so chooses, but every Christian should oppose the works of darkness wherever they are."

Joe looked at the stack of books he had plowed through since Robert's last visit. He thought about the legal battle with his mother-in-law that lay ahead. He thought about possibly losing his wife, and or child. He thought about the financial Grand Canyon he was in. "Well Paul, your Timothy has a question. How do I go about turning all this over to God? I mean, I'm ready, and I'm willing; but how do I go on from here? As I sat here listening to you, something just clicked. I mean, God brought to me an understanding I have not had before. I'm looking at all these trials and tribulations as separate things, but they aren't. I want to, I mean, I need to turn it all over. I can't go about this piece-by-piece anymore. I need to turn over the legal battle, the financial stuff, and the future of my child and my wife to God.

I cannot recklessly trust God in one area and trust in men, or my own wisdom, in another area. Robert, if I'm right about this, and please correct me if I'm wrong, this is a package deal, all or nothing, as they say. I have been letting things happen, and hoping for the best. That's not how this works is it? When you said it was God's plan for your little girl to get hurt so your family would be at the hospital to save Mary's life. . . . I just don't think like that, but I should, shouldn't I? What I'm trying to say is I can either recklessly follow God's plan, or I can stumble and muddle through life pretty much clueless. This isn't coming out very well, it's all jumbled up in my head and I can't make it come out of my mouth like I want to. I keep thinking about that parable about a wise man building his house on the rock. The floods came and the winds blew on both houses. The house built on shifting sand fell flat, but the one built on the rock stood firm even though the storm raged around it.

I don't know if you have ever been in the middle of a raging storm like this. Have you?"

"Well Joe, actually a few years back I was fighting multiple battles. I won't get into the details now, maybe later. I had just spent several days in the Neonatal Intensive Care Unit with one of my daughters. A few weeks later I was being investigated by DCFS. I said I had dealt with them previously — that was the time. I was overwhelmed and overcommitted on multiple levels. I felt so trapped and confused that I wondered, like so many people do, why is God letting this happen to me. I thought I was being faithful and trusting him for everything.

Then came the day when we had to evacuate our house. A fire was coming toward our home, and we had about 15 minutes to grab things before we had to evacuate. I didn't worry much: I thought our house was fireproof. Our pantry was full of food for the next two or three years. I had a store of solar panels for emergency electricity. All of our worldly possessions were in the house. We came back two days later when the police and firefighters would let us back in the area. Our home was gone. We had no debt on the house, but we also had no insurance on it. I won't go into great detail, but I caught a glimpse of what Job must have felt like. No, I didn't lose my family, but I lost everything else, except my faith. I had no savings, I had just lost my job, and I was battling it out with DCFS over my children.

There were several other battles, the details of which I won't bore you with. Everything I owned was burned in the fire on top of all that."

Joe looked at Robert in astonishment. "And you didn't take government aid or unemployment compensation in the midst of all of this?"

"Yes Joe, you are correct. My family and I had made a commitment not to do that, and believe me, I wasn't about to go beggin' to my estranged father for some of his borrowed money. You see Joe, this reckless life of total surrender isn't theory with me. It isn't some hypothetical what-if situation. I have been living it for years. And I know beyond a shadow of a doubt that building my house on the rock is the only way to live. I still don't know how things are going to turn out here on this earth. Every time I try to guess what God's plan is I have been wrong. Almost every single time he shows me that his plan is so much bigger, and so much better than anything I could possibly have imagined that I end up humbled, and on my knees crying out in praise and thanksgiving to my God.

I won't tell you it's not hard, because it is. You already know that. So many people read the Bible and see the miracles that happened back in Bible times because people had faith in God. Joe, God still performs miracles every day in my life. You need to look for them, even expect them. And when they happen, praise God for them, be thankful. There will still always be consequences for our past decisions that may not be pleasant, but I can assure you God has never let me down.

Have I been through terrible things? Yes. God will never give you more than you can handle if you rely on Him for your strength. If you are living a life of faith, God will always give you more than you can handle by yourself. We need Him, and we need each other. Joe, I have been praying for more than a decade that God would put together the people and the circumstances to expose the dangers of enslaving our children and our churches. Don't you see all of those things are coming together right before our eyes? If we will only be obedient and follow the path that He has prepared or is preparing for each one of us to walk in, miracles of biblical proportions will happen to us.

I would be honored to pray with you as you commit all of this to God. And I will, Lord willing, be there to rejoice with you when the miracles begin. I can't promise you that Mary will get better, but I can promise you that whatever happens, God's ultimate plan will be furthered if we are faithful and obedient. I think this would be a good time to pray."

Joe and Robert bowed their heads and went boldly before the throne of grace to obtain mercy, and find grace to help in time of need. As their Father heard their words, and looked into their hearts, He was pleased.

Early the next morning Mr. Verde marched into Joe's room followed by a small group of hospital employees from the legal and the financial departments. Mr. Verde began, "Mr. Smith, I'm here to help you. At this point you have amassed quite a large financial obligation to this hospital."

Verde turned to a young man carrying a clipboard. The young man read from the financial papers he held his hand, "To date, your financial obligations total $184,632.78."

"Mr. Smith," Verde began, "you have no visible means of paying the hospital for the continued care of your wife, and her insurance is expired. I am a compassionate man. I don't want to see a young man like you burdened with such a financial load. I also believe if the financial burden is lifted off of you and the hospital's shoulders, we will have a much better, workable relationship between us. These people have come down here at my request to assist you in filing for state and federal aid to help you in this time of need. I know filling out the forms can be an intimidating task, but it is their job to help people like you complete these forms. These forms have already been filled out with the data you have provided. We just need a few more pieces of information and your approval signature on these documents and we will take care of the rest." This group of smiling employees before him was ready and eager to help Mr. Smith in any way they could.

A pleasant-looking lady in her mid-40s walked up to Joe, "Mr. Smith we need your signature here, and here, along with your Social Security number in the highlighted box."

A stunned Joe Smith just shook his head. "I am sorry, I know you are probably just trying to help, but I have made a commitment not to accept state, or federal aid."

Mr. Verde just stared at Joe in disbelief. "Mr. Smith, I have gone to all this trouble trying to help you, and you're refusing?"

In a way very uncharacteristic of Joe, he stood up and said, "Yes, Mr. Verde, you seem to understand me very well. I refuse to accept state or federal aid. Now, if you have nothing further to say, I would like you to leave please."

Mark 13:11 sprang to Joe's mind — *Do not worry beforehand, or premeditate what you will speak. But whatever is given you in that hour, speak that; for it is not you who speak, but the Holy Spirit.* Joe knew the boldness to say what he had just said had not come from himself, but from God. He knew, just a few days earlier, he would have been intimidated into signing those forms, but not anymore. He breathed a silent prayer of thanks as the group followed Mr. Verde from his room.

Still following the leading of the Holy spirit, Joe grabbed his laptop and looked up the e-mail address of Mr. Verde on the online hospital directory and composed the following.

Mr. Verde

Thank you for your concern for me and your visit today. I know you were just trying to help. I am sorry for the inconvenience to you and your staff, but I am trusting God to meet my needs, not the government.

Joe Smith

Reading Joe Smith's e-mail was like rubbing salt in an open wound for Verde. He cut and pasted Joe's entire e-mail into his latest reply to Ken...

Smith is absolutely refusing to go on any kind of financial government program. This is infuriating! (See a copy of his e-mail below.) I will continue to pursue all other avenues.

Mo

CHAPTER 24

Shortly after Mary Smith's accident, Mr. Elder had sent an email to everyone involved with the school requesting prayer for the Smith family. Among the students, there had been much concern for their teacher, Mr. Smith. The students at Grace Christian Academy involved with their salt and light program had discussed at the summer meetings what they, as a Student Body, could do to help Mr. Smith. In the beginning, many of the students sent cards and letters of encouragement. In yet another update letter Mr. Elder had sent out, Mr. Elder had detailed the financial situation that the Smiths were now facing. After their late June meeting, the students had gone to their sponsors with several ideas.

A number of suggestions were made, but the three most feasible fund-raiser ideas seemed to be: having a car wash, having a garage sale, or doing odd jobs around town to make money. In the end, the students decided to do all three. With no objections from anyone, they obtained permission from the Board to use the high school gymnasium for their garage sale. They enlisted the help of most of the Student Body at Grace Christian Academy. Student volunteers did all of the work. Scouring the city far and wide in search of donations to put in the garage sale, many garages and attics gave up their long-held treasures for the cause.

The students divided up into groups. Mr. Elder, who had little to do with the whole effort, was impressed with the character qualities of responsibility and organization the students were exhibiting. One group organized volunteers, while another group was in charge of marking all the donated items. They decided to have a car wash at the same time in the parking lot across the street. Another group of students had a sign-up sheet for people to hire groups of students to do odd jobs over the summer. The group in charge of advertising was filled with overachievers. Indeed, it probably contained the entire art department at Grace Christian Academy. The students made enough signs to place one at every major intersection for 10 miles in every direction. All of the students involved agreed you'd have to be blind to miss those signs and this garage sale.

The students decided the garage sale would be three days, Thursday, Friday, and Saturday from eight in the morning to six in the evening. The week before the sale the students began e-mailing everyone on their address list. They posted notices online about the garage sale and stated who would receive the proceeds. On the day of the sale, students began posting signs before dawn, traveling in groups to cover the largest possible area in the shortest amount of time.

At eight o'clock there was a huge line of people waiting outside the gym. About ten minutes after eight, a police car pulled into the parking lot. The officer strode purposefully toward the gym, scanning the area as he walked. "Why don't you have your Permit clearly displayed near the entrance? And why are you starting an hour earlier than the city ordinance allows?" The students looked at one another, wondering who to blame. One of Mr. Elder's teenage grandsons spoke up for the group, "We didn't know we needed a Permit."

"We don't need a Permit," replied the faculty sponsor who had just walked up. Churches and schools are exempt from the ordinance. As far as starting early, I did not realize that times applied to us since we are both the church and a school. The school sponsor showed the officer a copy of the city ordinance. I'm sorry to bother you folks, I'm just trying to do my job. It's a great day for a sale. This is one of the biggest rummage sales I've ever seen.

"We're trying to raise money for one of our teachers whose wife was badly injured in a car accident," one of the students explained. "You're more than welcome to come back after you get off duty sir. The senior boys are even providing free delivery if you buy something large." The officer replied, "I may just have to do that" and returned to his patrol car and left.

Over the weekend, the school gymnasium became progressively emptier and the money box became progressively fuller. Not only did the police officer return after he got off duty, but almost everyone in the local community dropped by to see what was going on at the little Christian school. The car wash was a great success, and the volunteers had a full three pages of jobs to accomplish. The students borrowed a change machine used for the basketball and football games from the activities director. Still, it took them several hours to count the money and place it in coin rolls for deposit in the bank. When the counting was finally complete, the student council president announced to the group of students, "The grand total for the Smith fund-raising weekend is $5996.50!" At that point the sponsor reached in his pocket and counted out three dollars and fifty cents and added it to the pile exclaiming, "make that an even six-thousand!" The teller at the bank was slightly overwhelmed when they deposited the money in exchange for a certified check made to Mr. Joe Smith.

CHAPTER 25

Plead my cause, and deliver me: quicken me according to thy word (Psalm 119:154).

"But when you do a charitable deed, do not let your left hand know what your right hand is doing, that your charitable deed may be in secret" (Matthew 6:3&4).

Luke, an average looking blond teenager with an above average smile, navigated his $400 Toyota into the parking garage, and quietly found his way into the hospital. He knew the room number and exactly where he was going, but he felt nervous, perplexed, and unsure of himself now that he was finally at his destination. God had used Mary Smith's accident to make this young man think more seriously about life. Over the last two months, the Lord had been leading him to help Mr. Smith even before the garage sale. But right now, as he entered the floor Mary Smith's room was on, his courage and resolve were failing him. *Maybe this wasn't what God wanted him to do.* He didn't want to embarrass Mr. Smith. *How do you give someone $26,000?*

Luke's family wasn't wealthy, but Luke had been their only child. His parents, who owned a small appliance repair shop, had worked hard to provide an excellent education for him. He had been home schooled when he was in grade school. When he was older, he finished his high school education at Grace Christian

Academy, graduating just a week before the accident.

His parents had high expectations for him, and wanted to see him have the college education they had never been able to obtain, but for now that dream was put on hold. All of Luke's life, since he was a little guy, his parents had scrimped and saved to put back money in an account for his college education. The last three summers, he had mowed lawns and put his earnings in the account as well. He and his parents had this dream of him going to college debt free. But now, he felt God was leading him to give all of the money to his teacher, Mr. Smith. It had been a hard decision. Mom and Dad didn't understand at first, but eventually, the three of them had come to an understanding this past week. With much regret, but proud of their son, they had told him it was his money. He could give it away if he wanted to. If he felt God was leading him to give it away, then by all means he must follow God's leading.

God would provide other means for his college education. Looking at their current financial situation, it didn't look like he would be attending college this fall. It had not been the best year for their home business. There just wasn't enough money, and his parents weren't willing to get government aid or student loans. For Luke, this was a real step of faith because, although he was a diligent, hard worker, Luke wasn't the brightest or the most talented student. There was no big scholarship or free ride waiting for him now that he had graduated high school. Although he had applied for several scholarships, even one Joe Smith had helped him apply for, the only scholarship he had received was a small one at a private college out of state, that was three times the cost of any of the local schools. Definitely not a long term option! As Luke mulled over these issues in his mind, recalling the rumor that Mrs. Smith's bills were over $200,000, Luke wondered what his measly $26,000 would do for Mr. Smith's situation. Yet he was reassured, even now as he walked the halls of the hospital, that he was doing the right thing.

Luke paced back and forth in front of the nurses' station outside. He looked down the long hall of the hospital and knew Mr.

Smith and his wife were down there, the last door on the right. He had rarely been so nervous in his life. *How could he anonymously give Mr. Smith this money?* He thought about walking in and leaving it on the counter in the room, but he feared it might get lost; or someone on the hospital staff might find it and take it. Besides, if Mr. Smith did find it, he'd know where it came from if he'd been in the room for a visit. He didn't want Mr. Smith to feel under any obligation to him.

God had led him this far. Surely He would show him what to do next. "God show me what to do," he breathed a prayer under his breath.

The elevator in the waiting room dinged, and Luke lifted his eyes to see Mr. Cutler walking off the elevator toward Mrs. Smith's room. Luke didn't know Mr. Cutler personally, but he had seen him in the halls of GCA. He knew Mr. Cutler was the academy's lawyer, and he also knew him as Katie and Justin's Dad, but he had never talked to Mr. Cutler before. Even though Justin was ten years older than Luke, everyone at GCA knew about Justin, the soldier from GCA who had died in Afghanistan. Relief flooded Luke's mind. The lawyer would know what to do. Waving Mr. Cutler aside, he led him back to the empty hospital waiting room and told him his plan.

Corbin Cutler looked seriously into the eyes of the boy he knew only as a student from GCA. He knew the decision this young man had made, and he wanted him to carefully consider what he was doing. "Are you sure this is what you want to do, son?"

Luke returned the scrutinizing gaze and answered, "Yes sir, I know for certain this is what God would have me do."

Mr. Cutler continued his questioning, "And your parents are in agreement with this decision?"

Luke replied with firm resolve, "Yes sir, I've prayed with and visited with my parents at length about this. They also believe I should follow God's leading."

"Then come with me, and let's see what we can do, but not a word of this to anyone else, OK?"

Luke nodded his head in agreement and followed the big man like his shadow. The two of them got back onto the elevator and were carried down to the main floor of the hospital where they proceeded to the business office. Corbin wasted no time in stating their business to the girl in the office.

"My name is Corbin Cutler, I am a lawyer representing Joe Smith. We would like to know what you would settle for in cash today, if we paid all of the medical bills for Mary Smith."

The girl at the desk scurried off to talk with her administrator and came back and said, we'll take $40,000 cash today to pay all of Mrs. Smith's bills." The office girl was quite pleased with herself. She felt she had made a very reasonable offer to the lawyer.

Not wanting to seem rude, but really quite irritated with the girl, Corbin politely asked to see her supervisor. "That won't do, let me talk with your boss please," and Corbin almost managed a friendly smile.

Luke sat quietly on a bench against the wall with his head down, looking rather mousey on the outside, but praying like a lion on the inside. He had been obedient in what he had been directed to do, and he was having a heart-to-heart talk with God about it just then. Everyone in the office assumed he was the lawyer's son, forced to tag along with Dad, there only because he had to be. They had no idea he was a child of the King of Kings having a serious talk with his Father just then.

The girl soon returned with the office manager in her mid-fifties, a middle aged woman who could throw her weight around in more than one way. *Now we're getting somewhere,* Corbin thought to himself as he looked at the short curly graying hair and bifocal glasses on the lady before him.

Corbin addressed the lady with a smile, and all the civility he could muster. "What could you do for us in the way of a discount on Mary Smith's bills if we gave you cash today?"

Now it was the office manager's turn to look Corbin up and down and surmise the situation. Without saying a word, she looked at some figures on the screen of the office computer in front of her. Grabbing an old-time adding machine that spit a paper ribbon out the top, she began to calculate. Luke felt a knot rising in his stomach, and he felt like throwing up. All this intensity was about to kill him. "You have the cash in hand?" the woman asked, tearing the ribbon from the machine and raising her drawn eyebrows above the bifocals in disbelief.

"Yes, I can get it." Corbin wondered if he would get further if he told her how little cash they actually had.

"$38,000, if you pay it in full, now."

"We can't do that," Corbin hoped to strike a better bargain, but he realized his bargaining power was little.

The woman turned on him with cold, bitter, dark eyes. "$38,000 is all I can do Mr. Lawyer man. Mrs. Smith's bills are over $185,000. You should count yourself lucky we are willing to do that much for you."

It appears you need some more information Mr. Lawyer man, Mrs. Smith's bills currently exceed $185,000. We already received a $5000 payment from her car insurance, which leaves a balance of roughly $180,000. Mrs. Smith had insurance for the first month of her stay here which we are getting ready to file. The forms are on my desk right now, but her insurance is contesting her eligibility. If you pay this bill in full today, that means my staff and I don't have to fight, argue, and bicker with the insurance company for the next several months over these bills. You see Mr. Cutler, even if her insurance company finally admits she was eligible, her insurance company will try to force discounts on us which we don't allow. Often we have to contact them several times before we even talk to the right person. We have to fill out enough forms to float a battleship, often sending the same forms multiple times because they mysteriously 'get lost.' With a balance on account this large, the insurance company will most likely continue to contest payments and dispute bills for several months, possibly even years. This is very costly in man-hours to the hospital, and while we must still pay our employees NOW, if I am forced to file with the insurance we will not see any money in payment for several months or possibly years.

If Mr. and Mrs. Smith decide to apply for government aid my headaches and form requirements go up exponentially and the pay-out to the hospital in the end is even less. Mrs. Smith's policy co-pay is 20%, so if you don't take advantage of the discount and pay in full today, and we have to do battle with the insurance company, when we do finally settle Mr. and Mrs. Smith will still be responsible for as much as $36,000 in co-payments, plus any other expenses she's incurred after today. As you know, she no longer has insurance as of July 1st. It's not uncommon for these bills to take 20 to 24 months before the hospital billing office and the insurance processors finally agree on how much will actually be paid by the insurance company. Of necessity the hospital charges the maximum allowed on each individual item, so it can get the most pay-back from the insurance company in about two years from now. So in short, your client can pay $ 38,000 now or pay $36,000 in about two years. It would be much easier on us all if you paid now.

Corbin realized any more said would only provoke the woman and might close the window on any further negotiations for Mary's bills in the future. After all, she was still here and racking up new bills every day. "An even $38,000 pays everything through today?

"We will need your client's signature on some forms, but yes."

Can I have a few more hours to get that money to you?"

The woman softened a little as she realized Corbin, the hulk of a man before her, was actually trying to work with her.

"Yes, $38,000 even. You can have until five o'clock this evening, when we close the business office, to make payment."

Corbin slipped from the room and Luke didn't have to be told to follow.

"$38,000," Luke whispered in disbelief. That is quite a discount.

"Yes, they're willing to work with us."

Corbin seemed pleased, but Luke was discouraged. *Had they come this far only to lose the battle in the last five minutes?* "I don't have that much Mr. Cutler, and I don't know how we'll raise it," Luke said in despair.

"You don't have that much? I know that, but there's the $6000 from the garage sale and car wash the school had last week, and if you'll wait here, I think I know where we can get the rest of the money."

Corbin led Luke to the hospital cafeteria, bought him an orange juice and sweet roll and told him to wait there. Going back to his car, Corbin knew what he needed to do. Since the birth of their only daughter, his wife had been putting back money for their daughter's wedding. His wife had envisioned a huge church ceremony with a full meal afterwards at one of Chicago's finest restaurants. It was a nice thought, but not really necessary. Now that she was gone, she wouldn't be disappointed if that grand affair didn't happen.

Corbin pressed the speed dial and waited for Katie to answer. The conversations between him and Katie had been few and very strained over the last few weeks. Corbin wondered if she would even answer the phone. "Hello," Katie's familiar voice was refreshing to Corbin. "Sweetheart," all the irritation and anger was gone from Corbin's voice and the deep love he had for his daughter came through in his tone. "I've been thinking, well praying. I was wrong to try and prevent you from marrying David. I want you to know you have my blessing on your union." A defining scream of delight burst through the phone. Under any other situation, Corbin might have given his daughter a serious tongue lashing for screaming in his ear, but just now he felt her joy and wanted to be a part of it. He smiled to himself. It was nice to have his daughter back on his side.

"Thank you Daddy. I love you Daddy. You're the best Dad in the world," and she would have poured forth a gush of female emotion, praise, and gratitude, but Corbin cut her short. It was nearing four o'clock, and he needed thirty minutes to get to the bank and back.

"I'll tell you later what made me change my mind, but right now I need to talk to you on the level—no fluff. You know that case

I told you about where the woman's on life support? Could you do with about $6,000 less for your wedding? I'd. . .."

Now it was Katie's turn to cut her dad short, "Dad I already told you. We don't want a big wedding. Just about fifteen close friends and our families. I'd be thrilled to help this family if you feel it's a worthy situation."

"I love you sweetie. I need to talk to you and David some more later, but right now I've got to take care of something. Could you meet me at the house tonight for dinner? Catch you later."

Corbin closed his cell phone, ending the conversation. After a moment of silent prayer and thanksgiving, he started the car and headed for the bank, his bank. Thankfully, Corbin spotted a branch only a block from the hospital. He hadn't even known that branch was there. His thirty-minute drive had been turned into a five minute one. With the cash in hand, and a joy in his heart Corbin hadn't felt in years, and furthermore couldn't explain, he headed back to the hospital. Luke was only too glad to see Corbin return so quickly. In a matter of minutes he had rejoined Luke in the cafeteria and asked him to wait a few more minutes while he retrieved the garage sale check from Mr. Smith.

As Corbin rode the elevator back up to Joe's floor, he carefully organized what he would say to Joe. He didn't want to tell who the donors were, but he didn't want to lie either. In the end he decided to tell Joe some anonymous donors had agreed to pay Mary's hospital bills in full, if he would agree to sign the garage sale money over to the hospital.

Joe sat in stunned silence for a moment. With shaking hand, shocked, surprised, and relieved, he quickly retrieved and endorsed the check, making it payable to the hospital.

Joe handed the check to Corbin who, with a quick wave, made a hasty retreat down the elevator again to retrieve Luke. Together, they returned to the business office, Luke having given Corbin his college tuition money on the elevator trip down. As he entered, Luke quietly returned to the bench near the wall to watch the transaction.

This time he was wearing his above average smile from ear-to-ear.

The office manager, noticing Corbin's entry, came to wait on him herself. A look of panic and surprise crossed her face as Corbin produced Joe's certified check and the balance of the money in cash. He proceeded to count out thirty-two thousand dollars in cash right there on the counter. Cash payments of this size were such a rarity, and she was at a loss for a moment on how to proceed. Realizing almost too late she needed to fill out some government forms for large cash transactions, she immediately sent the money to be placed in a safe until it could be deposited in the bank.

Corbin was handed a set of duplicate receipts for payment marked, Paid-in-full, which he planned on presenting to Joe Smith as evidence of God's continuing grace and mercy.

As they left the business office Corbin handed the Paid-in-full receipts to Luke. "Would you like to give this to Mr. Smith yourself?"

Luke shook his head and replied, "No sir. I would appreciate it if Mr. Smith never knew where the money came from, at least my portion of it."

Corbin took the receipt back and separated the yellow carbon copy from the back, handing it to Luke. I think you should keep this in a safe place to remind you of this time when you were obedient to God, and God opened the eyes of an old cynical Christian lawyer who'd forgotten the joy of giving."

Corbin held out his hand to Luke and gave the young man a firm handshake. Corbin added, "God bless you young man, God bless you."

Luke looked up with tears in his eyes. "He already has sir. And thank you, too, for making up the difference." With that Luke left for home with joy unspeakable!

Corbin headed back for the elevator one more time while placing his own carbon copy carefully in his pocket. He whistled the chorus "God is so Good," to himself as he rode the elevator up to Joe's room after paying the bill. He hadn't felt this good in years.

Finding it hard to say what exactly had just happened, Corbin simply handed Joe the one remaining receipt marked "Paid-in-full" without a word.

Joe broke down and cried. A tremendous weight had been lifted off his shoulders.

Corbin, with a tear beginning to form in his own eye, looked out the window to see a beat-up old Toyota slowly leaving the parking lot, driven by a young man with blond hair and an above average smile.

Excusing himself, he left Joe's room with a joy and anticipation he hadn't known in years. As he headed for his home, he dialed up Katie again.

"OK girl, there are a few stipulations on this deal. Number one, you have to move back in until you get married. I'm not giving you up any sooner than I have to."

Katie's voice on the other end of the phone answered in the affirmative.

"And number two," Katie's heart raced in fear of what other condition her dad might put on her and David's marriage, "It's Chinese tonight, not Italian."

CHAPTER 26

Jesus I am resting, resting
In the Joy of what Thou art;
I am finding out the greatness
Of Thy loving heart.
Thou hast bid me gaze upon Thee,
And Thy beauty fills my soul,
For by Thy transforming power
Thou hast made me whole. —Jean Sophia Pigott

Lord We Would Ne'er forget Thy love
Who hast redeemed us by Thy blood;
And now, as our High Priest above,
Dost intercede for us with God. —James G. Deck

"Was there any change in Mary while I was gone?" Joe glumly
asked the kind blue-haired church lady with horn-rimmed glasses, who had given up an hour of her day to sit with Mary while he
took a shower. He seriously doubted anything had changed, but he
needed something to encourage him, something to feed his hope.
Another week had come and gone with little change in Mary's situation, and certainly no positive change. A load of worry had been
lifted off Joe's shoulders when Mary's medical bills were paid, but
there were still other mountainous loads to be borne by the young

man. Once again discouragement was creeping back into Joe as the weary days dragged on. The impending legal battle with his mother-in-law was heavy on his heart also.

"No, I can't tell any difference Joe," she said as she carefully put her horn-rimmed glasses back on.

Then trying to bring things to a brighter note she looked at Joe with her most serious face and said, "Joe I want you to know I'm praying for you."

Joe had heard this comment before. Instead of being encouraged, he felt a keen sense of loss, pain, despair, and downright annoyance at it and its bearer. Over two months had passed. Only a handful of patients had ever awakened after this length of time. In addition, there was the three-organ rule. Couldn't this elderly Christian see his situation was hopeless?

Indeed, the situation seemed hopeless from a human standpoint. *Maybe the doctors were right. Maybe the only thing she was good for was an organ donor.* As soon as the baby was big enough to be taken, Joe would have some tough decisions to make, but for now, just now, he couldn't bear the thought of what lay ahead.

As the church lady left the room, a nurse's aid came in to draw some blood. The orderly looked casually at Mary's charts. "Her renal levels are really bad. They may want to put her on dialysis."

Joe collapsed into the chair in silence. He was exhausted emotionally and spiritually, his injured arm was starting to bother him again, and now this one last blow seemed unbearable. Dialysis, in Mary's situation, was just one step closer to complete kidney failure. The nurse seemed eager to leave, and Joe made the necessary, polite thanks and responses to the questions concerning Mary's condition.

At this point, even though Joe had prayed and given the situation over to God, clichés like "It's in God's hands," had become a normal part of his daily conversation even when he didn't feel it in his heart. He uttered several of these strung together in a semi-coherent sentence, and the lady left. Now that he had the room to himself, he settled in for the long evening ahead of him. Joe started to look at a new book Robert had left him, but he quickly laid it down and sat down in the chair to stare at Mary.

Mary's face was puffy. Her facial features were swollen. Her lips weren't chapped or bleeding, and there was no spittle in the corners of her mouth as had often been the case when she was on the respirator. But her skin was not the beautiful ivory color it had once been. One of the elderly ladies who sat with Mary on a weekly basis had taken it upon herself to comb Mary's hair and braid it each week, giving her a more pleasant look.

Joe's mind flooded with questions. *Even if Mary did somehow survive, if her kidneys started working properly again would her mind ever be right? Would her intellect be permanently altered? Would she spend the rest of her life in some home, bed-ridden? Could she ever accept Jesus Christ as her personal Savior, or was it too late for her? Why had he fought so hard to preserve her life?*

There was nothing else he could do now. He had committed it all to God, but without a miracle, any thoughts of Mary recovering were futile. From a strictly human standpoint the coma had gone on too long for her to ever be normal again. Whatever happened, he would have to accept what God allowed, but somehow, just now, it didn't seem that easy.

Squeezing her hand, he once again reassured Mary of his love for her. Trying to focus his mind on something good, he picked up his Bible and read a chapter of Psalms aloud to her and the baby, but again his mind began to wonder as more depression and despair threatened to overwhelm him. He looked up at the water stains on the tile in the ceiling above him for what seemed like the thousandth time. How many times had he looked at those stains? He couldn't decide if they looked more like a dog or a fox.

The sometimes upsetting, but usually just political and social views of Robert Forbes were an interesting distraction, but what did it all matter? What was the purpose of man in the universe? Sin abounded. He had been taught the prince of the power of the air reigned and would continue to reign until the return of Christ, and the political and social issues of the world would continue to get worse and worse until the end. *Why was he living? What was his purpose? Wouldn't it be far better to be in the presence of his Savior than here in this wicked world? Job had said, "Oh that he had been a still born child."*

Joe slid to his knees and once again began to pour his heart out, as the tears poured out on the familiar vinyl chair.

"Oh God, what is my purpose? You seem to be letting my wife slip away from me into a lost eternity, and I can't do anything about it! My child's life hangs in the balance, and other than teaching some teenagers how to run a computer for God's glory, I have no purpose." *Even if the school did rehire him,* Joe mused, *if the school was even still there in the fall, would it be wise for him to return to that job? Wouldn't he just bring more scorn and criticism on the school?* "The world around me is filled with evil," Joe continued in earnest prayer, "and I have no desire to continue in it. Show me what your purpose for my life is, Lord."

As Joe cried aloud to the Lord, the door to the hospital room cracked open and almost unheard, Robert Forbes made his entrance. Prompted by the Holy Spirit, feeling Joe needed him at this time, he had left his home late on Saturday evening. Burdened by the Holy Spirit, he made his way to the hospital, not because he wanted to, but because he felt God was leading him to do so.

Silently, Robert knelt in prayer beside Joe. Joe didn't even realize he was there until he heard the Scotsman behind him praying in his native accent. "Savior, we praise thee for this short time Joe has been given with his wife and child. We thank Ye, that they were not killed in the automobile wreck immediately, and that Joe has had these few months to minister to their souls."

And then it happened, as Joe lay there wallowing in self-pity. From somewhere deep in his soul, the Spirit prompted him to praise and thanksgiving. At first the words were hard to say as Joe stumbled over them "Thank You divine Savior. . . for. . . these few months I have had to spend with my wife and son. Thank you Savior that I even got to find out Mary was pregnant with . . . ," and here he began to falter as the tears, so frequent these last few months, poured forth from the depths of his overwrought emotional soul, "my. . . our child. Thank You, Oh Most High God, Creator of heaven and earth, for the wonderful wife You gave me for the last three years." Three wonderful, yet sin filled and bitter-sweet years poured through his mind swiftly.

"And thank You Oh Savior for the godly friends and support You have sent to me in this great trial. Dearest Savior, I do not know or understand why You have allowed this trial, but I come before You to thank you for it and all it has taught me about You, my God. Forgive me for my lack of gratefulness. Lord Jesus I believe. Help my unbelief!"

And then as Joe prayed, another amazing thing happened. Kneeling there on the floor, he lowered himself into a prostrate position and continued to pray. Like David in 2 Samuel 12:20, in the time of greatest loss, his heart worshipped his Creator.

"We worship You Oh precious Savior for all you suffered on the cross to atone for my sin, for Mary's sin, for our son's sin, and for the sin of the world. Thank You Most High God for sending Your only Son to die for my sins. Thank You for loving me, a sinful wretch. I worship and love You God for Your sinless nature. Thank You for being so unselfish, and coming to redeem a fallen human race. Thank You for loving me when I didn't love You. Thank You for seeking me when I hated You." The tears became a flood that overtook him, and he wept tears of mingled joy and sadness in worship of his Savior and God.

The Holy Spirit had been working in Robert's heart as well, and he immediately picked up where Joe had left off.

"We worship You Oh God, because You are holy and just. You alone deserve our admiration. There is no other being in heaven or earth like You Oh Loving Father. You are just, sinless, pure, holy, all-knowing and omnipresent; and yet You love us and from the beginning of time You have set forth a plan of redemption for us."

Robert picked up a thin black hymnal he often carried with him and began to sing, "Abba Father we adore thee, in the Savior's precious name." Joe rose and sat in the chair next to him, wiping away the tears so he could read the words to the music, and together their voices lifted in songs of praise to their Creator. They sang another and another song. Joe read the words to the song "Emmanuel's Land." The words of one verse, "With Mercy and with judgement my web of time he wove and aye the dew's of sorrow were lustered by his love," touched the core of his emotions.

They lost all sense of time, and Joe couldn't remember how many songs they had sung. With the passing of time, Joe was growing hoarse from singing, and crying. What the two men lacked in musical ability, they made up for in sincerity of heart. Robert opened his Bible and, beginning in Genesis, he pointed out various passages, showing God and His redemptive work toward mankind. Then he offered another simple prayer of thanks to God for His love and redemption. As verses poured into Joe's mind, he shared them with Robert. Thus they continued for several hours, and amazingly enough, the hospital staff never interrupted them. Never did a nurse or orderly enter the room.

The scripture seemed to boil over with descriptive pictures and types of Christ in the Old and New Testaments. And these two New Testament priests to offer worship and praise to the Savior.

After a time, Robert walked over to the small refrigerator in the room and opened it. Annoyance rose in Joe's mind. How could Robert, at a special time like this, think about eating? Taking a bottle of grape juice from the refrigerator, and pulling the bread from a sandwich, Robert sat the elements before the worshippers. Then, saying a short prayer, he thanked the Father for the body of his Son, broken on the cross. Then, dividing the bread, he gave a piece to Joe and kept one for himself.

Without a second thought, Joe rose to his feet and lifted his hands in prayer, "Thank You God for the blood of Christ. Thank You for His allowing Himself to be crucified so His blood could cover my sin." As Joe sat down they ate the bread, then they both reverently took a drink of the grape juice. A sense of serene joy filled the two men. For these two men, it was not just an emotional experience, but instead a privilege they were given, an opportunity to show their love and devotion in a tangible form to their Savior.[1]

It was well after midnight when Robert silently slipped from the hospital room and made his way to the car. It had been a long night, and tomorrow would be a long day as he and his wife met with other believers to remember the Lord. But it had been worth it. His soul thrilled at being able to once again worship and remember his Savior, and this opportunity to encourage and strengthen Joe's faith had been an added bonus.

For Joe, a deep sense of loss still hung over his soul, but tonight his sight had been refocused, and he now had a joy and peace which he had not previously known. He had found his purpose in life: *the chief purpose or occupation of every Believer is to worship the Savior.* Come what may, whatever happened after Mary's death—if the child was mentally retarded, handicapped, or even died—he now knew that his highest occupation was to worship his Savior and Creator.

Mary heard every word that evening, and even though her body wouldn't obey her commands, her mind and spirit were alive and well. "God, I want an intimate relationship like Joe has with You. God, I'm so helpless. Help me. Forgive my sin." Silently, Mary's prayer floated up to the heart of God the Father.

With much effort, she managed to move her arm from her side to her somewhat stretched abdomen. Unable to fully control the muscles in her arm, it slipped from her side, back onto the bed where it had been. Joe was sure he heard a noise, a rustling of cloth. He looked behind him at Mary; he even went over to her side. *Had the sheets been moved?* Dejected he turned from the bed. *Had it only been his imagination?* He was sure her hand had moved. Checking the monitors he noticed her blood pressure and heart rate were up slightly. A glimmer of hope rushed into his heart only to be dashed by reality. Nevertheless, this had been an awesome night!

Turning one more time to the body of his wife, clasping her hand he prayed aloud, "Dearest Savior, I give You my wife and child. Do with them as You see fit. They are Yours O God, and I give them back to You."

Falling once more to his knees Joe cried out to his Creator, "You know best what to do. Amen." Joe looked at his watch. It was past midnight. Crawling into his chair, Joe was soon asleep.

CHAPTER 27

Whoever offers praise glorifies Me; And to him who orders his conduct aright I will show the salvation of God" (Psalm 50:23).

"The poisonous bile of her soul had affected her mind."
— *Debbie Pearl*

As the new week began, August was now well underway, and still, Jane Jones' lawyer had been unable to get the custody case into court. Jane Jones had lost some of her bargaining power since Mary was no longer on the respirator, but she was still arguing for the removal of the PEG feeding tube in Mary's stomach. In an attempt to buy some time, Corbin was doing everything in his power to stall the hearing. Corbin realized Robert had been right. This case was too great to leave it to the court of public opinion. After some prayer and consideration, Corbin agreed it would be best to try and settle the case outside of court first. Mary's mother, and her lawyer were contacted, and a meeting time was agreed upon. Corbin arranged for the meeting to take place at the hospital. He wanted to have the meeting, if at all possible, in Mary's room.

Since the day of the accident when Jane Jones came to the ER, she had not seen her daughter. Corbin wished to bring Mary's mother face-to-face with her daughter and her situation. Corbin hoped he might invoke some emotions of sympathy, pity, *Dare he hope—love* in this woman for her only daughter if she would only come into the room and see her?

However, true to form, Mary's mother refused to come into the room. A conference room was then decided upon. Corbin, the ever-prepared lawyer, anticipating this might happen, had already arranged for one of the ladies from the church to come over to stay with Mary while Joe went down to the conference room.

After some formal introductions, the four parties involved, Joe, Corbin, Jane and her expensive lawyer, Mr. Brown, sat down at a round table. Corbin began by activating his portable digital recorder. He then led the proceedings by asking what evidence Mr. Brown planned on sighting as proof that Mary's Mom should be given legal custody of Mary, instead of Joe?

After clearing his throat, Mr. Brown began. "First, Mary Jones-Smith fully intended to divorce her husband, Joe A. Smith."

"You still have no proof of this," Corbin flatly stated. "You have never found a lawyer who Mary Smith had hired or talked with about her alleged divorce, and there are no records of a divorce being filed in the state of Illinois."

Mr. Brown explained with a decided air of confidence, "My client Jane Jones had several discussions with her daughter indicating she intended to divorce her husband."

"Circumstantial evidence, next item," Corbin rebutted.

"Secondly," Mr. Brown continued, "your client refuses to receive state aid, and Mary Jones-Smith no longer has insurance. Your client is not financially able to care for his wife, and my client is more than able to."

Corbin pulled a photocopy of the "Paid-in-full" hospital receipt from his briefcase and explained; "As of last Friday, all of Mrs. Smith's bills have been paid in full."

"How did you do that?" Mrs. Jones' eyes glared at Joe. "That is a lie! He doesn't have the money."

Joe was silent. Corbin had told him not to speak. Mr. Brown put his finger to his lips in an attempt to communicate with his client. He had apparently made the same arrangement with Jane Jones, but she refused to obey her lawyer. The lawyer continued, "My client says, Mr. Smith was verbally, mentally, and physically abusive to his wife."

"Time and date." Corbin again flatly demanded.

The lawyer handed Corbin a written dissertation of the times and dates of the alleged abuses.

"Is your client willing to take a lie detector test to prove this is not just some story she made up?"

Mary's mother gave Corbin an icy stare. "I don't need to take a lie detector test. It's true. He's vicious! Besides, I know he wasn't faithful to my daughter."

Joe started to say something in his defense, despite the fact that Corbin had warned him not to speak. Corbin touched Joe's arm and calmly shook his head no. Joe wanted to scream, "That's a lie," but he swallowed his anger for the time being, and calmed down. Now was not the time to speak. "Do you have any proof of this?" Corbin asked.

Mary's mother again shot off her mouth. "I don't have to. I know it's true."

"Do you have any pictures, witnesses?" asked Corbin in his same emotionless way. Corbin Cutler remained calm and collected while Jane Jones was beginning to look rather silly.

"All you have is a lot of hearsay from your client," Corbin concluded looking rather smug as he smiled at Joe. "The judge will throw you and your client out of court if you can't produce one scrap of evidence."

Mrs. Jones' lawyer was about to make his next point and bring up the alleged Living Will, when Mary's mom spoke up. "I don't have to have evidence. It's true. Joe is a no good, religious fanatic, who ruined my daughter's life!" Rising from her chair, she rushed over to his chair and slapped Joe full in the face. With great anger, she began swinging wildly at Joe who slid his chair back in retreat.

Corbin grabbed her by the wrists and pulled Jane away from Joe and toward her chair. "Mr. Brown, you need to get control of your client, or I'll be forced to call the police." As he released her wrists, Jane took a swing at Corbin, but he stepped back and avoided the blow.

As an unearthly power guided her mind, Jane Jones' eyes narrowed to slits, and a look of terror came over her aging face, "I recognize you now. . . you sexually abused me as a child!" Corbin taken aback for a split second quickly regained his composure and asked, "And when madam did this happen, time and date please?"

"June 1, 1956 I was 14 years old."

"That's interesting, because I was only three years old," Corbin said with a smile at Mr. Brown.

Mrs. Jones' lawyer looked nervous and worried. Things couldn't get much worse. He had just learned the financial angle that had been the backbone of his case had been removed. Not only did he have little real evidence apart from his client's testimony, they were recording all the crazy things his client was saying, which would effectively destroy any credibility she had in court.

"Mrs. Jones," the lawyer said putting his arm on her shoulder, "Sit down, or I will resign this case immediately." Jane Jones looked like a caged animal; she kicked her lawyer in the shin and retreated into a corner of the room with her back against the wall.

Examining the injured shin, Mr. Brown spoke to Jane Jones, "That's it, Mrs. Jones. I resign the case." Picking up his briefcase and what few papers he had, he left the room, leaving his client alone with Joe and Corbin.

Corbin had no patience for this kind of behavior, especially when it came from a woman in her sixties. Mary's mom crouched in the corner with her back to the wall looking wildly back and forth, her arms extended in front of her as if to shield her from something unseen. "Get away from me, or I'll bite you!"

Joe didn't doubt for a minute she'd resort to biting given the opportunity. A torrent of profanity issued from her mouth.

"Mrs. Jones, this is your last chance. Stand up or I'll call hospital security."

More profanity issued forth along with, "Get me my counselor. I need my psychiatrist!"

Pity for the sinner caught in the chains of sin caused Joe to rise and try to help his mother-in-law. Stepping toward his mother-in-law, Joe reached out his hand to help her up, but she tried to bite him.

By now hospital security had come to see what all the noise and commotion was about.

"Protect me from these men!" Jane Jones screamed uncontrollably. "They are attacking me! Get my psychiatrist! These men are trying to hurt me!"

One of the officers tried to help Mrs. Jones to her feet. Taking a firm hold, she sunk her teeth into his arm.

Corbin fought back a laugh. He wanted to ask if she was current on her rabies shots, but he knew legal decorum prevented it. Instead he casually put his cupped fingers in front of his mouth to hide his smile. Several other security guards were called, and Mrs. Jones was removed from the hospital in restraints.

Corbin turned to Joe and explained, "It appears this case will never see a courtroom."

"Praise the Lord," was all Joe could say as he shook Corbin's hand and headed back to check on Mary.

Later that day, after being turned over to the Chicago city police, her psychiatrist recommended Jane Jones commit herself to another local hospital for psychiatric evaluation and treatment.

It was just after five o'clock. Mr. Verde sat at his desk wrapping up a few things. His new, attractive young secretary had already left for the day. Glancing at the file he had set up on Joe and Mary Smith he found the archived e-mail and began to re-read the old letter from Ken:

———————————

Mo

Sorry this reply is so long in coming. I took a few days off and went to northern Michigan, and did some sailing. When I got back,

I started looking into your question regarding the authority you possess to remove someone from life support. Traditionally, if the patient has no family, a hospital administrator and a doctor together have the authority to remove someone from life support, remove a feeding tube, etc.

In this case, the next of kin refusing doctor's advice presents a problem. The best option would be to use the hospital's resources to back the mother-in-law in her custody battle. If they were taking state financial aid, I could pull some strings and have this issue wrapped up by next weekend, but alas that is not the case.

If you took this case to court our mutual friends in the circuit court would do all they could to insure a favorable outcome, and set yet another good and needed legal precedent in our nation, but in your present circumstances, the time that it would take may be too long to be of benefit to the hospital.

I understand your concern over the people creating a scene outside the hospital, but I suspect that the group in question has been given more than enough distraction to prevent them from being a problem in this regard. I have been researching your question in admiralty/maritime law, and if this woman has a state birth certificate, which I suspect she does, the state has ultimate authority in this case. If you wish to take this case to court, please contact me and I would be glad to advise. If you have any more questions or problems, let me know. Ken

Mr. Verde realized he needed Ken's help and it was time to ask.

Ken

I see no alternative. We need to meet to discuss insuring a favorable outcome in court at your earliest convenience. It looks as if we are taking this case to court ASAP, to get this woman declared brain-dead, and give us authority to harvest her organs while they are still viable.

Mo

Mr. Verde closed the email program and sat back in his chair. He had heard about Joe's mother-in-law from his security guard earlier that day, sadly, for Mr. Verde's purposes, that avenue had become a dead end to him. It was time to begin legal proceedings of his own.

Bernard Thomas had been trying to call him every day this week. Now, he would have that liver for Bernard's wife one way or another. He just didn't know if he would be able to get through the court system in time. Mr. Verde looked at his schedule for the next day. He had a nine o'clock meeting, but after that was over, he would get the situation moving along.

It was unfortunate for him that Mary was now off her respirator. He needed a judge to declare her brain-dead ASAP, so he could harvest the organs while her heart was still beating to give Mrs. Thomas the best chance to survive the transplant. They would need to get that brain-dead woman into surgery, as soon as the court case was completed and get that liver removed. It would be tricky work, but he knew Dr. Bartlett would help him make it happen. In the meantime, the doctor was working daily trying to get that stubborn Joe Smith to do the right thing without taking him to court.

Later that afternoon, Joe sat reading his Bible as Dr. Bartlett came in for his evening rounds. For the first time in a long time, it seemed like all of Joe's trials had vanished away.

After a short examination, the doctor looked at his computer screen and then shook his head sadly. "Your wife's protein levels are way too high. I fear the kidneys will shut down any time." Not wasting any time, the doctor continued, "Your wife is not really a candidate for dialysis." The doctor looked at her blood pressure.

"Her blood pressure has been slowly rising over the last week. You know that her face is swollen, and as I already mentioned, she has proteinuria, and all of the symptoms of pre-eclampsia. I think we are very likely looking at the end."

"Pre-eclampsia, what's that?" Joe asked.

"It's a medical term for pregnancy toxemia," the doctor replied as he shut the lid on his laptop.

"Is there anything else we can do?" Joe desperately asked.

"No, not really. You need to think about some of the options we've talked about in the past."

Joe knew what the doctor meant. He didn't have to be told.

"When's the fetus due?" the doctor asked.

"Christmas," Joe mechanically mumbled.

Opening his computer again, the doctor punched in some dates. The baby ought to be viable by now, or very close. I'll call OB and see when they can work her in for a C-section. We need to get on this right way. Once her kidney's fail, it will only be a short time before your wife and the baby will both be dead. If we want to save the baby, we will need to act quickly. There is no way to save them both."

After the doctor left, Joe looked up pre-eclampsia on the internet. *Pre-eclampsia—a condition in pregnancy characterized by a rapid rise in blood pressure that can lead to seizure, stroke, multiple organ failure, and death of the mother and/or baby.* Death, the nightmare he had been dreading now faced him square in the face. Mary had come so far, for so long.

At first the doctors said she wouldn't even make it through the weekend. Now, thirteen weeks later, she was completely off the respirator. Had God brought them all this way to let Mary die now? So was this how it would all end? It seemed like he had just weathered through one trial to be faced with yet another worse trial.

Falling to his knees, Joe began to pray, *"Oh God, I have given you the life of my wife and child. I beg you to spare them. But if not, help me to accept what you allow."*

Dr. Bartlett called Mr. Verde on his cell phone. Mr. Verde was at home now enjoying a rum and coke by the pool. "After all the trouble we've had, I think you are finally going to have that liver," Dr. Bartlett told Mr. Verde.

"Really? Good work! Has Mr. Smith finally come around?"

"No, I don't think we will get him to change his mind, but the patient is developing pre-eclampsia. I think the patient might continue another two to three weeks in this situation with proper care and medication, but I am encouraging him to go ahead and schedule a C-section and take the fetus."

"So when do you think we will have the organs?" Verde continued.

"I'll check with OB tomorrow and let you know when we can schedule the surgery."

"Good. "Verde smiled, as he closed his cell phone. *This would be much better than a court case.*

Joe stayed on his knees and continued in prayer, seeking the Lord for another half hour. He wanted to have a pure, submissive heart, willing to accept whatever God allowed in this situation, but it was hard not to let his desires enter into the equation. As he sat there praying, it dawned on him that he needed a second opinion.

Reaching for his cell phone, he tried to call Rachel. Somehow he had to get ahold of Dr. Rodriquez. If Dr. Rodriquez felt they needed to do a C-section, then maybe he would consider it.

Rachel's phone rang and rang, but there was no answer. Joe called her every fifteen minutes for the next hour-and-a-half. Finally, after the sixth call, he left a message, pleading with her to return his call.

Not knowing what else to do, Joe called Mr. Elder and Robert Forbes and asked them to pray for him. If Joe had been thinking more clearly, he might have tried to analyze why Dr. Bartlett was suddenly so concerned about a baby he had only a few weeks before thought was dead.

A hard dilemma faced Joe. Did they let the doctors perform a procedure that would end Mary's life in order to save his child? He had clung to the idea for so long that he would do nothing to harm Mary or the child's life in any way. But now, if death was indeed unavoidable for Mary, would it not be wise to save his child while he could? Somewhere down deep in his soul the human side of Joe wanted to ask why God was forcing him to make so hard a decision. Joe walked the floor praying and beseeching his Lord and Savior for the life of his child.

Verde's friend Ken scanned through the messages on his private email account on his laptop as Joe prayed. It was a new laptop and he was still getting acquainted with his new track pad. He was scrolling down through the string of old e-mails from Mo, and deciding how to respond. As he scrolled up to begin his reply to Verde he unknowingly double-clicked Joe Smith's email address from an earlier letter, with a little help from one of the heavenly host who was there in response to Joe Smith's prayer.

Mo

I will get in contact with our mutual friends and see what I can do to expedite this matter.

Ken

As he clicked "send," the e-mail started its journey through cyberspace to two different recipients. The ongoing string of communication that had gone on between Mo and Ken was being sent to Joe Smith's email as well as going to its intended addressee.

Just after two in the morning when his physical body had no more strength, Joe moved the vinyl chair next to Mary's bed and laid down in it. Putting his hand on top of Mary's, he fell asleep. Unseen by Joe, spiritual forces were at work in the heavenly realms to carry out the plans of their Creator in response to the earnest prayers of this righteous man.

In Joe's inbox, Ken's e-mail waited to be discovered.

Chapter 28

Oh God help me. I'm in so much pain. Mary's mind was alert even if her body made little movement. *Joe where are you?* She wanted to scream, but her voice was weak from the respirator and weeks of no use. Instead, she made a faint moan, which sounded more like someone clearing their throat.

Joe moved in his chair, not yet fully awake and trying to get comfortable enough to go back to sleep. He'd only been sound asleep a few hours, and he had no desire to wake up now if he didn't have to. With one blurry eye open, he glanced at the clock. *It's only six o'clock. Way to early,* he thought. Without a second thought, Joe pulled the blanket over his head.

Where is he? Why doesn't he help me? A world of unending darkness had separated Mary from Joe for almost three months, but now a dim light was beginning to shine into her mind, and she felt certain Joe was closeby if she could just call for him.

"Joe the baby is coming." Mary wanted to scream, but instead a guttural hiss issued from her throat.

Joe sat up immediately. He had definitely heard something. There was no denying it this time. A sound had come from Mary. She had been trying to say something to him. The sleepy fog he had been in disappeared in an instant, Joe was wide awake now. Could it be true? Was Mary really waking up after all this time?

Jumping up, he shook Mary's arm, "Mary if you can hear me," he spoke in such a loud voice, it was a wonder he didn't wake the whole floor of the hospital, "blink your eyes."

Mary not only moved her eye lids, but attempted to move her head in an up and down motion.

"Dearest God, thank You!" Joe whispered a prayer of deep gratitude to the Savior, only to be interrupted by another moan, this time louder and more pronounced than the first he had heard.

"You're in pain. Something's wrong."

Again Mary gave a clumsy, half nod of her head in a slow deliberate way.

Joe glanced up at all the monitors. Everything seemed fine. Her heart rate was higher, about 90, but no beepers were sounding. Everything seemed normal. *What should he do?* His mind whirled. *Was this just a onetime thing? Would Mary slip back into unconsciousness again? If he called the hospital staff would they even believe him? What if Mary was unconscious again and he couldn't get her to respond to his voice?* He certainly had his doubts as to whether he could trust Dr. Bartlett and the rest of the hospital staff.

Dr. Rodriquez or Rachel would know what to do, but he hadn't been able to reach Rachel. Joe fumbled for his cell phone. Where had he left it? Retrieving it from the pocket of the shirt he had worn yesterday, he tried to call Rachel again. *Oh God help her to answer.*

A very sound asleep Rachel was suddenly aware of her phone ringing. She had forgotten to put her phone on the charger for several days, and when she had gotten back from the Crisis Pregnancy Center the night before, she had realized it was completely dead. Unplugging it from the charger, she answered the phone, trying to sound coherent.

"Rachel, hello?" The sleepy voice of Rachel on the other end of the line acknowledged him, "This is Joe Smith, the guy at the hospital."

"I know who you are," Rachel echoed back, as she rubbed her dark eyes, not sure what to think. "What can I do for you, Joe?"

"I need to get in contact with Dr. Rodriquez. It's an emergency. Mary's coming around, and she's in a lot of pain, and, oh my, the bedding is soaked . . ." Joe paused for a moment as he processed...

"Do you think she's having the baby?"

First time fathers are so clueless, Rachel thought as she rolled her eyes, shaking her head, but she checked herself, "Yes!" She yelled back emphatically, "You stay put. I'm calling him, and we'll be there shortly.

Did you try to call him yourself?"

"I can't find his number," Joe sadly replied.

Rachel quickly snatched her purse from the dresser. She had no time to lose. Searching through her purse, she quickly grabbed the piece of paper where Dr. Rodriquez had written his phone number many weeks beforehand.

Dialing the number quickly, she debated what she would say when he answered the phone. "Buenos Dias," a mysterious woman's voice spoke to her in Spanish. For a split second, Rachel's mind was paralyzed... so, there was a woman in his life.

Continuing in Spanish, the woman replied, "Joaquin is out on the patio having his breakfast, I will go get him."

Rachel took another deep breath, trying to calm herself, and put aside her own deep hurt and emotional tumult. Pressing her fingers to the bridge of her nose, she tried to focus on the issue at hand: Mary Smith needed a doctor, more specifically Dr. Rodriquez.

"Dr. Rodriquez," she managed to say, "Mary Smith has come around. I believe she's in labor."

Shocked, put pleasantly surprised to have Rachel call him, Dr. Rodriquez couldn't help but feel excited. "Rachel, I'm. . ." He hoped he didn't sound too nervous, too jubilant. *Here was his final chance. If she refused him now, he'd give her up forever. He'd ask her over to meet his Mom. No, no dinner first, then mom's place. He would do it now before she said anything else, and he lost his nerve. To Rachel, it was as if Dr. Rodriquez hadn't understood a word she had said.*

"Dr. Rodriquez," Rachel said more emphatically, "Joe Smith just called me. He needs you. Mary's water has broken. She's in labor."

Stumbling back into the world of reality from his day dreams, Dr. Rodriquez slipped into doctor mode, and all thoughts of his attraction for Rachel were held in check under the current crisis. Drawing in the reins on his strong emotions, his courage evaporated, and he felt his cold professionalism coming back. Rachel and he both knew what had to be done, but how? This was no time for romance.

"Would you please meet me at the hospital? I may need you to help me get into the ICU without being seen." *I might just get fired, too,* he thought to himself.

He may need me! Rachel's heart skipped a beat. *Maybe, just maybe he cared about her just a little, but then how could she hope for anything when he had another woman in his life?* "I'll be there in ten, north side of the employee parking lot," and just as abruptly as their conversation had begun, it ended.

Ten minutes later, Rachel was there waiting for him. Rachel was dressed in her purple scrubs and had her card ready to scan for entrance into the hospital through the employee back door when the doctor pulled into the parking lot. The doctor was dressed as a civilian, carrying a blue duffle bag under his arm. Rachel hoped his street attire would work to their advantage, although neither of them had thought that far ahead.

Without a hello or a thank you as Rachel opened the door for him, he started talking. His voice was nervous, worried, and strained.

"It's nearly seven. They should be changing shifts in the ICU soon. We need to get in there before there's a whole lot of staff on the floor who might recognize me. The less attention we have, the better." Rachel nodded and agreed.

"I don't know how I'm going to work this. This woman needs a C-section if anyone does, and I'm going to have to get her into the OB ward." Then, as an afterthought, he added, "If I lose my license over this one, I lose my license. We are going to do everything we can to save these two lives. I guess they'll let me practice in Mexico."

Putting her soft hand on his arm, she looked reassuringly into his dark eyes, "You won't go back to Mexico. They can't deport a US citizen. Anyway," trying to move onto something brighter. "You are the best OB doctor they have. I believe God is going to help us in this situation."

Dr. Rodriquez smiled back at her, following that gesture of encouragement.

Rachel's tender heart melted under that smile.

Dr. Rodriquez looked deeply into her eyes.

Rachel looked away in embarrassment.

His soul ached to say something, to draw upon this tender moment, but he didn't have time. *She is so kind—so kind and encouraging to everyone. How could she ever like a guy like me?*

Suddenly, they were at the door to the ICU. The round reception desk loomed ahead, but not a single soul sat at it. Rachel gently opened the door to the ICU without a sound, and left it partly ajar so the doctor could slip in unnoticed. Walking in, she moved to the far side of the desk and looked down the halls at the three remaining corridors. Not a single person in sight. This, in and of itself, was a miracle.

Rachel frantically waved to the doctor to come in. "Hurry," she whispered, "not a soul in sight. God is at work here."

In a matter of moments Dr. Rodriquez and Rachel were in the room. Joe held Mary's hand as she moaned in extreme discomfort. She seemed to be saying Joe's name over and over as she moved her head back and forth in slow uncoordinated jerks.

Dr. Rodriquez snatched a pair of gloves from the box on the wall and slipped them on in one smooth motion. "I didn't think this baby would come this early. Dr. Rodriquez pulled back the covers. Rachel gently pulled back the thin hospital robe Mary wore. Placing his hand on Mary to check her, a look of sheer fright crossed his face.

"This baby's crowning. . . .Push," he urged his reluctant patient. Whether Mary could hear and do what he requested or whether her body instinctively responded to the pain, no one knew. But the next thing Joe saw was his child issuing forth from the birth canal, covered in a thick white coat of vernix.

Dr. Rodriquez was nervous. Beads of sweat formed on his brow and face. *What attention would the baby need first? Would it even breathe on its own?* He didn't even have the NICU staff he so desperately needed. Picking up the small form, he motioned to Rachel.

"Rachel, in my blue bag..." He didn't even have to say it. She knew what he wanted. Quickly her fingers found a new suction bulb in its sterile container, and ripped back the plastic for him.

The doctor took the bulb and sucked the baby's nose and throat. Air poured into the tiny being's form, and her chest began to go up and down in a rhythmic motion. She cried a low beautiful note.

Joe stood dazed as the room swirled around him.

Rachel and the doctor worked on the baby. Dr. Rodriquez held the baby's head in one hand and the child's body in the other.

Was his son even alive? The tiny form looked so small and lifeless. Joe wanted to move forward, to take his child, to lavish the little one with affection. This might be his only chance to hold his child in this world, but his feet seemed glued to the floor.

"Check the heart rate Rachel." Rachel instinctively took the baby's pulse while she glanced up at the second hand on her watch."

Mary's weak hand brushed Joe's arm. He instinctively turned toward her. Joe looked into Mary's face. Her eyes were open. She was looking at him. A tear spilled down her cheek.

" Joe I want. . . ." Joe bent down close to Mary and kissed her face. He could barely hear her raspy voice, "... your God."

Now the emotional torrent within Joe broke and tears came streaming down his face as he shook uncontrollably, balancing himself with both his arms against the bed-rail of Mary's bed.

Rachel and the doctor were too focused on their small patient to notice or hear this intimate exchange between Mary and Joe. Her breathing was normal. This was a good sign. The doctor's form and features eased up.

"110," Rachel breathed out in relief—*a good heart rate for a newborn.*

Dr. Rodriquez cradled the little one in his arms now. The baby sneezed and then started to softly cry. Dr. Rodriquez wrapped the little bundle up in an extra blanket Rachel had retrieved from a cabinet in the corner of the room. It was a little large, but it worked.

"Here, take her," Dr. Rodriquez said, handing her to Joe.

Joe took his daughter, unsure of what to do or say. His mind was having trouble convincing himself this wasn't all a dream. "A girl? Here all this time I thought I was having a son," Joe mumbled in disbelief.

"It's a girl, let me assure you. I've delivered several of these, and I think I know the difference by now. Her color is great. She's pink from head to toe, and a good coating of vernix. She's moving her arms and legs. She has normal breathing and heart rate. She even sneezed. I don't think there is anything wrong with the child —except she needs some food, and some loving."

Then as an afterthought Dr. Rodriquez added, "She's rather small, but she'll catch up."

Dr. Rodriquez stopped talking and turned his attention to Mary. The doctor wanted to make sure the uterus clamped down and the bleeding stopped easily. With the little activity Mary had had over the past several months while she was unconscious in her severely-compromised physical state, she had very little muscle tone and she could hemorrhage easily.

"Rachel, get the chart there on the end of the bed. AB negative he muttered. Joe, what's your blood type?"

"What? What's my blood type?" Joe responded.

"What's your blood type," the doctor asked a little bit more short-tempered than he had intended.

"O negative."

"You sure of that?"

"Yes."

"Good. We shouldn't need a Rho-Gam injection."

Joe wasn't listening, and he probably wouldn't remember most of what the doctor had said. He was too busy staring at his two precious little ladies.

Rachel came over. As if she could read Joe's mind, she said reassuringly, "She's beautiful Joe, and the doctor's telling you he doesn't think there's anything wrong with her."

"That's right Joe. She seems perfectly healthy," Dr. Rodriquez agreed as he continued to massage Mary's abdomen. "We will do some more tests in a few days to be sure, but she looks great. Congratulations." Dr. Rodriquez gave him a sharp pat on the shoulders with his free hand.

Joe turned to Mary and lay the baby on her chest near her heart. "Our baby." She muttered in a voice only Joe could detect.

"Our baby," he repeated back. "She's beautiful. Thank you so much Mary. Thank for not aborting this child."

Mary only smiled and seemed to be lapsing back into her unconscious world of darkness. Worry again filled Joe. Was this it? Would his wife once again be an uncommunicative vegetable? Rachel perceived Joe's concern. "Let her rest Joe. She's had a full day."

"Her bleeding is normal and she has passed the placenta," Dr. Rodriquez said more to Rachel than Joe. Then, addressing Joe again he said, "She'll wake up and be able to talk more later on. It's better to take it slow at first with these accident patients."

"She doesn't even seem to notice you and Rachel are in the room. Is she going to be alright?" Joe commented in disbelief.

"We have witnessed two miracles today, a birth and an awakening. I suspect every day will show more and more improvement. Small amounts at first, but I feel confident in saying the worst is over. I think you have your wife back. And now," Dr. Rodriquez looked around the room, "I can't believe no one has been in here to check on us. Rachel, could you stay with Mary until I get a delivery room nurse up here? I want to walk Joe down to the nursery, weigh her, and get her a bottle.

"Joe, I'm a really big advocate of breast-feeding, but there's no way your wife can do that in her condition. You're going to have to bottle feed."

Looking over at Rachel, he displayed a playful grin. Rachel smiled back. The Doctor commented, "It is a shame they don't have a goat in this hospital. That's what my Mom says they use all the time in Mexico."

Joe thought of Proverbs 27:27. He knew where he could get some milk for his baby if the hospital would only let him.

The pressure was off Dr. Rodriquez, and he seemed to relax and be more at ease. He pushed the intercom button, alerting the nurses at the desk on the floor.

Dr. Rodriquez seemed to take great pleasure in announcing, "We just had a baby down here. Could you send someone in to clean up? Oh yes, and Mrs. Smith has come around. She's going to need some real food when she wakes up. Do you think you could arrange to have that on hand too?"

He turned the intercom off, so as not to hear the shock and disbelief on the other end. "Joe, we will take that PEG tube out of Mary in a day or so, as soon as she can take something by mouth, but first let's take care of your baby."

Joe walked numbly behind the doctor to the elevator, and down the hall, into another wing of the hospital to the nursery, carrying his tiny daughter. By now, several of the nurses on the hall had been alerted to the situation, and they looked on in disbelief as they hurried to Mary's room. The new baby was warm as she snuggled up next to Dad in her oversized blanket. She failed to notice everyone was staring at her. Instead, she seemed to be adjusting to the situation well, while Dad was still struggling to adapt to a world turned upside-down. This was more than he ever could have asked or imagined. Dr. Rodriquez turned to Joe and exclaimed, "NOW TO HIM WHO IS ABLE TO DO IMMEASURABLY MORE THAN ALL WE CAN ASK OR IMAGINE, BE GLORY, HONOR, POWER, DOMINION BOTH NOW AND FOREVER!"

CHAPTER 29

And, sir, when we think of eternity, and of the future consequences of all human conduct, what is there in this life that should make any man contradict the dictates of his conscience, the principles of justice, the laws of religion, and of God?" —William Wilberforce

"...in a time of deceit telling the truth is a revolutionary act." —George Orwell

The fluorescent lights of the hospital shone bleak, and this atmosphere brought no joy to the heart and mind of Bernard Thomas. It was early Wednesday morning. Bernard had flown in late the night before from Canada to be with Carol. The hospital staff could do little to manage the woman, and the two extra nurses he had hired to sit with her were both threatening to quit if something didn't change.

Carol lapsed in and out of consciousness. There was no need to sedate her for now; her mind was numbed by the pain medication which needed to be increased almost daily. When she was awake her mouth cursed God for her pain, and her disposition toward Bernard was almost as bad. She blamed him for everything. He relished the times she slept. It was better to have her asleep rather than deal with her in her bitter, wrathful, state of pain.

One of the plethora of doctors appeared at the door. After a brief exam of the patient, the doctor took it upon himself to prepare Mr. Thomas for the worst. It seemed inevitable. "If we can't get a transplant soon, I fear it will be useless to do one at all. Even now, I fear there is permanent damage being done to the rest of her body because of her damaged liver."

Bernard braced himself, and tried to show little emotion. He wasn't one given to letting out his deep feelings in public. The doctor slipped away after commenting that they would make her as comfortable as possible.

No need blowing up at this doctor. He was only a pawn in the whole scheme of things, but where oh, where was that liver that had been promised to them? They had wasted so much time here in Chicago when they might have been searching other places, Europe, or the orient, for that liver. He had heard he could buy a liver in China, but it was too late for that now.

Mr. Verde had assured him they had an exact match, an AB negative liver for them here at this hospital. Reaching for the phone, he dialed up the hospital administrator.

Mr. Verde looked at his phone. He didn't want to, but it was time he answered that phone call. It was time for him to face the music. The miraculous recovery of Mary Smith would make an excellent human interest story, and maybe he could salvage some publicity for the hospital and its staff, but now what was he to do about Mrs. Thomas? Secretly, he had hoped Bernard Thomas would donate the money for a long coveted new wing in the transplant ward. Clearing his throat, Bernard spoke with authority, "Almost three months ago you told me you had a liver from a brain-dead patient. We were assured that my wife would soon have that organ. What is the status on that?"

There was a long silence on the other end of the phone.

"The patient. . . . that situation is no longer available. I can't speak about it. It's highly confidential."

Bernard's eyes narrowed as anger entered his voice. "You know that money I was going to donate to the hospital? I don't think I will be able to do that now. The situation has changed, and I can't speak about it." Bernard threw the words back into the phone at the man. Without a word more, he slammed down the phone.

Despair filled Bernard. *Had they come all the way from Canada, and wasted almost three months in a Chicago hospital, only to let his wife die here in a country not even her own? When Carol was well enough, well enough . . . no, she would never be well enough. Next opportunity he got, he would fly them both back to Canada. It was too late now. Even if they could find an AB* negative *liver somewhere, it was doubtful there was enough time left. If she was going to die, she might as well die at home. And where was God in all of this?* Now even Bernard felt like cursing God.

Joe gradually began to adjust to the change of events, and by the time Dr. Rodriquez showed up the evening following his daughter's birth, he was able to ask a few more intelligent questions. Joy had replaced the worry that had robbed Joe of his strength for so long. Mary still slept, but she moved her arms and rolled her head slightly to one side, and everyone seemed to agree she would come around again.

"What happened?" Joe questioned Dr. Rodriquez, as he examined Mary. "My daughter doesn't seem premature."

"No, the tests showed she was about 37 or 38 weeks, a full term baby. At 5 1/2 pounds, she is rather small, but that's to be expected after all her Mom has been through and not eating regular, solid food during the last part of the pregnancy."

"I thought I knew when she was conceived, but I guess I was way off," Joe confessed. "That means she was pregnant before we split up. Did Rachel know all this?"

A pang of guilt plunged into Dr. Rodriquez's heart at Rachel's name. He hadn't even really properly thanked her for all her help. When he returned to Mary's room after escorting Joe to the nursery, she was gone and an OB nurse was there. Now that the Smith's baby was here, he wouldn't have any good reason to be around Rachel or communicate with her. *How was he going to get to know her better?*

Why couldn't he ever seem to bridge the gap and tell her how much he really admired her?

"I don't know what Rachel did or didn't know. I told her we wouldn't determine the age of the baby, for fear that would give more reasons for the powers that be to force you to abort the child. However, I suspect she did know. She is very good at what she does."

"I was all prepared for a handicapped, mentally-retarded child, if the child lived at all. Now, I don't know quite what to do with myself, except to thank God that she seems healthy."

Dr. Rodriquez picked up the baby again. Just to be cautious, Dr. Rodriquez had kept the baby on the Neonatal Intensive Care monitors. In order to enable Joe to stay in the ICU with Mary and care for his newborn daughter, Dr. Rodriquez had insisted the NICU monitors be moved down to the ICU ward. It had taken some doing to convince the nurses he should and could do this, but he felt it was what needed to be done. Dr. Rodriquez smiled as he looked at the even heartbeat and rhythm of the child's breathing and respiration on the monitors.

"She is fine. Look at those vital signs. Just keep her warm, love her, and feed her." Then as an afterthought he said, "What are you going to name her?"

A dumb look spread across Joe's face. "I don't know. I had some names picked out for a son, but I never imagined we would have a daughter."

A nurse came in to make a routine check of the baby and Mary. "Mrs. Smith sipped some protein shake this morning when she was awake," the nurse said.

Dr. Rodriquez asked the nurse, "How much?"

"About fory five cc's," the nurse replied.

"Good." Then Dr. Rodriquez instructed, "As soon as the PEG tube is out, I've signed the paperwork to have Mrs. Smith and the baby downgraded. There is no longer any reason to have her in ICU at this point." Dr. Rodriquez left.

It was a comfort to Joe to know Dr. Rodriquez was now their

primary doctor. It had taken some persuasion, but Dr. Rodriquez would now be Mary's regular doctor and Dr. Bartlett was out of their life for good.

Joe picked up the phone and called Robert. Robert was over-joyed for Joe.

Then Joe called Mr. Elder at home. More congratulations fol-lowed.

Joe didn't know which he was more excited about: the fact Mary had awakened, or the reality he had a healthy newborn baby.

Next, he called his mother-in-law in the psych ward. His moth-er-in-law took the news coolly saying she always knew Mary would pull through. It was as if she didn't remember what had happened the last three months. His mother-in-law seemed to have little inter-est in her new granddaughter. She yelled at Joe, blaming him again for where she was. Joe hung up the phone; he would not allow her to spoil his bliss with her revengeful raving.

Picking up his laptop, Joe spammed everyone on his email list with the good news.

A few floors below, in a fit of desperation, Bernard called out to God. *God if you are real, show yourself to me.* He picked up the Gideon Bible and started reading on the page where it fell open.

"I am the resurrection and the life." *If this Jesus is the resurrection and the life, why can't He save my wife? People talk about being saved. What does that mean? Saved from what? All their religion certainly hadn't saved Carol from the threat of death.* Bernard slammed the Bible shut. He must be making arrangements to return to Canada. *Tonight, yes, tonight, if he could get the plane and the pilot here in time.*

Then it happened! At the last possible moment, when things seemed the bleakest; as Bernard pushed God out of his mind and started to make the final plans to return to Canada, the phone rang. Bernard answered it, little suspecting how it would change their lives.

On the phone was the head doctor of the transplant center and not Mr. Verde. An AB negative liver had come available in a car accident, which would fit Carol's needs, and by some miracle, the liver was only a few hours away by flight. If they would accept it, a pilot was on standby to fly it in.

"But would they still want the liver?" the doctor asked. He had heard about their plans to return to Canada.

"Want the liver? Of course we want the liver!" There was no question about that. This liver was their only hope for any type of a normal life together. All of the recent tests showed the cancer was still localized in the liver; there were no indications that it had spread. *Once Carol got that liver, everything would be normal again,* Bernard thought.

He could hardly believe what was happening. It seemed inconceivable that another AB negative liver was available. For one brief moment, his thoughts were open to the idea of a merciful Creator somewhere in the universe, but he had no time to contemplate God right then. Carol had to be awakened immediately to be prepped for surgery. Bernard tried to explain and make her understand what was happening, but she was in too much pain and discomfort. After trying to explain it to her, he wondered how much she really understood.

Hospital staff members were buzzing in and out of the room, taking vitals and labs on Carol before she was taken to pre-op, while mountains of legal documents were brought in for Bernard to sign. The hospital staff members were as surprised as Bernard at finding a matching liver. In this case, Carol's blood type had worked to her advantage. There were no other people in this region with her blood type needing a transplant, and her case certainly was critical. Carol hardly knew what was happening. One moment she was trying to rest in her bed, and the next she was in pre-op. A little more than two hours later, the liver was at the hospital. Bernard paced the floor with beads of sweat dripping from his forehead during the lengthy procedure. He feared at any moment a doctor might emerge to tell him the bad news. He feared Carol might die on the operating table. She was so frail, so fragile now. He didn't know if she had the strength to make it through the surgery.

Bernard walked on pins and needles, fearing the worst. After several hours, the doctor did come out to speak with Bernard. He was dreading the possibility of bad news. The doctor's conversation was optimistic, but tentative, as he explained to Bernard, "Carol's life is hanging on by a slim thread. If infection does not set in, and her body does not reject the liver, there is a chance for recovery."

The first day was the hardest. Carol remained sedated and senseless for most of the time. Bernard had nobody—no family, no friends, no God to comfort him. All his hope lay in Carol recovering, surviving, and living a normal life. All his happiness seemed wrapped up in her life continuing. He couldn't bear to think of what would happen if she didn't survive. *What if her body rejected the liver?* There was no turning back now, and somewhere in the middle of all these deep emotions, Bernard found a few moments to wonder about the God of the universe. *Did he really care about a man and his wife in a hospital in Chicago? Maybe he did. Otherwise,* Bernard thought, *what would you call the events of the day, except a miracle?*

CHAPTER 30

But evil men and seducers shall wax worse and worse, deceiving, and being deceived (2 Timothy 3:13).

"No people are so hopelessly enslaved as those who think themselves free." —Gothe

Any society that would give up a little liberty to gain a little security will deserve neither and lose both." —Benjamin Franklin

Joe stretched and yawned as he woke up from a short nap. Easing up slowly from the vinyl chair, he gently deposited his soundly sleeping baby in the hospital crib. It was now Monday afternoon following the birth, and his daughter was nearly a week old. Joe had finished covering her with a fuzzy pink blanket when his phone rang. Quickly, he stepped out into the hall of the hospital so as not to wake the baby or Mary.

Robert Forbes' familiar voice greeted Joe. Robert had come up to the hospital a couple of days after the baby's birth, but extenuating circumstances at home and frequent teaching sessions with Corbin Cutler had kept him from being a frequent visitor at the hospital like he had in the past. "How are you lad, and how's the babe?" Robert asked from the comfort of his living room.

"Good. It's hard to believe she's almost a week old," Joe replied.

"What did you name the wee lass?"

"Dorea," Joe replied, "it means. . . ."

"Gift from God," Robert finished Joe's phrase for him. "That's a beautiful name for a little lass."

Joe stood in the doorway to the hospital room. As he was talking with Robert the dietitian and a nurse approached, wanting to talk with him. With all the commotion in the doorway, little Dorea began to wake. Robert could hear her fussing in the background. Joe walked back into the room and over to the crib. He picked her up, holding her in his arms while he balanced the cell phone between his chin and shoulder.

"I've got to let you go, Robert, but watch the news tomorrow night. We're supposed to be on it."

"Really now?" Robert said in disbelief. "Let me know which channel and what time."

"I'll email you later," Joe said as he hung up the phone.

Robert hung up and sat back down on the living room couch. He wanted to ask Joe if he had filled out the baby's birth certificate paperwork, but he felt like it just wasn't the right time or place. Bending down on his knees there in his living room, he poured out his heart to God: *Savior and Provider, give Joe wisdom as he makes these decisions. Be with Mary and Joe, roll back the veil, and help them to understand what is really going on in our world, and help me to know how to get this message out to others.* Robert went outside and called his daughters. It was time to go milk the goats.

The dietitian and nurse talked with Joe about a plan to get Mary back on solid food. As the nurse and dietitian were leaving, the phone rang again. It was the reporter from the TV station, confirming the time for the interview. After setting a time with Joe, the spokesperson on the other end of the line told Joe she had already spoken with Mr. Verde, the hospital CEO, about the interview time. Joe started to ask why, but then checked himself. He hadn't realized Mr. Verde would be part of the interview. He thought it was a little strange. *What did he have to do with the story?*

Since the birth of Dorea, a new optimism had filled Joe as he went about the daily drudgery of the hospital routine. Yes, the hospital was still sterile and dismal, but he could now look forward to the day when he would leave this place with Mary and their little girl, and be a family. There was hope!

Each day Mary seemed to improve. Some days she would be awake for only a few hours at a time, then lapse back into sleep for a few hours. During the times when she was awake, she was often confused about her surroundings. Slowly, the intervals became longer, and within five days of Dorea's birth, Mary was often awake and coherent for five or six hours at a time.

With a new-found interest in spiritual matters, Mary enjoyed having Joe read the Bible to her. No longer was there the bitterness which had once prevailed in their conversations about God. No longer did she doubt His existence. She was even glad to receive visits from Joe's "religious friends," but these visits had to be brief for the present. There was so much to get caught up on, and then too, there was so much that went unsaid. Joe found it hard to even begin to tell Mary about the problems with her mother.

The first week passed by quickly. Their new baby girl spent the first two days of life outside the womb on the infant monitors commonly found in a hospital NICU. These machines, though sometimes necessary, made Joe's job as a new father far more difficult than it needed to be. Dorea was very fussy and didn't sleep well. The monitor strips failed to stick to her the way they should, and when they came off there was an annoying alarm that went off and brought nurses and hospital staff rushing into the room.

The baby many thought would never draw a breath was now the center of attention. After two days of this torture, Dr. Rodriquez mercifully decided Dorea had a normal heart rate, respiration, and oxygen levels, and could be taken off the monitors.

The first night off of the monitors, little Dorea started out in the hospital crib. One of the nurses had told Joe it was wise to make

Dorea sleep in her own bed, but that didn't last very long. It soon became obvious neither Joe nor Dorea was happy with the crib arrangement. Her favorite place to sleep was next to Daddy's heart, on his chest, with her head snuggled up in the crook of his arm while Daddy slept in the familiar vinyl chair. Waking every couple of hours to give her a bottle was hard work, but Joe didn't mind. The arrangement suited them both well, and neither of them complained. His injured arm was healed now, and he was glad to use it to hold his little girl.

The next day, as Joe finished feeding little Dorea, he was startled by a knock. Several strangers carrying boxes and cases of equipment waited outside as the reporter introduced herself. They began with pictures of Joe holding Dorea as he burped her and changed her diaper. They then attached a microphone to Joe and asked him a series of scripted questions. Trying not to sound too cliché, Joe made a point of giving God the glory for the miracle that had taken place.

About the time Joe was answering their last question, Mr. Verde appeared at the door in an immaculate black suit. Without waiting for Joe to finish the sentence he was speaking, the reporters immediately turned their attention to Mr. Verde.

"Let's get a shot of Mr. Smith and me, the baby and Mrs. Smith," Mr. Verde instructed.

Joe gently woke Mary so she would be awake for the picture. Walking over to Mary's bed, as if it had all been prearranged, Mr. Verde put his arm around Mary's shoulder while Joe stood on the other side.

Speaking with what would appear sincerity to the rest of Chicago, Mr. Verde turned to the camera and said, "Our hospital never gave up on this precious family. Our staff has done everything humanly possible to preserve the life of Mary Smith and her little baby." Mr. Verde left as abruptly as he had entered.

One of the crew removed Joe's microphone as they packed up their equipment. "Thank you Mr. Smith. This should air during the five o'clock broadcast. It may run at ten, also, if there is an open slot, and there is a chance it will run on the national news tomorrow morning," the reporter said as she handed him her card. The television crew filed out of the room, leaving the Smith family alone once again. Joe fired up the computer and shot Robert a quick e-mail to let him know the time and channel of the news story. He then closed his laptop and laid it aside.

Aa few minutes before the broadcast, Joe turned the TV on for the first time in more than three months. He was eager to see the story. It wasn't every day you were given an opportunity to praise God on television for so obvious a miracle. As he endured the wait through the weather, the sports, and the sound bites of what passed for news on that particular day, he wondered when their story would be on. After a particularly long string of commercials that shocked and offended Joe so much that he wanted to turn the TV off, the news program resumed and the wait was over.

Joe was disappointed to find that every reference he had made to God had been deleted from the interview, and the bold-faced lie told by Verde and the false compassion he showed went completely unedited. Joe was sorry he had agreed to the interview. That opportunistic Verde had hijacked the interview. The glory which should have gone to God had ended up being given to Mr. Verde and the hospital staff. The thought of Verde made Joe sick to his stomach.

Joe needed to put the thought of the interview behind him. His Creator knew what he had said even if it had been edited out by the news people. Getting angry would do no good. He had tried to give the glory to Christ Jesus, and he was disappointed, but as the saying goes, life would go on.

"Time to eat!" Joe turned toward Mary and asked what she would like for supper.

As Mary pondered what to eat, Joe thought back at how supper for Mary had changed over the last week. At first a sip of protein shake was all she could manage. Gradually, they worked her up to puddings and Jell-O, and then on to soft fruits.

Joe remembered Robert bringing in the fresh goat's milk, but getting Mary to try it had been next to impossible. Joe had coaxed and pleaded to no avail. Finally he downed an entire glass as she watched in stunned amazement. Mary knew her husband to be quite particular about the milk he drank, so when he chugged a glass to show her how good it was, she reluctantly agreed to try it. Since that time, Proverbs 27:27 milk, and that special green cheese Robert was making for her had become two of her favorite foods.

Robert had started making a dark green cheese with something called spirulina mixed in it. Mary insisted, "It doesn't change the taste at all."

Robert explained when he had brought the cheese, "Spirulina is a super-food. It's very nutrient dense, and will be good for your body as it replenishes and repairs."

On his last visit, Robert brought her something that looked a great deal like runny yogurt, or a very thick milk shake. Robert instructed, "It is called kefir. Drink a cup twice a day. It will help!"

Mary was drinking it twice a day. She said it was an acquired taste. She didn't care for it at first, but now she was actually enjoying drinking her kefir.

Mary's answer snapped Joe back to the present. "I would like some banana, some green cheese, and a slice of that wonderful wheat bread the Forbes girls baked for me. Oh, and a cup of Kefir."

Joe took great joy in preparing their meal. Joe smiled as he thought to himself, *There is not one thing on this plate Mary would have requested for supper before the accident.*

Every day was a new challenge, every day a step toward a more normal life. The difficulties would have seemed overwhelming, but in light of all they had been through, they were a welcome change. Physical therapy seemed to be the biggest challenge ahead of them. Since the medical staff had not expected Mary to live, several things which should have been routine for an accident patient in her situation were left undone. Mary had a lot of work ahead of her to get her muscles back in shape. Indeed, the physical therapist feared she may take years to regain all the muscle tone she had lost.

After two weeks of therapy, Mary had enough muscle tone and control to hold little Dorea on her lap while the bed was placed in a raised position.

Robert Forbes' wife had been up to see the precious little bundle, and had given her some little cotton sleepers complete with soft eyelet lace that she and her daughters had made. These were nothing like the tiny hospital T-shirts they had for newborns. With a pink headband in her fuzzy brown hair, and a little pink sleeper, Joe thought *She is the most beautiful baby in the world.*

Between caring for the baby, and looking after Mary, Joe had little time to think about all the legal information he had studied during Mary's months of unconsciousness. Those things didn't seem so important right now. He had no legal troubles now. The suit had been dropped when his mother-in-law was admitted to the mental hospital. He could hash over how to make the world a better place with Robert later, when he had some spare time. He was too busy living his life to worry about study right now.

Joe was glad to see Mr. Elder had dropped by for a welcome visit.

"Mr. Smith, there is a job waiting for you when you are ready to return. The school's legal problems are being dealt with now, and soon, LORD willing, they will seem like only a bad dream. The school is in the process of changing their name and starting over as an unincorporated church under the sole authority of the LORD Jesus Christ. It might take some time for the state of Illinois to admit they no longer have legal jurisdiction over the school, but Corbin and Robert are both confident the situations with the state will eventually work themselves out."

At that point, Mr. Elder glanced at Mary and said, "Mrs. Smith do you mind if Joe joins me for a walk down the hall?"

"No, I don't mind at all, Mr. Elder, have a nice walk."

As they walked, Mr. Elder explained, "I didn't know if it would be upsetting to your wife to hear of her mother being in the hospital, so I thought it better to continue our conversation where we would not upset Mrs. Smith." Joe nodded in agreement.

Mr. Elder continued, "Shortly after your custody case was dropped, Mr. Cutler discovered that Mr. Brown was both Iris Wethers' and Jane Jones' lawyer. In a phone conversation, he had candidly asked Mr. Brown about the connection between the two women. Mr. Brown declined to comment, but said his client had decided to drop the "discrimination in hiring" lawsuit. Mr. Cutler suspects your mother-in-law had been providing the money for Iris Wethers to sue the school."

"Thank you Mr. Elder for not upsetting Mary with that news. She still is not handling the hospitalization of her mother very well." With that the two men parted, and Joe returned to the hospital room. The last great burden in Joe's world had been removed during his visit with Mr. Elder.

Because Mary wasn't on the OB floor, and Dorea wasn't in the nursery, there had been a delay in getting Joe and Mary's signatures on the Birth Certificate. The Thursday after the television interview, a nurse called from the nursery. The hospital had some forms for Joe and Mary to sign, and the nursery would be sending someone right up. With clipboard in hand and a friendly smile, the nurse appeared at the door of their room. She seemed pleasant enough, she was just doing her job. Joe smiled back a cordial smile. He couldn't be happier. "So what do you have for me?"

"These are just routine forms everyone has to fill out when they have a baby, but since your wife didn't give birth on the OB floor, we hadn't gotten them to you yet. You need to double check the spelling when you fill these out and print neatly, because they go into the state."

Joe nodded his head, not even thinking about what he was doing. Dorea was about to empty the bottle, and he was debating in his mind whether or not she needed some more milk, or if that would be enough for now.

"Well, I can tell you're busy. I'll get back with you before I go off shift."

"Thanks," Joe said as Dorea finished the bottle. Joe burped her and changed her diaper.

"Dorea, my own little personal gift from God," he spoke to Dorea in a loving tone as he patted her little bumper. Dorea snuggled into his chest and gave one last trusting look up into Daddy's face before shutting her eyes and drifting off to sleep. Joe sighed peacefully. *Was there anything better in the world?* And to think, all that time she had been inside Mary, Joe had been convinced she was a boy.

Thinking back over the struggles of the last few weeks, Joe remembered how close he had come to losing the members of his little family, and not just once. He shuddered at the thought of what could have been if he had followed Dr. Bartlett's medical advice, or if Robert had not been there that first night. That would have been murder, he understood that now.

Dorea shuddered on her Daddy's chest as if she read his thoughts. Joe looked down into her face. "Don't worry girl. I won't let anyone take you away. God gave you to me to protect."

Joe reached for the clipboard with the "routine forms everyone has to fill out." Seeing the Birth Certificate application information on the clipboard, Joe gave it a close look. Robert claimed this Birth Certificate application would somehow enslave little Dorea. Robert had said a certificate showed ownership—in this case, the ownership of your child. He flipped to the pages beneath. They were paperwork to apply for a Social Security number. Then, picking up the pen, he mechanically started filling out the forms. Joe had no interest in the legal battles with the world, particularly the Social Security number and Birth Certificate debate.

When Joe thought Dorea was going to be a handicapped child, he seriously considered not getting her a Social Security number, but now, when she was born a normal, healthy child he wanted Dorea to have a normal life. He wanted her to be able to get a passport, travel, and go on mission trips. Yes, the registering of his daughter with the government may be wrong, but you have to choose your battles, and he had concluded this battle wasn't one worth fighting.

Joe didn't want Dorea growing up with a complex, and feeling different than all the other children she would be around at church, or the Christian school. He wanted her to be able to fit in with other children her age. And what if she never got married? She might have to support herself and get a job. She would need to have a Social Security number then. He wouldn't want to handicap her in this way.[1]

As Joe continued filling out the forms, he became aware of a strange uneasiness in his heart and mind. *What had he just promised his daughter? He would protect her from harm, but would he be able to protect her from the state?*

He forced the thought out of his mind. He had already made his decision. It was done. He and Mary would sign the forms. Joe didn't like being different, he had no desire to be a martyr, and he certainly didn't want that for his daughter. His little Dorea would be like all of the other children. *Why did he suddenly feel so guilty?*

Joe remembered reading all the information Robert had given him. His mind began to consider what he was doing. He put down the pen and prayed, *"God what would you have me do?"* Proverbs 15:22 came to his mind, "Without counsel, plans go awry, but in the multitude of counselors they are established."

He needed counsel. Reaching for his laptop, he opened it up and noticed it was still open to his e-mail program from when he had written to Robert. As he scanned the contents of his inbox he noticed a strange e-mail there, from someone he didn't know, in the midst of all of the ones from friends congratulating him on the birth of his baby. He usually deleted these without opening them, but something in his spirit told him he needed to open this one. He scanned the e-mail, and he was astonished to find his name. This caused him to continue to read more carefully. It was a series of e-mails between Mo and Ken.

Ken,

I spoke with you the other day about that situation here at the hospital. The situation is no better, and the foreign clients grow even more impatient as the days go by. What is my legal recourse? I want to get this situation resolved and deliver the product to the buyer. What legal rights do I have?

Mo

Mo

Sorry this reply is so long in coming. I took a few days off and went to northern Michigan, and did some sailing. When I got back, I started looking into your question regarding the authority you possess to remove someone from life support. Traditionally, if the patient has no family, a hospital administrator and a doctor together have the authority to remove someone from life support, remove a feeding tube, etc. . . . In this case the next of kin refusing doctors' advice presents a problem. The best option would be to use the hospital's resources to back the mother-in-law in her custody battle. If they were taking state financial aid or social security, I could pull some strings and have this issue wrapped up by next weekend, but alas that is not the case. If you took this case to court our mutual friends would do all they could to insure a favorable outcome, and set yet another good and needed legal precedent in our nation, but in your present circumstances the time that would take may be too long to be of benefit to the hospital. I understand your concern over the people creating a scene outside the hospital, but I suspect from what you told me that the group in question has been given more than enough distraction to prevent them from being a problem in this regard. I have been researching your question in admiralty/maritime law, and if this woman has a state birth certificate, the state has ultimate authority in this case. If you wish to take this case to court please contact me and I would be glad to give you advice. If you have any more questions or problems, let me know.

Ken

Ken

I cannot wait on the custody battle, transplant needed ASAP. The patient has a huge debt to the hospital. I will see what I can do to *encourage* next of kin to apply for state aid. We need to meet to discuss what strings will need to be pulled as soon as they are on state aide at your first possible convenience.

Mo

Ken

Smith is absolutely refusing to go on any kind of financial government program. This is infuriating (see a copy of his e-mail below)! I will continue to pursue all other avenues.

Mo

Mr. Verde

Thank you for your concern for me and your visit today. I know you were just trying to help. I am sorry for the inconvenience to you and your staff, but I am trusting God to meet my needs not the government.

Joe Smith

Ken

I see no alternative; we need to meet to discuss ensuring a favorable outcome in court at your first possible convenience. It looks as if we are taking this case to court ASAP to get this woman declared brain dead, and give us authority to harvest her organs while they are still viable.

Mo

Mo

I will get in contact with our mutual friends and see what I can do to expedite this matter.

Ken

Joe saw his name at the end of what he had sent to Mr. Verde. He soon realized what he was reading, and it sent shivers up his spine. These were e-mails between Verde and some friend of his in the legal system named Ken. His heart began to beat wildly. A sick feeling rose in the pit of his stomach.

Rising, Joe paced the floor in the room.

His thoughts were a jumbled mess as he thought about the methotrexate incident, and how God had sent Dr. Rodriquez to save the life of his precious Dorea. They, Mr. Verde and who knew who else, were trying to murder Mary to harvest her organs for some foreign clients, whatever that meant.

These e-mails were so vague in spots, he couldn't tell what exactly had happened or when. But he now realized that Robert had been right about total surrender to God. If he had accepted financial aid, Mary and Dorea would be dead right now. If he was reading between the lines well enough, it was either Mr. Verde or his friend Ken who were responsible for the state investigation and problems at the school and church.

Verde had been near the point of taking him to court, and Dr. Bartlett was just waiting for Mary to die, so he could use her as spare parts for transplant. This pre-eclampsia was probably another lie as well. There was probably more he was missing; but he was too distracted and upset to read those e-mails again right now. He forwarded the series of e-mails to Robert and Mr. Elder. They would be able to advise him what to do later.

He had gotten the counsel he had been seeking. God had given him a precious gift. He had allowed him to see behind the scenes—in the form of an e-mail that was obviously not intended for him. The e-mail showed him the plans of the Evil One that had been thwarted by his obedience, and total surrender to God.

Dorea was his gift from God. She did not belong to the government. He now understood why he could never surrender one of his greatest gifts from God to the state. *How could he willingly sign Dorea over to them? He could not sign her into their control—*

knowing what he knew to be the truth! Dorea, his gift from God! He would stand before God and give an account for what he had done in this life, how he had raised her, and for her spiritual state. *Could he now turn that responsibility over to the state by letting them register his daughter?*

Joe looked at the final form. It was a form to file and get a Social Security number for Dorea. Joe's face grew red as he pulled the two forms off the clipboard, and with one swift motion, he ripped the forms in half, stuffing them in his pocket. *Never!*

He then realized he had been thinking like a pagan in assuming mankind and the government were basically good. The Bible told him man was sinful and evil. Without Christ making them a new creation, all men are slaves to sin, and most are deceived into becoming the slaves of other men. Come what may, Dorea was his gift from God, and he would not sign her up to be a slave to the fraudulent government system.

CHAPTER 31

"...a soul is forever."—Doug Phillips

For once the white walls of the hospital seemed invigorating and energizing and not bleak to Joe. The warm September sun shined in through the windows, warming the nursery crib that held Joe and Mary's most precious earthly possession. Little Dorea looked the picture of health. A rosy pink color enveloped her fat cheeks and body, and her mousey brown hair was now long enough to be put in a cute little pink bow instead of shooting up in a haphazard way all over her tiny head.

The "old" Joe was back. The serious, but yet happy-go-lucky young man of former days had returned. The physical wear and tear of the past three months was no longer obvious at first glance. This was a day for rejoicing; they were finally going home. Dorea slept soundly while Joe scurried about the room making sure everything was in order for them to leave.

Mary, despite all she had been through, looked the picture of radiance as she sat smiling in the familiar vinyl hospital chair. She couldn't help but wonder how Joe had slept in one of these for the last fifteen weeks.

The beautiful pink cotton dress Joe had bought her accented the radiant healthy glow which was slowly returning to her cheeks and joyous face. Her shoulder length blond hair was clean and glimmered in the sunlight as she patiently tried to comb it. It took work, but she was now able to brush her own hair, and it felt good to be able to do something for herself instead of being so dependent on Joe, and the nurses.

Though Mary's physical steps were still somewhat wobbly and unsteady, her spiritual steps were now placed firmly on the straight and narrow path. Sure, it would be a long time before she was back to normal, in a physical sense, but in a greater spiritual sense she knew she would never be truly "normal" again. Her life had turned a corner when she met the Savior and a new and different life lay before her, Joe and Dorea.

A month of physical therapy had done wonders to help her regain muscle tone and dexterity. Mary would continue physical therapy treatments three times a week for at least another three months, then continue at home for many more.

Little Dorea was gaining steadily. Although still only six and a half pounds, she had made a lot of progress and the hospital staff was not at all concerned about her going home with Mom and Dad. She was beginning to smile and coo, and she was the favorite of all the nurses on the floor. Many had commented on her alertness and physical development. They seemed surprised that despite all she had been through, she was thriving, even excelling. Joe and Mary could only smile proudly and thank the Lord for their precious little gift.

Joe had spent what seemed like weeks, but was actually only a month, talking to Mary and getting her caught up on all that had happened. The last month had not been without its trials. First, there was the unhappy story of Mary's Mom. Still in the mental institute, she had spoken with Mary several times on the phone. Short of Jane Jones getting saved, there seemed little hope of their relationship being reconciled, and yet, despite their obvious differences, she was still Mary's Mom and Dorea's grandmother.

Secondly, there was the issue of the Birth Certificate which the hospital administration was making an issue of. Several "associates" had been down to talk with Joe about his refusal to sign the Birth

Certificate. At first it came as a gentle reminder. "You really need to get this in, or your child won't have a valid State Birth Certificate."

When Joe frankly replied they weren't going to give the child's name on the Certificate for "religious reasons," the director of the department of records paid a call to Mary's hospital room to explain the importance of the document. Joe tried to explain his reasons to her, but she ended up leaving convinced this Dad was a religious nut case.

Eventually, DCFS even sent down a caseworker to interview Joe and Mary, and explain to them the child would not be eligible for state aid if they didn't get a Birth Certificate. Joe kindly thanked the caseworker, and sent her on her way.

Last, but not least, the hospital sent a series of certified letters to Joe and Mary. At first the letters kindly asked Joe and Mary to comply and dutifully fill out the appropriate documentation, and return it to the hospital. Later, as more letters were sent, they came as formal commands and sounded rather threatening.

Joe carefully and prayerfully read each letter, and then he placed them in a file for safe-keeping, just in case he ever wanted to prove his child had been born at that hospital on that particular date.

Dr. Rodriquez had been more than happy to sign an affidavit of live birth, and Rachel had said she would stop by today to put her signature on the document as well. Joe wondered if Rachel would make it to the hospital before they left?

Packing their bags wasn't exactly what Joe was doing. In his excitement, he was randomly stuffing things in the bags. He and Mary would sort things out when they got home. Tonight they would sleep in their own bed, together!

Mary, with a smile on her face, wondered, as she had so often before, how someone so meticulous in computer programming could be so careless and disorganized at packing.

Nurses and hospital staff bustled in and out of the room. The patient, everyone thought was dead, Mary, with a smile on her face, wondered as she had so often before, how someone so meticulous in computer programming could be so careless and disorganized at packing, and say one last goodbye.

Dr. Rodriquez had already signed Mary's release forms, but Joe hoped he would be by to see them one more time before they left. As eager as Joe was to leave, he didn't want to leave without seeing Rodriquez if at all possible. The bond between them had become a special one. Joe had called Dr. Rodriquez, and he was supposedly on his way over, but he still hadn't come. Joe placed the last item, his Bible, in Mary's bag. He then sat down on the edge of Mary's bed to wait for Dr. Rodriquez to show up.

A light tap was heard on the door, and Joe quickly went to answer, hoping Dorea wouldn't wake up until it was time to leave. Mr. Elder smiled warmly at Joe, Mary, and little Dorea. Mrs. Elder handed a slim book to the Smiths saying, "This is one of the best child training books I've read."

Joe glanced over the title before giving it a toss into the open suitcase. *To Train Up a Child* by Michael and Debbie Pearl. "This sounds interesting. Thanks," he said without ceremony. The Elders only stayed for a few moments more.

It was obvious Joe and Mary were ready to leave and eager to be on their way. The phone in Mary's room rang as Mr. and Mrs. Elder were getting ready to leave. Joe waved good bye, and Mr. Elder said, "See you next Monday, Joe."

"Mr. Smith." It was a very excited Luke on the other end of the phone. "I got that computer graphic arts scholarship you helped me apply for."

"What?" Joe couldn't believe what he was hearing. "I thought you said they had given it to someone else?"

"They had," Luke said, "but the kid backed out at the last minute, and the financial aid office called me yesterday and asked if I wanted it? It's a full ride for tuition, and the school is just ten minutes from my house. I can live at home."

"Man, that's great Luke. God sure does provide. I'm so happy for you."

"I couldn't have done it without your help, Mr. Smith."

"No," Joe commented, "It wasn't me. It was a God thing."

Mr. and Mrs. Elder meandered down the hospital hall, holding hands. For once, Mr. Elder didn't seem to be in a hurry. Mrs. Elder suggested they go by the nursery and look at the babies in the nursery window. As they were entering the OB ward, Mr. Elder noticed Misty Sellers, the social worker who had given him so much difficulty weeks before. She was much more modestly dressed than the last time he had seen her.

Absorbed in her own thoughts, Misty walked down one of the parallel corridors on the other side of the glass enclosed nursery. Misty had not noticed the Elders, but they noticed her. Mr. Elder leaned over to his wife, and explained to her in a whisper who Misty was. Misty was obviously upset about something, and Mr. and Mrs. Elder prayed quietly for her unknown hurt.

The source of her grief lay behind the doors to the Neonatal Intensive Care Unit. A child, not three weeks old, lay in the NICU of the hospital. A week earlier, Misty had removed the baby boy from his home while the poor single mother had looked on in tears. Though no one knew why, the baby had taken a mysterious fall in the foster home, and was now in the NICU, with a fractured skull.

The mother had left the NICU only ten minutes before, with a silent icy stare at Agent Sellers, the woman who had taken her baby away. Misty had been called in to monitor this visit between the mother and her child. The tear-stained face of the mother as she placed her hand on the almost lifeless form of her child haunted Misty, and for one brief moment, she was beginning to question the wisdom of the social service system in removing children from the birth parents.

Mr. Elder need only nod his head in the direction of the woman and whisper in his wife's ear again, and Mrs. Elder went to see what she could do to comfort this obviously hurting young lady. Leaving her husband standing in the hall outside the nursery, she approached the woman while Mr. Elder waited out of sight and prayed for both of them.

"Miss," she spoke, heralding the woman.

Misty turned to see who was talking to her.

Mrs. Elder with her short curly gray hair, and pleasant smile approached and asked, "Are you alright?"

Misty wiped the trail of mascara from her cheek unsure of how to answer as she tried to appear to be in control of her emotions.

"I know you don't know me, but I can see you are hurting and I just want to help if I can. My name is Esther. What is your name?" Mrs. Elder continued in a friendly way.

"My name is Misty, and there is a baby boy on the other side of those doors over there that may not live much longer. I thought . . . I was protecting him, and now he might die. Watching his Mother just stand there and weep for her son, I felt so helpless. Esther, you remind me of my dear friend, Dr. Astra. She is dead now, and I miss talking to her."

"I am a good listener. I have had lots of practice. Would you like to get together for lunch, sometime this week? I know this may be rather strange, but you remind me of someone very special, too. Misty, I enjoy giving gifts, would you receive a gift from me today?" Mrs. Elder pulled from her bag a carefully wrapped gift. "This is for you. These are the two best books I've ever read," she said as she handed her the beautifully wrapped package containing a *One Heartbeat Away* book and a compact Bible. "My name and phone number are written on the inside front cover of the heartbeat book. I lead a book study for young women about your age every Tuesday. We are just starting a new study on the heartbeat book I just gave you. I would like to take you as my guest. We usually meet over lunch in the back of this little tea room my friend owns. I could come and pick you up, or you could meet us there. OK?"

Misty stared at the strange woman before her, a little dumbfounded. Any other day she would have thrown the gift on the ground and walked away, but now something vulnerable inside of her was struck by the care this woman showed for her. Pulling a business card from her pocket, she handed it to Mrs. Elder. "I'll have to get back with you on that one Esther. I need to go now," and she silently walked away holding the gift close to her breast.

Mrs. Elder tucked the card securely in her wallet. She would call Misty when the LORD indicated the time was right.

Down in the transplant center another family was getting ready to leave. Carol had finally stabilized enough to fly home to her beloved Canada. Her liver rejection medications had been adjusted several times, but her test results were within normal limits now. A new level of hope radiated from Bernard and it even rubbed off on the cynical Carol, a little. The doctors had given them some hope during their last visit.

The new liver would buy Carol a few more years of life in this world. No nurse would fly home with Carol and Bernard. They would enjoy the time alone together. Carol sat on the edge of the bed buttoning her imported silk blouse, one of the few things she was strong enough to do without help. She thought to herself, this was the first time in months she had worn real clothing.

"Carol, what would you have me do with these?" Bernard gestured toward the drawer next to Carol's bed containing the Gideon Bible and Christian literature Carol had been studying.

"Go ahead and pack them. I'll probably just round file them when I get home."

Bernard stepped out of the room for a few minutes. He still needed to go to the business office and finish paying for Carol's lengthy stay in the hospital. Carol felt an uneasiness deep inside her. The Bible and the Christian literature brought back memories to her mind she would rather not think about, but she felt as if she had no choice but to consider what she had read. If all that stuff was true, hell and a lost eternity had loomed very close to her a few weeks ago.

Was there really a righteous God waiting on the other side of death to condemn you to Hell when you died? If she was bad enough to warrant sending to Hell, why would. . . how could He love her enough to send His Son to redeem her? Could one sinless Man's death really pay for all the sin and wrong in the world? She still struggled with the question: *How could a loving God allow her and others to be sick and suffer as she had suffered?*

Repentance. The thought welled up inside Carol's heart as the lump rose in her throat. Tears began to slip down her face. Carol fought to wipe them away so Bernard would not see her weakness. For the first time in her life, Carol realized she was a sinner. A life of wrong and selfish sin confronted her. No longer could she make excuses for faults—the Holy Spirit was convicting her heart. But still many struggles and snares lay before her.

Oh God! she cried within herself. *If you are God, show yourself to me! I don't know if all of this is true, but if it is, have someone, today —before we leave this hospital building—come up and tell me about you. I have so many questions. I need to know if you are real. If you are really an all-powerful God, you should be able to manage that.*

A mixture of anger, defiance, dread and hope swelled within Carol. She shouted out loud for the first time in this audible exchange with God.

"God, Jesus, whoever you are, if you are real, show me. I'm giving you thirty minutes to prove yourself God! If you can manage that, I will give you my eternity. If not, I guess I'm hopeless, and you don't want to love a selfish spoiled wretch like me."

A few floors above, Dr. Rodriquez gave a rap on the door as he pushed it open. "Ah, Senorita Smith, you look beautiful today." He bent over and planted a playful kiss on the forehead of the sleeping Dorea.

Mary willingly handed her sleeping bundle to Dr. Rodriquez who examined her one last time, more out of habit than concern. After a moment he handed Dorea to Joe.

"She's fine. She will be out playing in the yard before you know it."

"Dr. Rodriquez," Joe's voice cracked with emotions, "I want to thank you for ....."

Dr. Rodriquez interrupted, "Thank me? You haven't gotten my bill yet," he said in a playful tone.

Joe smiled, realizing the doctor was trying to lighten the moment.

Another gentle knock on the door, and in slipped Rachel. She placed her blue handbag on the end table by the door. Her brown skin was smooth and flawless, and a white headband held her tight curls back to reveal her beautiful smiling oval face.

Dr. Rodriquez suddenly grew awkwardly silent.

Rachel paused for a moment; the silence was a bit awkward. She had hoped she wouldn't have to face Dr. Rodriquez today. In her mind she feared her deep admiration for him would show all over her face, again. *Why did it have to be so hard to get to know this man? They had worked so well together at Dorea's birth. Why couldn't they just talk like old friends?*

"I," she began softly, "just wanted to say goodbye and sign that paper Joe asked me to sign." Reaching out her hand to Rachel, Mary pulled her to her chest and gave her a warm embrace that radiated the thanks Mary felt inside.

"I want to thank you Rachel. You gave Joe hope when few others did. Without you, I don't know what would have happened." Joe dug out the affidavit and Rachel affixed her signature with a smile next to Dr. Rodriquez's name.

"Don't count God out of the picture," Rachel reminded as she handed the paper and pen back to Joe. A silence again settled over the room as no one knew quite what to say.

Joe picked up Dorea and ever so carefully snapped her into the car seat. "Well, thanks for stopping in everyone," he said as he began to gather the last of their belongings from the room, shaking hands as he made his final circuit around the room. "Our one remaining car is loaded and waiting downstairs."

Mary had risen slowly from the uncomfortable chair to the wheelchair with Rachel's help. Rachel bent over and gave Mary one last warm embrace as she sat in the wheelchair.

Mary whispered into Rachel's ear in a voice only they could hear. "Give Dr. Rodriquez a chance Rachel. He has a crush on you the size of the Grand Canyon, and your beauty leaves the man speechless."

Rachel stared at Mary in stunned silence not knowing what to make of that comment. "Time to go sweetheart," Joe said as he pushed her and the baby through the open door held by Rachel. And with that simple motion, Joe, Mary, and Dorea began a journey to their new life outside the hospital walls.

Rachel paused, still holding the door. "Are you coming doctor?" She smiled.

A confused, jumbled mess of emotions welled up in the doctor's chest. So many times he'd wanted to get to know Rachel, to be her friend, to tell her how he really felt about her. . . *oh why couldn't he say anything when he had the chance?*

"No," he replied meekly. "Go ahead. I want to make a few more notes on this chart." It was a lame excuse, but it was all he could think up on short notice. And then, through the open door, she passed into the hall, and she was gone once again.

A failure again, his mind tormented him. *Why couldn't I talk to her like a normal person? But then*, he reasoned, *she is so beautiful. What would she want with a short Hispanic man like me? She probably has dozens of men after her.* "LORD, help me," he whispered. Calmness covered Dr. Rodriguez as he glanced up and saw the blue purse left on the table. Snatching it up with a smile and new-found confidence, he dashed down the hall.

"Rachel," he raced up behind her, "you left your purse."

Ducking her head in embarrassment, Rachel turned and looked at the doctor as he held out his blue leather offering. He was such a peculiar person with his determined black eyes and olive skin. *Why would he joke with everyone else, but always fall strangely silent around her? Could what Mary said be true?*

Why would he never talk with her? She thought she must really be repulsive to him with her black skin and flat nose. Mary's words echoed in her mind. *Did he sense how much she cared for and admired him?* She feared her interest in the good doctor was written all over her glistening face.

"Thank you, doctor. You're so thoughtful." Looking at the floor, without a word more she turned to leave.

"Rachel, could I buy you a cup of coffee?" The words came pouring out of Dr. Rodriquez's mouth so fast he wondered if she could even understand what he had said. Then for a split second of dread he wondered if in his haste—had he spoken in Spanish instead of English?

A brilliant smile made up of gleaming white teeth spread across Rachel's still blushing face and her eyes sparkled, "Are you asking ME out, for coffee?" she stammered in disbelief with her head slightly tilted.

"Well uh, yes," came the only words his suddenly dry throat could utter.

"I don't drink coffee," Rachel said in her matter of fact way.

He thought to himself, this was a stupid idea! Why would she want to go out for coffee with a loser like me? She just doesn't want to be seen with me. She's trying to think of a nice, polite excuse to get away. Dr. Rodriquez felt his ego and self-confidence deflating.

"But, I would love a cup of tea." She smiled, hoping the offer was still good.

The tension was broken, and Dr. Rodriquez quickly found his voice again. "Coffee, tea, milk, juice, Ice cream, a chocolate malt, or a full meal at the restaurant of your choice, I don't care! I just want an opportunity to get to know you better Rachel. I've FINALLY, with God's help, screwed up enough courage to ask you for an opportunity to spend some time with you, and get to know you better. I don't care what you order, or where we go!"

A stunned and confused Rachel flashed that winning smile and whispered a silent prayer inside her head, *Thank you Jesus,* and swallowed hard. *Mary had been right.* She timidly said, "I am available for any or all of those, except the coffee, doctor."

Feeling a little more courageous, Rachel asked, "What about the woman on the phone when I called your house for Joe that Sunday the baby was born? You don't have someone else?"

Dr. Rodriquez laughed out loud. "That was my aunt, my Mom's older sister. She was visiting from Mexico, and she doesn't speak English."

"Really? she sounded young."

"She is, just forty eight."

Rachel gave the doctor an astonished look. "How old is your Mom?"

"forty six."

Rachel looked even more amazed at the doctor.

"My Mom came to America when she was sixteen. She was pregnant with me out of wedlock. All the medical professionals advised her to abort the baby, but she wouldn't. Some Christians took her in, helped her, and led her to the Lord. I guess that's why I'm such a strong pro-lifer. By the way," Dr. Rodriquez flashed a charming smile. "Did I mention you're going to meet her this evening after dinner?"

As they made their way to the hospital cafeteria, the good doctor could be heard proposing they get an ice cream now, and have a nice dinner later that evening. He would be off his shift in a couple of hours, and it was a wonderful day for a walk on the lake front.

For Bernard and Carol, life was not as hopeful, or carefree. Neither one of them was so starry-eyed as to believe this was the last of their troubles. Sure, the liver transplant had bought them some more time, but it wasn't a permanent solution to Carol's health problems. Pushing Carol's wheelchair, Bernard dejectedly pressed the "down" arrow on the elevator. *The limo driver should be waiting in the limo downstairs with the luggage*, he thought to himself, as he waited for the elevator.

As the chime sounded, Carol's heart beat faster with anticipation. She couldn't wait for that elevator door to open. *Would her prayer be answered?* The thirty minutes was almost up. She hoped there was a God. She hoped there was an answer for all her questions, but she didn't really believe there would be.

The elevator doors slowly opened revealing an empty elevator. Bernard moved his jacket from one arm to the other and pushed Carol over the gap into the elevator.

Carol looked at the ground with a sigh, "I should have known." *God, You're not real, and even if you are real you don't care about me!*

Bernard said in a loving and patient tone, "What was that sweetheart?"

"Nothing, never mind, it's really nothing," Carol sighed.

Without a second thought Bernard turned to press the "L". The door slowly closed crushing the last small glimmer of Carol's hope of ever finding God. Now, the repeated chiming sounds in the elevator only aggravated her more.

In anger, Bernard slammed his fist against the button on the wall. "Where is this thing taking us? We're supposed to be going down, not up."

"What the..? You stupid machine!" Bernard vented the frustration he had been feeling for so long on the elevator door with a kick. Bernard began pumping the "L" button like the fire button on a video game. Still, the elevator lumbered slowly upward as Carol watched her annoyed husband's hammering. The numbers on the floor indicator and Bernard's frustration both continued to increase.

With another annoying chime, the doors slowly opened.

In front of Carol was a young woman, in a pink dress, smiling at a baby in the infant seat on her lap. The young husband beside her looked pleasant enough. They were so happy. At least they had a child.

Joe tried not to stare at the obviously frustrated Bernard who was smoothing his hair and trying to regain his composure. "Mind if we join you?" he inquired.

Bernard could not help but laugh as he asked, "Are you going up or down?"

The question was a simple enough one to Bernard and the odd

look Mary flashed at Joe puzzled him. With a winning smile, she smiled at the older man before her.

"We're both going up now," she commented without further explanation.

Joe looked at Bernard and chuckled, "Lobby, please."

Bernard calmly pressed the button he'd been all but beating on just a moment before. Carol looked at Mary. She obviously was not completely well. The woman's arm was weak and shook as she held the baby carrier on her lap. Carol couldn't help but wonder what was wrong with such a young woman. The baby seemed small, but healthy enough. How could she be so happy when she suffered so much?

"I thought you said you were going up?" Carol managed to say.

"We are, when the final trumpet sounds, when Jesus returns. My wonderful husband was just reading that to me from the Bible. I guess it was still in my head. You see, I've just become a Christian recently. A lot of things have changed, but I don't suppose an elevator ride is quite long enough to explain any of that right now." With a shaky arm, Mary extended her hand to Carol, "My name is Mary Smith."

For a moment Carol forgot all her sorrow and disappointment. Carol smiled and took Mary's hand, "Carol Thomas."

Carol pointed with her gaze, "My husband, Bernard."

Mary was again silent for a moment. Her heart felt burdened for this lady beside her who seemed so weighed down with care. Mary felt a strange prompting in her heart as if she was supposed to ask Carol something. The elevator was almost to the lobby, but try as she might, Mary could not escape the feeling nor could she find the right words to say.

Summoning all her courage as she saw the elevator was nearly to the lobby, she began, "Carol, Are you going up or down? Have you put your reservation in with Jesus? Do you know Christ? If not, I would love to tell you about Him."

A chill ran down Carol's spine, and a sweat broke out on her forehead. *How could she deny the existence of God now? He had made the elevator go the wrong way just to arrange this meeting with Mary.* A hundred questions raced through her mind. She took a deep breath and decided to answer the first one she had been asked.

"Right now, I'm afraid I'm going down, but I desperately want to go up. I have been reading, and I'm so confused. I have so many questions. I don't know this Jesus you speak of, but I desperately want to. In my room just now, I made a request of God; actually it was an ultimatum. Then the elevator went the wrong way, and YES! I would love for you to tell me about this Jesus."

Mary smiled at Joe, and said "I may need a little help."

Bernard stared at Carol in a stunned and amazed silence as the elevator doors opened. He hadn't seen this type of earnestness, this vigor for life in his wife in years.

Carol begged her husband, "Can I take a few minutes to talk to this young lady, please?" All of a sudden the limo and limo driver didn't seem to matter. The private pilot and jet could wait. Nothing seemed to really matter right now except finding out the truth.

Bernard stated flatly, "I would like to hear what she has to say as well."

Joe glanced up and saw an arrow pointing to the hospital chapel and said, "I know just the place, follow me!"

And the two gentlemen wheeled their ladies into the chapel to introduce Carol, and perhaps Bernard as well, to the Lord Jesus Christ.

EPILOGUE

Many of our friends have asked what led us to investigate these issues and write this book? It certainly wasn't an abundance of free time! We had plenty of activity to fill our days with running a small goat dairy, building a debt free home, raising and home schooling our six children, and Darren working full time outside the home as a science teacher. In 2000 we began to study freedom, the constitution, and the code of federal regulations. This eventually led us to study socialism, communism, and the new world order. As we studied these topics, we saw an evil nobody seemed to be warning others about: the slavery of the church and the slavery of the common man. As a family, we have done what we could to protect our own family. As any follower of Christ should do, we began to warn friends and family of the dangers we could so plainly see facing our civilization. Most of our warnings fell on deaf ears.

It would seem few people want to consider the possibility they may be slaves. We felt the conviction of the Holy Spirit to write a novel to try and convey some of these truths to other freedom loving Christians, who might be open to the truth. As the task became long and arduous, we prayed time and again that God would raise up someone else to proclaim this message to the nation, and yet, God would not release us from the burden we felt. After the passage of the Patient Protection and Affordable Care Act, better known as ObamaCare, we felt even more compelled to warn others of the dangers of enslaving our churches and our children. In this book we have only given you a small taste of the body of knowledge that exists on these two topics. Our prayer is that each of you, as individuals, will take the time to study out not only the dangers of church incorporation, but also the dangers of social security numbers and birth certificates. Why social security numbers and birth certificates? Because, these documents are the foundational documents for the enslavement of this generation and the next.

Some topics you might want to start your research with:
birth certificates and bank notes or bank securities
Slavery by Consent
Maritime law
admiralty law
Uniform Commercial Code (UCC)
The truth about your birth certificate youtube
Shadow Government by Cloudten pictures
information on getting a passport without a birth certificate

ENDNOTES

Chapter 1

A good video on schools is *IndoctriNation Public Schools and the Decline of Christianity in America* by Gunn Productions.

Chapter 2

1 Recommended reading : *A Full Quiver* By Rick & Jan Hess & *Family UNplanning* By Craig Houghton.

Chapter 3

1 What Every Parent Should Know About Childhood Immunizations by Jamie Murphy.

2 www.unhinderedliving.com/statevaccexemp.html

3 I took a class . . . a social worker was in charge of one hour of the training, and her topic was, what is the typical abusive family? What are the ingredients? The last had three categories. One category was the parent who abuses alcohol or drugs. You know this kinda thing. It was obvious there would be child neglect problems. Then the second category was, it was a family who home schooled, who went to church regularly, many times served as an elder or deacon in their church, used the scripture to control their children. I

couldn't believe it. That's what they are training. Chris Klicka from a talk at the OCHEC Home School Convention May 2008 titled The Good the Bad and the Ugly.

5 Some states are now wanting to require psychological evaluations for all home schoolers after an investigation by a state social worker even when nothing was found wrong in the home. —Chris Klicka from a talk at the OCHEC Home school convention May 2008

Chapter 4

1 An excellent source of information on parental rights and who really controls our children under the laws of the constitution is ParentalRights.org.

The movie *Overruled: Government Invasion of your Parental Rights* is a must see. So what are we as Christian parents to do if the united States Constitution is done away with or ignored, and if or should we say when the UN Convention on the Rights of the Child is ratified? What are our other options?

Chapter 5

1 An excellent source for end of life decisions is Vision Forum's DVD, *Should We Starve Grandpa?*

2 www.drdino.com Creation Science Evangelism has a great DVD Creation Seminar boxed set by Dr. Kent Hovind

3 Different states have differing guidelines stating how long one can stay on life support if they are on state aid.

4 The authors have been using Samaritan ministries for their health coverage and are quite pleased with it. Tell them Darren Grant recommended it to you. www.samaritanministries.org/my/

5 Watch the DVD *Agenda: Grinding America Down* by Curtis Bowers

Chapter 6

Chapter 7

1 A longer, more detailed work on the issue is *The Tragedy Of American Compassion* by Marivn Olasky, Regnery Publishing, Inc.

Chapter 8

1 Maritime law is quickly replacing the constitution in the United States. Have you ever wondered why the court systems don't follow the constitution any more. It's largely because they follow maritime law, or the international law of nations for the high seas and trading by ships. . . . research this out for yourself.

2 A Durable Power of Attorney is a document designating an agent who will make healthcare decisions when the patient is unable to do so not only in terminal illness but also in any crisis. One can also include written instructions or a letter for your DPAHCD. In addition, a Protective Medical Decisions Document(PMDD) is wise to attach to your DPAHCD. This document prevents assisted suicide, euthanasia, direct and intentional ending of life, authorization of lethal injection or drug overdose, and denial of food or fluids for purposes of starvation or dehydration. www.internationaltaskforce. org/pmda.htm and the Patient's Rights Council offer more information on this topic.

3 An excellent video discussing bioethics, organ transplants, and the abuse going on in our medical system from a Christian perspective is *Should We Starve Grandpa* by Vision Forum Ministries.

Chapter 9

1   http://www.worldviewweekend.com/test/register.php?testid= WORLDVIEW&groupreg=19684d78c

Chapter 10

1 Section 702 of the Civil Rights Act of 1964 exempts religious organizations from Title VII's prohibition against discrimination in employment on the basis of religion. This could be repealed or

amended at any time, however.

Chapter 11

1 See the video: *The Money Masters—How International Bankers Gained Control of America* DVD available from www.themoney-masters.com, and also the book End the Fed By: Ron Paul)

2 realmilk.com. www.raw-milk-facts.com

Chapter 12

Chapter 13

Chapter 14

1 *Debt Virus* is a good, easy to understand, book on what is wrong with our money, Another excellent book is *Whatever happened to Penny Candy?* by Richard J. Maybury

Chapter 15

Chapter 16

Chapter 17

1 *What He Must Be . . . If He Wants To Marry My Daughter* by: Voddie Baugham Jr. is a great book

2 http://www.everettramseydd.com/lessonsfromlouisville.html A small part of this web site is listed below.

It was well into this case in the year 1983, after I had already been to jail a couple of times and I was serving my third round of contempt of court, when the honorable Judge Raymond Case asked the Sheriff to bring me one night from the jail cell, about 10:00 PM, to his office on the second floor of the Cass County Court House. As I came to the door the Sheriff left; the Judge invited me in, spoke to me in very humble terms and said he wanted to visit with me for a few minutes. He then asked me to pray before we had our meeting. We both got on our knees and prayed that God would direct our discussion.

He first began by asking me to close the school. When I refused, he asked if I would move it outside his jurisdiction. Again, I refused.

He then made a statement that got my attention. He said, "Pastor you're 95% right in your arguments, but you are 5% wrong."

I responded, "If you can point out where I am wrong, I will repent and make changes."

He then pulled from the file the pleadings that had been filed and asked me to read the heading.

I read, "The State of Nebraska et. al., Attorney General Paul Douglas vs. The Faith Baptist Church, a Nebraska Corporation."

At that point he stopped me and said, "Would you read those last few words again?"

I read them again, "Faith Baptist Church, a Nebraska Corporation."

He then asked me, "Is that a heavenly corporation?"

I replied, "No!"

He asked me again, "Is that an angelic corporation?"

I replied again, "No!"

He asked me thirdly, "Well, what kind of corporation is that?"

I responded, "According to the heading, it is a Nebraska corporation."

He then asked me a strange question, "Who owns your buildings?"

I answered, "The Faith Baptist .... Ah, I'm beginning to see the light. The corporation owns the property."

The Judge responded, "Who owns the corporation?"

I said, "Ah, Nebraska." He said, "That's right."

He told me that he was going to padlock my church again and he wanted to explain to me that that was the most charitable thing he could do since the leaders in Lincoln, Nebraska have requested that he bulldoze it down and burn it, and the State had the jurisdiction and authority to do so because those properties belong to a corporation owned by the State of Nebraska and it is breaking the laws of the State of Nebraska which the charter forbids it from doing.

Well, I didn't have to call my religious guru to find out if I should unincorporate. I unincorporated the church and it began to turn the case around from that point; not in the Courts, but God stepped in and ended the matter very quickly after that.

Now, we have had a tremendous battle trying to educate Pastors about this whole concept of the Lordship of Christ and the corporation and any other ties with the government.

3 The Supreme Court has ruled that churches which incorporate are not viewed as churches, but rather as corporations, and are no longer protected by the Constitution, but are subject to Corporate Law (Hale v. Hinkle, 201 US 43 at 74, 1906).

4 For the whole message see link http://www.sunnetworks. net/~ggarman/madison.html

Chapter 18

1 Edward Mandell House established another set of house rules for real life see

http://www.gemworld.com/EdMandellHouse.htm

2 http://nogreaterjoy.org/articles/holy-matrimony/ this is a great article on this topic.

Chapter 19

1 The authors personally know several pastors that are knowingly violating the law in an effort to bring about a court case so the issue can be battled out in court in an effort to set a legal precedent, or challenge the constitutionality of the law. They are taping their sermons and mailing them into the IRS.

2 If a true church is not incorporated, the government will often still try to bluff and intimidate, but without willingly submitting the church to their jurisdiction, the church is NOT subject to their authority. Church incorporation is discussed in greater detail later in the book.

Chapter 20

1 On a rabbit trail, there are many good books on the power of prayer. The authors would humbly recommend *Praying Successfully* by Charles Spurgeon, the Autobiography of George Muller.

Chapter 21

1 *New World Order: What Do You Believe?* By disinformation (warning) Alex Jones uses some unappropriate language in this video, but it gives a good overview of what is really happening with the New World Order for those who are interested in what is going on, and for those who might be skeptical of its existence. He also deals with the cover-up of the 911 events, etc,

2 Ron Paul speech "imagine" http://www.youtube.com/watch?v=XKfuS6gfxPY

3 www.exposingterrorism.org and the short video by the same name, *Exposing Terrorism* by The John Birch Society are excellent sources of information on what is really going on in our country.

4 Alexis de Tocqueville, *Democracy in America*

5 *A foreign Policy of Freedom Peace, commerce, and honest friendship* by Ron Paul. The part Justin is referring to is on page 364 at the top.

6 "Anti-Biblical worldviews have infected virtually every arena of life-law, science, economics, history, family, social issues, education, and religion—and these worldviews consistently connect back to four major forces destroying America from within. The government-corporate complex(Corporate Fascism), which includes the State itself, non-government organizations, trade unions, and the UN; occultism and pagan spirituality, the apostate Church; and the educational establishment. These forces have attacked on all fronts, aggressively helping national and international governments accomplish their ultimate goal of global control." This idea is from Brannon Howse, *Grave Influence*, p.22

7 McArther's sermon he gave while in Japan on when it's right to go to war.

8 Watch the video LOOSE CHANGE on the internet to learn more about the truth of 9-11.

9 See the movie *Agenda: Grinding America Down* by Curtis Bowers

10 The New American Magazine is published by the John Birch Society.

Chapter 22

Chapter 23

1 *Indoctrination Public Schools and the Decline of Christianity* in America is an excellent video on this topic.

2 Another excellent source for American history is William Bradford's *Of Plymouth Plantation*

3 *The Money Masters—How International Bankers Gained Control of America* DVD is a great resource for looking at the history of the world's money problems.

4 Mark 4:16-19

5 There is a great deal of misinformation and bad information put out there to distract someone from finding the truth. Please be careful as you search for the truth.

6 A good resource on this is *Grave Influence* by Brannon Howse.

Chapter 24

Chapter 25

Chapter 26

1 Some excellent books on the subject of true worship are *His Dying Request* by David Dunlap, *Worship and Remembrance* by Daniel Smith, and *Worship The Christian's Highest Occupation* by A.P. Gibbs

1 A social security number is not necessary to get a job in the 50 states unless you wish to work for the government, or contract with the government as part of your job.